THE HEIR OF

BROWNLIE
Manor

OTHER BOOKS/AUDIO BOOKS BY ANITA STANSFIELD

THE HEIR OF
BROWNLIE
Manor
A NOVEL

ANITA
STANSFIELD

Covenant Communications, Inc.

For Evelyn Alexandria

Cover image: *English House* © RMAX, courtsey of istockphotography.com

Cover design copyright © 2016 by Covenant Communications, Inc.

Published by Covenant Communications, Inc.
American Fork, Utah

Printed in the United States of America
First Printing: July 2016

22 21 20 19 18 17 16   10 9 8 7 6 5 4 3 2 1

ISBN-13:978-1-52440-013-2

Chapter One

SEEKING PURPOSE

Hampshire, England—1808

THOMAS QUINCY FITZBATTEN PUSHED HIS steed upward against the steep incline and halted abruptly as he came to the crest of the hill. This view of Brownlie Manor and its surrounding lands was deeply familiar to him, and therefore of great comfort. He drew that comfort into his aching spirit and sat atop the fidgeting horse for more than a minute, just gazing at a view he'd not been privileged to see for nearly three years.

The manor where he'd been raised was breathtaking, and he loved it dearly. But it was not its majestic structure and unique stonework, nor the lush gardens and grounds surrounding it that warmed his heart. He'd known perfect love and tenderness from parents who were less than perfect but who had given their whole hearts to him for as long as he could remember. Unlike many families of substance with whom he'd been acquainted throughout his life, the Fitzbattens were well-known—often with disdain from others—as kind and generous people who treated every member of the household as family. Even the boys mucking out the stables and the girls scrubbing pots in the kitchen were known by name to Thomas and his parents—which made Brownlie Manor a coveted place of work for the serving class, and a place looked down upon by many of those belonging to the upper classes. For these reasons more than any other, Thomas was proud of his upbringing. He far preferred the company of those who lived and worked at the manor than he did of those who lived in similar grand structures in the area who considered themselves entitled to a better life simply as a result of being born with a proper name and a large bank balance.

After breathing in the palpable solace of the view, Thomas stirred the horse to a brisk gallop, suddenly anxious to be surrounded by his family. He'd been born and raised an only child, but he'd never wanted for company or love in a house full of the numerous trusted people who had been carefully chosen to care for the multitudinous needs of a manor house so large and complex. As he came closer to the manor, Thomas realized that he'd never considered his home extravagant or lavish but rather a grand place of refuge and beauty. Brownlie Manor was like an island of stability and strength in the sea of a wavering and ill-fated world. Thomas had once heard his father say that he didn't see the vast amount of servants in his employ as people being there to serve his family's needs; he rather saw Brownlie Manor as the means to give good people honorable employment for fair wages—and a place to offer *them* a refuge from the horrors that were more often than not the fate of the lower classes. Thomas had never completely understood what his father had meant until he had fully ventured out into the world himself. After what he'd experienced during these years while he'd been away, he longed for the security of home and felt no desire to ever leave here again.

Thomas dismounted some distance from the stables and led his horse by the reins, ambling slowly while he breathed in the Hampshire air and took in the beauty of his surroundings, blanketed by a typically overcast sky. He finally saw his first sign of human life when he stepped through the open stable doorway. At the other end of a long row of stalls stood Chip, noisily repairing a hinge on a stall door. Chip was at least ten years older than Thomas, lanky and bald, with a wife and children who lived in one of the many small homes situated on Fitzbatten land.

Thomas smiled while observing Chip, who had grown balder but no less lanky. He finally shouted to be heard over the clanking of Chip's tools. "Can a man get any decent feed and water for his horse around here?"

Chip turned with a start, broke into a grin, and set aside his tools before he strode eagerly toward Thomas, his hand outstretched. "Well, I'll be!" Chip said, shaking Thomas's hand firmly. Thomas was so glad to be home that a handshake didn't seem sufficient, so he put his other arm over Chip's shoulders and gave him a warm, manly pat.

"Hello, Chip," Thomas said, stepping back from their quick embrace.

"Well, hello there, Captain!"

"Oh, please, please . . . don't call me that." Thomas shrugged his shoulders, which bore the weight of the red coat of his uniform, and absently pressed a hand down the standard white waistcoat. "I can't *wait* to get out of this uniform, and I'll be glad to set aside everything that reminds me of it."

Chip's eyes showed a glimmer of concern, but he smiled it away and said, "Then I'll settle for saying welcome home, Thomas. It's good to see you alive and well and back here where you were sorely missed."

"Thank you, Chip. And I've missed all of you . . . and everything here . . . more than I can say. You look well. How is Agnes? And the children? I believe Mother wrote to tell me that you were blessed with another son while I was away."

"Indeed we were," Chip said proudly. "Three boys now. And they're all doing well."

"I'm glad to hear it," Thomas said.

"You must be tired," Chip said, taking the reins of the horse. "You look downright worn out, I'd say. Best get yourself into the house."

Thomas's heart quickened at the thought of seeing his mother and father, and he was glad to leave the horse in Chip's care, suddenly wanting to break into a run. "Are my parents—"

"Oh, sir," Chip interrupted, looking grim. For a moment Thomas feared that something terrible might have happened since he'd last received letters. But Chip only said, "I fear they're not at home. Vacationing, they are. Went across the channel. Be gone a month or so, from what I understand."

"I should have considered such a possibility when I decided to surprise them." Thomas swallowed the depth of his disappointment, hoping it wouldn't be too evident in his voice. "It's my own fault for not writing ahead to tell them when I was coming."

"They'll be mighty sorry to learn they weren't here when you returned."

"I'm sorry for that too," Thomas said, trying not to betray how *deeply* sorry he was. Not wanting to draw any attention or pity from Chip, he smiled and added, "Their return will give me something to look forward to."

"Indeed it will," Chip said. "Indeed it will."

Thomas thanked Chip and walked the short distance from the stables to the house, entering through a door most commonly used by the servants. He knew well where he was most likely to find friendly faces gathered and hurried down the stairs to the kitchen. A pleasant aroma greeted him, but he could hardly recall a time when he'd gone down to the kitchen without the lure of good food wafting through the air. He approached quietly and hovered discreetly in the doorway, taking in the pleasing and familiar sight of Deloris Darby—the head cook for as long as he could remember—chatting and laughing with Candy, her most trusted assistant of many years. Liddy and Selma worked as maids in the house, and they were obviously enjoying their morning tea. There were nearly a dozen people—both men and women—gathered around the large table, and Thomas knew them all. There was Dawson the head butler, and Clement and Crawford, who did whatever Dawson asked them to do. Sitting among them was Gib, the driver who cared for the carriages, and Fletcher, who was the head gardener, and Ernie, who assisted him. Thomas knew there were more than twice this many who worked the house and the grounds, and it was typical for them to take their breaks in shifts. But Thomas had had the good fortune of coming upon some of those who were dearest to him, and he breathed in the sights and the sounds of home. Short of seeing his parents, this was the sweetest form of reunion, the kind of scene he'd imagined while he'd been away. And now he was here, and everything that had been horrible and wretched felt far away and unimportant.

Thomas couldn't hear anything that was being said, but a sudden roar of laughter from the group made him smile. Unable to recall the last time he'd genuinely felt the urge to smile, he felt his face threaten to crack, which could perhaps explain the sting of tears in his eyes. Swallowing his emotion, Thomas bellowed lightly, "The mice do indeed play when the cat's away."

All eyes turned toward him as he stepped into the room. In a flurry, the servants pushed their chairs back, and they all rushed toward him, offering warm greetings, firm handshakes, and a few embraces. He felt surrounded by aunts and uncles and cousins, even though he shared no blood with any of them. But he had no blood relatives to speak of, and this was indeed his family. He was easily coerced into joining them for tea but resisted any questions about his time away, insisting instead that each of them give him a quick update of what had taken place in *their* lives while he'd been gone. They all had something to tell him of his parents, of their travels, of the parties they'd thrown, of the cold his father had endured a few months earlier just as winter had been turning to spring. Now spring had fully taken hold, and the good weather had drawn Quincy and Yvette across the channel to bask in the sun in one or more of their favorite travel destinations, which meant they were either in France or Spain. Thomas missed them, but he didn't long to be accompanying them. He was glad to be home and felt no desire to leave—perhaps ever again.

Thomas finally told them all to get back to work, pretending in the lighthearted way he'd learned from his father to be the tyrannical master of the house. But they all saw through him and laughed as they scattered away to their duties and Thomas went up the back stairs to his own rooms. He found fresh water in the basin there and wondered who had sneaked up here while he'd been having tea. Everything was tidy and free of even a hint of dust, and he knew his personal living space had been kept consistently cleaned in anticipation of his return. He considered—not for the first time—how it might have been for the people he loved if he'd *not* returned. Knowing beyond a doubt of the sorrow he would have left behind, he could only figure it was an indication of how thoroughly he knew he was loved. If not for that love, he wondered now if he could find the will to live and to believe that life might bring joy again. Physically he'd come home, safe and sound, but no one here knew of the inner festering wounds he'd brought with him. And he far preferred to forever keep those wounds to himself and prayed that with time they would heal.

Thomas gratefully peeled off every stitch of his uniform and tossed it in a heap at the bottom of his wardrobe, resisting the urge to burn it. Had there been a fire in the grate, he might have. He washed up and dressed in clothes that had once been familiar and comfortable to him, clothes that had never seen the ugliness of war or the depravity of which some men were capable.

Buttoning a brocade waistcoat of dark green, Thomas pondered his reflection in the mirror. The dark shadow on his face betrayed his avoidance of a razor these last few days while he'd only wanted to get home. But shaving could wait until the next morning. His nearly black curly hair was in sore need of a trim, which left it mostly a windblown mess—but then it usually looked like that unless it was cut very short, which was a look his mother had always declared did not suit him well.

Thomas debated whether to lie down and rest for a while, feeling indeed tired from his journey, or go back to the kitchen in search of something to eat, now realizing he was also hungry. He was pondering whether fatigue or hunger would dominate when he answered a knock at the door and Liddy entered the room with a tray.

"Mrs. Darby thought you'd be hungry," Liddy said, setting the tray on a table near the window where he often ate breakfast or lunch when his parents were away. "You know we'd never let you starve."

"I would never worry about that," Thomas said. "Thank you, Liddy."

"Will you be wanting to take your supper in the dining room?" she asked on her way back to the door. "Or should I bring that here as well?"

"I'll come to the dining room, thank you," he said, even now dreading the thought of eating there alone. In spite of the camaraderie in the house, there was still a division between classes over certain matters, and none of the servants would ever sit at the formal dining tables. But he could remedy that. "Actually, Liddy, would you tell Mrs. Darby that I loathe eating alone and I would like to join the rest of you in the kitchen when you have *your* supper?"

Liddy smiled. "I'll tell her, sir. That'll be at seven o'clock, sir."

"I'll be there," he said. "Thank you."

Thomas relished the bread and stew that tasted of home. It was as if Mrs. Darby had some secret ingredient that made everything she cooked taste differently—and better—than he could ever find elsewhere.

With his stomach full, Thomas stretched out on top of the bedspread, pulling up a blanket that had been neatly folded at the foot of the bed. The room wasn't cold enough for a fire, but it was still a bit chilly. By the time the sun went down a fire would be welcome, but he was home and he knew that everything would be taken care of. Feeling completely safe and secure for the first time in years, he drifted into a pleasant slumber, but he came awake sometime later, breathing harshly and overcome with a cold sweat. He could only recall bits and pieces of his dream, but those fragments meshed into the actual memories that haunted him. His surroundings had a calming effect, although the angle of the sunlight in the room indicated he'd slept a long while.

Before supper, Thomas wandered idly through the house, merging his memories into the present reality of truly being home. He lingered in his parents' rooms, missing them but comforted to know that it wouldn't be so many weeks until they returned. He ended up in the library, which had always been one of his favorite rooms for relaxing, either alone or with his parents. A fire was lit and lamps were burning there, and he smiled to think how someone had anticipated he would come here.

Thomas perused the vast shelves of books, recalling all of the adventures and learning he'd gleaned from these pages. He was a little startled to turn and see the usual decanter of liquor and clean glasses sitting there. They'd always been found in that exact spot, but he felt a little taken off guard in light of how he knew he'd taken to drinking too much in order to dull his senses, and now he felt as if he'd confronted an enemy here among his safest surroundings. He stared the golden liquid down for only a moment before it conquered him, and he poured himself a glass and sat down to drink it, enjoying its soothing effect far more than he knew he should. He promised himself that he wouldn't get carried away and felt certain that being home would help him keep his drinking to a minimum.

Thomas enjoyed supper in the kitchen, and he enjoyed a good night's sleep in his own bed. He was only awakened once by a nightmare and was quickly able to go back to sleep. Following a shave and a hearty breakfast, Thomas knew he needed to find something with which to occupy himself. He helped Chip and Herman in the stables, then he helped Gib repair an axle on the wagon used for acquiring household supplies in town. After lunch, Thomas helped Fletcher and Ernie in the gardens, pulling weeds from around the vast array of rose bushes where buds of many colors were just starting to appear.

Thomas enjoyed listening to the lighthearted banter between Fletcher and Ernie, who had been friends all their lives since they'd both grown up on this estate, the children of people who had worked for Thomas's father and grandfather. Both men occasionally asked Thomas a question to include him in the conversation, which he would politely answer, then fire questions back at them, far preferring to just listen and be distracted from the dismal tendency of his thoughts.

Fletcher interrupted his own topic of conversation to say, "Well, would you look at that!"

"Oh, my giddy aunt!" Ernie declared with such enthusiasm that Thomas turned to see what all the fuss was about. "It's rare to see a blue one at all, and I don't know if I've ever seen one so early in the year."

Fletcher chuckled. "Must be some kind of good luck, eh?"

"Right you are," Ernie agreed.

Thomas felt entirely confused until he realized they were looking at a butterfly with bright blue wings flitting about in front of them. He too became fascinated with the brilliant color of the little creature's wings, as much as with the way it kept hovering nearby, as if it were as curious about the men pulling weeds in the garden as they were of it. While Thomas was staring at this wonder of nature, it lighted on a rose bush directly in front of him. Its delicate wings glimmered in the sun while Thomas dared to imagine that it might be some kind of mythical creature come to bring him a secret message. At the very moment he scolded himself for having such a vivid imagination, he heard Fletcher say, "Would seem the good luck it brings belongs to the young master, here."

"I'd say so, for certain," Ernie replied. "Just you wait and see, Thomas, something good'll come to you. A blue butterfly 'tis better than throwing a coin in a fountain, it is."

"Is it now?" Thomas asked absently, hypnotized by the butterfly and its apparent contentment to remain so still and clearly in his view. He watched it for a few seconds that seemed like much longer, wishing from an aching place deep inside himself that what Ernie had said might be true. Oh, how he needed something good to come to him! He needed purpose and meaning. He needed some kind of redemption to purge away the guilt and remorse he felt over events he couldn't bear to think about but which wouldn't leave him in peace. He had everything here that a man could ever want, and yet he had nothing when it was all so brutally overshadowed by memories that haunted his mind night and day.

Bring something good to me, Thomas silently pleaded, wondering if this little butterfly might carry his hope upward to the God who he wanted to believe existed. The dainty wings suddenly fluttered and took flight, disappearing so quickly from sight that it was easy for Thomas to believe he might have imagined it. Fletcher and Ernie spoke of how they would later tell their wives and children about the untimely appearance of the little blue butterfly, reminding Thomas that it really had happened. But within minutes, he'd convinced himself that the strangeness he'd felt had all been in his mind, likely a part of some inner illness he'd developed that had irrevocably changed him and would be prone to haunt him for the rest of his life.

* * *

Five days following his return, Thomas began to feel he was on the brink of insanity. He'd taken to avoiding conversation or even interaction with anyone in the household as much as possible, if only to conceal his increasingly foul mood. He wanted to talk to his father, knowing that he too had endured the harshness of war, and perhaps he could help Thomas put the things he'd seen and done into perspective. His mother was too fragile for any such talk, but her guileless love for him would have surely helped soothe his wounds. He considered the possibility of talking with one of the other men in the household. He was close enough to more than one of them that he knew he could trust them with his deepest thoughts and feelings. But he felt hesitant to trouble anyone else with what burdened him. As it was, he felt alarmingly alone.

Thomas took many long, brisk rides, pushing the horse sometimes to exhaustion until they would both rest in shaded grass near a stream. The sound of the water was soothing to Thomas, and sometimes he rode in the other direction, going as far as the sea. He would stand on the rocks above the waves and look out over the vast power of the ocean and feel so helplessly small. With every wave that rolled into and then receded from the shore, with every hoofbeat of the horse when he rode, with every sunrise and sunset, Thomas became convinced that the only way to ease his pain was to find some greater meaning or purpose in his life. It was as if something indefinably deep in his spirit believed that if he could do something meaningful with his life, he might feel worthy of being redeemed from the choices he'd made that could not be undone.

On Sunday Thomas went to church; his hair was trimmed and he was wearing his finest clothes. He received warm greetings from many people he knew, but the level of society he technically belonged to had an air about it that heightened his guilt. He'd been blessed with so much while so many in the world suffered. And these people with their lavish clothes and outright obsession with formal parties and politics were entirely oblivious to anything but their own comforts. He'd never been more grateful to have been raised by parents who had taught him the equality of all humankind; who had taught him that when people were blessed with greater abundance than others, they had an obligation to *do* more, and to *give* more. But Thomas was doing nothing. He'd been raised to be a gentleman, and it was somehow—for reasons he would never understand—considered honorable and appropriate for gentlemen to *do* nothing.

Thomas tried to focus on the sermon, but it felt so pious and full of hypocrisy. He wondered how Jesus would feel about the people of high society blandly putting a few coins into a collection box and treating their servants badly, and never even glancing toward beggars in the streets when they went into the cities. And Thomas wondered when and how exactly he had come to feel responsible for all of it. Every injustice in the world felt like a burden upon his own shoulders. He knew it *shouldn't* feel that way, but it did. And he didn't know what to do about it. He blocked out the sermon and silently prayed for hope, for understanding, for peace.

The following day, Thomas felt no better. He rode to the sea and back. He helped in the stables and in the gardens. He wore himself out, but he still felt burdened by emotions that seemed as if they might explode. He went to the library after supper and poured himself a large drink, certain the servants knew how much he'd been drinking. Someone had to refill these decanters he was emptying. He slouched onto a comfortable sofa and stacked his booted feet on the table in front of him, gazing into the fire as it hissed and crackled. He didn't realize he wasn't alone until he heard a man clearing his throat in a way that was obviously meant to signal his presence.

Thomas looked up without moving. "What can I do for you, Dawson?" he asked and took a long, slow sip of his drink. Frederick Dawson was a burly man who looked more like a rough sailor than a butler. But his dress and manner were always perfectly proper, even when he was expressing kindness—which he did often and with great finesse.

"I *do* have something I want to ask," Dawson said seriously, "but first I think that I *must* ask if you're all right."

Thomas forced surprised innocence into his expression, but it quickly became evident Dawson wasn't fooled. Thomas looked back at the fire. "I'm fine," he lied.

He heard Dawson sigh before he said, "Do you think you're the first man I've seen come back from war with that look in his eyes?"

Thomas said nothing, but he felt like a guilty child. He suddenly felt certain that Dawson had been on to him the moment he'd come home. And if he could see *that look in his eyes*, then surely others did as well. Still, he didn't know what to say.

"It's not my place to intrude, sir," Dawson said, "but I hope you know that I'm not just here to keep the house running smoothly."

Thomas sighed and felt softened. "I know that, Dawson. Thank you. I'm certain I just need some . . . time." He wasn't certain that was all he needed, but he had no other solution.

"I will say this much, sir," Dawson added, "only because I know for a fact your father would not be happy with me if I *didn't* say it."

"And what's that?" Thomas asked.

"The drinking will never make the pain go away, Thomas. And the more you drink, the more you'll feel the need to keep drinking."

"And what *will* make the pain go away, Dawson?" Thomas asked in a tone of mild pleading, even though in his mind he heard the words sounding snide and spiteful. But he knew better than to behave like an arrogant child with Dawson—or anyone else in the household, for that matter. No matter what the person's occupation or position, speaking unkindly to anyone in this house was strictly forbidden.

"Perhaps if you could talk about it, sir," Dawson said, and Thomas felt as if his mind had been read. He *wanted* to talk about it, even if he didn't know where to begin or what to say. "Again, I'm here, sir . . . should you feel the need to talk . . . until the time that your father returns."

"Thank you, Dawson," Thomas said, feeling the tiniest bit better. Enough to at least set down his drink. Trying to draw the attention away from himself, Thomas asked, "Now, what did you want to ask me?" In a light voice, he added, "Are the kitchen maids arguing? Is the butcher trying to cheat us again? Give me a problem to solve, Dawson. I'll give the maids a talking to and challenge the butcher to a duel."

"All is well with the maids *and* the butcher," Dawson said.

"I'm glad to hear it." Thomas motioned to a chair. "Please . . . sit down. I get the feeling you've come to me as a friend; at least I hope you have. Or if you've come to me as your employer, I shall do my best to fill my father's shoes fairly in his absence."

"I wish to speak to you as a friend *and* my employer. I *would* have taken this to your father if he were here, but it is a great dilemma, and I don't know if there's anything that anyone can do; however, your father has made me promise many a time that if I ever needed help I should come to him."

Thomas scrutinized Dawson's countenance and felt a little unnerved. The man was leaning his forearms on his thighs, rubbing his hands together nervously, staring at the floor. The confident and proper demeanor he'd worn only moments ago had completely vanished. Whatever the problem might be, it was weighing on Dawson heavily, and Thomas hoped that he *could* help.

"Out with it, man," Thomas said gently. And to make a point, he added, "If you expect me to be willing to come to you and talk about my troubles, you must be willing to do the same."

"Thank you, sir," Dawson said.

"Stop calling me sir and tell me what's wrong," Thomas said. "Are you in some kind of trouble?"

"Not me," Dawson said, still looking at the floor. "It's my niece; my brother's daughter. He died some years back in a mining accident, and I promised his wife that if they ever needed anything, they could come to me. And now little Ruthie has shown up at the kitchen door just a while ago with a letter from her mother and a very big problem. I took her to my room without anyone seeing her, and I got her something to eat, but I need your advice, Thomas. I don't know what to do. I can't hide her here past breakfast, and the problem isn't going away, and I just don't know what to do."

"What exactly *is* the problem?" Thomas asked.

Dawson looked up at him. "She's pregnant . . . and not wed."

Thomas sighed. "I see. And how old is Ruthie?"

"Nineteen, twenty, I believe. According to her mother's letter, the father of the baby is a scoundrel who had convinced the poor girl he loved her and was intent on marrying her, but he's moved on. And there seems to be some concern for her safety."

"She fears the baby's father will harm her?" Thomas asked with all his forlorn feelings about the plight of humanity pressing down on him again. He wanted to demand to know how people could be so cruel and selfish. But there was no one to whom he could put such a demand.

"That's the impression I get, yes," Dawson said.

Thomas sighed again and pondered for a long moment. He couldn't change the plight of humanity, but he *was* in a position to help one poor girl who had been cruelly taken advantage of and abandoned.

"Dawson, listen to me," Thomas said, and the men exchanged a gaze worthy of the bond they shared. "I'm glad you came to me, and I will gladly do what I believe my father would have done. If what I've been blessed with can help this poor girl, then I am happy to do it. Are there not places she could go to live until the baby is born? Are there not good people who will adopt unwanted babies?"

"I believe it's possible, yes," Dawson said. "I know little of such things, but I'm certain we could find out. But there must be a great deal of cost for such things, and I could never ask you to—"

"You don't have to ask me, Dawson, because I'm offering. I will gladly cover all of her expenses so she can make a fresh start of her life. I can't do anything about the emotional impact of such an event in her life, but I can make certain her physical and financial needs are met, as well as those of the child. It does seem the best option . . . as opposed to her raising the child without a father."

"It does," Dawson said. "I agree. I . . . don't know what to say. I was hoping for advice. I did not expect such generosity."

"Would my father not have been generous?" Thomas asked. "You have been with this family since before I was born. You are family to us. Have you *ever* asked for anything you haven't worked for?"

"A man *should* work for what he receives, should he not?"

"In theory," Thomas said. "But what have I ever done to deserve having more money than I know what to do with? I would be a fool and a hypocrite to think I'm more deserving of it than you or your niece . . . What did you say her name is?"

"Ruthie."

"Ruthie." Thomas stood up, inspired by a surge of that sense of purpose he'd been seeking. "Come with me now."

Dawson followed Thomas to his personal office, where Thomas unlocked a safe and took out some bank notes. He counted them out on the desk and put them into Dawson's hand, chuckling at the butler's astonished expression. "It's only money, Dawson."

"And people starve without it, Thomas," Dawson said, almost looking as if he might cry. "To say I'm grateful feels so inadequate."

"Perhaps when I start complaining to you about all of my woes— as you so kindly offered—you will quickly feel that we are even."

"Never," Dawson said.

"I'm thinking it might be wise to take her discreetly into town tonight to stay at one of the inns until arrangements can be made. And I'm also thinking that you are in need of a few days off. I'm certain everyone will manage without you for that long, and I assure you the house will still be standing when you return."

"Thank you, sir," Dawson said and surprised Thomas with a warm embrace, the kind that Thomas was looking forward to receiving from his father when he returned.

"I'm glad to be of service," Thomas said. A thought came into his mind, seemingly out of nowhere, and he put a hand on Dawson's arm to stop him from moving toward the door. "Wait," he said. "I know there is a certain respect and trust among the household, but I also know that gossip is abundant. It will seem strange for you to leave this evening, so unexpectedly, and so late. It would be terribly out of character for you and might start the servants chattering. I know how damaging even a little bit of scandal can be, and I don't want this to fall back on you or your sister-in-law. Let *me* escort her into town. Tell the others I've decided to visit the pub, which I've not done since I returned, and I prefer going by carriage just in case I get too drunk to ride home of my own accord. Tell only Gib that I'm helping your niece. He'll not ask for details and he can be trusted. Go and speak to your niece and discreetly get her into the carriage before I leave." He pulled his watch out of waistcoat pocket at the same time Dawson glanced at the clock on the wall. "Say, nine o'clock?"

"Yes, sir. Thank you, sir. It's good that one of us is thinking clearly."

"And tomorrow at breakfast you can announce you're taking some time off, that your sister-in-law needs you, and you can leave without any fuss and meet your niece and take care of the details. Take as many days as you need."

"Thank you, sir."

"Stop calling me sir . . . at least when we are alone. This is all a matter of friendship, my good man."

"Thank you, Thomas," Dawson said, again looking as if he might cry.

Thomas hurried up to his room to make himself presentable enough to go to the pub, even though he had no intention of going there—or perhaps he might for just a few minutes, if only to give his story the ring of truth.

Thomas stepped out the front door of the manor at exactly nine to find the carriage there, with Gib sitting atop it, the reins in his gloved hands. Clement was standing at the carriage door, ready to be of service, but Thomas knew that neither Dawson nor Gib would have told him anything of the truth.

"Good evening, Gib," Thomas said. "I hope I didn't upset your plans for the evening."

"Not at all, sir," Gib said. "'tis a fine evening for some fresh air." He tossed Thomas a subtle smirk that implied he was enjoying his part in this haphazard rescue of a damsel in distress; his expression was completely missed by Clement, who was looking the other way. "To the pub, then?" Gib asked.

"To the pub," Thomas said, and Clement opened the carriage door for him.

Thomas stepped inside, and the door was closed behind him before Clement stepped away. Since it was dark inside, Thomas saw only the vague outline of a figure in a hooded cloak, but the very mysteriousness of the moment made his heart quicken. He sat down across from the young woman, and the carriage rolled forward.

Determined to not let this situation become awkward, he decided to try to initiate some simple conversation. "Hello," he said. "I'm Thomas."

"I know who you are," she said with a melodic voice that was heavy with sorrow. "I'm Ruth . . . Dawson, of course."

"It's a pleasure to meet you, Miss Dawson," he said, wishing he could see her face. And he was glad she'd not introduced herself as Ruthie. He far preferred calling a grown woman by a proper name. "Ruth," he added, both to hear himself say it and to make it clear that he preferred their encounter be on a first-name basis.

"My uncle told me what you're doing for me," Ruth said from out of the shadows. "I never imagined anyone could be so kind."

"The cruelty with which you have been treated has led you to expect the same from others. In spite of my own keen awareness of how dreadfully unkind some people can be, I really do believe that many people—if not most—are good at heart. I'm only sorry that you find yourself in such unfortunate circumstances."

"You're very kind, sir. But did I not bring this upon myself? I was foolish and naive."

"As we all are at some point in life."

"And I *did* make a terrible mistake . . . committed a terrible sin."

"You were deceived, were you not? I have seen many things, Ruth, and I have come to believe that accountability is rarely black and white. From what I understand, whatever mistake you may have made was never with ill intent. Consequences often far outweigh the choices that precede them."

"Perhaps," she said as if she didn't believe him. "And now my only choice is to raise an illegitimate child in poverty, or give my child away and never see it again."

Hearing it put that way, Thomas felt heartache on her behalf. He wished there was some other option. He felt compelled to say, "The very idea of giving your child away must be very difficult for you."

"I cannot fathom it," she said, "and yet, the loving decision—the *right* decision—is to give my child a chance at a good life, and I can never offer that." He heard her sniffle and could see enough movement to know she was pressing a handkerchief to her face. Following a passage of silence, she added stoutly, "Forgive me, sir, for running on with complaints. Truly, your kindness will never be forgotten. Whatever happens, Mr. Fitzbatten . . . Thomas . . . I will always remember your goodness and generosity."

Thomas let out a shallow gasp before he even recognized the reason for it. His heart quickened even before his mind recalled vividly the moment he'd been staring at that magnificent little butterfly, and his silent, urgent plea. *Bring something good to me.* The memory flashed so clearly into his mind that ignoring it was impossible. It was as if the finger of God had tapped him on the shoulder while a powerful voice echoing within himself whispered, *Take notice of this moment.*

"Is something wrong?" Ruth asked him.

"No," he said, so overcome that he never could have begun to explain. He was still thinking about it, trying to convince himself that it meant nothing, when the carriage halted. Perhaps with the hope that he could figure out what he was feeling, he wanted to prolong their time together a little longer.

Gib opened the carriage door, and Thomas stepped out while Gib said, "I will be glad to escort the lady to the inn while you make an appearance at the pub, sir. Both are within walking distance of here."

"Thank you, Gib," Thomas said, "but I will escort her myself. I will meet you back here."

"Very good, sir," Gib said, and Thomas reached his hand into the carriage to help Ruth step out. He felt her fingers slip into his, and a warmth rushed through him that seemed an echo of what he had felt moments ago. He felt drawn to her for reasons that made no sense. He felt responsible for her when he'd not even known of her existence earlier this evening. And he hadn't even seen her face. As she stepped into the glow of a street lamp and pushed back the hood of her cloak, his mind quickly tallied her features. She was average. Average height, average build, average brown hair plaited and pinned up. She was pretty in an average kind of way; the type of woman to get lost in a crowd and never be noticed. She then turned to look at him, as if to assess him with the same kind of appraising gaze. And when he looked into her eyes he saw nothing average at all. If the eyes were indeed windows to the soul, then her soul surely had a depth and breadth he could never comprehend. But when she looked up at his face, those fascinating eyes widened as if in terror. She gasped aloud and stepped back from him as if she feared he might harm her.

"What is it?" he asked, glad that Gib had gone off in the direction of the pub. "What's wrong?"

"Forgive me," she said, one hand over her heart and one over her belly as if it might protect her unborn child. "It's just that . . ." She didn't seem to want to explain, but neither did she stop staring at him. "Forgive me," she said again and looked down, laughing tensely to cover her embarrassment. "You just . . . look so much like someone I know. The resemblance is striking. It caught me by surprise, that's all."

Thomas could accept her explanation—most of it, anyway. Something about her reaction left him uneasy, but he couldn't put a finger on it. Hoping to ease her discomfort, he told her in all honesty, "I met a man in France once who looked so much like my dead uncle that for a moment I thought he'd come back to haunt me. Given what a stodgy old thing he'd been, I was truly terrified."

His little story made her laugh, which eased the tension. "I've heard it said we all have someone in the world who is our double."

"Yes, I've heard that too," he said and offered his arm. "Let me see you safely to the inn, Miss Dawson, and your uncle will come for you in the morning."

"Thank you," she said and put a hand over his arm. She appeared to be relaxed, but he distinctly felt her hand trembling.

Chapter Two

ARRANGED AND CONVENIENT

By the time Thomas had escorted Ruth Dawson the short distance
to the inn, he was feeling the very thing he'd been longing to feel ever
since his return: purpose and meaning. Perhaps it was simply being
able to help this woman and her child in a way that would spare them
both from a life of misery. He told himself that's all it was, while at
the same time he felt so keenly aware of her that he had to focus on
his breathing enough to remember to exhale.

As they approached the door to the inn, she stopped walking and
put a hand over her mouth.

"Are you ill?" he asked, having heard that pregnancy could affect a
woman adversely in many ways.

"Truthfully . . . I just need a little something to eat. They serve
meals here, do they not?"

"They do, but . . . I thought they'd given you a good supper at the
manor."

"Oh, they did," she said. "Thank you. I just . . . perhaps if I
could just get some bread to take to my room, I'll be fine. There's
no need for concern." She moved toward the door and away from
him as if to imply that he'd done his duty in escorting her safely
to her destination, but he opened the door and followed her in,
which seemed to surprise her. He insisted that she sit down at one
of the tables across the room from the few remaining customers. He
arranged for her room and asked that some bread and cheese and
milk be brought for the lady. He sat down across the table from her,
which also seemed to surprise her, but when she looked at him he saw

that hint of terror again. Whoever it was that he strongly resembled was not someone she liked; of that he was certain.

"Why are you doing this?" she asked in little more than a whisper before she glanced around the room as if someone might be watching. "Aren't you afraid that someone will see you, that scandal will come from this?"

"I have never cared what people think of me, Miss Dawson."

"But . . . surely . . . you don't want to be seen at an inn with . . . a woman like me."

"Like you?" he countered, perhaps wanting to test her true feelings on such matters.

"You can't be so naive, Mr. Fitzbatten. It only takes a glance to see from the way I'm dressed that I do not belong in the company of a gentleman. You have been *so* kind. I don't want to cause further trouble for you. I assure you that I will be fine."

"Your manner of speaking is rather refined for a *woman like you*," he finished with light sarcasm.

"The lady I've been working for helped me with that so that I could get better positions."

"And you left that job?"

"I had no choice."

"Did this lady who employed you not care enough about you to help?"

"She would have thrown me out. At least leaving on my own allowed me to leave with some dignity."

"And do you think that I would be like her? Like the people you worked for? Just because of my wealth? My name?" She said nothing, and he couldn't help sounding mildly snide. "You can't answer that because you would have to admit that you have assumed all people of my class are arrogant and selfish. Truthfully, I didn't notice how you're dressed, because I was looking at *you*. And again . . . I don't care what anyone thinks, or what they say. It is *your* reputation and your *safety* that concern me. I will leave when I know that you are well and have all that you need. That's what a gentleman does. It has nothing to do with social class." She looked mildly stunned, and he couldn't resist adding, "I can't help wondering *which* social class begat the man who treated you so cruelly."

"Does it matter?" she asked with shame in her eyes.

"Not to me, it doesn't. *Any* man who treats any woman with such disrespect should be held responsible. And yet he walks away and you are left to suffer the consequences."

He saw a glimmer of tears in her eyes before she looked down abruptly to hide them.

"Forgive me if I'm being insensitive," he said.

"What makes you think you're being insensitive?" she asked with no hint of defensiveness, but she still wouldn't look at him.

"It wouldn't be the first time," he admitted.

"You weren't insensitive," she stated firmly, and he decided he liked her straightforward manner. "I just hate to think of *my child* being a distasteful consequence. It's a child . . . a human being. And however ill-begotten it might be, it deserves a good chance at life."

"I agree," he said, and she met his eyes briefly, then looked down again.

"And thanks to you it will have that."

Thomas tried to think of an appropriate comment, but he couldn't. He was thinking of the sacrifice she would be making to give her child a chance at a good life. What little money he was giving to aid her cause was nothing compared to what a woman must experience in giving up a child. He'd never thought too deeply on the matter before, but he was thinking of it now. Looking at this dear, sweet young woman, it was tempting to let his heart break on her behalf. She seemed to represent the very feelings he'd been struggling with. His anger and confusion over the injustices of the world. His inability to do anything about them. This opportunity to help her made him feel better about himself than he'd felt in a very long time, but it still felt so tiny and minuscule, so insignificant in contrast to what she yet had to face.

A serving maid set the food Thomas had ordered on the table, and Ruth looked pleasantly surprised. "A little bread would have sufficed."

"Perhaps," he said. "I'm certain you have plenty to be concerned about without having to feel ill. If a little food will remedy that, so be it. I recommend taking what you don't eat now to your room so that you'll have something should you need it before breakfast is served."

"Your thoughtfulness is . . ."

"What?" he asked, not certain if her hesitation was due to chewing the bread she'd just taken a bite of.

After she had chewed and swallowed she said, "Surprising."

"And what if I told you it was for purely selfish reasons?"

"What do you mean?" she asked with alarm, as if she feared he might expect something unsavory in return. After what she'd been through, he couldn't blame her.

"I mean that I've been . . . rather out of sorts since I've returned from the war. I have felt terribly useless. Doing this for you is the first thing I've done in a very long while that has actually seemed truly worthwhile. But in truth, all I'm giving up is a little money I won't miss; therefore, it's certainly no personal sacrifice."

Her eyes widened slightly, and from the glow of the lamp on the table, he believed them to be a dark hazel. Average in color, perhaps. But not at all in their expressiveness. "You are not just giving of your money, sir. You have personally escorted me here, provided me with a room for the night and food to eat, and you are sitting here with me for reasons I cannot begin to understand. I'm certain you could be having a far better time down the road at the pub . . . doing whatever it is men do at pubs."

"I think I far prefer the company here as opposed to a bunch of men drinking too much and laughing uproariously at ridiculous jokes. And yes, that would be a fair description of what men generally do at pubs."

"You are a rare breed, Mr. Fitzbatten," she said and continued to eat while she seemed to be assessing him—or perhaps assessing him again now that they'd actually shared some honest conversation.

"Am I?" he asked. "If by that you mean I'm different than most of the people of my class, I will take it as the highest compliment. I am very blessed to have wealth and privilege, but I *do* consider it a blessing. Beyond that I rather loathe the society I am supposed to fit into. I far prefer associating with . . . *real* people; people like your uncle. Hardworking, honest people who have no reason to put on airs and snub their noses at others."

Ruth nodded with her mouth full. The silence provoked him to say, "Forgive me for my vehemence. I'm likely talking far too much."

"Not at all," she said and kept eating. He was rather amazed at how much a woman so small could eat, especially since she'd had a large supper not so many hours ago. But he supposed that must be the way of pregnancy. "I'm enjoying your company," she said. "May I say that I didn't expect to?"

"You may say anything you like."

"Then I will also say that this is the first time I haven't felt completely alone for weeks now. I don't know why you're so easy to talk to, but you are."

Thomas felt taken aback all over again. The sensations he'd felt earlier in the carriage rushed over him again as she admitted to sharing his own feelings of being completely alone. She wasn't talking about the absence of any people around her; it was rather the feeling of being unable to speak openly of emotions, a dilemma that left a person standing in a crowded room and feeling completely isolated. He wanted to explain all of that verbally but reminded himself they had only known each other for about an hour—even if it didn't feel that way.

Instead he asked, "How long has it been?"

"About a month now," she said, shame clouding her countenance again, "since I realized I was pregnant. And that was the same week he unexpectedly left his job at the same manor where I was working . . . with rumors about his reason for leaving being another woman."

"I'm so very sorry."

"It's not your fault."

"I was not apologizing; rather expressing . . . my sorrow on your behalf."

"And why should you feel sorrow on my behalf?" she asked and quickly wiped a hand over both cheeks before he even realized that tears were falling. "We are practically strangers."

"Practically," he repeated. "And yet I do . . . feel sorrow."

Silence fell while she stopped eating quite so voraciously but continued to pick at the bread and cheese in front of her. Reason told him he should leave now. She was surely tired and needed her rest. There was no logical reason for him to linger. He could insist on escorting her to the door of her room to know that she was safe, and beyond that the situation was simply none of his business. Giving her money had not given him any rights or privileges in regard to her personal life. But he felt as if he'd turned to stone—a statue with its gaze permanently fixed on her. He couldn't look away, and he couldn't brush off the overwhelming sense he had that this was not chance or coincidence. Her needing help and his ability to give it felt to him like fate or destiny somehow. But he didn't believe that fate or destiny existed as some kind of abstract force in the universe. If they did exist, they were simply words used to explain the hand of God in people's lives when no other explanation was possible. Thomas had many times sought to question his belief in God when he'd been assaulted by the horrors of the world. But he'd never been able to let go of something deep within his spirit that intrinsically knew He existed, even if he couldn't begin to comprehend. And now, his gaze fixed like stone upon Ruth Dawson, contemplating her plight, his belief in God felt renewed and strengthened. This was no coincidence, and he knew it with all his soul. But what could that possibly mean? He had given her uncle the money to send her away until she gave birth to her baby. He considered it a possibility that he could find her in a year when this was behind her. He knew her uncle well; he would always know where to find her. Wouldn't he? But that solution felt so out of his control, so subject to chance. And wrong somehow.

While Thomas sat like carved marble and Ruth randomly picked at the bread and cheese, putting little pieces into her mouth and looking everywhere but at him, he silently uttered a prayer. He wanted to know what God would have him do with this moment of divine destiny. He felt himself at a crossroads. He could let her go, or . . .

Before his next thought could fully articulate itself in his mind, he heard himself asking, "Do you *want* to give away your baby, Ruth?"

She looked astonished, then upset, but he still couldn't regret asking it. He needed to know how she would respond to such a question.

"No, sir," she said and made no effort this time to wipe away the tears that oozed from her eyes in great abundance. "However wrong the existence of this baby might be, it is growing inside of me. It is a part of me. I will do whatever I can to give it the best possible chance at a good life, and for your help in that I am grateful. But I would *never* choose to give away my baby."

Thomas considered that while he handed her a clean handkerchief from his pocket, since her own handkerchief already looked well used.

"Thank you," she said and dabbed at her tears. "Forgive me . . . for getting so upset."

"No apology necessary," he said. "I asked a question; I appreciate an honest answer."

"I'm feeling very tired." She gathered the remaining bread and cheese into a napkin and folded it into a little bundle before she stood and he did the same. Looking down at the table, she picked up the key to her room, then looked back up at him. "Thank you . . . for everything. I will never forget what you've done for me."

"It's been a pleasure," Thomas said, and she moved toward the stairs. He didn't want to let her go, but now even the idea of walking her to her room felt awkward and unnecessary. He felt almost panicked to let her out of his sight and blurted, "I'll see you in the morning."

Ruth turned back, surprised. "You will?"

Thomas stepped closer so they wouldn't be overheard, even though no one was nearby. "I want to discuss with your uncle the best possible options for your care, and see what I can do to help see you settled." Knowing he needed to leave, he repeated, "I'll see you in the morning," and hurried out of the inn and down the street, wondering why it felt literally painful to leave her behind. Had he gone mad? Had he lost his mind since suppertime? Or had his madness been slowly coming on? He thought about how he had poured himself a drink earlier this evening in the library, and he felt like a different man entirely.

Thomas found Gib in the pub, leaning against the bar with a tankard of ale in front of him, exchanging some light banter with the man at his side.

"We can go whenever you're ready," Thomas said to him.

Gib replied, "You won't be wanting a drink first?"

"No," was all Thomas said, and Gib looked surprised. Thomas didn't have to wonder why. He quickly added, "I just . . . don't feel the need for one. If you would like some more time, I'll wait in the carriage."

"I'm ready when you are," Gib said, and they walked together toward the door. "I appreciate your kindness, sir, but don't be forgetting who's the master and who's the servant."

"Can we not just be friends?" Thomas asked, wondering why he felt so agitated.

"Friends, yes," Gib said as they walked up the street at a brisk pace. "But I still work for you, and we both know that a ship needs a captain."

"What do you mean by that?" Thomas demanded.

"Now, don't go getting all high and mighty on me just because I remind you of something I know your father taught you well. The serving folk at Brownlie are surely the most blessed in all the world, but we need to know that someone's in charge and that there's order in the way things are done."

Thomas took a deep breath. "Yes, of course." His father *had* taught him that, and he knew it well. "But that doesn't mean we can't share a drink at the pub once in a while."

"But you didn't *have* a drink," Gib said lightly.

"And I didn't want to interrupt your conversation."

"That weren't no conversation; that were passing the time," Gib said as they arrived at the carriage. Gib opened the door and Thomas stepped in.

"Thank you, Gib," Thomas said before the door was closed, "for everything."

"A pleasure, sir," Gib said, and they were quickly on their way home.

During the drive, Thomas's thoughts swirled and danced and gained volition. They raced like a horse galloping at full speed and crashed like ocean waves against the rocks at high tide. Again he prayed, as if God and only God could lift him up out of this ceaseless internal roiling enough to see clearly and discern madness from reason. Before the carriage halted in front of Brownlie Manor, his prayer had been answered. He knew what he had to do, and he knew it was right. He only needed the courage—and a certain amount of craftiness—to move forward.

Thomas opened the carriage door himself before Gib even had a chance to get to it.

"Thank you," Thomas called and hurried into the house. At such times when he wanted to find someone or get to a certain place in the manor quickly, he sorely disliked how wretchedly enormous the place was. He felt as if he'd walked a mile before he crept quietly, holding a lamp, down the hall where the single male servants of the household had their rooms. He knew well which room belonged to Dawson, but he didn't want anyone else in nearby rooms to overhear him knocking at the door, so he took the risk of simply going in and closing the door quietly behind him.

"Dawson," he whispered loudly. "Dawson, wake up."

He heard Dawson mutter some mild cursing under his breath as he sat up, looking rather startled and dazed. "What in the name of heaven and earth are you doing?" Dawson growled in a low whisper. Thomas chuckled. There was no distinction of servant and master in *that* comment.

"I need to speak with you," Thomas said, "and it can't wait until morning."

"Very well," Dawson said a bit begrudgingly—likely because he was still half asleep. Thomas knew well enough that Dawson was generally up and busy very early in the mornings. "Is Ruthie all right?"

"She is for now," Thomas said and set the lamp on a table before he sat down in one of the two chairs available.

Dawson grabbed a robe and pulled it on over his nightshirt before he sat in the other chair and waited for Thomas to speak. Thomas hesitated a long moment, silently recounting his decision, his plan, the steps he needed to take. As soon as he allowed the words out of his mouth, there would be no turning back. He had to be absolutely certain. And it only took him a long moment to know that he was. With confidence, he said, "You told me that when your brother died, you promised his wife you would look after the family if the need arose. That's why she sent Ruth to you."

"That's right."

"Since you have assumed that responsibility, it is you I must speak to if I wish to marry her."

Dawson gasped. He stared at Thomas as if he'd broken out with the pox. In what could only be described as a shouting whisper, he finally said, "Have you taken complete and utter leave of your senses?"

"Am I not good enough for her?" Thomas asked, keeping his voice low.

"Good enough?" Dawson echoed. "In my opinion you are one of the finest men in England, which is the very reason you should not be impulsively wedding yourself to a servant girl who has gotten herself into trouble. The trouble is temporary. Marriage is for life."

"The child *is* a life, Dawson. And giving up that child will leave a hole in Ruth's heart that will never heal."

"And . . . so . . . what?" Dawson motioned elaborately with his hand. "Her plight gives you some kind of . . . purpose? Some chance to be a hero? Your feeling lost and disconnected right now is something that will pass. Don't be fool enough to think that doing such a thing will magically solve what's not right in *your* life. Don't be a fool at all."

"For this, Dawson, I will be a fool if that's what it takes." Dawson looked as if he were about to explode and the need to not be overheard might actually cause his eyes to burst out of his head. Thomas prevented him from being able to speak by forging ahead with all that he needed to say, "Listen to me, and listen well. Arranged marriages and marriages of convenience happen all around us all the time. It sickens me to see the reasons why some people will marry each other. Do you honestly think I would want to marry any one of the women who have thrown themselves into my path simply because I have the wealth to maintain their audacious and pretentious lifestyle? Never! So, call this marriage arranged. Call it convenient. Fine."

Dawson sighed but appeared more calm. "The two of you do not even know each other. How can you possibly have any idea if you would not drive each other mad?"

"A great deal can be learned about a person through an hour of honest conversation."

Dawson's countenance was softening, and his eyes betrayed mild intrigue. He was thinking about it.

"She's your niece. I honestly don't know how often you've been in contact with your brother's family. How well do *you* know her?"

"I keep in touch as much as I can, and my time off has been spent visiting them. She's a good girl with a good heart. She's kind and honest and knows how to work hard."

Thomas breathed that in, feeling it assuage him with added validation that his instincts were not out of tune. "That's all I need to know," Thomas said firmly. "As I see it, anything else can be worked out."

Dawson leaned closer and gave Thomas a piercing gaze. "And what of love, my boy?" He asked the question just as Thomas imagined his own father would have asked it if he were here.

"Is it mad to say that I could feel love—or at least the spark of it—in so short a time? I'm not naive enough to believe that feeling drawn to her now—or perhaps drawn to the desire to help her— will carry a relationship for long. But you know my parents better than anyone; you know the example with which I was raised. Trust, respect, and commitment—that's what my father told me are the makings of a good marriage. He told me more than once that love can grow out of those elements and it will die in the absence of them. Do you not believe I am capable of that? Do you not believe Ruth capable of that? I've only known her a few hours and *I* believe her capable of that. Is it so wrong of me to want to devote my life to the care of a good woman and a child who needs a father and a name? If it's a mistake, then it's a mistake I am willing to make, and I will always know that my intentions were from the heart."

Dawson was quiet for many minutes, and Thomas had nothing more to say. Dawson finally sighed loudly and muttered, "You make a strong case, young man. I cannot fault your thinking. I just . . . never dreamed . . . When I came to you for advice, I did not expect financial assistance, and yet you gave it so generously. But this . . . this . . . I never dreamed . . ."

"Well, I can assure you it was not in *my* plans when I left here with her earlier. But I know it's right, Dawson. It feels more right to me than anything ever has."

Dawson took hold of Thomas's hand and squeezed it tightly. "Then I give you my blessing and my gratitude."

Thomas smiled, then chuckled, feeling deeply relieved and even happy. There were many details to work out in order to avoid any cause for scandal. He didn't want people ever speculating or wondering about their first child being born far too soon after the wedding. That could be a taint for the child—and for Ruth—in and of itself. And there was also one other very big thing to consider.

"I haven't actually asked her," Thomas said. "I feel like I should make arrangements quickly, and I need to come up with a believable story right away. But should I be doing that without talking to her first? Maybe she wouldn't *want* to marry me?"

"If you believed that, you wouldn't be here convincing me it's the right thing to do," Dawson said. "Given the choice of marriage to a fine man and giving up her baby, which do you think she'd choose?"

Thomas didn't even have to think about it. He knew the answer. He knew it was right. And it seemed a gesture of faith to go boldly forward with his plans. If she was angry with him for not consulting her first, then their first order of business as husband and wife would be his begging her forgiveness.

Thomas talked with Dawson for a long while, coming up with a detailed plan on how to go about this. It would require some deception and some fairly good acting on their part, but they agreed it was all for a good cause and it was certainly feasible.

When Thomas finally rose to leave, Dawson stood as well and offered Thomas a fatherly embrace. He took Thomas's shoulders into his hands, saying with a tenderness that rarely showed, "You've always felt like family to me, my boy. I never imagined it could actually happen."

"Nor did I." Thomas chuckled. "With any luck, she'll have me."

They agreed that they both needed to try to get some rest. Tomorrow would be a big day. Thomas quietly crept the lengthy distance to his own room, where it took far too long to relax enough to sleep, but he awoke with a shock to his heart. He was getting married today! But before that happened, he would be putting on an elaborate charade and he had to face convincing the potential bride.

Thomas had everything under control and a bag packed for travel before he went down to the kitchen, knowing the majority of the servants would be gathered there. He didn't have to wonder if Dawson would have efficiently done his part in all of this scheming. Dawson had never fallen short of a task in his entire life.

Thomas stopped partway down the stairs and took a deep breath, rehearsing again in his mind what he intended to say. Brief and to the point. No over-the-top explaining. He could do this and be convincing.

Stepping into the kitchen, he found most of his staff seated around the huge table, eating their breakfast. They all stood when they saw him.

"No, no, please sit down," he said but remained on his feet.

"Would you like to join us, sir?" Mrs. Darby asked.

"Thank you, no. But I'll take a little something for the road. Gib is harnessing the carriage as we speak. I'm going to the cottage to stay for a while; I'm not sure how long. Dawson has sent word to Barclay there to let them know to expect me. And now—" he took a deep breath and put a smile on his face that didn't feel at all fake—"I have some news to share with you all that I have been keeping a secret. You have all seen me moping about since I've returned, and perhaps this will help explain my reasons. You see . . . I wanted my parents to be the first to know, so I didn't say anything. But now . . . before I go, I think it's only proper for you all to know that I was recently married, and . . ." He paused while the small crowd muttered their surprise, but they all seemed pleased. So far so good. "My wife was needed at her family home, and I thought it wise to come back and tell my parents the good news before bringing her here. I've missed her terribly, and I've had a devil of a time trying to keep quiet about it, but I received word just yesterday evening that her obligations at home are taken care of, and we will be going to the cottage for a long-overdue honeymoon. I've left a letter for my parents explaining everything. I would ask that no one break the news to them until they've had a chance to read it upon their return. Well," he chuckled, "that's all. I'll look forward to bringing the new Mrs. Fitzbatten here to meet you all."

His news was well received, and he graciously accepted offers of congratulations and well wishes, trying to imagine that it was all deserved if only a little ahead of its time. As the flurry was winding down, Thomas said casually to Dawson, "Since I'm taking the carriage and you're off today to visit family, why don't you ride along? Unless you prefer to leave later as you'd planned."

"I can be ready quickly, sir," Dawson said as if their going together had not occurred to him until that moment. "Thank you."

Once both men were seated in the carriage, Thomas looked across the way at Dawson and asked, "So, how do you think that went?"

"I didn't sense even a smidgen of doubt," Dawson said proudly. "As if they would ever doubt your honesty."

Thomas sighed and looked out the window. "All for a good cause," he said. "Now let's hope Ruth doesn't make a true liar out of me."

* * *

Ruth finally gave up attempting to sleep when the room began to grow lighter with the coming of day. She was glad for the bread and cheese left from her late-evening snack, but eating it reminded her of the time she'd spent with Thomas Fitzbatten, and she'd spent all night trying not to think about him. She had told herself a hundred times at least that it was his kindness and generosity that had drawn her to him. No man beyond her own father and uncle had ever treated her as he had. And with her father such behavior had been rare. Surely that was reason enough for Thomas's behavior to have left an impression. But a woman would have to be blind to look at a man like Thomas and not see how remarkably handsome he was. Even now she could close her eyes and his image became clear in her mind. The dark stubble on his face suggested he hadn't shaved for two or three days. His curly hair had a windblown look, as if the thick waves refused to be controlled. His dark brows would furrow closer together when he became thoughtful, and the corners of his full lips would turn down at the same time. She believed his eyes to be a grayish blue, but she couldn't be certain given the dim lighting of the inn. But she remembered how tall and strong he felt as she'd walked beside him, her hand on his arm.

Ruth groaned and pushed her hands through her rumpled hair as the most likely possibility for her obsession with Thomas Fitzbatten forced its way into her mind. His uncanny resemblance to Lucius was haunting at best. In reality, it was nearly frightening. How could it be possible for two men, unrelated and unknown to each other, to look so much alike? And how could it be *probable* that one of those men was guilty of taking advantage of her and then fleeing, while the other had offered nothing but kindness and concern?

Realizing she had no idea when her uncle might come for her, Ruth hurried to get cleaned up and dressed for the day—wishing she knew what this day would bring. Her uncle had told her they would travel out of the area before they inquired too much about the possible places where she could go to endure her confinement and childbirth, so as not to arouse local suspicion. Ruth didn't care *where* she was going. She only wished she could somehow leap forward a year in time and have it all behind her. The very idea of nurturing this life inside of her—all the while knowing it would be taken away—already felt like too much to bear. But she had already debated this issue a thousand times, at least inside her mind. She had even written down lists of why she should or shouldn't keep this child. The love she felt for her baby already was more than sufficient to make her choice clear. She would not have her child raised in derision and shame, and penniless as well. She could never hope to find a decent husband while caring for a child conceived in scandal, which meant she would always be working to provide whatever meager living she might manage. Ruth had seen beggars on the streets of London, and she'd seen how servants were treated when such a child was a part of their lives. Some respectable homes wouldn't even consider hiring such a woman, and where would that leave this little one growing inside her? No, she could not keep it. The choice was simple. It was far from easy, and she believed her heart would be forever broken, but at least she would have the peace of knowing that someone, somewhere, was giving her child a better life.

While Ruth was eating breakfast in the dining room, at the same table where she'd sat the previous evening with Thomas, she kept expecting her uncle to show up and find her there. Then she remembered that Thomas had said he would see her. She felt almost panicked at having forgotten. Would he truly come with her uncle and add to her tumultuous thoughts and feelings? She couldn't begrudge his help; she certainly was in no position to question that. But she was in no position to be distracted by a kind, handsome man.

And even if she *weren't* unwed and pregnant—the worst predicament a woman could find herself in—he was not the kind of man to ever seriously take an interest in someone like her.

As if to contradict her thought the moment it entered her mind, she immediately recalled Thomas saying, *I didn't notice how you're dressed because I was looking at you.*

Ruth sighed and hung her head, when all she really wanted was to scream and run away from there. If she had any more than a few coins in her possession, she might have seriously considered just walking away before her uncle arrived. As it was, she needed his help—and she also needed the funding that Thomas Fitzbatten had so generously donated on her behalf. But the turmoil associated with the situation felt as if it would devour her from the inside out.

Having eaten every bite of her breakfast and getting some extra biscuits to stow away for later, Ruth returned to her room, wishing she'd been given a specific time to anticipate her uncle's arrival—and heaven forbid that of Thomas Fitzbatten, perhaps. They'd both said *morning*, but looking at the clock with hours of morning left to go, it felt far too long and too vague. She felt her life and her future hanging in the balance and couldn't force herself to even sit still. With her bag packed and set near the door, she paced the room, looked out the window, which faced the opposite direction of the street, then paced some more. When there was finally a knock at the door it startled her. She took a deep breath, pressed her hands down the front of her dress, and opened the door, both thrilled and horrified to see Thomas standing there with her uncle.

"Good morning, my dear," her uncle said and hugged her. "How are you this morning?"

"Nervous," she admitted. "But I'm all right. At least I think I am."

"Did you get some breakfast?" Thomas asked.

"Good morning, sir," she replied, curtsying slightly as a habit she'd acquired working in a manor house. But a disapproving gaze from him made her think that he'd perhaps found the gesture somehow mocking.

"Good morning," he said and repeated, "Did you get some breakfast?"

"I did, thank you. And I've got biscuits tucked away in my bag."

"Good," Thomas said with approval, and she wondered why he'd taken it upon himself to be concerned about her eating habits. Given the situation, his concern for her—albeit comforting in a way—was only adding to her growing turmoil.

"May we come in?" her uncle asked. "Thomas wanted to talk with you for a few minutes before we set out."

"Of course," she said and stepped aside for the men to enter the room. It was small and looked even smaller with two tall men now filling the space. There were only two chairs, so Ruth sat on the edge of the bed, fearing her knees might give out otherwise. She felt suddenly so nervous that she had to focus on keeping her breathing steady. The men moved the chairs and sat on them so that they were both facing her directly, and she wondered what could be so serious.

"Miss Dawson," Thomas began, looking at her with a directness that was almost fierce, but in a caring way that didn't at all frighten her—completely opposite of his look-alike. Even from his eyes she could tell immediately it was not the same man, in spite of the uncanny resemblance. "I have given a great deal of thought to your dilemma, and may I say that I have prayed?"

"Of course."

"Do you believe in prayer? In God?"

"Very much, sir," she said and heard him sigh. It seemed important to him, and she wondered why.

"We talked last evening of how limited your choices are in regard to this situation, and neither path before you is a good one. I would like to offer you a different option. It may sound strange . . . even shocking." He glanced at her uncle. "Heaven knows Dawson was shocked when I first proposed it to him, but he's come around, and I hope you will too."

Ruth was surprised by the way he took her hand and leaned forward, but she was more distracted by her reaction to his touch and his nearness. "What is it?" she asked when he didn't speak right away. "You're making me terribly nervous." She hoped that would explain the way her hand was trembling in his.

Thomas lifted his chin and drew back his shoulders as if to add strength to what he was about to say. "Miss Dawson . . . Ruth . . . I propose that you might do me the honor of becoming my wife."

"What?" she gasped and pulled her hand from his. It was absolutely the last thing she'd expected to hear; she'd never even imagined such a possibility, and the very idea made her almost dizzy. "No!" she insisted. "No, no, no, no, no."

She noted her uncle looking distraught as he said to Thomas, "I don't think she meant that as an answer to the question."

"I most certainly did!" Ruth said and shot to her feet. Thomas came to his feet to face her, but she began to pace even though she hardly took her eyes off of him. "You must be mad! This is taking kindness too far, Mr. Fitzbatten."

"I ask that you hear me out," he said, sounding calm but betraying his nervousness with the fidgeting of his hands.

"You cannot truly mean to create a . . . *marriage* between us simply for the sake of . . . of what?"

"I'll tell you what if you'll let me speak," Thomas said.

"Ruthie," Dawson said. "Let the man speak his piece."

Ruth stopped pacing and folded her arms. "Fine. I'm listening."

"To answer your question: for the sake of allowing you and your child to be able to stay together and to be cared for. I suspect you're thinking I must have some kind of motive, so I'll just tell you what my motives are so you can stop wondering. I'm not asking you to marry me as some great sacrifice on my part, Ruth. What I hope to gain is purpose and meaning in my life. I need to feel needed. And I'm tired of being alone. I want companionship. And I want to share my life with a woman whom I have come to see—in a very short time—is very much the kind of woman I would choose to spend my life with. That's what I want, Ruth. If that makes me selfish, so be it. I also want to help you. I genuinely want to help you. And let me make it clear that if you do not desire to marry me I will not be offended, and I will still do everything in my power to make certain you and your child are cared for. However, last night I was thinking that perhaps in a year when this is over we might be able to see each other again, and perhaps something good might come of the spark of what I have come to feel for you already. And then I realized that it was ridiculous to wait when I already know in my heart that you and I both have what it takes to make a good marriage and a good life, and if I can give this child a name and a father, that is all the better. My condition would be that no one who doesn't already know you're pregnant will ever be told the truth. If you agree to marry me, this child will be mine, and it will never know differently. Never! You would never lack for anything, Ruth. I would care for you, provide for you, protect you. I would devote my life to your happiness. I realize you don't know me well enough to know whether or not you can trust what I just said, and after what you've been through I can understand why it might be difficult for you to trust *anything* a man said to you. But as God is my witness, I am genuinely offering all that I have if you would consider being my wife."

Ruth was stunned beyond belief and unable to speak. She looked up at this man standing before her—an aristocrat, no less—offering her everything that any right-minded woman would ever want. It was the answer to her every prayer in regard to the sorrow and dilemma she was facing. Yet it all seemed too good to be true. She finally found her voice enough to ask, "Why me, Thomas? Why would you choose me?"

He sighed as if the answer to her question had deep significance. "Sometimes," he said, "something good comes to you at exactly the right moment. I believe we need each other. I feel it very deeply or I would not be standing here."

Ruth felt weak and fumbled her way back to the edge of the bed. She'd be a fool not to accept such a proposal, and even though she was willing to pay a high price to be able to keep her child and live a comfortable life, there were certain matters she knew she could never live with. And she had to make those matters clear now, before any agreement was made.

Ruth looked up at Thomas and pulled together all of her courage enough to say, "I'll not be living life with my husband treating me like a wretched sinner. That's what my mother called me. A wretched sinner. I sinned, I know. But I carry enough guilt and remorse in my heart already; I'll not have it be any part of my marriage—even if that means I *never* marry."

"Ruth," Thomas said in a gentle voice and sat back down, scooting his chair close enough to take her hand. "I don't see you that way; I would never treat you that way. We are all human, and we all make mistakes. It's what we learn from our mistakes and how we rectify them that determines our character. Heaven knows I've committed my own share of sins."

At the mention of his confession, Ruth was startled to see regret, sorrow, turmoil, and grief all pass through his eyes in a matter of seconds. She wondered what his past might entail, and if it might ever come to haunt her if she chose to be his wife. But he was a man willing to take on another man's child. He summed up her thoughts perfectly when he said, "I say that we work together to put the past behind us and create a new life."

Ruth took a moment to ponder that. It all sounded so perfect; she wanted to weep with joy and relief and drop to her knees at his feet to express the depth of her gratitude. She managed to keep her emotions in check and turned to look at her uncle, who had been silently observing the drama.

"And what do you think of all this, Uncle? You must approve or you'd not have brought him here."

"My dear girl," he said, leaning more toward her. "Your life has been hard, but you've always handled it well for the most part. I'd say it's about time something good came to you. In all honesty, if I were to arrange a marriage for you and I were given the option of choosing any man of all the men I know, I could not choose anyone better. I've known him since the day he was born, and he has his moods." Her uncle winked at Thomas. "But he's a good man, Ruthie. Mark my word."

Ruth turned to look again at Thomas, as if she could discern a firm answer by just observing him. Recalling how memories of his handsome face and kind words had kept her awake most of the night, she wondered if she would be so willing to consider his proposal if he were homely and gruff. As it was, she couldn't think of a single reason to decline and figured she would forever regret turning him down if she were fool enough to do so. But there was one more question she needed to have answered. It took even more courage than the last one, but she needed to know exactly where they would stand on such an important matter.

"I assume," she said, "that you are speaking of marriage in every respect . . . that you would expect to share a bed . . . to have more children and—"

"Ruthie!" her uncle interrupted, looking embarrassed. "It's not proper to speak of—"

"No, it's all right, Dawson," Thomas said. "I admire the way she speaks her mind, the way she wants everything to be clear. And it's certainly a valid question." He tightened his gaze on her in a way that made her heart quicken. "Yes, Ruth, I would expect this to be a marriage in every respect. However, given that we barely know each other, I would think it wise to give *that* matter some time. When we are more comfortable with each other . . . when you feel ready. If we are going to be married, we *should* talk about such things. Far better than trying to ignore them, especially given that this is a . . . unique situation."

Ruth stood again and walked to the window, which left her back turned toward the men. She needed a few moments to think and to feel what her heart might be trying to tell her. And she could think much more clearly without having to look at her uncle and her potential husband. *Husband.* It all felt like a dream. Until this conversation had begun it had all been a nightmare. And now it was a dream. She wasn't fool enough to believe that taking this step would mean a life of ease and bliss. She had much to overcome, and he'd admitted to the same. She knew he had wealth and position, but she also knew that such things brought with them a different kind of challenge than what she'd been accustomed to. She wondered how she might fit into his world. Even though he clearly held no regard for social status, others from both classes certainly did, and they would likely have to face the reality of that for the rest of their lives. But in her heart she knew this was a good choice, the right choice. She had no reason to believe his proposal hadn't been given for all the right reasons, and she needed to recognize answers to prayers when they were presented to her.

Ruth turned to look at Thomas. The expectancy in his countenance was as touching as the vulnerability in his eyes. She truly believed he would be devastated if she refused him. It was what every woman wanted to feel when she received a proposal of marriage. She took a deep breath, drew back her shoulders, and said, "I thank you for your honest and sincere proposal, sir." She watched him closely and saw a trace of fear, as if he expected her to add a *but* to that sentence. She was glad to be able to say with full purpose of heart, "I will do everything I can to be a good wife to you."

She saw more than heard him take a sharp breath before he let out a small laugh of relief and looked down as if to conceal his emotion. He looked back up and stepped toward her, taking her hand, which he pressed to his lips without taking his eyes from hers. "Oh, I am very glad to hear it," he said without letting go of her hand.

"When?" she asked, looking away and removing her hand, fearing the physical weakness she was beginning to feel from all of this. A quick glance at her uncle let her know he was both pleased and relieved. She knew him to be a good man, and trustworthy. His endorsement of this marriage meant a great deal to her.

"Today," he said. "If that is agreeable to you."

"Of course," she said, not wanting to have to wait and wonder if it would really happen.

She wondered exactly what his plans were and was glad when he told her. "Your uncle has discreetly made arrangements with the vicar in the next village, not far from here. Gib, my driver, will take us there and act as a second witness. We will be able to come and go unnoticed. The vicar is bound to confidentiality with his position and has assured your uncle that he will be discreet."

"He's a kind man," her uncle said. "He assured me that this sort of thing happens far more than most people would imagine, and he was glad to help put things right. I'm certain he can be trusted."

"After the marriage, your uncle will take a much-needed vacation, which will include a visit to your mother to inform her that you are well and very much married. Gib will return to Brownlie Manor, and you and I will take a hired coach to a cottage owned and kept by my family for a retreat. We should arrive before the sun goes down. We will remain there for as long as we choose, until we both feel comfortable returning to the manor without arousing any suspicion."

An obvious problem occurred to Ruth. "But won't everyone realize the baby was conceived many weeks before we were married?"

"I recently returned home after nearly three years' absence," Thomas explained. "This morning I told my household that I had been married before I'd returned and I'd not mentioned it because I had hoped to be able to tell my parents first—but they are traveling abroad. I told them my wife had been needed at home to take care of an obligation with her family, and she would be meeting me today, and we would be going to the cottage for a long-overdue honeymoon." He bowed slightly and smiled, as if he were just the tiniest bit proud of his outlandish tale. "They were all overjoyed at my happiness."

"Indeed they were," her uncle added.

Ruth put her hands on her hips and said with a scolding tone, "And you told them all of this before you'd even asked me to marry you?"

Thomas was quick to say, "All the while praying you would accept my proposal and forgive me for being presumptuous."

"I'll have to think about that," she said, trying to sound serious as she picked up her bag and opened the door.

"I'll take this," Thomas said and did, carrying the bag for her.

Walking down the stairs, Ruth felt Thomas take her arm, as if he wanted to be certain she descended safely. *It is a dream*, she thought again. *A remarkable, miraculous dream.*

Chapter Three

THE COTTAGE

IN THE CARRIAGE RUTH SAT next to her uncle, which gave her a perfect view of Thomas Fitzbatten while he mostly gazed out the window. She tried not to stare at him, mostly not wanting him to catch her at it. But he was about to become her husband and she barely knew him. She almost felt as if the more she just looked at him, the more likely she would be able to accept that this was really happening. When he glanced her way, she looked out the window, and her mind went to the baby she carried. She'd endured nothing but turmoil and agony throughout the weeks since she'd discovered her pregnancy—and her abandonment—and she had been torn apart inside over the choices before her, both of which had seemed impossible to accept. She believed that some women might have the strength to raise an illegitimate child and do it well, even under the strain of society's injustice and intolerance regarding such matters. And she believed that some women might find peace over giving a baby away, perhaps coming to know that it was God's will. She had been praying that with time she would come to feel such peace. But as of yet she had felt exactly the opposite, as if letting go of her child would have been all wrong. Still, she'd been backed into a corner due to her foolish and sinful behavior. And now, suddenly, like a lightning strike out of a blue sky, she had been offered a way out of that impossible corner. She couldn't foresee her life beyond this day, but she instinctively knew that whatever it might entail would be far better than the way things might have turned out without the intervention of this good man.

They arrived at their destination more quickly than Ruth had expected. Thomas stepped out of the carriage first and helped her down before he left her in her uncle's care, saying that he had some things to arrange and they would meet at the private entrance of the church, just as they had previously arranged with the local vicar. With her hand on her uncle's arm, Ruth walked just a short distance to an inn, smaller than the one where she had stayed the previous night. There were almost no customers inside, which made her glad for the quiet solitude of the place; that likely wouldn't be the case at other times of day. Her uncle ordered some food for them to eat, asking also for food that could be taken with them to eat while traveling. She was grateful for his insight on that count, since she invariably became hungry—and therefore nauseous—so frequently.

While they waited for their food, Ruth used the available facilities and was able to freshen up. She looked at herself in the dingy mirror in the tiny room and considered that she was about to become a bride. She'd never been one to dream of elaborate gowns or huge celebrations, but neither had she imagined being married wearing one of the two dresses she owned, looking no different than she did every day of the week. She attempted to smooth the hair that had worked its way out of the plaiting and pins she'd put in place not so many hours ago, but it seemed hopeless. Deciding that Thomas was willing to marry her whether or not her hair was perfectly in place, she sighed and turned away from the mirror. She found her uncle eating and sat down across from him, once again feeling hungry because of the child growing inside her but having little appetite due to her nerves. She forced herself to eat and was glad to know that the bag her uncle carried with him out of the inn contained food that would tide her over when she needed it.

Again they walked together while her uncle said little. He asked if she was all right, and she insisted that she was. As the church came into view, he stopped walking and turned her to face him. "Are you absolutely certain this is what you want, my dear? It's all happening very quickly, but if you feel any doubts . . . any concerns . . . I need you to tell me."

Ruth thought about it a long moment and assessed her feelings carefully, which wasn't easy considering how overwhelming all of this was proving to be. She looked up at her uncle and said, "You've told me he's a good man. You know him as well as anyone, and I trust you. Under the circumstances it seems a miracle that he would be willing to do this for me . . . for the baby."

"It is a wonder, indeed," he said, "but it's a lifetime, Ruthie. And I just have to ask . . . do you *want* to marry him? We both know it's a better option than any other, but do you *want* it?"

Ruth was able to say with a conviction that surprised even herself, "I do, Uncle. I want to marry him. It feels right to me, even if I can't explain it. I know it may not be easy, but it *is* by far the best option. I do believe it's good and right, and I can only feel grateful."

He sighed and nodded as if her reassurance meant a great deal to him. He hugged her as her father might have if he'd still been alive. Ruth missed her father, but in truth she wasn't sure he wouldn't have reacted the same way as her mother had over the unwanted pregnancy. Being in her uncle's care seemed a blessing not only in the kindness and lack of scolding he'd offered but in the way he had gone to his employer for help—which had resulted in a miracle.

Together they walked on toward the church while Ruth tried to accept into her mind and heart that her life was about to be changed forever. She wondered what it might be like to be Mrs. Thomas Fitzbatten. She honestly had no idea. She had worked in manor houses much like the one in which her uncle worked—a servant to her intended husband. She couldn't imagine uniting herself with any man she had ever worked for; it was a world she had never wanted any part of. She'd seen servant girls coveting the gowns and jewels of the women they served. She'd heard them speculate over the handsome and wealthy bachelors who lived under the same roof but had absolutely nothing else in common with them. Ruth had never shared their views or sentiments. But Thomas was clearly nothing like any man of his class she had ever encountered. If he was, she would be far more reluctant to accept his offer. She might have married such a man for the sake of not having to give up her child, but she would have considered it a sacrifice that would have been difficult to bear. As it was, she felt no trepidation. More than a little nervous, certainly. But not afraid.

As they came around the corner of the back of the church, Thomas was waiting near the door, and Ruth was taken aback to see him holding a bouquet of mixed blooms in a variety of colors. He smiled when he saw her and held out the flowers. She took them and he said, "I'm certain this is not the wedding you might have dreamed of, but a bride should at least have a bouquet."

"Thank you," she said, unable to express how much his thoughtfulness meant to her. She smiled at him, hoping he might read appreciation in her eyes. He surprised her again when he took a blue hydrangea out of the bouquet and tucked its stem carefully into her hair where it was pinned to the back of her head. She felt certain the size of it must look ostentatious, but she *was* getting married.

"There." He smiled, proud of his handiwork. "Very pretty." She found herself staring at him while she wondered if he meant her or the flower. But then, he was staring back. It seemed they were still both trying to accept what they would mean to each other's lives. Without taking his gaze from her, Thomas said, "Doesn't she look pretty, Dawson?"

"She does, indeed," her uncle said. "The blue is lovely on you, my dear."

"Thank you," she said and closed her eyes to inhale the mixed fragrances of the bouquet in her hands, if only to break away from Thomas's gaze.

"Shall we?" Thomas said. "I believe they are waiting for us."

Ruth took a deep breath and went inside, overcome with a fluttering in her stomach. They walked down a hallway and around a corner, coming into a chapel from the front near the organ. There were many candles lit, and light streamed through a stained glass window that depicted Adam and Eve, their faces barely visible among the lavish garden of foliage and flowers in which they stood looking at each other. No one was in the chapel except a man in clerical robes who was obviously the vicar, and Gib, the man Ruth had met the previous evening who was a driver for the Fitzbattens—and obviously well trusted by Thomas.

Ruth was mostly oblivious to the conversation taking place among the men regarding the marriage document that was being prepared. She just sat down and waited, holding tightly to her precious bouquet, wanting to remember every detail of its beauty, knowing it was the only tangible evidence that her wedding was taking place.

"Are you ready, my dear?" her uncle asked, offering his hand. She took it and stood, hoping he wouldn't notice that she was trembling.

There was no music, no walking up the aisle—just her uncle ceremoniously placing her hand into Thomas's as they stood before the vicar. Ruth kept her eyes on Thomas throughout the ceremony, glad that he returned her gaze, hoping the words had meaning for him as they did for her. For all the haste and necessity of this unlikely marriage, she took these vows very seriously and hoped he did, as well. She wondered for a moment if he might one day grow tired of her, if he might be the kind of man to cheat on his wife or maintain a marriage only for the sake of public appearances. She wondered if he might break her heart, or if she might break his. She wanted to believe that their hearts were not involved; they'd only met last evening. But she couldn't deny that she wanted with all her heart for love to grow out of this union; she wanted happiness for herself and her child. And she believed he wanted it too. If their hearts were not already invested, there was the hope that they would be. But that required the risk of opening their hearts to each other, and she wondered if it might be possible. She had been wounded cruelly and yet felt eager to trust Thomas Fitzbatten. He had admitted to unsavory facets of his own past, and she wondered what wounds he might be holding within himself. Had a woman broken his heart? Would his heart, then, forever belong to another? Was he willing to marry a damsel in distress because he could not have the woman he loved?

Ruth's list of questions began to grow more ridiculous, and she forced her mind to focus only on the words being spoken by the vicar. And then it was time for her and Thomas to speak their vows. She had no trouble speaking her part with conviction and felt some relief to hear equal conviction from him. She was surprised to see Thomas pull a ring from the pocket of his waistcoat at the appointed time. She'd felt certain there wouldn't have been time to acquire such a thing.

At her questioning gaze, he said quietly, "I brought it from home. It was my grandmother's. It was always meant to be for my wife. If it doesn't fit, we can have a jeweler adjust the size."

Ruth nodded, then looked down to watch him place his grandmother's ring on her finger, feeling unworthy of such a lovely and meaningful heirloom. The gold band was wide with an ornate design carved into it, and on the top was a small blue jewel, not dissimilar in color to the flower she wore in her hair. She wondered if he had planned that, or if it was merely coincidence. Whether he'd planned it or not, nothing about this event seemed to be coincidental—a thought that sent a warm chill over her shoulders as the ring slid into place and Thomas said with a smile, "It *does* fit. It would seem that it was meant to be yours."

Ruth found the statement ludicrous under the circumstances, but at the same time it felt strangely right. The contradiction puzzled her, but it flew away along with every other thought when she heard the vicar say, "I now pronounce you, Thomas Quincy Fitzbatten, and you, Ruth Hollis Dawson, man and wife, till death do you part."

Ruth's heart quickened and her stomach fluttered again at the sense of finality. She saw nothing in Thomas's expression to let her know how he might be feeling, but she distinctly saw a glimmer of intrigue in his eyes. Far better that than some kind of grim and begrudging duty—which was what Lucius would have felt if he had actually been man enough to marry her.

Ruth was thinking that would be all and felt a little startled to hear the vicar say, "You may now kiss the bride." She wanted to say that wasn't necessary; she wanted to avoid such an exchange of affection—especially here in front of her uncle and these strangers. But she knew that for all intents and purposes the vicar had been led to believe that this secretive, hurried wedding was due to her being pregnant with Thomas's child and that love was the motive behind this marriage.

She closed her eyes as Thomas bent forward to kiss her, expecting it to be brief and to the point. While his kiss did not last longer than might be appropriate for a wedding, she felt a tenderness in it that surprised her. It quickened her heart, and tears tingled in her eyes;

tears that he surely noticed when she opened her eyes to find him watching her, as if he were looking for some evidence that all of this meant something to her. She assumed that he found what he was looking for when he smiled slightly and said, "Shall we go home, Mrs. Fitzbatten?"

Ruth was afraid to speak for fear of betraying a sudden rise of emotion. All of the fear and shame she'd been feeling for weeks had rushed up unexpectedly to be greeted by the inexplicable relief of this moment. But she swallowed any temptation to cry and nodded with a smile that genuinely expressed how she felt in that moment.

When everything had been taken care of with the vicar, Ruth left the church with her new husband holding her hand, and Gib and her uncle following. Once they were outside, Gib offered a handshake to the other two men, congratulating them as if this were truly a cause for great celebration. He nodded and smiled politely toward Ruth before he left to take the carriage back to Brownlie Manor, having pledged to not breathe a word of the scheming he'd been privy to. He seemed a kind man and loyal to Thomas, and Ruth suspected he enjoyed having such a secret to keep and that he was very good at keeping things to himself.

Ruth listened as her uncle made Thomas promise to always take good care of his little Ruthie and Thomas promised with vehemence that he would. Thomas then reminded Ruth—as if he might have sensed that she needed the reassurance—that her uncle was taking advantage of a few days off to go and visit her family and see that all was well. He would tell them of the marriage, which she knew would come as a great surprise to all of them. Of course, only her mother knew of the pregnancy, and she would die of shame before she'd ever tell a soul. All of Ruth's brothers would simply be surprised to hear that their sister was married.

"Tell them we will come to visit at a future date," Thomas said to her uncle. "It's certainly right that I should become acquainted with the family."

"I will pass that on," Dawson said, nodding at Thomas.

"Tell my mother I love her," Ruth said. "I don't know if she'll believe it, but tell her anyway."

"And why would she not believe it?" her uncle asked.

"I've disappointed her so very much," Ruth admitted, her voice breaking. She felt Thomas squeeze her hand in response.

"I'm certain she loves you no less," her uncle said. "And will she not be pleased that you've married such a fine man?"

"We will hope for that," Ruth said and was glad to have her uncle on his way, if only so they could stop talking about her mother. Their conversation following the revelation of Ruth's pregnancy still haunted her, but she would save coming to terms with that until another time. For all its strangeness, this was her wedding day.

Ruth watched her uncle walk away and only then realized that she and Thomas were standing among some very old gravestones that were situated just next to the church. The intermittent clouds overhead were more decorative than threatening, and a pleasant breeze carried the vague hint of nearby flowers to her nose. Or perhaps it was the flowers in her bouquet that she could smell. She lifted it to her face and breathed in, thinking it was the most beautiful collection of flowers she'd ever seen. She wanted them to never die or fade.

"Shall we be off?" she heard Thomas say and wondered how long it would take her to get used to the idea that he was her husband.

"Of course," she said, and he kept hold of her hand as he led her in a different direction from that which they'd come, through the graveyard and toward a road on the other side. "Where is it exactly that we're going?"

"It's a cottage owned by my family," he said, and she recalled now that he'd mentioned it earlier. "We keep it for occasional retreats and such, and we don't use it nearly as much as we should. It's maintained by a lovely family who lives there always. It provides a good living for them even if it serves little purpose otherwise. I thought it would be a good place for us to get away for a while and let people lose track of how long we've been married—although I did tell my household that I was married before I ever came home."

"You lied to them, then."

"Yes, I did," he said almost proudly. "And as long as we remain vague on exactly when and where we met and married, no one will ever be the wiser."

"How far is the cottage?" she asked, walking beside him at an easy pace.

"It's not far from the sea. With stopping for a good meal on the way, we should still easily arrive before sundown."

"And they're expecting us?"

"Yes, I sent word ahead with a messenger."

Before embarking on their journey, Ruth was able to once again use the facilities at the inn, and with some extra food tucked away, she felt as ready as she could be to set out. An older woman who wore far too much perfume and a ridiculously ugly dress laden with frills was also in the coach, which made it necessary for Ruth to sit next to Thomas. But she didn't mind. His closeness had a way of making her feel safe, although she doubted that she could ever tell him why.

The woman across from them noticed the flowers in Ruth's hand and commented on them, but it didn't seem to occur to her that they might be a wedding bouquet—probably because neither Thomas nor Ruth were dressed the way one might expect of a bride and groom. She did, however, look inquisitive, as if the couple she had no choice but to look at had caught her interest. Ruth couldn't blame her. They likely appeared a strange pair.

Thomas put all matters to rest when he said, "The flowers are lovely, are they not?"

"Indeed, sir," the woman said.

"When I saw such a fine bouquet, I could not resist buying them for my wife. A man shouldn't need any other excuse than that to get flowers for the woman he holds most dear."

"Certainly not," the woman said and smiled as if she'd just been included in some kind of real-life romantic tale. Perhaps she had.

Ruth felt certain the woman would be appalled to know the truth, but she didn't care. Instead she chose to ignore the possibility and looked up at Thomas, quietly echoing his last words, "Most dear?"

"Indeed," he said with conviction, as if the reasons for their hasty marriage meant nothing in light of the vows he had declared at the altar.

Thomas made Ruth feel a little more like his wife when he put his arm around her and urged her head to his shoulder. "You must be tired, my dear," he said as if they'd been married for months. She accepted the term of endearment as a form of acting rather than any real indication of his feelings. But she *was* tired, and the comfort of his shoulder made it easy to relax.

Her next awareness occurred when she was jolted awake by the coach passing over a rather nasty bump in the road. She found herself still clutching her flowers and Thomas's arm still around her. And the woman across the way still observing them while her perfume overwhelmed the confines of the carriage.

"Are you all right?" Thomas asked.

"Yes," she said, trying to ignore the nausea with which she always awakened. "How long was I—"

"Nearly two hours, I think," he said. "We should be stopping at an inn in just a short while, I believe, where they'll change horses and we can eat and freshen up." He placed a folded napkin on her lap as if he'd predicted her next thought. "Hopefully this will tide you over until then."

"Oh, thank you," she said with enthusiasm, not wanting the embarrassment of having to ask for the carriage to stop so that she could heave at the roadside. That would certainly not be a pleasant addition to her wedding day! "You think of everything."

While Ruth was eating the buttered bread with an enthusiasm that she doubted was very ladylike, the woman said, "Might I guess that you're expecting?"

"You guess correctly," Thomas said, which prevented Ruth from having to speak with her mouth full. "You must have experience with such things."

The woman began talking of her own children, who were now all grown, sharing details that Ruth found tedious and uninteresting—especially when this woman was a complete stranger. But Thomas remained politely engaged in the conversation until the coach blessedly drew to a halt and they were able to part company with their perfumed companion, who would now be traveling in a different direction.

"May the earth have mercy," Ruth muttered as soon as the woman had walked far enough away that she wouldn't be overheard.

"If I'd had to smell that perfume another mile I'd have lost my breakfast all over that ridiculous dress she was wearing."

As soon as she'd said it, Ruth wondered if Thomas would find such words unbefitting of his wife, but he chuckled and said, "Then we can be grateful we have arrived with her perfume *and* her ridiculous dress intact."

"It seems I have much to learn about proper fashion, but—"

"Ruth," he interrupted with another chuckle, "the dress *was* ridiculous."

She laughed with him and was so glad for the comfort of the inn in spite of its crowds. Fresh water and good food went a long way in helping her feel better and more prepared for what the rest of the day might bring.

On the chance that the remainder of their journey might also lack privacy, Ruth took advantage of being alone with Thomas during their meal to say, "Tell me a little of what to expect of the cottage, so I won't be too terribly nervous."

"There is no need for that, I can assure you," he said. "It's very small in contrast to Brownlie Manor, but I think you'll like it immensely. It's secluded and rather quaint. That's the word my mother has always used to describe it. *Quaint.* I have many memories of going there with my parents—all through my youth."

"Tell me about the family who cares for the cottage," Ruth said, not wanting to embarrass herself with her ignorance on the details of his life.

"Young Barclay runs the place. Actually," Thomas chuckled, "I suppose I should get used to just calling him Barclay. His father was always the caretaker, and so we naturally called the son *Young* Barclay. But my mother informed me in a letter that the elder Mr. Barclay passed away while I was gone, so the son has taken over his father's job. According to my mother's letters, Barclay was also married since I last saw him—a girl from the nearby village. Apparently they've known each other from childhood and no one was surprised by the union."

"Just like us," Ruth said with light sarcasm, and Thomas chuckled.

"Yes," he said and took her hand across the table. "Just like us."

She was glad that he could laugh with her over the situation. If his response to her little joke had been stuffy or awkward, she would have found the entire situation more difficult.

"I'm afraid I can't remember her given name. If I've ever met her I don't recall. But we'll meet her soon enough. Barclay's mother, Starla, is still living and is in his care, but I understand her health is failing. And . . . that is what I know."

"So . . . they live in the cottage to care for it on the chance that you or your parents may decide to pay an occasional visit."

"That is true," Thomas said.

"I would like such a job as that," Ruth said.

"Would you, now?" he asked. "Well, you are the wife of Thomas Fitzbatten and you shall *never* be required to ever work again in your life."

Ruth felt more than a little astonished at the implication and felt compelled to say, "But is work not good for the soul, and all that? I have no desire to spend my life being waited upon while I sit about doing nothing at all."

"Let me clarify something, wife," he said, and she liked the way he called her that. "While I'm well aware that most people of my class consider it some kind of honor and privilege to do absolutely *nothing* productive with their lives, I am not one of those people. I enjoy work and do so wherever I may be needed. There are also certainly times when you and I will need to appropriately fulfill our roles as the owners and residents of Brownlie Manor with all the finery and pomp that goes along with such things, but—"

"How on earth will I ever do *that*?" she asked.

He chuckled. "We will cross that bridge when we come to it. There is no need to trouble yourself, my dear. As I was saying . . . except on certain occasions and in regard to certain things—of which I will properly inform you and not leave you to embarrass yourself—you may work at whatever you please. What I want you to know is that you are not *required* to work. There will never again be the need for you to do menial labor in order to provide a meager living for yourself. I will see to your every need. But whether we are at the cottage or the manor, there will always be gardens that need tending, animals to be cared for, and kitchens that have work aplenty. Those who work *for* me and my parents are well accustomed to having us frequently work *with* them. I'm certain they won't be put off by having my wife do the same."

"I'm glad to hear it," she said. "I can't very well imagine having someone else wash my underclothing for me. I think I'd much rather do it myself."

Thomas smiled at her, and she asked, "Is that funny?"

"Endearing," he said, but she couldn't be sure what he meant. "Although, you shouldn't be at all embarrassed about letting someone else do your laundry—*all* of your laundry."

"And should I be embarrassed to discuss such a thing as my underclothing with my husband?"

"Not in the slightest," he insisted and she was glad of that. She'd never had any trouble speaking of feminine things around her brothers; she certainly didn't want to have to mind her words too carefully around this man who was now meant to be more important to her than any other. It crossed her mind that perhaps once they were settled at the cottage he might simply leave her to her own resources; that the companionship she was growing accustomed to was only due to their traveling together—and the fact that they'd been married this morning. Perhaps she was a fool to think that it would always be this way. If he were disagreeable and gruff—as Lucius had often been—she might have preferred it that way. As it was, she found herself wanting to always know that Thomas was nearby; she enjoyed his company as well as his kindness. But in truth she had no idea what his expectations were in regard to this marriage, and she could only be grateful for all he'd done for her and try to make the most of however it managed to turn out.

"There is one more thing," Thomas said, "before we go—on the chance that we're not alone in the coach."

"Yes?" she asked, fearing what he might say.

"I just want to remind you that Barclay and his family—and anyone else we might encounter—are meant to believe we've been married for months. Not only do we need to be vague about how and when we met and married, we need to behave as if we *are* married."

Ruth took in that implication but didn't know what to say. She simply nodded and said, "I'll follow your lead and do my very best acting."

"I suspect that within a day or two it won't take any effort at all," he said.

She wished there was time to have him explain what he meant, but it was time for them to leave, and she wasn't certain she would know *what* to ask even if they'd had more time. He took her hand to help her to her feet, and she picked up her bouquet from the table. The serving girl provided them with some food for the road that she'd had prepared according to Thomas's request, and they were soon on their way again, this time riding with a middle-aged couple who seemed rather ordinary and quietly kind, saying little beyond minimal greetings. Ruth preferred it that way and was glad to again find Thomas's shoulder readily available for her head. The combined exhaustion of pregnancy and sleepless, worry-filled nights quickly put her to sleep.

Ruth stirred when the coach stopped, giving them a few minutes to get out and stretch their legs, but they were quickly back on the road, this time with no other passengers. Still, Ruth was glad that Thomas sat next to her instead of across from her. She ate the food they'd brought with them, offering Thomas some of it, but he assured her he was fine. With her stomach settled again, she was quickly back to sleep against Thomas's *other* shoulder, amazed at how quickly his closeness had become so familiar and comfortable to her.

Thomas marveled that Ruth could sleep so deeply in spite of the bumpy roads. He was aware that pregnancy caused fatigue in women, but he also suspected that she had likely been losing sleep due to the worrisome predicament she had been in. Her ability to sleep now left him already feeling as if the decisions he'd made were good. The way she slept against him, with his arm securely around her, seemed symbolic to him of the commitment he'd made to always care for her. Her very ability to relax so completely within his grasp implied that she was free of worry and agitation, and that alone gave him some sense of purpose.

Thomas couldn't deny that he also felt something else from her closeness. He wasn't a man to get caught up in carnal desires; he'd been taught from a very young age to harness such feelings appropriately. But there was no avoiding the fact that he was glad to know that Ruth was his wife. Of course, they barely knew one another, and he would—as he'd promised—give her all the time she needed to feel ready to share that kind of relationship with him. He didn't feel impatient or concerned in any way; only a vague kind of comfort in knowing that what Ruth was awakening inside of him did not have to be temporary. Even as he'd made his plans to marry her and had been as certain then as he was now that it was the proper course to take, the possibility of such feelings had barely crossed his mind. Now, as he held her close while she slept, he couldn't imagine anything else he could be doing in that moment that might give him more satisfaction or a sense of hope.

The sun was creeping toward the western horizon when the scenery outside the carriage windows became familiar. Thomas couldn't even recall the last time he'd been here, which would have been long before his military duty had taken him away. Having that and all of its associated horrors behind him was one of many reasons he was glad to be returning here. Returning with a wife made him feel all the more blessed. The charade of pretending they'd been together for months now didn't feel as challenging as it had earlier in the day. He was growing more comfortable with her as each hour passed—even while she slept.

When the cottage came into view in the distance, he gently urged Ruth awake. "We're almost there," he said. "Do you want to see it?"

"Oh yes," she said and leaned over him to look out the window in the direction he was pointing. Much of the house was hidden by the surrounding high grasses and foliage, but the peaks of the roof and its chimneys rose past the height of the nearby trees.

"Oh, it's lovely, Thomas," she said with an enthusiasm that warmed him. He had no doubts that most of the women who had tried to charm him into marriage in years past would have found the place barely habitable, let alone lovely.

"It *is* lovely," he agreed. "I'm glad to be back. I do hope you'll like it here."

"I'm certain I will," she said and took his hand in a natural way, as if she'd not thought about it but had simply done it. He squeezed her hand and watched the details of the cottage become more visible as the coach got closer. When it stopped at the edge of the walk—which was more like a rough footpath from the road—Thomas stepped out and held up his hand to help Ruth step down.

Ruth took in the view of the home in front of her and tried to imagine it as hers. She almost laughed aloud to think of Thomas saying that the cottage was very small in contrast to Brownlie Manor. The cottage was large and beautiful in contrast to the home where she'd grown up. She had believed that today she would be on her way to some detestable home for wayward single mothers, and here she was, her husband beside her, about to step into a place his mother had described as quaint. Already she agreed. It certainly was quaint.

While Ruth stood to admire the cottage, clutching her bouquet of flowers in one hand, the driver handed Thomas their bags, which weren't very heavy. The carriage rolled away while Thomas led the way up the path to the front door. They had almost reached it when a man came out to meet them, wearing a grin that revealed crooked teeth, which didn't detract at all from the bright, welcoming appeal of his smile. He was as tall as Thomas but more broad in his build. His hair was tied back with a ribbon, but much of it had fallen out and hung at the sides of his round face, likely the result of a long day's work.

"Hello, Barclay," Thomas said.

"Master Thomas," Barclay said with genuine enthusiasm. "'Tis a pleasure indeed to have you come to the cottage at last."

"And a pleasure to be here," Thomas said while Barclay took the bags from him. Barclay tossed a curious glance toward Ruth, and Thomas was quick to add, "May I present my wife. There's no need to tell you her formal name. I think she prefers to simply be called Ruth."

"Good evening to you," Barclay said and nodded.

"And to you, Barclay," Ruth said.

Barclay hurried into the open door of the house as if he didn't know how to walk slowly. Thomas took Ruth's hand to follow but paused and asked, "What do you think so far?"

Ruth was touched to realize that he actually cared about her opinion. He'd rescued her from a terrible fate, and here he was, concerned about her comfort and preferences.

"Oh, it's lovely, Thomas," she said with all of the enthusiasm she felt. "And rather grand. I think I might be far more suited to such a home as this, as opposed to Brownlie Manor."

"You only say that because you haven't yet lived at Brownlie Manor," he said. "I doubt it has much in common with wherever you may have lived and worked before."

"I daresay I believe you," she said, certain that everything to do with Thomas Fitzbatten was likely different from anything she had previously encountered.

They stepped inside, where Barclay had set their bags at the foot of the stairs. To one side of the hallway in which they stood, Ruth saw a cozy parlor with many comfortable places to sit, arranged prettily with little tables and simple decor. A fire was burning in the hearth. To say the room was inviting after a day's travel seemed an enormous understatement. In that moment, Ruth could imagine endless hours spent in such a room—reading, visiting, or just relaxing. On the other side of the hall she could see what appeared to be a fine dining room, with a table large enough to seat ten or twelve; she didn't actually count the chairs. There was a lovely carved sideboard and a large vase of fresh flowers in the center of the table. Both rooms had large windows through which the evening sun was shining brilliantly, illuminating every detail that added to Ruth's delight.

Ruth moved dreamily into the parlor, randomly touching the delicate porcelain pieces and crocheted doilies that added a homey touch. She ran her hand over the blue velvety fabric of a sofa and touched the blue-and-gold brocade draperies.

"It's beautiful, Thomas," she said, and he seemed pleased.

"At the back of the house is the kitchen and washroom, where the laundry is done. Upstairs are bedrooms and bathing rooms. Barclay's family occupies the rooms to the south, and we will use the rooms to the north."

"I must apologize, sir," Barclay said, hovering nearby and sounding decidedly nervous.

"Is something wrong?" Thomas asked him.

"It's just that . . . I assume you know my father passed."

"Yes, my mother wrote to tell me. My condolences for your loss."

"Thank you, sir. He lived a good life. I believe he was ready to go. The thing is, my mother's not doing well, and it's taken a lot to care for her properly."

"I'm sorry to hear that," Thomas said. "Is there anything we can do?"

"We're managing fine," Barclay said. "It's just that . . . my wife, Bertie . . . I'm hoping your mother wrote of her and—"

"She did, yes," Thomas said. "And I congratulate you on your marriage. And a child coming too, I hear."

"Yes, sir. Thank you, sir. The thing is . . . Bertie's coming near her time and hasn't been up to doing much. What I'm trying to say, sir, is that things are not as in order as we would have hoped for your visit."

"There's no need to apologize for that, my good man," Thomas said, and Ruth felt proud of him. How glad she was to have a husband who treated his servants like human beings and was understanding of their challenges. "I'm certain everything is fine, and you should know me well enough to know I don't expect to be waited on hand and foot, and I'm rather adept at helping when I need to."

"You're very kind, as always, sir."

"And my wife is not unaccustomed to helping when need be," Thomas said, reaching for her hand, which she gladly gave. "Are you, my dear?"

"Not at all," Ruth said. "Is there anything we can do to help this evening?"

"Oh no!" Barclay said. "Everything is fine for the moment. I just wanted you to know that things are not in quite as good of order as we'd hoped. We'll see what tomorrow brings. There's some stew on the stove for you; I'm certain you must be hungry. And Bertie's just brought biscuits out of the oven a short time ago. She manages fine so long as she doesn't overdo."

"That sounds lovely," Ruth said. "We thank you."

"And we only had time to put the one bedroom in order . . . air it out and get rid of the dust, but knowing that you're just newly married and all, my Bertie assured me that would be fine. I do hope it is."

"Of course it is," Thomas said, discreetly squeezing Ruth's hand as if to assure her that they would find a way to manage. She hadn't really thought about how they might go about handling such things, but thankfully she felt comfortable enough with Thomas to know that she could be forthright about her feelings on the matter.

Bertie came into the room, looking very pregnant and uncomfortable with every step she took. Barclay introduced her proudly, and she explained that her given name was Bertha but she couldn't tolerate that and had chosen to be called Bertie instead. She had blonde hair that was excessively curly, and a face that was more kind than pretty, but she seemed well matched with Barclay, and their happiness was evident. They seemed especially happy to have Thomas and Ruth there, as if their presence in the cottage was a privilege and not a burden.

"Oh, your flowers are lovely," Bertie said, taking note of the bouquet Ruth was holding.

"They are," Ruth said. "Thomas was kind enough to get them for me this morning, but I fear they're a little the worse for wear due to the journey."

"Let me put them in some water for you," Bertie insisted and took the bouquet into what was apparently the kitchen. Barclay exchanged small talk with Thomas until his wife returned, then Thomas encouraged Bertie to sit down and Barclay insisted his wife put her feet up. Ruth sat with her and asked, "When is the baby expected?"

"Two or three weeks, from what I estimate," Bertie said.

"Then we shall have to take very good care of you," Ruth said to Bertie and glanced at Thomas, wondering after she'd said it if that was all right.

She caught a subtle nod of approval from Thomas just before he said, "We are expecting one of our own, though not for some time yet, as you can see."

"Oh, how wonderful!" Bertie said.

"Finally a child to carry on the Fitzbatten legacy," Barclay said with joy.

"Yes, finally," Thomas said, sounding enthusiastic, but Ruth had trouble looking at him.

Bertie tried to get up to serve them their meal, but Thomas insisted they could manage just fine and she should rest. Barclay helped make certain they had all they needed to sit in the kitchen near the warm stove to eat their stew and biscuits. He then left them to eat, saying that he and his wife and mother had already eaten.

"I'll just take your bags up to your room and light the fire to take off the chill," Barclay said.

"Thank you," Thomas said, and Ruth was left alone with him in the kitchen. Ruth noticed that her wedding bouquet was in a vase of water on the table where they were eating. It seemed appropriate.

"How are you so far?" he asked quietly.

"Oh, they're lovely people," Ruth said. "And it's a lovely house. I couldn't be more grateful."

"You're an easy woman to please," he said.

Ruth felt confused. "What do you mean?"

"I mean that before I went into the military, there were high society women all vying for my hand in marriage, thinking I would be impressed by their tawdriness and pretentious ways. They were shallow and they disgusted me. I can't help thinking how any one of them would loathe sitting here in such a small home, eating stew and biscuits she had to serve up herself, and not having someone wait on her, hand and foot. And here you sit expressing gratitude. It would seem I made a fine choice in a wife."

"Did you?" she couldn't help asking.

"At this moment it seems so," he said and took a bite of stew. "So, let us enjoy this moment, Mrs. Fitzbatten."

"As you wish," she said, and enjoyed filling her stomach with such delicious food.

When they had finished their meal, Ruth followed her lifelong habits and cleared the table and started washing dishes. She expected that Thomas might stop her, but he just helped, surely thinking they didn't want to leave a mess for Bertie in her condition.

Barclay came in as they were finishing up and looked embarrassed—but unmistakably grateful—for their help in the kitchen. He told them that Bertie had gone up to bed and his mother was already asleep. "But I'm sure she'll want to see you and meet your bride in the morning," he added with enthusiasm.

"We'll look forward to that," Thomas said.

"I thought you must be tired, long day and all that," Barclay said. "Your room is ready. I will see you in the morning unless there's something you need in the meantime."

"No, thank you, Barclay. Everything is more than fine. Please don't concern yourself. We appreciate your efforts."

Barclay nodded and left the room. Thomas held out his arm for Ruth. "Shall we retire then, wife?" he asked, sounding mildly facetious.

"It would seem wise, husband," she said in the same tone and took his arm, walking with him up the stairs.

Chapter Four

TOGETHER

At the top of the stairs there was a closed door to the right that Ruth assumed was the entrance to the private bedrooms and bathing room for Barclay and his family. To the left was a similar door that had been left open. They passed through the door and Thomas closed it. They moved past three closed doors, which he explained were other bedrooms that were likely in need of cleaning, as Barclay had implied. They peeked into a bathing room with a large tub and a stove for heating water, along with an abundance of many other necessities.

"How nice," Ruth said.

They then went through the open door at the end of the hall, which was obviously the bedroom where they were meant to stay together as husband and wife. A quick glance told her this room was every bit as cozy as the parlor, with a small table and two chairs that seemed meant for sharing breakfast. There were soft, comfortable chairs as well, a little desk, and some book cupboards, along with a large, beautiful bed and matching armoire. The fire burning in the grate and candles lit throughout the room added to the warm effect, now that the sun had gone down.

As Thomas closed the door, he said, "As far as I've ever known, my parents have had a good marriage. But they often kept separate rooms, mostly due to their preferences for dramatically different sleeping schedules. My mother likes to sit up late and read and sleep in, often having breakfast in her room. My father is quite the opposite, wanting to go to sleep early and get up at the crack of dawn. They've told me that getting their sleep was more conducive to a better marriage, and they seem to exemplify that." He paused as if to emphasize a point. "If you prefer separate rooms, I'm certain we can arrange it tomorrow and not appear terribly conspicuous—even if that might seem a bit strange because we are newly married; I'm certain we can find a way to explain ourselves—if that's the way you want it."

Ruth preferred to be with Thomas as much as humanly possible, but she didn't feel ready to cross boundaries with him that she knew were expected in marriage. She wondered how to clarify that but simply said, "It is a bed made for two people, and it appears to be rather spacious. I can manage if you can—unless that makes you uncomfortable for some reason."

She sat on the edge of the bed, mostly because she was feeling tired and didn't want to stand any longer. An awkwardness descended between them that was surprisingly unusual for what they had been through together today. Ruth wondered what to say and what to expect. She hoped he would take the lead and clear the air of this deepening tension around them.

"Ruth," he said and sat on the edge of the bed beside her, taking her hand. "I want to make something very clear; I don't want there to be any room for misunderstanding or any reason for awkwardness between us." She nodded, wondering if he was referring to the very thing she'd been thinking about. "We are husband and wife, yes. And it appears we will be sharing a bed—which, if nothing else, will waylay any suspicions or questions regarding our hasty marriage. But I want you to know that I have no expectations in that regard. I can assure you I have enough self-discipline and respect for you to sleep in the same bed and mind my manners. Eventually, yes, I want to share such things in our marriage, the way God intended a marriage relationship to be. But I want you to know that I don't believe the vows we exchanged today automatically give me any rights in that regard. I know you've been through a great deal, and I want you to feel ready. I will wait for you to let me know when the time is right—perhaps after the baby comes and you've had time to recover." He looked down, which was his first hint of embarrassment over the sensitive topic. "Or perhaps I shouldn't be trying to put any time frame on it at all."

Thomas looked back up at her and asked, "Are you all right with that? If there's anything you want to say, Ruth, you must speak your mind. We are far more likely to have difficulties between us by keeping our feelings silent than if we talk to each other and try to sort them out."

"I agree," she said. "And I promise to share any thoughts or feelings I have in regard to our marriage."

"Very good," he said but kept looking at her, as if he sensed there was something she wanted to say now. She was amazed by his insight and glanced at the clock, wondering if they'd even known each other twenty-four hours yet. Just barely, she noticed by the position of the hands.

"What is it?" he pressed.

"It's only that . . . your kindness continues to . . . surprise me," she said.

"Why would that be?" he asked.

"I suppose that . . . with few exceptions . . . the men in my life were *not* kind—in one way or another. It's as if women are raised knowing they *must* be kind in order to be considered acceptable, and men can choose whether or not kindness suits them."

"Was your father not kind?" Thomas asked. "Knowing his brother as I do, I can't imagine Dawson being *anything* but kind. He's very rigid at times, but I always assumed that was due to his position."

"As I understand it, my father and his brother were dramatically different from a very early age. My father always wanted to be working with his father, out on the farm, taking pride in any little thing he could do from the time he could stand—that's what I was told. But Uncle preferred his mother's company and helping with his mother's work—which was something his father always ridiculed, calling him less than a man and horrible things like that. As the story goes, Uncle left home as soon as he could manage on his own and found work serving in one of the big houses. According to my mother, it made him happy and he'd found his place. My father was at home on the farm, and that's what made him happy. It's not so unusual for brothers to be so different."

"No, it's not. And Dawson is *very* good at what he does. Few people could run such a large household with as much efficiency as he does. But it's more than that; he truly is like family to me."

"As you and your parents are to him; he's told me as much many a time." She sighed. "But you asked about my father. I would never describe him as unkind—not in the way that some men are, at least. He never raised a hand to us, and we all knew he loved us. But he was gruff and not very warm. Well, he had *moments* of warmth and kindness. But more likely he showed his love by making sure we were all fed and cared for and by making sure we knew how to work hard so we could care for ourselves when we came of age. I don't ever remember him speaking to me particularly kindly; I just knew that he loved me. I think when I was old enough to be drawn to seeking the attention of young men, I must have sought out the kind who were like my father. Don't they say we do that?"

"I believe I've heard such things."

"I seemed strangely drawn to men who were gruff and lacking in affection. I suppose I just assumed all men were that way, and that underneath it all, it didn't mean they didn't care for me. After what happened with Lucius I certainly realized the hard way how very wrong I'd been." She turned her focus to Thomas. "But you have been so kind to me in every way, and it continues to surprise me."

"You've not known me long enough to see me lose my temper," he said with a smile.

"And I'm not fool enough to believe that you never would. Still," she said and briefly touched his face, "you've been very kind, and I would be remiss not to tell you I'm grateful."

"I'm only trying to be the man my parents taught me I should be. I long ago realized they were among the best of people in this world, and I do not take for granted the privilege of being their son. I would never want to let them down."

"Then I shall very much look forward to meeting them."

"I dare say they will take to you immediately."

"Let us hope so," she said.

Thomas stood up and said, "I will give you some privacy to change for bed."

"Thank you," she said, and he left the room.

Ruth had very few possessions, but she did own a nightgown that had been prudish enough to wear around the house in front of her father and brothers and not feel inappropriate. She was glad to have it now under these strange circumstances, which she could never have predicted.

Once changed for bed, Ruth sat at the little dressing table where there was a mirror. She reverently removed the blue hydrangea from her hair and held it to her nose. It looked somewhat bedraggled from the rigors of the day, but she felt excessively sentimental over it and set it on the table in front of her before she removed the pins from her hair and allowed the long braid to fall down her back. Normally she would have unwound the braid, brushed it through, and rebraided her hair before going to bed, but she felt tired and not certain what to expect and decided to leave it as it was for now.

Ruth stood at the window attempting to take in the view, even though it was mostly the shadows of trees and shrubbery in the darkness. Thomas came into the room after knocking and sat down to take off his boots and stockings. He also removed his tie and waistcoat, having discarded his jacket earlier. She was relieved when he climbed into bed still wearing his shirt and breeches, then wondered why she might have expected anything less when to this point he had been perfectly respectable and respectful in every way.

"The bathing room is free now," he said, "if there's anything you need to—"

"Yes, thank you," she said and hurried out of the room, taking her toothbrush with her.

Ruth returned to the bedroom and closed the door, not even glancing at Thomas as she climbed into bed and turned down the wick on the lamp to darken the room. She was grateful beyond words to note what an enormous bed it was in contrast to those in the home in which she'd grown up. She'd often wondered how her parents even had space to roll over without disturbing each other. But in a bed such as this, she felt sure that she and Thomas could both sleep comfortably and peacefully. Despite the fact that the need to share a room had turned out to be a necessity under the circumstances, she felt glad for it. She didn't want to admit to how lonely she'd felt since Lucius had abandoned her and her mother had turned her out. She'd not had a friend to speak of in a very long time. No one to turn to or talk to. But in the course of a single day she felt as if Thomas had become her best friend, someone she could be honest with and with whom she could feel comfortable. She didn't want to be alone and wanted to tell him so, but she simply said, "Thank you, Thomas, for everything. Today has truly been a blessed day for me."

"And for me," he said, and she wanted to ask what he meant exactly, but her instinct told her it was best to get to know him better before probing too deeply about the truth of his inner self.

Ruth was surprised to feel his hand find hers beneath the covers. He squeezed her fingers and said with the barest hint of vulnerability, "It's nice not to be alone."

"Yes," she agreed and squeezed back. "It *is* nice."

She fell asleep with his hand still in hers and woke to find the room filled with daylight, her husband sitting in one of the comfortable chairs she'd noticed the previous evening, his booted legs crossed, as he read a newspaper.

"Good morning, husband," she said, just loving the way it felt to say such a word and have it connect her to this man. She knew well enough from marriages she'd observed throughout her life that such a connection was often considered an imprisonment of sorts, a symbol of being bound to someone who was unkind, or neglectful, or even someone who considered that marriage gave him the right to control and dictate a spouse's every move in life. She didn't know Thomas Fitzbatten well enough to know if he might eventually turn into such a man, but from what she already knew of his character, she considered it highly unlikely. As it was, being able to call him *husband* meant only freedom from shame and poverty, and a promise of care and security for herself and her children. The very idea of having more children with him only added to the serenity she felt at watching him now and thinking of herself as his wife.

"Good morning," he said, darting his eyes toward her before he even set the newspaper aside—as if whatever sentence he might have been in the middle of reading didn't hold nearly enough interest to keep him from turning his attention to her. "And how did you sleep?" he asked.

"Delightfully well," she said. "And you?"

"The same," he said.

Before another thought could enter her mind, a sudden bout of nausea reminded her that this situation was not as ideal as she might have wished. As if he'd been more mindful of it than she—and well prepared—he pointed to a bucket on the floor near the bed, saying with a little smirk, "Just in case. And Bertie prepared some food for you and sent Barclay up with it a while ago. He told me his wife understands these things."

"I dare say she does," Ruth said and leaned against a stack of comfortable pillows propped against the headboard before she moved the small tray to her lap and lifted off the cover to find buttered dark bread, two kinds of cheese, and some sliced apples. "Oh, bless her!" Ruth said and hurried to eat enough to calm down her smoldering stomach, taking care to remember that she should eat like a lady while in the presence of a gentleman, although his chuckle made her believe that he enjoyed her voracious appetite and would not be disappointed no matter *how* she ate.

Thomas returned to his newspaper, and Ruth hurried to the bathing room, needing to make quick use of the facilities available— another ailment that had come with pregnancy. She washed up and returned to the comfort of her bed and the delicious food waiting there for her. While she was eating, Thomas said, "Careful that you don't fill up too much. You wouldn't want the *real* breakfast Bertie is cooking to go to waste." He tipped down the corner of the newspaper and smiled at her. "Although I dare say you'll manage."

"Should I be apologizing for my excessive obsession with food?" she asked with her mouth full.

"Not at all," he said, returning to his reading. "Far better that you and that baby remain healthy and strong than you eat like a bird for the sake of some imagined propriety. Eat away, my dear. There will always be plenty of food, I can assure you."

Ruth didn't know why his last comment provoked her to tears, but it did. She was trying to figure out how to hide them from him when he once again tipped down his paper as if to investigate the reason for her inability to keep from sniffling.

"Whatever is wrong?" he asked and set the paper aside, moving to sit on the edge of the bed, where he took her hand as if they *had* been married for months.

"I'm not sure," she said and sniffled again, wiping her eyes on the edge of the sheet under which she was lying. "I've heard it said that pregnant women cry more easily, and to tell you the truth, I've cried buckets of tears—mostly before you came along and rescued me. I've managed to keep them mostly in check while I've been with you, but sometimes they just . . . spring out of nowhere and—"

"There is no reason to ever hold back for my sake," he said.

"You might regret that when I have cause to lose my temper," she said with complete seriousness, but he chuckled.

Then, more seriously, he wiped at her tears and asked, "Why are you crying now, my dear? Is it something I said?"

"I suppose it was . . . your saying there will always be plenty of food." Her emotion gained momentum. "When my mother learned of my being pregnant, she told me I would starve on the streets and my child with me." Thomas urged her face to his shoulder and she took hold of his strong arms, relishing the comfort they offered. "I've never had cause to believe my mother didn't love me. She could sometimes be cross, what with all of her worries and caring for a family on her own after my father's death. In my heart I know she said the things she did because she was afraid for me, but . . . her words have haunted me." She looked up at Thomas, knowing full well that a steady stream of tears still flowed down her cheeks. "I've asked myself if I agreed to marry you simply to be sure that we never went hungry. I'd be dishonest if I didn't admit that it had something to do with it. But it was so much more than that. Still, even the promise you've given me . . . that there will always be enough to eat is . . . no small thing, Thomas. You must know that."

"There is no need to fear on *any* count," he said, and Ruth held more tightly to him, hoping he wouldn't consider it inappropriate. Married as they were, she had to remind herself that legally and in the eyes of God there was nothing at all untoward about sharing such a tender moment with this man. It was only the short amount of time they'd known each other that made it strange. But he had a way of making her feel so comfortable that even taking the brevity of their acquaintance into account couldn't force her to feel awkward with the way he held her and whispered tender reassurances.

Ruth didn't know if it was her need to ease the tension of the moment or her genuine concern for Bertie that took her mind back to what he'd said a moment ago. Either way she drew back and muttered with alarm, "Bertie's cooking breakfast? She should be doing no such thing in her condition."

Thomas chuckled. "I had the same thought, but Barclay has assured me she's fine and he'd already tried to talk her out of it. My secret plan was for you and me to insist upon cleaning all the dishes afterward—although perhaps I should consult you before I go making any such plans, secret or otherwise."

"It's an excellent plan, husband," she said. "I assure you that if you make any plan to which I disagree, I will certainly let you know."

"I dare say you will," he said and ate a piece of cheese from the tray nearby on the bed. He then put a piece of cheese into *her* mouth and watched her eat it.

Thomas told himself to go back to his chair and his newspaper—but he didn't want to. He was utterly fascinated with his new wife and trying very hard to figure out why. When he'd offered to marry her, believing at his core that it was absolutely the right thing to do, he'd imagined making certain her needs were met while each of them went about their own business. Although now he couldn't imagine exactly what *their own business* might entail. He had no predetermined use of his time, and now that she was his wife, there were no restrictive requirements on *her* time. He realized now that he hadn't really thought through the details of how their lives would play out beyond their arrival here. He'd known of married couples who managed to spend practically no time together at all, and he'd known the opposite—of couples who could hardly bear being apart. His parents fell mostly into the latter category. With the exception of their often sleeping in separate rooms, simply because of their dramatically different sleeping habits, they were practically inseparable. Thomas had grown up observing them rarely do as much as have a cup of tea without the other one nearby. There were certainly times when his father was occupied with the business of the estate and his mother had other things to do during the hours when he was absent. But in their leisure time, if he went riding, she went along—although that had become less frequent as she'd gotten older and more frail. But if she went for a walk in the gardens, he accompanied her and held her hand. Was it some kind of subconsciously ingrained habit or expectation that made him want to be with Ruth, no matter what their day might entail? Perhaps. But if he found her company disagreeable he surely would have been more than happy to establish habits of separateness for both their sakes.

As it was, Thomas only wanted to look at her and hold her hand and know her every thought. He didn't want to ever be too far away from her, instinctively wanting to be certain that her every need was met, her every whim catered to. The very fact that she was a woman who was well accustomed to meeting her own needs and never indulging in a whim made the idea all the more intriguing. He cautioned himself against getting caught up in such feelings simply because the situation was new and therefore occupied his thoughts and stifled his boredom. He didn't want to establish a pattern between them that he would then need to uphold after the novelty of their marriage wore off and he might feel drawn to spend his time elsewhere. He determined that he was intelligent enough to establish some kind of proper balance, and he also felt confident that he could appropriately communicate with Ruth should any misunderstanding or need for change arise.

Thomas left Ruth to prepare herself for the day and found Barclay in the barn, seeing to the animals housed there.

"What can I do for you, sir?" Barclay asked.

"Carry on," Thomas said. "I was more wondering what *I* can do for *you*."

"I don't understand," Barclay said, holding a pitchfork midair.

"I've noticed the cottage is in need of some repairs; a coat of paint wouldn't go amiss. And the gardens are in need of some attention. I was thinking that—"

"I apologize for that, sir," Barclay said. "We've just not quite been able to set things right since my pa passed on, but—"

"Barclay," Thomas interrupted, "there is no need to apologize. My mention of it was not to criticize. You've been caring for your family, and that is by all means exactly what you *should* have been doing. I'm saying that while Ruth and I are here, perhaps we can help get things in better order so you'll not have such a burden. I'm certain we can hire some local help for part of the work."

Barclay had managed to stick the pitchfork in the ground and was leaning on it, but he seemed to have gone dumb. Thomas simply asked, "Would that be all right with you, Barclay?"

"'Tis your cottage, sir," Barclay managed.

"And I could not ask for a finer man to watch over it," Thomas said and left Barclay to his chore, taking mental notes regarding what needed to be done as he returned to the house. Given the circumstances, perhaps his idea to come here had been inspired. And since that decision had been closely tied into his idea to make Ruth his wife and take her away for a while, he felt added peace over *that* being inspired as well.

Breakfast was delightful, especially since Thomas insisted that Barclay and Bertie join them. They talked and laughed, and Thomas saw a new side of his wife in the way that she conversed so easily with these people—not just because she understood the workings of the serving class but because she had a completely artless way of drawing them into easy conversation and getting them to talk about the *real* feelings and challenges associated with the passing of Barclay's father, of his mother's failing health, and of Bertie's frustration in having her pregnancy cause such limitations when she felt far more at home keeping busy. It seemed the more he learned about Ruth, the more impossible it became to deny that the hand of God had surely been present in bringing them together. Even now—not even married twenty-four hours—he was already thinking that he couldn't have handpicked a woman more perfect for him if he'd had several dozens to choose from.

Ruth continued to solidify his beliefs on that count when, after breakfast was finished, she insisted that Bertie put her feet up on an extra chair and keep Ruth company while she cleaned up the kitchen. She told Thomas that he needed to go and see what Barclay might be doing and give him some help.

"We've got women's work to do," she said, waving her hand toward the door as if she were quite accustomed to ordering him about. "Now get out of here and make yourself useful elsewhere," she said with playful severity.

Thomas helped Barclay create some order in the barn while they made a list of supplies they needed from town. The men returned to the house to find the women sitting with the elderly Mrs. Barclay in her upstairs bedroom, the three of them laughing like a gaggle of little girls. The laughter finally quieted when the women realized the men had entered the room, and the elderly woman held out her arms toward Thomas in a motherly way that warmed him. She had helped care for him during his visits to the cottage for as long as he could remember. And she was so glad to see him that tears filled her aging eyes and she touched his face as if to be reassured she was not hallucinating.

"And you've got yourself a lovely wife," she said to Thomas.

"I do indeed," Thomas said, glancing briefly toward Ruth.

"Does she know what a fine catch you are?" the woman whispered in a teasing way, as if Ruth might not be able to overhear them, even though they both knew she could.

"I believe it is the other way around," Thomas whispered with another glance at Ruth, which revealed a rare hint of shyness.

"Well, I'm glad you didn't marry one of those snooty young misses who was always vying for your hand," Mrs. Barclay said. "I doubt such a woman would have cared much for the likes of us."

"Which is exactly why I never would have married such a woman," Thomas said. He hurried to change the subject. "I hear you've not been feeling well."

The old woman made a scoffing noise. "I'm older than a tree; a woman's got a right to be down and out when she's lived three lifetimes and more. Doctor says I've not got long, as if it might take a trained eye to know *that*. But you mustn't worry about me, Master Thomas. I'm ready to meet up with my sweet Mr. Barclay on the other side just as soon as the good Lord sees fit to call me home. Until then, I've got such fine children to care for me. And who could ask for more than that?"

"Indeed," Thomas said and kissed her frail hand. "After living three lifetimes, who could possibly ask for more?"

Thomas heard sniffles in the room and quickly turned to see Barclay and Bertie both wiping their eyes. He was a bit surprised to see Ruth wiping hers as well—until he recalled her confession to being overly emotional. He kissed Mrs. Barclay's brow and wondered if he might one day be privileged enough to pass away from this world surrounded by loved ones to care for him and knowing he would be met with love on the other side. She was certainly right. Who could ask for more than that?

* * *

Days passed quickly, accompanied by a stretch of fair weather. Thomas kept busy helping Barclay with some needed repairs to the house and barn and diminishing the unruly accumulation of weeds that were being the most bothersome. The two of them took the wagon into town for supplies, a variety of things that were needed for both the animals and the household. While there, Thomas made arrangements for some temporary hired help to do some repairs on the roof of the house and to give both the house and the barn a fresh coat of paint. He saw a few people he knew from his youth, and all who remembered him wished him well in having returned safely from serving his time in the military. And Barclay was quick to inform others that Thomas had gotten married and was expecting a child, which always brought a hearty round of congratulations from anyone nearby—whether they knew Thomas or not.

While Thomas and Barclay kept busy during the days, Ruth seemed content to be left to assist Bertie in doing whatever she might need help with in the house. At mealtimes when the four of them were together, they'd share reports of what they'd accomplished. Bertie felt badly about how much Ruth was doing, but Ruth was all aglow with feeling useful, and she rather appeared to be enjoying herself. In Bertie's condition it was much easier for Ruth to go up and down the stairs to see to Starla's needs, and it was evident Ruth had taken quite a liking to the old woman—and the other way around. Bertie and Ruth had apparently become good friends, with much in common and a great deal to talk about.

Bertie bragged about how Ruth had done most of the cooking since Bertie could hardly get on her feet anymore without "waddling like an old cow," and Thomas couldn't help being impressed to realize that his wife was more than a fair cook. When Barclay commented about Thomas finding a wife who could cook, Thomas pretended to have already known of her competence, and Ruth just smiled at him the way she did when their mutual secret was so gracefully avoided.

Thomas's favorite time of day was in the evening after he'd taken advantage of the bathing room to clean himself up; he'd return to the bedroom wearing fresh clothes that he would sleep in. Usually he would find Ruth sitting in front of the mirror performing what he now knew was a nightly ritual with her hair. The hair that he would have described upon meeting her as *average brown* proved to be anything but average when she set it free. At first she would remove more hairpins than he could count that held her hair coiled tightly against the back of her head. With the pins absent, a thick, silky braid fell down her back, and he wagered that it nearly came to her waist.

Thomas usually sat in bed with a book while she took care of her hair; that way he could discreetly watch her but pretend to be reading should she chance to glance in his direction. But the words on the page held no interest for him as she untied the ribbon at the bottom of the braid and efficiently unwove the plaiting that kept her hair in place. And then she brushed it. From top to bottom, over and over in long, efficient strokes, she brushed and brushed. There was a practiced efficiency to the task that was typical of her personality. But there was also a beauty to it that was so thoroughly feminine and fine. He could almost believe she did it solely for his entertainment, except that she'd obviously been doing it years before they'd ever met. And since they'd not yet known each other a week, he knew it had absolutely nothing to do with him.

When she considered her hair sufficiently brushed, she quickly wound it again into a long braid to keep it from tangling while she slept. The only break he'd noted in her routine regarding her hair was on the days she washed it. Then she performed the ritual earlier in the day when heating and carrying the water was more convenient. Given that he'd offered to help her with the water, he'd seen her hair wet and realized that the beautiful waves were not natural but rather a result of her hair drying while it was plaited. In its natural state her hair was like a length of satin. And there was absolutely nothing average about it.

But then, there was absolutely nothing average about Ruth. She was as kind as she was hard working. While she was not one to keep an opinion to herself, he'd never heard her utter an uncivil word to anyone—not even a rude woman they encountered when he took Ruth into the village for a little outing to acquire some much-needed clothes. He insisted that she get new *everything*, to which she protested and he won. In the end she couldn't hide her delight over the new dress and shawl she wore as they left the shop. She was equally thrilled with the other items they'd ordered. She simply said, "You're too good to me, Thomas. Should I not feel guilty for being taken off the streets by such a fine gentleman and then lavished with an abundance of gifts?"

"No, you should not!" he told her. "You're my wife and I will buy you whatever I choose." He made a scoffing sound, realizing he actually felt mildly insulted. "And I did not *take you off the streets*."

"Seems so to me," she said.

"And it's time you put all of that behind you," he insisted. He added more softly, "Your kindness to Bertie and Starla—and to Barclay as well—is worth a thousand new dresses."

"It takes no effort to be kind to them, Thomas." Now it was *she* who sounded insulted. "Do you think I do such things to earn your favor?"

"No," he said and took her hand. "Which is exactly the point."

Ruth seemed confused on *the point*, but he changed the subject.

The following day they attended church, and Ruth admitted while they were on their way to the village chapel that she was nervous.

"There's no need to be," he said. "Just be yourself and all will be well."

In a tone that was slightly teasing but mostly accusing, she said, "Is that why you bought me this new dress, Thomas? So, I'd not embarrass you at church?"

"You look lovely in the dress, wife. But I wouldn't care if you wore rags to church. One of these days perhaps you'll figure out what kind of man I am."

"I'm not sure that's possible," she said, and he chuckled.

Following the service, they encountered a few people who showed less-than-subtle disapproval over Thomas's choice of a wife—but he'd expected as much and actually felt some pride in getting such a reaction out of those people. He told Ruth so on their way home and was glad to hear her say, "Oh, I don't care a bit about what people like that think of me, so long as you don't." She smiled at him and added, "It was nice to be at church and not feel so all alone."

"Yes," he said and smiled back, although their smiles faded long before they stopped gazing at each other, "that *was* nice."

After church it was Ruth's idea that they take Sunday dinner up to Starla's room so they could all share a fine meal with her. Barclay helped Bertie up the stairs and made her comfortable, and Starla's face lit up at the announcement of their plans. After a few trips up and down the stairs by those who were able-bodied, they all sat around Starla's bed, and Barclay spoke grace over their meal, including a sincere thanks to God for his mother and all the good she had brought into their lives. They all chimed in with an enthusiastic "Amen" and shared a good deal of conversation and laughter, not only while they ate but long afterward. Starla ate very little, which had been typical for a number of weeks, according to Bertie. But she reveled in the company, and her eyes looked half the age of her frail and weakening body.

The following morning Barclay found his mother dead. She had a peaceful countenance that implied she had gone to sleep and never awakened, and it had likely been hours before morning when she'd left, since Barclay had found her skin already very cold.

Thomas felt the weight of his own grief at Starla's passing, but he couldn't comprehend that of Barclay, who had already lost his father. Thomas offered to take care of arrangements with the vicar and the undertaker, and this man who was usually hesitant to take help from anyone readily agreed.

With Barclay and Bertie left to their grieving—and Bertie's necessary rest—Ruth took over the running of the household with an efficiency and drive that left Thomas somewhat stunned. He never caught her sitting down unless she was eating or brushing out her hair. But the day after Starla's death it rained as if the sky itself were grieving, and Thomas searched the entire house for his wife, wanting to ask if there was anything he could do to help. He finally caught a glimpse of her out the kitchen window, and was taken aback by what he saw.

Thomas stepped quietly outside, not wanting to alert her to his presence too soon and deny her this moment. If he had to guess, he believed the rain had spoken to something inside of her and had lured her out into this downpour, and she was oblivious to how completely wet she was from head to toe. With her face turned to the sky and her eyes closed, she sobbed and heaved, her arms wrapped tightly around herself. The depth of her grief implied that she had known Starla for a lifetime; it also prompted his own tears that had been hovering just below the surface since word had come of Starla's death yesterday. But he stepped into the rain, and the downpour quickly disguised them.

"Ruth," he said, at the same time gently setting a hand on her shoulder. She was startled only a moment before she took hold of him and cried and cried. He just held her and let her cry, understanding without any words why the bathing downpour of rain had a soothing effect in light of such grief.

"Why do you cry for her so deeply?" he asked and pressed a kiss into her very wet hair.

"I don't know," she admitted. "I don't know. She was so kind and good, and the love that Bertie and Barclay have for her makes it evident how well she loved them. Perhaps I just needed to cry."

"In the rain?"

"It seemed fitting," she said and held to him more tightly.

Minutes passed before she spoke again, saying, "I'm so glad we were here, Thomas. What would they have done? Bertie grows more uncomfortable every day, and Barclay can hardly put a thought together."

"I agree," he said. "I'm *very* glad we're here. And you do very well at keeping everything under control."

"As do you," she said.

He wanted to point out how well they worked together, managing to see that everything was taken care of without hardly having to communicate over who would do what. He wanted to tell her that an hour didn't pass without him thinking that his decision to marry her was the best thing he'd ever done. But it had been so short a time, and trying to put a voice to such words made him fear sounding like a fool. He'd been carefully taught the difference between love and infatuation, but now he wondered if he was infatuated with his own wife. He thought of her continually, and when he wasn't with her he wanted to be. She did everything that impressed and pleased him without even trying, and she was mesmerizingly beautiful. When he looked at her now he didn't see anything average or ordinary. He could only see the promise of his life stretching out before him, with her always at the center. He was blessed to already be married to her, and to know that she would always be with him. But whether or not what he felt was love—or anything akin to it— deserved far more time and consideration.

Chapter Five

THE WRONG ORDER

THE DAY OF STARLA'S FUNERAL was heavily overcast, but not one drop of rain fell from the sky as her casket was carried to the church graveyard and laid to rest. After the funeral service, many people from the village came to the house to pay their respects. On the previous day while Barclay and Thomas had remained busy with other preparations, Ruth had helped prepare cakes and biscuits that could be served to the guests. Bertie had been able to do some of the work as long as she remained sitting, but she had done well at giving Ruth careful instructions on how to make things she'd never made before, and between the two of them they had come up with an appropriate offering for such an event. When the time came, some of the guests brought plates of food that could be shared, and they ended up with a feast. While the rain continued to hold off, some people gathered in the yard while others filled the main floor of the house, mingling and visiting and sharing memories of Starla and the good life she'd lived.

Ruth kept busy serving the food and seeing that Bertie was all right. Even though her heart still felt heavy with losing Starla—her new and dear friend—she was coming to find joy in having known her at all. And she was overcome with the kindness and well wishes of the community on Starla's behalf.

After everyone had left, rain finally started to fall, as if it had been waiting for its cue to come only when the social gathering was done. The men pitched in to help clean up, and Bertie was left to rest on the sofa in the parlor. She confessed to feeling so utterly exhausted that she doubted her ability to climb up the stairs to bed when the time came. Ruth often watched Bertie, taking in the details of her condition, and wondered how she herself might fare when her pregnancy overtook her so completely. She also wondered how it might have been if she'd been living in some tucked-away home for women of ill repute who'd gotten themselves pregnant while the fathers of said babies were off living their lives, free of any encumbering consequences. She'd heard that such places more often than not had despicable living conditions, and she would have lived every day with the knowledge that her pregnancy was nothing more than a temporary incubation for a baby who would be taken from her without so much as a hello or a good-bye.

Ruth had to force such thoughts away, fearing they would reduce her to helpless sobbing—both in sorrow at the possibility of what might have been and in gratitude for the present state of her life, all thanks to the kindness and generosity of Thomas Fitzbatten. He would tell her he'd felt compelled—perhaps inspired—to make her his wife. And maybe that was true. Considering how blessed she felt, she would not dispute it. But there was something deeply comforting—if not difficult to comprehend—in thinking that God had been mindful enough of her to inspire this good man to offer her a life such as this. Caring for her new friends through their grief and Bertie's present condition was a blessing in itself. Remaining busy and needed by others kept her mind from going places she far preferred to avoid.

As the dark of evening settled in, Bertie's discomfort increased until it became evident that her time had come and this baby was on its way.

"We must send for the doctor," Thomas declared.

"I'll not have that doctor anywhere near me!" Bertie practically shouted. "He's a charlatan if ever there was one. And his medical practices are rooted in the dark ages, I tell you."

"Then what will you do?" Thomas asked, and Ruth looked at Bertie, silently echoing her husband's question.

"We got it all worked out," Barclay said with a false confidence that Ruth assumed was meant to help keep his wife calm. "We've been talking about it and we know what to do."

"I believe now would be a good time to let us in on your plans," Ruth said, betraying her agitation in light of her concern.

"I've been trained in midwifery," Bertie explained. "Helped deliver lots of babies."

"And you're telling me this now?" Ruth countered.

"Forgive me, Bertie," Thomas said, "but isn't that entirely different in regard to giving birth to your own baby?"

"I'll help her," Barclay said, but he didn't sound very sure of himself. "She can tell me what to do, and I'll do it."

"There's no need for such a fuss," Bertie said, clearly in pain. "Women have been giving birth to babies since the world began. Who do you think delivered Eve's first baby? Unless there's some part of the story missing from the Bible, I don't think anyone would have been there but Adam."

Ruth looked at her husband, glad to see her own concern reflected in his gaze. But what could they do but honor Bertie's wishes and hope for the best?

"Fine," Ruth said, knowing her terseness was only a mask for her fear over how exactly this might all turn out. "If that's how you want it, Bertie, who are we to argue? But I'll be helping as well. It's about time I learned something about bringing a child into the world. Just tell me what to do."

"And what am *I* supposed to do?" Thomas asked.

"Whatever you're told, presumably," Ruth said.

Their first order of business was to get Bertie to her bed before she was hurting too much to get up the stairs. The men helped her up the stairs and into bed, after which Thomas stepped into the hall where Ruth was standing, and he offered to make some coffee.

"Remarkable," Ruth said quietly to him.

"What?"

"A nobleman who knows how to make coffee," she said.

"Very funny," he replied in a tone that indicated he didn't think it was.

"I meant it as a compliment," she said, putting a hand on his arm.

Thomas met her eyes and felt a wild spectrum of emotions swirling around and between them. Today they had honored the ending of a life, and now they would help bring a new life into the world. But in the flurry of existence surrounding them, he felt for a long moment as if they were together in the calm eye of a storm, silently sharing thoughts that required no words. In so many ways they were practically strangers, and yet he honestly couldn't remember in that moment what his life had been like before her nearly magical appearance. He gave no thought or premeditation to kissing her; he just did it. The meeting of their lips was brief and lacking in any hint of passion or intimacy. It was the kind of kiss a man would give his wife in passing—if he were about to leave for the day, or if he'd just returned. It seemed completely natural and perfectly appropriate for the relationship they shared. And yet she looked completely startled by it, and he felt a little startled himself.

"Should I not have done that?" he asked, still holding her gaze as if that might give him some clue as to what she was really thinking.

"On the contrary . . ." she said but didn't finish the sentence. Her eyes narrowed as if she were trying to figure out *why* he'd kissed her. He had no explanation to give her, so he just kissed her again, this time daring to make it last an entire second or two longer than it had before.

Again their eyes met and the moment became too much to try to analyze or understand. He was glad when she said, "I . . . should help Bertie."

"And I should make some coffee," he said and hurried down the stairs.

By the time Thomas arrived in the kitchen he had to take hold of the counter with both hands to steady himself. He glanced toward the stairs as if just looking in that direction might help him understand what he had just done and why. *It was just a kiss*, he told himself. Two, to be precise. *Just a kiss*. And yet the present agreement between them was that they were living as husband and wife in name only and using what pretenses were necessary to make the arrangement believable. What had just happened had not been for anyone's benefit but his own. It was as if having her as a wife had come to feel so completely natural that kissing her the way he'd seen his father kiss his mother every day throughout his life had been an impulse that perhaps in his mind had already seemed a part of the life they shared. But he'd be a fool to think she had seen it that way. She'd not seemed put off by it at all, but he'd told her—in no uncertain terms—that he would leave it up to her to let him know when she was ready to cross certain boundaries. And as simple as a quick kiss might have been, he felt as if he'd crossed that boundary and therefore broken his word.

Resigned to the fact that he could do nothing about it right now, he set to work preparing the coffee. He suspected that the pain of childbirth would keep Bertie wide awake, but the rest of them might need a little assistance.

* * *

Ruth stood in the hallway long after Thomas had gone down the stairs. She touched her lips as if doing so might reassure her that they had indeed been kissed—not once, but twice. She tried to figure out what he'd meant by such an impulsive gesture. He'd shown her respect and kindness in ways she'd never imagined. They'd grown comfortable with their routine here at the cottage, and even with sleeping in the same bed in their completely platonic way. She'd come to enjoy his company and felt entirely comfortable around him, and she'd had no reason to think he didn't feel the same. He'd told her that he expected matters of affection to evolve between them with time, and his very reticence over the matter had increased her respect for him. She suspected that many men would need no more than the formality of knowing a woman was his wife to expect every right and privilege associated with marriage. But Thomas had made it clear before their marriage that he had no such expectations, and he had subsequently reiterated his feelings regarding the matter. What then, exactly, might it mean for him to kiss her? Not for the sake of upholding pretenses. And with no apparent motive at asserting his right to do so as her husband. It had seemed nothing more than a spontaneous expression of affection—an idea that spurred a fluttering in her stomach that made it difficult to even move.

Ruth had grown increasingly comfortable with Thomas, and there was no doubt about him being an attractive man. That wasn't to say that she'd actually felt attracted to him—at least not that she'd consciously thought about. But his kiss had awakened something in her that she'd never felt before. She had believed she'd felt it, but now in contrast she had to admit that this sensation coming to life in her was entirely unfamiliar—and completely delightful.

Ruth heard Bertie crying out and went tentatively into the room to see what she could do. Barclay was handling the situation with surprising efficiency, and it was evident the two of them *had* talked about this and made plans on how to get through it without a doctor's intervention. But it also quickly became evident that a woman's touch was perhaps better in regard to some things, and much appreciated by Bertie. Ruth felt certain they would have managed without her there, but being there was making it easier on all of them. And she was glad for that.

Throughout the night as Bertie's labor intensified, Thomas kept them supplied with coffee and hot water and clean linens and whatever else Bertie asked for. While Ruth and Barclay took turns sitting at Bertie's side and resting in the big chair in the room, Ruth knew that Thomas was resting a little here and there down the hall with the door open so that he could hear someone call him if he was needed. Everything between them had been all practicality since their brief, tender moment at the beginning of this drama, but given all that was going on, she could hardly expect any opportunity for quiet conversation with her husband.

When Bertie's pain became unimaginable to even observe, Ruth was glad for the way that Barclay kept saying his wife had warned him of this, and that the pain was just a normal part of bringing a child into the world. They kept talking of how it would all be worth it when that baby finally arrived, and of the love it would bring into their home. As much as Ruth appreciated knowing that the pain was not an indication of a problem, she couldn't help thinking almost every moment about the fact that she herself was pregnant, and she would inevitably have to endure this experience as well. The actuality of giving birth to a baby felt entirely impossible to imagine at the moment.

While she followed Bertie's instructions on checking to make certain everything was as it should be, Ruth fought to remain calm and reassuring. But in her mind she kept imagining herself going through this in some strange, dark, emotionless place where babies were taken from their mothers and women were expected to return to some kind of normal life with empty arms and a permanent hole in their hearts. She knew as she'd always known that for some women the decision to give their baby to a childless couple was the right thing to do, and they could find peace with that decision. But she'd never felt that way for herself, and thoughts of it haunted her even now, in spite of knowing she'd been blessed to never have to face such an ordeal.

Somewhere in the darkest part of the night, Bertie gave birth to a healthy baby boy. Seeing the baby actually took Ruth by surprise—it was as if somewhere in her mind she'd never been able to fully connect the facets of pregnancy and childbirth to a child as the end result. A living, breathing, moving child. He was tiny and helpless and oh so strong and beautiful! And Ruth felt utterly and completely in awe.

* * *

Throughout the course of Bertie's ordeal, Thomas had tried in vain to get some rest. Only once did he doze for a short while. But it didn't seem right for him to be sleeping while everyone else in the house was either consumed with pain or doing everything possible to ease it. Occasionally Ruth came looking for him, appearing distraught as she requested that he bring something from downstairs or do some task that would help. But for most of the night he was left alone and feeling helpless, doing little more than pacing the hallway at the top of the stairs, wondering how it might be when Ruth gave birth to the child she was carrying. Given that he'd not been tutored by a midwife on how to assist in the process, he would likely never be allowed anywhere near the birthing chamber. There was also the fact that he was not in actuality the child's father. Of course, no one was to know that. But he could hardly expect to be involved in something so intimate as childbirth when he'd never shared any degree of intimacy with his wife. While a part of him hoped that might change prior to the birth of the baby, he thought it more likely that it wouldn't. For more reasons than he had fingers to count, it was easy to imagine himself doing this very thing when Ruth's time to deliver finally came. Unable to help, left alone, pacing and fretting.

The aching of his legs provoked Thomas to sit on the floor with his back against the wall and his head in his hands. He felt sleepy but restless and wondered if a new day would dawn with this still not having ended. He had no idea what time it was when a baby's cry startled him into a heart-pounding alertness. He jumped to his feet, but then nothing more happened for many minutes, and he felt certain there was a great deal going on in the bedroom where he was not allowed.

As if Ruth had known he would be anxiously waiting, she came out of the room, removing an apron, which she tossed onto a chair. "It's a boy," she said tiredly. "And it appears they both came through just fine."

"Oh, praise heaven!" he said, and she threw her arms around him, laughing with relief. He lifted her feet off the floor and swung her around before he set her back down and their eyes met. "And you?" he asked, looking at her in the dim glow of a nearby lamp. "Are you all right?"

"I am now," she said and swept a hand over her cheeks to wipe away a sudden flow of tears. "I just . . . wanted to let you know. She needs me, I think."

"Of course," he said. "Thank you. Is there anything I can do?"

"I'll let you know," she said and hurried away, grabbing the apron and closing the door behind her.

Thomas sighed and uttered a silent prayer of gratitude that all was well. He slumped back down to the place where he'd been sitting on the floor and prayed that all would continue to be well for these good people.

Sooner than he'd expected, Ruth came into the hallway and declared, "I believe I've done all I can for now. Everything is in order and the baby is sleeping—which is what the rest of us should be doing while we can." She held out her hand, and he took it as he stood. "Come along, husband. I do believe breakfast will be served rather late tomorrow."

"You mean today," he said, liking the way she kept hold of his hand as they moved in the other direction down the hall. "Perhaps we should just forgo breakfast and prepare a hearty lunch."

"What an excellent idea," she said through a yawn.

She spent a few minutes in the bathing room, but he noticed she did nothing with her hair, nor did she change out of her clothes. She only kicked off her shoes and crawled into bed, and within a moment she was asleep. It had indeed been a long day. For a few minutes he watched her sleeping, wondering where life might take them given the choices they had made to share their lives together. Recalling his impulsive kiss—no, two—he felt just a little giddy for a moment before he turned down the wick on the lamp and got into his side of the bed, where he too fell asleep almost immediately.

* * *

Within days, Bertie was up and around, declaring she felt better than she had in months. It seemed that just getting that baby out of her had relieved her ailments immensely. They all still kept an eye on her and insisted she take it easy, and the time she took just caring for and feeding the baby gave her little choice but to remain sitting.

While Bertie managed well at caring for herself and the new baby, Ruth kept the household functioning smoothly, and she served three meals a day with no apparent difficulty. She became adept at ordering the men about, seeing that they brought in plenty of firewood and water, and she made it clear that if she was working in the kitchen she'd not be out in the barn milking the cows or gathering eggs. Thomas had no problem with assisting Barclay in seeing to Ruth's edicts, but he did love teasing her about it.

When they were alone in the kitchen while she was preparing supper, he sidled up next to her and whispered, "I do believe you rather enjoy ordering me about."

"And I do believe you rather enjoy letting me get away with it," she said.

He chuckled but couldn't argue. "I do believe you could get me to do just about anything, wife."

"Is that a fact?" she asked and held up a knife so abruptly that it startled him. "How are you at carving a leg of lamb? Because it's about to come out of the oven."

Thomas chuckled again. "I confess I've never done it before, but I'd be willing to give it a go."

"You might as well take it out of the oven too," she said, nodding toward the towel nearby, which he could use to protect his hands. "Don't burn yourself; I haven't got time to be nursing a burn."

"I'll do my best," he promised and managed to get the lamb successfully out of the oven and sliced into edible pieces without botching it too badly.

After supper Thomas noticed that both Barclay and Bertie looked especially tired. The baby hadn't been sleeping well, and Thomas insisted they both go up to bed and he would help Ruth in the kitchen. Barclay's protests were brief when Thomas reminded him who he worked for.

"Thank you, sir," Barclay said. "I don't know how we'd have managed these weeks without you and your good wife."

"I'm glad we were here when we were needed," Thomas said. "Although I'm certain the majority of the credit goes to my good wife."

Barclay nodded toward Ruth before he escorted Bertie and the baby up the stairs. Thomas started helping Ruth clear the table. They were nearly finished cleaning the dishes, which she washed and he dried, when he realized how silent it had been between them.

"What are you thinking of, wife?" he asked. "It's not like you to remain so quiet for so long."

"Nor you," she said.

"I asked you first," he said and took a wet plate from her to dry and stack in the cupboard near his head.

"Little Warren is nearly three weeks old," she said.

"Has it been so long?" he asked. "The time has flown."

"Do you not want to even hold him?" she asked, and he stopped what he was doing to look at her, realizing now that something heavy was weighing on her—and that she was far too sharp for him to think he could conceal his own concerns and not have her guess that something was amiss. "Barclay has offered to let you hold him a good many times, but you decline. Do you have some aversion to babies?"

"He's just so . . . small," Thomas said. "I have no experience whatsoever with babies. I fear that I'll . . . do something wrong."

Ruth looked up at him and asked a question that pierced him—and she knew it. "Will you not hold *our* baby? You did say you considered it to be *our* baby."

"I plan to, if that's what you're asking. I've just not quite . . . become accustomed to the idea of being a father."

Ruth looked at the water in the sink and tossed the dishrag into it. "Do you think it will magically be different when it is your wife who gives birth to a child who is small and fragile, as any baby would be?"

"No, of course not."

"Then the problem would be that most men become fathers by doing things in a different order, and therefore become more accustomed to the idea of becoming a father. Most men would meet a woman, get to know her a bit, court her, become engaged, and then get married. And *then* babies come, so there's plenty of time to be prepared. Yes, we have skipped some obvious steps, or perhaps it's that we're doing them in the wrong order."

Thomas took all of that in while he finished drying the goblet in his hands and put it away. "My father often said that any decent man has the good sense to listen to what a good woman tells him, because women have a way of seeing things that men are often oblivious to."

"Do you believe that's true?" she asked.

"More every day," he insisted and turned toward her. "Ruth," he said as he took her hand, "I can't know if something upsets you if you don't tell me. I had no idea that my avoidance of giving attention to the baby would be interpreted in such a way. It is my sincere desire to be a good father to our baby, but I need you to help me."

"Well, it's not like *I've* done this before."

"But you have little brothers. You help Bertie with the baby. You know far more than I do."

Ruth looked up at her husband and wondered why expressing her opinions had made her expect an argument. Perhaps because that's how it had usually happened with her own parents. She knew now that she'd been allowing herself to feel on edge and defensive before she'd even given him a chance to know what she was feeling. But their entire situation was so beyond anything normal or expected that it was often difficult to know what to say or do.

Trying to keep her focus on one problem at a time, she simply said, "I just think it might be good for you to hold little Warren now and then. It's a good opportunity for you to become accustomed to a baby. I suppose that's all. Forgive me for making mountains out of molehills. It's just that . . . as you said . . . time has flown . . . it is flying, Thomas." She took his hand and pressed it over the unmistakable mound of her belly, which she'd been able to keep well hidden by hiking her skirts above it. But it wouldn't be long before she'd have to start wearing the dresses they'd ordered that had been made to accommodate pregnancy, and there would be no hiding it then.

"Ruth," he whispered and kept his hand tightly against where the baby grew while he looked into her eyes.

"I feel it moving inside me, Thomas, and I can't help but feel afraid."

"Afraid?" he echoed, not because he didn't know there were many possible reasons for fear, but because he wanted to understand exactly what *she* was afraid of.

"After seeing what Bertie went through," she admitted. "I don't know if I can do it, Thomas. She's so strong and brave and—"

"And so are you," he insisted, unable to admit that he was afraid for exactly the same reasons. He'd not been in the room during Bertie's labor, but he'd heard her crying out, and the very thought of Ruth enduring that much pain was as frightening to him as anything he'd ever felt on a battlefield.

"When the time comes," Ruth said, turning back to the dishes, "I hope you will remind me of that."

"I will," he promised. "And before the baby comes we will be at Brownlie Manor. There is a doctor available there who is a fine man and the best at what he does. He has attended our family for many years. And there are so many there who are like family; you will love them and they you. I promise you, Ruth, that you will not be left to face it alone. I promise you."

She nodded, and it seemed he'd offered the reassurance she'd needed, but she was still quiet as they finished the dishes and made certain all was in order for morning. He sat in the parlor to read a newspaper that was a few days old, but he'd not had time to peruse it as he usually did. He felt distracted by the very fact that Ruth was in the room with him, but that wasn't unusual. He discreetly glanced at her more than once while she was mending something with a needle and thread held close to the lamp at her side. That wasn't unusual either. But it occurred to him that these quiet moods of hers were becoming more frequent, and he wondered how long it might have been that way and he'd not noticed. His father had taught him that when a woman was behaving unusually it was most likely a sign that something was amiss, and that any man with a brain would wheedle it out of her. Thomas didn't know that his father was an expert on women in general, and he felt sure they were certainly not all alike. But his father had successfully kept his mother happy for a great many years.

Considering that Ruth *had* become far more quiet than usual, Thomas felt that something more might be bothering her— something more than her concerns about having a child and what his place might be in all of that. He tried to remember what else she'd said in the kitchen, if only to find a place to begin a conversation. When the recollection came, he wondered if she'd hinted at something they truly needed to talk about. Whether or not it was weighing on her, it certainly came to *his* mind often enough that he figured it should be addressed.

Since the direct approach had always seemed to work best with her, he cleared his throat and said, "So, which stage do you think we're at exactly . . . wife?"

She looked up at him as if she had concerns about his mental well-being and said, "I've no idea what you're talking about."

"You said in the kitchen that we had skipped some steps, or perhaps done them in the wrong order. If we're hoping to eventually . . . get all of the proper steps in, I just wondered what step you might think we're at."

He could see that she now understood, but she also looked annoyed. Or was it embarrassed? She focused her attention on her mending, but he felt confident he was on the right course toward "wheedling it out of her," as his father might say. "We met. You mentioned that as a step. We certainly did meet."

"We certainly did," she said with mild sarcasm. "And twenty-four hours later we were here pretending that we were wildly in love with each other and had been married for quite some time. Oh yes, we certainly did meet."

"You sound angry, Ruth," he observed. "Will you set aside the sewing and tell me why? Or is there some exclusion I don't know about in our agreement to always be honest with one another?"

"I'm not angry," she said in a voice that contradicted the statement. More calmly she said, "Just . . . concerned, perhaps; confused."

"Talk to me." He leaned toward her. "One of the reasons I knew that marrying you would be all right was the way we could so easily talk to each other. We must *never* stop talking to each other." He sighed deeply and said, "Tell me why you are concerned and confused."

He gave her some time to speak, and watched as she visibly drew courage. Was this so difficult for her—whatever it was?

"Life is good here for us, Thomas, but I know this is not where we're meant to live most of the time. I feel as if we're adrift in a little boat, surrounded by the sea and all is well, but eventually we will come to dry land and I will have to face what it *really* means to be your wife. You talk of the manor and the people there, and of your parents with such fondness—but they are all strangers to me, Thomas. You are my only link to anything that feels sure and steady, and . . ." She paused and pressed her fingers over her eyes, a sign he recognized as her effort to control her tears.

"And what?" he pressed gently.

"How do I truly step into your world with you when I don't even know where things stand between us? Are we friends? We are; I know we are. But it's more than that; it's different. We both know it is."

"We are husband and wife; of course it's different."

"But we are *not.*" She sprang to her feet and began to pace. She took a deep breath and admitted, "This is difficult for me to say. I ask for your patience."

"Of course."

She kept pacing, deliberately avoiding any glance in his direction. "You've told me that you want this marriage to become everything a marriage should be, and I want to believe you, because that's what I want. But there are doubts in my head, Thomas. Everything happened so quickly that I start to wonder if you've changed your mind now that you've come to know me. Everything will be different when we return to the manor, but I wonder what that means exactly. I've worked in more than one such grand house and I know the reputation of so many men of your class. I don't believe it possible of you, but my head starts to tell me things, and . . . I wonder if that's the kind of marriage this will be. I'm grateful for all you're doing for me, Thomas, but I don't know if I can still be your friend if I know you're turning to other women for—"

"Other women?" He shot to his feet, and she stopped pacing. Once he knew exactly what she was trying to get at he felt furious and ultimately insulted. "I can assure you, Mrs. Fitzbatten, that I am not nor would I ever be *that* kind of man. I would live a life of celibacy before I would betray my marriage vows, and I take *our* marriage vows very seriously. I would hope you do, as well."

"I do," she said with tears growing in her eyes. Looking at her face and recounting all she'd just said, he could see the vulnerability of a servant girl becoming suddenly and unexpectedly wed to a man who belonged to a social class he most often found distasteful. He knew of the reputations she spoke of, and he found it disgusting. He'd heard men bragging in public houses and gentlemen's clubs of their philandering as if it were nothing more than a silly distraction, no different than sneaking out to play cards or get drunk. He knew Ruth's concern was not a personal affront to him, but a need to understand something that was considered normal in situations to which she'd been exposed.

Thomas took her shoulders into his hands and said with gentle firmness, "My dear Ruth, I can assure you there will never be any woman in my life but you."

"I'm so glad to know it," she said, putting her head to his shoulder, although he suspected it was mostly to hide the fact that she was crying.

Thomas put his arms around her and said, "The more I get to know you, Ruth, the happier I am that I married you. If you ever have doubts about *anything*, you should come to me."

"Yes, I should," she said.

"And the same for you," she said and looked up at him. "Just in case you ever wondered, I feel the same. I'm increasingly happier every day that I am blessed to share my life with you."

"Then all will be well," he said. "You mustn't worry about the future, my dear. I will always be at your side to help you adjust. One day you won't even be able to remember life before we were married."

"I do hope for that," she said.

Before letting her go, he said, "Perhaps the step we missed is courting."

"What?" she asked, confused at the dramatic change of topic.

"We became engaged and married very quickly. Perhaps what we missed is courting."

He stepped back and bowed elaborately. "Would you do me the honor of allowing me to court you, Mrs. Fitzbatten?"

She laughed, which he considered a good sign. "And how exactly would we go about that when everyone knows we're already married?"

"Perhaps we could start with a picnic," he said. "It would be a crime to spend all these weeks at the cottage and not have a picnic where we can look out over the sea. It's one of the highlights of this place that cannot be missed. We can go on horseback, and we can go tomorrow, if you like. I do believe Barclay and Bertie can manage without us."

"It does sound lovely," Ruth admitted with a smile that lit her eyes. "I only see one problem."

"What is that?"

"I've never ridden a horse, husband."

"Then we shall have to remedy that straightaway, wife," he said.

Chapter Six

COURTING

THE FOLLOWING MORNING BERTIE HELPED Ruth pack some food into a spacious set of saddlebags. Bertie seemed almost as excited as Ruth about the prospective day out, saying in earnest, "The two of you haven't had much of a honeymoon with all that's been going on here. A day near the sea will be good for the both of you."

"Perhaps it will," Ruth said, feeling a little giddy to recall Thomas's mention of courting. They had come to know each other well in many respects; they even slept side by side. But in spite of an occasional and subtle implication, their relationship had not become what Ruth would ever describe as romantic. Now that the idea of *courting* had come up, she found the idea of exploring some form of romantic relationship with Thomas intriguing, and it did help to ease her doubts in regard to his feelings toward her. She didn't know if he could ever love her—but she hoped so. Surely everyone wanted to love and be loved. She only hoped that could be possible within the marriage they had chosen.

When it was time to leave, Ruth felt more than a little intimidated to look up at Thomas mounted on a large, magnificent steed. She was relieved at least that there was only one horse and she would not be expected to ride on her own with absolutely no idea how to do so. Before she could ask him exactly how she was meant to get up there with him, Thomas held out his hand toward her and said, "Take hold of my arm, put your left foot into the stirrup, and swing your right leg over the horse."

With only a little hesitance, she said, "I'm trusting you, husband. You'd best not let me fall."

"Never," he said, and she did as he'd asked.

A breath of exhilaration rushed out of her as she flew—mostly by the force of Thomas's strength—onto the back of the horse. She laughed spontaneously at her success in ending up exactly where she'd been intended to, and she barely had time to take hold of him before he eased the horse into a trot out of the yard. Once the moors opened up before them, he heeled the horse into a gallop and Ruth's exhilaration magnified. She wrapped her arms around his chest, as much to keep herself steady as to feel more as if they were one in sharing the experience. Of course, this was nothing new for him. He'd been raised with horses and had traveled with their aid for the whole of his life. But for her—a servant girl raised by servants, for whom a horse would have been a luxury far beyond their means—she had trouble catching her breath as they rode at remarkable speed toward a destination completely unknown to her, but it was obvious he knew exactly where he was going.

"Are you all right?" he asked over his shoulder a few minutes into their ride.

"I'm wonderful," she said, and she couldn't hold back a laugh. He laughed in response, and she considered that, so far, being courted by Thomas Fitzbatten was proving to be a worthwhile endeavor.

Just at the point when Ruth began to feel uncomfortable— unaccustomed as she was to straddling a horse—Thomas drew the animal to a halt and dismounted before he turned to help her down by putting his hands at her waist.

"Are you *still* all right?" he asked.

"Ask me tomorrow when we'll see how well I'm able to walk," she said, and again he laughed, a perfectly genuine and delighted laugh that let her know he was truly enjoying himself.

"If that is the case," he said, "I shall prepare you a hot bath, and once you've had a long soak, I shall wait on you hand and foot."

"How very gallant," she said. "And do such extravagant privileges end when we are no longer courting?"

His answer surprised her. "I think that once you meet my parents you will stop asking such questions. If you believe that I consciously try to emulate them, you will never need to wonder over such things."

Ruth just smiled, not wanting to admit that she was very nervous about meeting his parents. Despite all the praise she'd heard about them, she couldn't help fearing that they might not approve of their son's choice of a wife. They also might be prone to ask more questions than others had about how this marriage had come to pass. Ruth both dreaded meeting them and longed to have it over. According to Thomas, as soon as he got word that Quincy and Yvette Fitzbatten had returned to Brownlie Manor, Thomas and Ruth would be returning there for her to meet them, and for her to become accustomed to life in the home that would be hers for life. She thought—not for the first time—that she preferred to stay at the cottage forever. But she knew its purpose, and she would simply have to insist they visit as often as possible.

With both feet firmly on the ground, Thomas motioned with his hand and said, "What do you think?"

Ruth caught her breath so sharply she put a hand over her heart. The angle of the hill on which they'd been riding had made it impossible to see the view until now. But here, near the edge of a sharp, rocky decline, the ocean lay before them in all its glory, glistening in the late-morning sun.

"Oh, Thomas!" she murmured. "It's spectacular!" She took a deep breath; now that she was paying attention she could smell the salt in the air. "I've never seen the ocean before."

"Never?" His astonishment was evident.

"And why would I?" she asked. "I've been working to earn my keep for as long as I can recall. We didn't have the luxury of going on holiday." Ruth heard her own tone of voice and quickly added, "Forgive me for sounding sharp. It's not your fault. I should learn to mind my tongue."

While she couldn't take her eyes off the continuous roll of waves against the shore, she heard him say, "You should always say whatever you wish to say—at least to me. And while it may not be my fault, that doesn't mean it's right—or that you don't have a right to feel some anger."

"I'm not angry, Thomas," she said, looking out over the view. "Right now I'm only grateful. It's beautiful. It truly is."

"Let's walk," Thomas said and took her hand after he'd tethered the horse in a small grove of trees where it could graze in the shade.

They said little as they ambled slowly along the top of the cliffs, without getting too close to the edge. When Ruth admitted that she needed something to eat, they returned to where they'd left the horse and Thomas spread out a blanket, where he emptied the contents of the saddlebags. Ruth was eager to eat, while Thomas took on the ritual more slowly and seemed more content to observe her. She'd grown accustomed right from the start to the way he often watched her, and she was generally inclined to just watch him in return, as if to maintain some kind of common ground with him. Although she couldn't figure why. In truth there was a great deal she couldn't figure out about Thomas Fitzbatten. He was overtly open and forthright in most ways, but there was a part of himself he kept hidden away, and she longed to know what it might be. She could hardly begrudge his keeping secrets when she had some of her own. Still, she longed to know.

Trying to keep her thoughts more in the present, she interrupted the silence by saying, "So, this is courting."

Thomas chuckled. "Some form of it, I suppose. I can't say for certain since I've never courted a woman before."

"Not once?" she asked. "There must have been eligible ladies falling at your feet."

"Assuming you mean *falling at my feet* as metaphorical, I suppose there were. But it was all so pretentious and utterly ridiculous. I can't recall a single lady I ever felt any desire to share company with after a few minutes of conversation made it readily evident she was simple-headed and entirely superficial. I can't blame the women, really. Women of my class are raised to behave like simpering fools, believing that the acquisition of a good marriage is their only worthy goal in life."

"And by a good marriage you mean wealth and title."

"Exactly!" he said, pointing at her with a leg of cold chicken in his hand. "And since I had the curse of having both, I often felt like social gatherings were some kind of auction and I was on the auction block. It was expected that I should be perfectly happy to marry a woman who could look pretty in a parlor, serve tea correctly to guests, and embroider cushions and other odd little projects that were apparently of great importance."

He sounded mildly angry, but Ruth let him speak. He was talking about himself and his views on the life he'd lived. And she felt oddly comforted to know how much he detested the very kind of woman she was *not*.

"I stopped attending *any* social events of my class long before I went into the military. They held no interest for me. When my parents and I were invited to some kind of social gathering among the farmers and tenants of our estate, we were generally always pleased to attend."

Ruth opted to voice something she had thought many times. "It's as if you were born into the wrong class, husband, and yet your wealth gives you the opportunity and privilege to assist those in need. Far better that someone like you is blessed with wealth than those who would spend it on meaningless frills and nonsense."

"How observant you are, wife," he said, smiling at her. "My father taught me that very thing. I've often wondered if the attitudes I carry are a result of something born inside of me, or the teachings and example of my parents."

"I would guess that it's both," she said. "Have you not seen cruel and selfish people come from kind and decent parents? And the other way around?"

"Yes, I certainly have." He took a bite of chicken and chewed and swallowed it. "Like you, for instance."

"What about me?"

"You have described your father as gruff and occasionally unkind, and your mother turned you out right at the moment when you most needed a mother. I know they both have good qualities, because you've told me that as well. And yet I cannot imagine you ever exhibiting any of their negative traits."

"Perhaps you've not yet seen my temper unleashed, Mr. Fitzbatten," she teased.

"And perhaps I know you better than you think I do," he countered.

A long moment of silence allowed for a change of topic, and Ruth asked something she'd always wondered. "Why did you join the military?" She was surprised at how quickly he shifted the way he was sitting and looked pointedly away from her. But she ignored his apparent reluctance to talk about it and added, "Given your background, I assume you purchased a commission."

"I did," he said.

"And it is quite evidently your least favorite topic of conversation."

He looked surprised but admitted, "Right you are. They are years I wish I could forever erase from my memory *and* my life. But you *are* my wife and you deserve to know why I did what I did. So, I'll tell you. This dreadful business with Napoleon just never seemed to end, and I considered it my duty to do my part. As you have mentioned, I was blessed with great privilege. And with that comes great responsibility. It was expected of me, and so I was committed to do my part. I served my time and likely would have served longer if it weren't for my nearly dying."

"No!" she muttered, horrified at the very idea now that she'd grown to care for him as she did. "What happened?"

"A very close encounter with a saber belonging to an enemy soldier. I was saved by one of my comrades in arms—a man who remains a dear friend to this day. But I spent many weeks in one of those makeshift army hospitals before I was finally sent home." In a tone of caution, he added, "My parents know nothing of this yet, Ruth. I pleaded with my commanding officer not to send them word of my injury, and since it was evident I would survive and return home, he agreed. It was the reason for my returning earlier than they'd expected."

"Otherwise they likely would *not* have been traveling upon your return."

"Precisely," he said. "I will tell them when the time is right."

"I'll not say a word, of course. Will you tell me what happened?"

"It was dusk and difficult to see, so the details are somewhat foggy in my memory. But I recall facing off an enemy soldier, and I thought I was getting the better of him when the point of his saber pierced me, and I thought I was drawing my last breath. But the man was killed from behind, and my wound was serious but not fatal."

"You mean your friend killed this enemy soldier?" she asked, sobered by such talk of death and killing. She knew it was a part of war, but imagining Thomas in the middle of it made the horror far more personal.

"That's right."

"And had he not, this enemy you were fighting, he would have killed *you*?"

"Yes, Ruth. That's the truth of it. When I look back at the battles I fought, I find it a miracle I'd not fallen long before then. But apparently there was some reason I'd been meant to return home alive and well."

Ruth wanted to believe that reason was her, but she thought it would sound presumptuous to assume his only purpose for living was to care for her.

"Where were you wounded?" she asked.

He wiped his hand on a napkin and unbuttoned the top few buttons of his waistcoat, and then those of his shirt. He pushed both aside to the left, revealing a nasty scar below his collar bone. "Doctor said it missed my lung by less than an inch. If the saber had gone all the way in—as it had clearly been intended to—then it *would* have pierced my lung and I'd have died in minutes."

Ruth lifted her hand to touch the scar but hesitated, considering that perhaps he wouldn't feel that doing so was appropriate. "May I?" she asked.

"Of course," he said in a tone that implied there should be no need for her to wonder.

Ruth gently fingered the discolored skin that surrounded the cavity that remained as a permanent reminder of the wound—and the incident that had caused it.

Without moving her hand, Ruth asked, "Will you tell me the name of the man who saved your life?"

"Of course," he said. "It's Theodore Grayson—although he prefers being called Teddy. I first met him during our training, so we began our service together, and we always ended up posted to the same places at the same times. We joked about it being fate." He laughed. "Or perhaps some kind of curse that we couldn't get away from each other." More seriously he said, "Of course, if it was fate that my most trusted ally was there to save my life, I'll not give any argument to that. There were other men we became close to through the years, but some had been there longer and had already returned home. Some arrived long after we had and continued their service. Some were posted elsewhere, and of course . . . many died." He drew a strained breath. "But Teddy and I seemed inseparable." More lightly Thomas added, "He has plans to travel to Brownlie Manor sometime in the future."

"Then I shall be able to thank him personally," Ruth said, still unable to pull her fingers away. For some reason this tangible evidence of how close he'd come to dying had affected her deeply and she was finding it difficult to accept.

Ruth was surprised when Thomas put his hand over hers, pressing it more tightly to the wound. In a quiet voice he said, "It bled so much I thought I would bleed to death there on the battlefield. Teddy promised me over and over that he would not let that happen. The next thing I knew, I was in a bed and bandaged up, with Teddy sitting at my side, holding my hand as if he were my brother."

"Does it haunt you?" she asked and made no effort to hide a sudden swell of tears.

"Yes," he said, "but not nearly as much as other things do."

"What things?" she asked.

"Perhaps another time, my dear," he said and pulled her hand away before he refastened all of the buttons. "That's enough talk of war for one day." He touched her chin to make her look at him at the very moment tears spilled down her cheeks. "You mustn't be sad, wife. It is all in the past."

"I was just . . . wondering what might have become of me if you had died that day."

"There is no need to ever wonder any such thing."

"And I can't imagine how horrible it must have been for you." She touched his face without even thinking about whether or not she should. "I don't want you to ever hold back from talking to me about your experiences in the war simply because you don't want to upset me. I would far prefer to share your burdens than to think of you carrying them alone."

"That is very likely one of the kindest things anyone has ever said to me." He touched her face, as well, and she hoped he would kiss her. But he didn't. Instead he leaned back on one elbow and looked out over the sea. Ruth wondered what it might be that haunted him, if nearly dying on the battlefield was not the most difficult thing he'd encountered during his years at war. She wanted to ask, but she also needed to believe they were just beginning a life together, and this was likely the first of many conversations they would share about his wartime memories.

When the silence grew long, Ruth decided she would likely get no better opportunity to bring up something she'd thought about far too much. That impulsive moment between them on the night little Warren was born had crept into her thoughts every hour of every day. The memory was pleasant and stirring, but it was also confusing. And truthfully, it had been a strong contributing factor for talking to him just last night about her confusion and concerns regarding their relationship. She'd been hoping that *he* would bring it up, since it was he who'd done the kissing. It wasn't like him to let things go unspoken, which made her wonder if he didn't know what to say any more than she did. And yet it needed to be talked about, and she was determined to make that happen. Here with only the sun and the sea and the sky, there would be no interruptions, and she'd regret it later if she didn't take advantage of the moment.

"There's something important I need to ask you, Thomas," she said, and he immediately drew his attention from the view to look directly at her.

"I'm listening," he said when she didn't go on.

She drew in a sustaining breath and let the words out on a lengthy exhale. "Why did you kiss me?" He said nothing, didn't even change expression. "On the night Warren was born, why did you—"

"I know when you mean," he said.

Suddenly nervous and made more so by the silence, Ruth said, "Given that the only other time you kissed me was in front of the vicar when we exchanged vows, I should *hope* you'd know when I mean. But you can't blame me for wondering why you did that, and why you've never explained yourself since. It's not like you to—"

"Because I don't *know* why," he said and turned again to look at the sea. "At least not in any way that I could put into words." He chuckled with no hint of humor. "Perhaps this sort of thing is one of the drawbacks when courting is skipped over. If we'd been courting, then perhaps such a kiss might have been expected."

"If we'd been *properly* courting we'd not have been left alone without a chaperone—at least not in *your* world. And we certainly wouldn't have been working together to help our friends bring their baby into the world."

"No," he chuckled, which eased the tension—if only slightly. "We likely wouldn't have been doing *that.*"

Thomas looked again at her and said, "I didn't even think about it, Ruth. I just did it. At the moment it just felt right and I did it . . . without even thinking."

Ruth could accept that explanation. They'd been living like husband and wife in most respects, and it had been a very husbandly kind of kiss. But that didn't explain all of what had happened, and now that the subject was opened, she hurried to say, "But you kissed me again. You must have thought about *that.*"

His silence again provoked her to nervous chatter. "Maybe it's not that important, and I shouldn't be making such a fuss over it. Perhaps my wondering over it at all is a silly, womanly kind of thing and I should just—"

"I wanted to," he interrupted.

"What?"

"It felt so right the first time, that I just . . . wanted to do it again. I did it because I wanted to. And I'm not certain what to think about your categorizing your wondering over this as a silly, womanly kind of thing, because I have wondered every day how I might explain myself, and I've never been able to come up with anything. When we were married I made it clear that it was up to you to let me know when you were ready to cross certain boundaries in our marriage. I know you've been through a great deal, but the truth is I have absolutely no idea what your relationship was like with the man who fathered this child. I don't know if you loved or hated him; if he broke your heart or simply left you stranded and alone. I want to forget he ever existed, but his child is a part of our marriage. And I wonder if you think about him. Do you miss him? Do you wish it was him in my place? I wonder things like that, Ruth. Is that silly or womanly? Or just human? I want to believe that you hate him, that you're glad to have him out of your life for good. But I know what you shared with him is no small thing, no matter what the circumstances—or your feelings—might have been. And I'm afraid to ask. Because if I ask, then perhaps you'll tell me a truth I don't want to hear. I kissed you that night because I wanted to, but I immediately felt as if I'd broken my word to you, as if I'd offended you somehow by crossing a boundary I had told you was yours to cross. The things you said last night . . . about being confused and concerned about how our future would play out. I feel confused and concerned, as well. But I don't know if it's for the same reasons. I want the kind of marriage I've seen my parents share, and I want to believe that's possible with you and me. I believe we are well suited for each other, but I'm haunted by your memories, Ruth—even though I don't know what they are. And I'm afraid to ask if you are haunted by them too."

Ruth took in his string of confessions with a mixture of shock and awe. She felt breathless but fought to disguise it, holding herself upright with her hands planted firmly on the ground, trying to accept the implications of all that he was saying. She had married him for security and the means to erase her shame. She had hoped they could share a marriage of trust and comfortable companionship. She had not expected to feel the way she had come to feel for him, but even less had she expected him to feel such things for her—and so soon. She couldn't keep herself from staring at him, as if she might find evidence in his eyes that might contradict everything he'd just said. What she found was the opposite. Her heart quickened and her stomach quivered.

The silence between them became so taut she felt certain it could have been struck with a hammer and shattered. He'd confessed a great many feelings, and she could see vulnerability in his eyes. It was her turn to speak, to offer some kind of response. And if she had any concern or compassion for him at all, she would have the decency to reassure him that he was not alone in his feelings. But no words came to her tongue that didn't sound like girlish nonsense, and the more she tried to think of something to say, the more muddled her thoughts became.

It then occurred to Ruth that no words at all were necessary. Before she had time to talk herself out of it, she moved on her hands and knees toward him and kissed him much as he'd kissed her that night in the hallway.

"Before you ask," she said, sitting beside him, noting the question in his eyes, "there's no need to wonder if you offended me. If you were leaving it up to me to cross this boundary between us, I just did."

"So you did," he said and kissed her in return. She felt relief in his kiss—both from him and within herself. It seemed to hold promise for both of them that this marriage might yet be everything they had ever hoped a marriage could be.

Since he'd made it clear that it was up to her to declare the boundaries between them, she felt the need to say, "I do believe it would be wise to take matters slowly—or at least not rush too quickly. But I see no reason why a man should not kiss his wife if the mood strikes him."

"Or the other way around," he said, seeming more relaxed than he had in quite some time—perhaps since the night Warren had been born. Had this been weighing on him so heavily?

Ruth put a hand to his face, loving the way that being his wife made it acceptable for her to touch him this way. "I think I like courting, Mr. Fitzbatten."

"Yes," he said with a little chuckle, "I think I like it very much." And, as if for good measure, he kissed her again.

* * *

Thomas looked into his wife's eyes, overcome with a heart-quickening realization that he was not alone in his feelings. And with that realization came the most likely reason he'd felt afraid all these weeks, and why fear had kept him from bringing up what had happened between them. If she'd told him she was agreeable to be his wife in every way—in spite of having no actual feelings of attraction toward him—he believed his heart would have been broken. He'd been unable to acknowledge—even to himself—that his heart could be so completely invested in a woman he'd married impulsively and mostly with a desire to rescue her from a dire situation. He'd told himself that only a fool would become so thoroughly dependent upon—and attracted to—a woman under such circumstances. And it was those feelings he'd been hiding from. But Ruth had challenged his reasons for behaving as he had, and he was more relieved than he could admit that it was now openly acknowledged. But even with the words spoken between them, it was what he saw in her eyes that quickened his heart and brought him to the realization that he was not alone in his feelings. He was not alone in his vulnerability or his concerns. And he was not alone in this attraction that consumed him.

Thomas considered this ritual of courting they had mutually decided upon to be a wise course in their relationship, and he believed even more now that it certainly was good for them to spend the time together that couples usually spent prior to considering engagement and marriage. And yet he was so deeply glad to know she already belonged to him. There was no question at the end of this courtship—only what he hoped would be the evolution into a real marriage in which they could both be happy and content. The attraction and intrigue he saw in her eyes when she looked at him only solidified his hopes on that count.

Thomas wanted to kiss her again. And again. He wanted to never stop. Knowing she was his wife made self-discipline all the more difficult to reason with. So he kissed her once more and shot to his feet, taking her hand as he did.

"Come along, wife. It's a crime that a woman of your years has never once beheld the sea until today. Perhaps it would be well for you to get a little closer."

"Truly?" she asked with a girlish excitement as he helped her into the saddle behind him, leaving the remnants of their picnic to be gathered later.

Thomas guided the horse some distance up the length of the cliff, then carefully down a steep trail. He reminded Ruth that he knew every secret of this place, having come here a great deal in his youth. When they emerged onto the beach, she laughed aloud and the contagion of it made him laugh with her. They galloped the length of the beach before he helped her dismount at a place that was dry where he could tie off the horse and know it would be safe. He knelt and began to unlace her shoes.

"What are you doing?" she demanded.

"You can't come all this way and not get your feet in the water, Mrs. Fitzbatten. I assure you there is nothing like it."

Once her shoes were unlaced, he turned his back while she removed her stockings and he sat to pull off his own boots and stockings. He set them all aside where they would stay dry, then suggested she hold her skirts high enough to keep them from getting wet. He considered how scandalous some people might think it to be that he could see her lower legs, but that only made him laugh again. She was, after all, his wife.

"Just stand right here," he instructed and took hold of her arm. A moment later a low wave rushed over their bare feet and she laughed like a child.

"Oh, it's cold," she declared.

"Yes, indeed," he said, but she stepped out farther, and the next wave came almost to her knees. And she laughed again.

They laughed and played in the waves, and her efforts to keep the bottom of her skirts dry quickly proved fruitless. She was reluctant to put her shoes and stockings back on, but it was late enough in the day that he insisted they had to leave soon or they'd not get back to the cottage before the sun went down. They stopped to gather up their belongings from the picnic, and Ruth was glad to find some bread and butter wrapped in a napkin still in Thomas's saddle bag. She ate it while he kept the horse at a steady gallop toward home.

"It was a lovely day, Thomas," she said when the cottage came into view in the distance. "I shall never forget it."

"Perhaps you can tell our grandchildren about it," he said.

"Perhaps I shall," she said and laid her head against his back while she tightened her arms around his chest.

Thomas headed up the hill toward the cottage, firmly deciding that he liked the idea of courting his wife. In fact, he concluded it was likely a tradition they should manage to observe for the rest of their lives.

* * *

Thomas and Ruth returned to the news that a letter had arrived by way of a courier from Thomas's parents. Since it had been addressed to Barclay, he'd taken the liberty of reading it.

"And a good thing I did, too," Barclay said. "Otherwise we'd have not been ready nearly in time."

"In time for what?" Thomas asked, snatching the letter from Barclay's hand.

"What does it say?" Ruth asked, and he read it aloud for her benefit.

"*My dear Mr. Barclay, we have just returned this morning from the continent to the news that our Thomas has come back from the war far sooner than we had anticipated, and he is now on holiday at the cottage. As anxious as we are to see him, we will be setting out straightaway and plan to stay at the Rutherford Inn tonight. We should then arrive sometime tomorrow before noon, and hope that this will not pose any imposition upon you and your good wife. We understand congratulations are in order for the recent birth of your son, and do so look forward to meeting the little one, as well as seeing you and dear Bertie again. We also offer our condolences at the passing of your mother and find peace in knowing that she is surely now with your dearly departed father in some great heavenly realm.*"

Thomas stopped and looked at Barclay with a smile. "I suppose we don't need to wonder which of my parents actually *wrote* the letter."

"No, sir," Barclay chuckled. "Your dear mother certainly does have a way with words."

Thomas cleared his throat and continued. "*Since we have read the letter that Thomas left for us, we are also aware that he has taken a wife prior to his return home, and we are filled with delight at the prospect of meeting her. Perhaps some time at the cottage will give us all an opportunity to become acquainted. As ever, we don't wish for you or Bertie to fuss over our visit. We will be glad to offer our assistance upon our arrival, as needed. With fondest anticipation, Yours Respectfully, Lord and Lady Arrington.*"

"Arrington?" Ruth asked. "That's a name I've not heard before."

"You'd best get used to it, my dear. It will one day be your title."

Before she could question him further on that, Barclay reported, "Me and Bertie have got the rooms that the lord and lady prefer all aired out and ready for them, and we went into the village and got some extra food, proper things we know they like. You needn't worry about a thing, sir. We're all set for their arrival."

"And how good it will be to see them!" Bertie said, as if nothing could have made her happier.

Thomas felt rather happy about it himself and was thoroughly pleased with the prospect of Ruth finally meeting his parents—and vice versa. During supper and long afterward they speculated about where Thomas's parents had been traveling, how thrilled they would be to see Thomas again, and how the news of Thomas's marriage would have surely made them happy. Bertie was quite set on how thrilled the lord and lady would be over the prospective arrival of their grandchild, and Barclay mentioned there was surely hope that it would be a son to carry on the family title and traditions.

Later that night, after Ruth had doused the lamp and climbed into bed, Thomas said to her, "You're nervous."

"Are you a fortune teller now?" she asked.

"It doesn't take a fortune teller to see that you're nervous. You cover it well, mind you. But I can tell. And I assure you there is absolutely no reason to be. They will adore you."

"Are you certain, Thomas?"

"I am very much like my parents. If I've managed to tolerate your company this long, I doubt it will be much of a problem for them." He laughed at his own sarcasm, then laughed harder when she slugged him in the shoulder. "Although I wouldn't suggest behaving like *that* when they're around."

"I'm certain they'd not deserve it," she said with a little laugh and settled back onto her pillow.

"It will be all right," he said. "I promise."

When several minutes passed, he thought she might have fallen asleep, but she said, "We've never come up with a story of how we met and married. No one has asked the details of us. But I suspect your parents will want to know. I hate lying to them, but I suppose it's necessary."

Thomas leaned up on his elbow to look toward her silhouette in the darkness. "Let's not think of it as a lie; let's think of it as you said—as a story. Our little secret."

"A secret we should be letting my uncle in on once we return to the manor."

"Yes, we likely should." He sighed. "So, where did we meet, wife? I was recovering from a war wound. Where were you?"

"Oh, I know," she said, also leaning up on her elbow so they were facing each other, even though it was too dark to see more than shadows. "Is it plausible that you were staying with one of your comrades in Portsmouth who had gone home on leave, getting your strength back before returning home?"

"I don't believe I have any comrades from Portsmouth, but we could pretend that's possible."

"And I went to Portsmouth on holiday, because I have an imaginary cousin there who was ill and needed my assistance. I looked familiar to you because I'd once been to Brownlie Manor to visit my uncle and we had crossed paths briefly."

"Excellent," Thomas said. "And we shall have to inform your uncle of his part in the story at the first opportunity."

"So, we met again in Portsmouth and knew right away that we couldn't live without each other, and so we were married. When you returned to the manor to tell your parents of the marriage and surprise them with your return, I went to see my mother and brothers to tell them the same, and it was our plan all along to meet up and come to the cottage."

"That sounds fairly convincing," he said, and they talked a while longer, coming up with names of their imaginary friends and relations in Portsmouth and the actual date when they were supposedly married, which would have been some weeks before Ruth's baby had been conceived.

"Do you feel less nervous now?" he asked when she relaxed onto her pillow. He did the same, wishing this bed weren't quite so large— but at the same time feeling grateful that it was.

Chapter Seven

ON BUTTERFLY WINGS

THE FOLLOWING MORNING WHILE RUTH was pinning up her hair, Thomas's face appeared in the mirror beside hers as he took hold of her shoulders. "Are you still nervous?"

"Yes, but not quite so much now that I know we have a story to tell them that won't leave us looking like fools."

"It will take very little time for you to feel completely comfortable with them, I promise."

"I'll hold you to it," she said, and he chuckled as he left the room.

About halfway between breakfast and lunch, a hired coach stopped in the drive at the other end of the footpath. Barclay and Bertie were like a couple of children, barely containing their excitement. Thomas managed to remain more composed, but Ruth had no trouble seeing how thrilled he was to see his parents. They all went down the footpath to meet Lord and Lady Arrington as they alighted from the carriage. Ruth held back, preferring to observe from a distance at first.

Bertie held the baby while Barclay helped the coachmen take down the luggage and set it aside to be carried into the house after greetings had been exchanged. Thomas helped his mother step down from the carriage and immediately wrapped her in his arms, lifting her off the ground with a burst of laughter and twirling her around twice before he set her down and helped steady her from her dizziness.

Ruth couldn't hear what they were saying, but she was glad for the chance to see Thomas's mother—and the charming way he interacted with her. Yvette Fitzbatten looked a little taller than Ruth, and thinner. Her clothing was fine but looked as though it had been created more for comfort than show, which certainly didn't surprise Ruth. Her graying dark hair was done up tightly, and pinned to it was an intricate lace bonnet that revealed more hair than it covered. Her features were fine and delicate, and she had a frail look about her that had not been evident in the enthusiastic greeting with her son.

As Thomas's father stepped out of the carriage, Ruth turned her attention to him. He met Thomas eye to eye, and his gray hair showed only hints that it had once been as dark as his son's. But it was evident where Thomas had gotten his curls. Quincy Fitzbatten had that same impossible-to-control look to his hair, which Ruth found endearing. Thomas bore a strong likeness to his father in his features, as well. Even though she could see a hint of Yvette in Thomas's face, he definitely favored his father. The two men laughed and embraced, and Ruth had to remember this was the first time they'd seen Thomas in years, and they had likely wondered if they would ever see him again.

Yvette started up the walk while the carriage rolled away, and Thomas and his father collected the luggage. Barclay had already carried a trunk into the house, and Bertie had followed him. When she saw Ruth, Yvette stopped walking, put both hands to her face, and let out a joyful noise.

"And this must be our Ruth," Yvette said and hurried to close the gap between them. "Oh, my dear girl!" Yvette said and took Ruth's face into her hands. "What a beautiful and precious thing you are!"

"It is so good to finally meet you," was all Ruth could think to say.

"And you, my dear," Yvette said and laughed. "Although I didn't know about you until yesterday; still it is grand to meet you." Putting her arm protectively around Ruth, Yvette called to her husband, who was almost up the walk with a piece of luggage in each hand. "Look, Quin, look. It's our Ruth. Isn't she just precious?"

Thomas's father set down the bags as if he had to do so in order to fully appreciate the moment. He looked at Ruth with intrigue sparkling in his merry eyes, saying firmly, "You *are* just precious, my dear."

"It is such a pleasure to meet you, sir," Ruth said, nodding toward him. "But I must protest your declaration of my being precious.

You've barely met me." She lightly added, "Perhaps I have hidden vices or a nasty temper."

"Oh, I do like her," Thomas's father said to him.

"I knew you would," Thomas said, winking at Ruth.

Quincy stepped forward and took both of Ruth's hands into his. With full sincerity, he said, "If our Thomas chose you to be his wife, then you are most certainly precious. I'm absolutely certain of it."

"You are very kind, sir," Ruth said.

"Now, there'll be none of that." He lifted a finger. "Either call me Quin or Papa, if it suits you. But I'll not be 'sirred' by my own daughter."

He picked the suitcases up again and took them into the house while Yvette held the door.

"You'd best do as he tells you," Thomas said quietly to Ruth as he passed by, also carrying luggage.

Ruth stood outside the door a long moment while Yvette's *our Ruth* swirled around in her mind along with Quincy's *my own daughter.* And Thomas had not seemed at all hesitant or ashamed of them doing so. If anything, he'd seemed proud of her—and this while she was pregnant with another man's child and their marriage had begun as a charade. But if it had ever *felt* that way, it didn't now. In that moment Ruth felt like a part of this family. During the simple exchanges of just a minute or two, she felt loved and secure; she felt as if she belonged. And if she thought about it a moment more, she would dissolve into uncontrollable tears until Thomas would have to come searching for her, and she would need to try to explain. Instead she forced back any need to become maudlin over all of this and went into the house.

Ruth found that the men had taken the luggage upstairs; she could hear their booming voices filling the upper floor with teasing and laughter. Yvette was seated in the parlor and just now saying to Bertie, "Come sit down, my dear girl, and let me see that baby."

Ruth tried to imagine—in the households where she'd once been employed—the lady of the house being seated with a servant, fussing over the baby as if they were friends. It never would have happened; it wasn't considered respectable in polite society. But here was Yvette Fitzbatten, Lady Arrington of Brownlie Manor, holding little Warren on her lap and fussing over him, declaring him to be the cutest baby she'd seen since Thomas had been that age.

Ruth moved discreetly into the room and sat down to observe, but both women glanced her way and Yvette said to her, "Isn't he just the sweetest thing, my dear?"

"He is, indeed," Ruth said. "We've all been enjoying him very much."

"Ruth helped deliver him," Bertie told Yvette proudly. "You know how I feel about the doctor here."

"I do, and I heartily agree," Yvette said.

"Since I've had me own training, I thought we could manage on our own. And we did. But I know it would have been much harder on me if it hadn't been for Ruth." Bertie smiled toward her. "She's as kind as she is capable."

Yvette took a long look at Ruth and said, "I'd not expect my Thomas to marry anyone less than that."

"Certainly not, m'lady," Bertie said.

Yvette smiled at Ruth as if to punctuate that she truly meant it, then she turned her attention to Warren, talking to him in a funny voice and touching his every finger as if to be assured they were all as perfect as they appeared to be.

"I'm so happy for you, Bertie," Yvette said, giving the baby back to his mother as he began to fuss.

As always when the baby needed feeding, Bertie was quick to unfasten a few buttons of her bodice and lead the baby to her breast. Once he was situated, she tossed a shawl over her shoulder, since the men were likely to return to the room before the baby finished nursing. Being able to nurse the baby with or without men in the room was one of many skills that Ruth was taking note of as she observed Bertie with her baby. The time was creeping closer far too quickly, and in fact she had barely been able to make herself presentable in the dress she was wearing and felt sure that tomorrow she would opt for wearing one of the dresses Thomas had ordered for her to accommodate her increasing size. For reasons she couldn't define, she hadn't wanted his parents to meet her with her pregnancy blatantly obvious. They were family, and perhaps once *they* knew, she would feel a little more comfortable with being publicly pregnant and pretending that Thomas was the father.

Once Yvette was no longer distracted with the baby, she turned toward Ruth and physically moved on the sofa to put herself closer to where Ruth was sitting in a nearby chair. "Now, you must tell me all about yourself, my dear," Yvette said. "You can't imagine our surprise to return home and learn that Thomas had come back and we'd not been there to greet him. And then to read his letter and discover that he'd come home to us with the best surprise of all." She reached a hand toward Ruth, who took it and smiled, a little overcome with this woman's kindness, but at the same time thinking that meeting Thomas's parents had made *his* natural kindness make perfect sense. "Tell me about your family, Ruth," Yvette prodded.

"I'm one of six children," Ruth said, "and the only girl."

"Oh, my," Yvette said. "What an adventure that must have been!"

"It certainly was," Ruth said with a little laugh. "They're all old enough to work in the mines now; two of them are married and the others live at home with my mother."

"That's not an easy life," Yvette said with compassion.

"No, but the mines have provided well for my family, in spite of . . ."

"Of what, my dear?"

"My father was taken in a mining accident some years back."

"Oh, you poor dear," Yvette said. "And your poor, dear mother."

Ruth only said, "The mine gave us a compensation, which helped immensely, and they are all managing well enough."

"I'm glad to hear *that*," Yvette said. "We must arrange to meet your family as soon as possible."

"Of course," Ruth said, thinking that it was likely proper; but that didn't mean she necessarily ever wanted it to happen.

"And tell me about you, my dear," Yvette urged, and Ruth was grateful for the opportunity she'd had to observe Thomas's mother with Bertie and to know that his parents were not the kind of people who cared a whit about marrying outside of one's social class.

"My story is nothing unusual," Ruth began. "I started working in a manor house at rather a young age, and worked my way up. I went to a different home when a better opportunity came, and eventually I was assisting a lady's maid."

"Well, you appear to be as refined as any lady I've ever met," Yvette said. "Not that it would matter to me." She squeezed Ruth's hand. "If my Thomas loves you, then nothing else matters."

"I can attest that she is very much a lady," Bertie said, "but not afraid to get her hands dirty, neither. She kept the household running while I was recovering. Don't know what we'd have done without her." Bertie chuckled. "And she does well at ordering the men about when there's chores to be done."

"Good for you, my dear," Yvette said with a delighted laugh, and Ruth knew by then that she couldn't have disliked her mother-in-law for any reason. She'd certainly not expected to, but the evidence was comforting—especially given the strain Ruth had felt with her own mother at their last parting.

Hearing the men coming noisily down the stairs, the women ceased their conversation, and Ruth observed the light and comfortable interaction Thomas had with his father. She also noticed that Quin treated Barclay much like an old friend—just as Yvette behaved with Bertie. They were all seated in the parlor, although Thomas took Ruth's hand and urged her to sit in a different spot on one of the sofas so he could sit right next to her. He kept her hand in his and smiled at her as if he felt no nervousness or discomfort at all, even though she knew they were both about to expound upon the lie he'd begun in the letter he'd left for his parents.

They shared small talk about the people in the village, the repairs that had been done on the cottage and barn, and the birth of little Warren. They also spoke solemnly of Starla's passing, although Yvette declared that Starla was surely an angel watching over the new baby and his parents. A moment of silence and a few sniffles implied a mutual agreement even before Barclay said, "I'm certain you're right, m'lady. I've thought many times that I wish she were here to see him, and then it occurs to me that she's likely looking in on him all the time."

"I'm certain she is," Yvette said.

Bertie declared that the baby was asleep and she needed to check on some things in the kitchen, and Barclay followed her out of the room, as if they both knew when it was the right time to see to their duties as employees of these people and leave them to their time together as family.

They'd not been gone half a minute before Thomas said, "Now that we're all together, I'm certain you have many questions. So let me begin by telling you that *yes*, I did come home earlier than I had anticipated. And when I got it in my head to surprise you, it hadn't occurred to me that you might be traveling. It *should* have occurred to me, but it didn't. So I apologize for my poor timing."

"No apology necessary, dearest," Yvette said.

Quin piped in. "It would have been as foolish of us to be sitting at home waiting for you as it would have been for you to think that your return had to be perfectly timed. It couldn't be helped. We're together and happy for it."

"It is *so* good to see you alive and well, my boy," Yvette said.

"It is good to *be* alive and well," Thomas said and went on to tell them the story of his being wounded on the battlefield, although he was a little less graphic about it than when he'd told Ruth, which she felt certain was for his mother's benefit. Yvette still wept and thanked God aloud more than once that her son's life had been spared. Quin said as much himself, and Ruth noted that the love these people had for Thomas was readily evident. She felt immensely privileged in that moment to have married into such a family and wondered why, of all the women who had found themselves in such dire circumstances, she might have been blessed enough to be rescued by Thomas Fitzbatten.

Quin and Yvette were then full of questions about how Thomas had met Ruth and how they'd fallen in love. There was that word *love* again. He just smiled at her as if it perfectly described everything they felt for each other, then proceeded to tell their manufactured tale of how they'd met and married in Portsmouth. When they came to the part about how they'd looked familiar to each other, Thomas's parents were thrilled to realize that she was a niece to their long and trusted servant and friend.

"Imagine him not telling us!" Quin said in a tone of teasing.

"He was sworn to secrecy," Thomas said. "And we all know that Dawson can keep a secret better than the average ten men."

"That he can," Quin said.

Yvette asked more questions about the marriage and what had led up to it. Thomas smiled at Ruth and then at his mother. "It all happened very quickly, but you always taught me to follow my heart and to trust my instincts." He looked again at Ruth. "I'd barely spent an hour with her before I knew that marrying her was the best thing I could do with my life."

Ruth was taken aback to look into his eyes and realize he was telling the absolute truth. He had no regrets or doubts. She wanted to hold him close and tell him how very much that meant to her, how grateful she was to feel the same, and to have good reason to hope they could share a good and loving lifetime together. As it was, she just smiled, glad to see him smile back before he turned to his parents and added lightly, "Good thing Dawson considered me a suitable match, or we'd have had an uproar at Brownlie Manor to be sure."

Yvette laughed softly, but Quin apparently thought it was extremely funny. His laughter was deep and hearty and apparently contagious because Ruth found herself laughing as well. And so was Thomas. She loved it when he laughed.

When the laughter finally died down, Quin said to Ruth, "If Dawson gives you any trouble, my dear, you let me know."

"I'll try not to be too hard on him," Ruth said, and they all laughed again.

Ruth considered that a great source of the laughter was simply the joy these people had at being reunited with their son—and the other way around. She wondered if Thomas had imagined this reunion with a pregnant wife at his side, but she chose to think instead of the conviction she'd seen in his eyes only moments ago when he'd declared his belief that marrying her had been the right thing to do.

When silence settled again, Thomas said, "I don't know if you can take any more happiness in one morning." His parents both looked at him, aghast and expectant. "But it's about time you know that you're going to be grandparents."

Ruth wasn't surprised by the way Yvette put a hand over her heart and got tears in her eyes, but she hadn't expected Quin to do the same. In response to their silence, Thomas put his arm around Ruth's shoulders and said, "I'm going to take that to mean you're pleased. And it's high time you knew. Ruth is about to burst out of the seams of that dress she's wearing. It was impossible to not tell Bertie and Barclay, but we *did* want you to be the first to know—as much as that was possible."

"Oh, my dear!" Yvette murmured and crossed the room to sit on the sofa on the other side of Ruth. She embraced Ruth tightly and said, "You dear, sweet thing. I doubt anything could make me happier."

Ruth returned Yvette's embrace and then nodded at her in response, overcome with her own tears.

"This is joyous news, indeed," Quin said. "It's high time the halls of Brownlie Manor had more family to fill them up, and what could be better than the laughter of children?"

"Indeed," Yvette said. "And the crying." She smiled at her husband. "Babies cry as well, my dear. I'm sure you remember."

"Oh, I remember," Quin said. "But this time we're the grandparents. We aren't required to take care of the crying. We can just . . . go for a walk, or something." Quin laughed and added, "Congratulations . . . to the both of you. This is a joyous day!"

"Yes, it is," Thomas said, and Ruth once again found him looking at her. She returned his gaze for a long moment, until the shame she felt over her secret roiled up inside of her, threatening to smother her joy.

Ruth stood and said, "I'll let you all do some catching up and see if Bertie needs any help." Yvette moved to stand, but Ruth motioned for her to remain seated. "No, you've been traveling. Visit with your son. Everything is under control."

Yvette smiled and nodded, and Ruth hurried into the kitchen. Bertie assured her there was nothing to be done except keep an eye on the food to make certain it didn't burn, and Bertie had that under control. Ruth was secretly glad and hurried quietly up the stairs, wanting to be alone.

Once in the bedroom she tugged frantically at the lacings down the back of her dress but couldn't reach well enough to do any more than give herself a little more breathing room. Thomas had been helping her with them, since she always wore a chemise underneath and she'd never felt exposed, but she wasn't about to go find him and ask for help while she felt as if something hot and volatile inside her might explode.

Ruth kicked off her shoes and lay down on the bed, curling around the mound of her baby, feeling torn and confused. How could she be so thoroughly blessed and feel that everything was so dreadfully wrong? Tears came with force, and she had no strength to hold them back, glad to know that the house was big enough—and the walls thick enough—that she could do so with some privacy. But she jumped and nearly screamed when she felt a hand on her shoulder and turned to see Thomas. Her crying had blocked out the sound of his coming into the room and closing the door behind him.

"Can't a woman have a good cry in secret around here?" she snapped as she turned away from him.

Thomas sat on the bed beside her and said, "As soon as you can tell me why you're crying and I'm assured it has nothing to do with me, I will gladly leave you in peace."

When Ruth could only keep crying, she felt Thomas loosening the laces down her back. "Here, at least let me help you. I told you this morning when you put this on it was ridiculous. It can't be good for you or the baby."

"I didn't want your parents immediately seeing that I am enormously pregnant," she said through a whimper and sat up so that she could shimmy out of the dress. Even though the chemise covered everything to her elbows and nearly to her ankles, Thomas still wouldn't look directly at her when she wore it with nothing over it. He opened the wardrobe and took out a lovely red print dress that had been hanging there for weeks in anticipation of her growing waistline.

"Here," he said, then added after she'd taken it from him, "And what was your excuse the day before that? And the one before that? Sometimes I wonder if you wish that you *weren't* pregnant."

Ruth barely had the dress over her head before she looked at him in astonishment, but he still wouldn't look at her so she stood up and let the dress fall over the chemise. "I'm covered now, Mr. Fitzbatten," she said with a snarl. "If you would do the honor?"

He fastened the back of the dress while she considered how to respond to what he'd said—and how angry it made her. "I don't think I've ever seen you so upset, *Mrs. Fitzbatten*." He mimicked her tone perfectly.

"I would *never* wish for this baby to not exist, Thomas. I feel it moving and growing inside of me, and I . . ." She started to cry again, and he urged her to sit on the edge of the bed, sitting beside her with his comforting arms wrapped around her.

"Tell me why you're so upset," he said, "and accept my apology for being so insensitive. We men are just a bunch of insensitive fools, you know. My mother has told me so."

"I'm certain she never meant it of you and your father."

"There may have been moments," he said. "I can't say I've never been an insensitive fool, and I may yet be again. It's a wife's job to point out when her husband is behaving badly."

"And a husband's job to do the same for his wife?" she asked and sniffled.

"Perhaps," he said and repeated, "Please tell me why you're so upset."

"I feel terrible having to lie to your parents, Thomas. If my uncle and my mother know the truth, shouldn't they? Surely you can trust them." She looked up at him. "Surely they would understand." At his alarmed silence, she stated the obvious, "You don't think they *would*?"

"I don't know, Ruth," he admitted. "I need . . . to think about it; obviously I didn't think it through as well as I should have." He sighed and lowered his head into hands.

"I meant no grief to come into your life, Thomas. If I could have—"

"Listen to me, Ruth," he said, turning toward her. "I *chose* to do this. Do you think for one moment that I *regret* that choice?"

"You don't seem to," she said, "but . . ."

"Ruth," he said, turning on the bed to take hold of her hands. "Tell me what you think, now that you've met them. You've brought up a valid point, and we need to consider it. But I need to know what *you* think; I need to know what you want."

Ruth couldn't take her eyes off of him while she pondered his question, and then she turned her gaze downward, unable to look at him at all. The truth swelled inside of her, along with the answer to his question. But the strangeness of the situation had made it so difficult to talk about—even though she knew it shouldn't be. He'd never given her reason to be afraid to tell him the truth.

Keeping her eyes focused on the floral pattern of her dress, Ruth spoke from her heart. "I want our story to be true, Thomas. I want us to have met in Portsmouth, to have fallen so quickly and deeply in love that we couldn't get married fast enough. I want this baby to be yours and for everything in our lives to be as perfect as it seems." Now that she'd said the difficult part, she looked up at him. "But it's a lie; we'll always be living a lie. And what can be worse than lying to people you love and respect? How can you live your life, allowing your parents to believe a lie about something so vital and important to them? And what if this baby is a boy? Don't think I haven't thought about what that means. Can you truly stand by and allow a child with no Fitzbatten blood to inherit everything your father will leave to you? Including a title? Can you? Because I don't know if I can! There," she finished firmly, "that's what I think."

Thomas looked deeply into her eyes, as if he were trying to measure everything she'd just said. "I *do* need to tell them the truth," he said. "I can see that now. I just . . ."

"Don't know how?"

"I just . . . have to do it—as difficult as it might be. But . . . there is something I need to do first. I only need a little time . . . to think . . . to pray, certainly. But I will tell them soon, I promise."

"I need to be with you when you do," she said, and he looked as if he might protest. "I must!" she insisted. "We are husband and wife. We are in this together."

He nodded before he embraced her, and she could feel hesitancy and fear in the way he held her. But she also knew he would do the right thing. She wanted to be close to his parents, and she knew she never could be if they didn't know the truth. She could only hope and pray that when they *did* know the truth, they would still feel about her the way they did now.

* * *

Ruth observed that lunch went smoothly while Thomas asked question after question of his parents about their travels and didn't give them a moment to notice that both he and Ruth were a little on edge. After they'd eaten, Quin and Yvette both declared the need for a nap, which they admitted was often their habit even when they hadn't been wearing themselves out with travel. Ruth helped Bertie in the kitchen for a while, and Thomas went out to the garden to pull weeds from around the rose bushes. When Bertie no longer needed her help, Ruth found him there, his sleeves haphazardly rolled up and his waistcoat unbuttoned since the day was warm.

"Are you thinking or praying?" she asked, standing above him.

"I've been doing both," he said.

"Would you prefer that I leave you alone?" she asked.

"No . . . thank you. I think I would now prefer some company." Ruth knelt nearby and began pulling weeds as well. He added, "You don't have to work in order to keep me company."

"And you don't think I need something to occupy my hands every bit as much as you do?" she countered. She picked up a little pair of clippers that he'd left on the ground and began removing all that was no longer useful on one of the bushes.

Thomas stopped pulling weeds and brushed the dirt from his hands, suddenly no longer needing to keep them occupied. While he carefully considered all he'd been pondering, and his hope that God would guide him and help propel him forward, he sat on the ground to simply watch his wife as she clipped away all that was dead and dying on the rose bush that was currently the product of her tender care and pruning. How could it be that he had married a woman so impulsively and yet had grown to respect and admire her more every day? And her declaration in regard to his parents had only made him respect and admire her all the more. How could it be that he believed his heart would irrevocably break if he were to ever lose her or see her harmed in any way? What kind of magic had brought them together and made him feel this way?

He was so entranced with his study of her beautiful face and tiny hands at work that he was startled when she laughed and looked up, saying with glee, "Oh, my! I've not seen one like this in such a long time; years maybe." She laughed again, her dampened mood completely absent. "It's beautiful."

"What?" he asked, turning to see what had her attention.

Something eerie and remarkable and strange enveloped him with wonder as his eye caught the butterfly with bright blue wings flitting around over the bush that she'd been tending to, as if it might be inviting her to play. How could he ever forget the last time he'd seen such a butterfly? The bright blue wings were rare and unmistakable. He'd been in the garden at Brownlie Manor with Fletcher and Ernie, feeling terribly low and sorry for himself. And the butterfly had come, seeming to bring with it a message in the way it had lighted in front of him as if to stare him down. *Something good will come to you*, he'd been told. And it was not many days later that Ruth had appeared in his life. He didn't believe in magic or mystical things. But he did believe that butterflies were God's creatures, just as men and women were, and he couldn't deny—though he could never explain without sounding crazy—that the blue butterfly had seemed to bring him a message that day that had given him hope. And now a butterfly of the same breed was here, many miles from Brownlie Manor, delighting his wife with its fluttering dance.

Thomas wanted to tell her about his thoughts, and perhaps eventually he would. For now, he was content to simply watch and take in the moment. He'd known even before she'd come outside to join him exactly what he needed to do—or rather say. And he knew it had to be done before he could face his parents with the truth and the necessary conviction to make them believe him. But now, rather than feeling any concern or even fear over what he needed to do, he felt entirely calm and at peace. Caught up in a sensation that was almost magical, he was taken aback to hear Ruth say, "It's the same color as the flower you put in my hair just before we were married."

"So it is," he said, wondering why he'd chosen *that* flower from the many different colors available in the bouquet.

"Which matches the stone in the ring you gave me," she added, still watching the butterfly as if she dared not look away. The little creature finally seemed satisfied with its exploration of that particular rosebush, and it flew quickly up and away, gone from sight in seconds. Ruth turned to him and asked, "Did you plan that?"

He said facetiously, "I am capable of a great many things, my darling, but I have no control over butterflies."

She laughed and held her hand toward him to display her wedding ring, as if he might not remember what it looked like. "Did you pick the blue flower because it matched the stone in the ring?"

"I wish I could say I'd been that clever," he admitted, taking her outstretched hand to kiss it before she returned to her work. "Although . . ." he drawled, "maybe I picked the blue hydrangea to match the butterfly so that this moment would remind you of our wedding."

"That *would* be clever," she said and laughed again. Oh, how he loved to hear her laugh!

He continued to watch her until she turned to look at him and asked, "Why do you sit there and stare at me? You aren't getting very much done."

"Sometimes a man's thoughts are so overwhelming that it's impossible to do anything but think."

"And what of a woman's thoughts?" she asked, setting the clippers on the ground before she sat to face him.

"I can only speak for myself," he said.

"Then tell me what you are thinking about so seriously, Thomas Fitzbatten. You told me you needed to think, but now you look absolutely resolved—and dare I say cheerful?"

"I would say that's accurate—of you as well as me."

"I just . . . believe everything will be all right," she said.

"So do I," he admitted. "But there is something I need to say."

"I'm listening," she said, and he hoped that speaking his mind would not darken her mood. He felt suddenly vulnerable with the idea of sharing his thoughts with her, but at the same time he desperately needed to speak them. And he knew it was right.

"I love it," he forged ahead, "when we can just be together this way. I love the way we can talk and laugh over everything and nothing. I love how quickly we've grown to be so comfortable with one another. I love the way we can work side by side at any task and feel as if it's always been that way."

She smiled, which he considered a good sign. "I love it too," she said, and he sighed. So far so good.

Becoming more serious, he added, "I don't want any of that to change, Ruth. You have become my best and dearest friend, and I want it to always be that way."

She took his hand but said nothing, even though she seemed to silently agree. And he pressed on. "I think that something in me fears . . . saying what I really want to say . . . because it might . . . change what we've come to share."

Her countenance darkened as if she now realized the seriousness of what he was trying to get at. "We have agreed to be honest with each other," she said. "If you hold back things you wish to say, is that not some form of dishonesty?"

"Perhaps," he said. "Or is it just discretion? Wisdom, maybe. Or sensitivity in knowing that the re might be a right time or a wrong time to say certain things."

He saw her shoulders rise and fall as she drew in a deep breath and let it out. "Are you leading up to whatever it is you need to say to me before you can tell your parents the truth?"

"I believe I am." He couldn't deny it.

She asked with severity, "Have you been keeping secrets from me, husband?"

"And if I have?"

"I could not deny that we are guilty of the same failing. Perhaps for the same reasons."

While he couldn't be certain they were talking about the same thing, her words gave him the fortitude he needed to go on. "I cannot hold it inside any longer, Ruth. I must tell you that . . . I did not expect this."

"*This?*" she echoed as if she feared he might admit to having some repulsion to their marriage.

"I expected that . . . over time we would . . . gain some degree of affection for each other; or at least I hoped for it. I did not expect to feel the way I do . . . and after so short a time." He chuckled to cover a sudden nervousness. "But how could I expect something I've never known before? For all that a person may hear things described and talked about, until it happens to that person, the explanations of others can't possibly have any real meaning."

She sounded mildly nervous herself when she said, "That sounded awfully vague and hypothetical, Thomas. Why don't you just tell me what you're trying to say?"

He knew she was right. He just had to get to the point and pray that it *didn't* change anything between them. "I don't want to offend you, Ruth; I don't want to frighten you or put distance between us, because I've grown to depend upon your company so completely. But I have to say what I feel. I just . . . find myself wondering . . . every day . . . how it could be possible that I chose a wife so impulsively . . . and that before even a season has passed . . . I have grown to love her and need her beyond anything I ever comprehended possible."

Thomas held his breath while he heard her sigh loudly. She looked down, and his heart beat wildly with fear and expectation. He'd sensed her feelings for him in the way she looked at him, the things she said. But he wondered now if what she felt did not equal all he'd just confessed. He feared his confessions would create an awkwardness between them that he would find unbearable.

While looking at the ground, she asked, "And . . . you felt the need to tell me this . . . before we speak to your parents."

"Yes, Ruth," he said. "If we are going to be completely honest with them—and with each other—then I need to be able to tell them how I really feel. And I couldn't say it to them until I'd said it to you."

Ruth finally looked up at him with tears on her face. He wondered about their source until she said, "How well you have put words to my own feelings, Thomas." She shifted onto her knees and put a hand to his face. "As long as we are making confessions, there is one more thing I have to say. The thought has rumbled inside of me for so many days now."

"Say it," he challenged in a husky whisper.

"Oh, Thomas," she murmured, "if you do not kiss me, I fear that I will die. And I don't mean in the way you've kissed me before; I mean the way a husband should kiss his wife. Like a plant in need of water, I thirst for your kiss, Thomas, and I feel as if I will wilt and shrivel into nothingness without it."

While he was checking his mind to make certain he'd heard her correctly, he saw a sparkle of sincerity in her eyes, and a smile lit up her beautiful face. "Because," she said in little more than a whisper, a sound that reminded him of the movement of that little butterfly taking flight, "I love you, as well, Thomas."

He took her face into his hands and heard himself laugh with relief before he realized the sound had come out of his own mouth. "You do?" he asked.

"Oh, Thomas," she continued in that breathless whisper of a voice, "I knew before we stood before the vicar that I would grow to love you, and I was praying you would grow to love me. As desperate as I felt, I could not have spoken such vows with any conviction if I'd not felt something already, if I'd not believed it was possible."

Thomas echoed what she had said only a moment ago. "How well you have put words to my own feelings, my darling Ruth."

Now that he'd said what he'd needed to say, and she'd told him what he'd hardly dared hope for, he had no reason not to heed her request. He pressed his lips to hers, meekly at first, as he'd kissed her many times. He then pressed his hand into her hair, not caring that he might leave it mussed and pull it loose from its pins. With no regret behind him and only hope ahead, he kissed her as if the little butterfly had left a portion of its magic behind; he kissed her as she'd asked—as a husband should kiss his wife. Her response was intoxicating and soothing to his spirit, making him believe that his life had only truly begun when he'd first seen her lovely face, or perhaps when he'd looked into her eyes that were anything but average. He loved her, and she loved him. Now he could face anything.

Chapter Eight
SECRETS

RUTH SAT IN THE GARDEN holding her husband's hand while they talked and laughed, and even cried a little, and she felt as if she were living in a dream. Occasionally he would kiss her, as if doing so was a great privilege that he now intended to take full advantage of. It all seemed so perfect that she chose not to think about how his parents might feel about her once they knew the truth, and while she didn't doubt Thomas's commitment to her—or his love—she wondered what he would do if his parents were unhappy about the marriage— or more specifically the fact that Ruth's baby was not their grandchild. She knew how dearly he loved and revered his parents, and she prayed this would not cause any kind of difficulty between them that couldn't be overcome.

Ruth and Thomas were both surprised when Bertie called them in for supper, and they hurried to put away the gardening tools and get cleaned up. Yvette didn't come down from her room to eat with the rest of them, but no one seemed surprised by this.

Quin informed Ruth, "She gets worn out easily. Bertie's already taken up a tray for her."

Later, while Thomas was helping Ruth put freshly cleaned dishes away in the kitchen, he explained to her quietly, "My mother is more frail than she often lets on. It's nothing serious medically; she's been this way for as long as I can remember. She will put forth a great burst of energy for things that are important to her—like coming here and meeting you. And then she needs time to recover. She'll be fine, although you should know that I've spent far more time visiting with my mother in her bedroom than any other room in the house. You will likely need to become accustomed to doing the same. She gets very bored and lonely and appreciates it when those she cares about come to spend time with her."

"Assuming she'll ever want to see me again," Ruth replied, barely above a whisper, "after we tell her the truth."

"You mustn't worry," he said and embraced her. Oh, how she wanted to believe him!

Thomas then told her that his plan was to talk with his parents the following afternoon, since he'd learned that Barclay and Bertie were going into the village together after lunch to take care of some personal errands. Given the personal and complicated nature of the conversation, he felt it was best they endeavor to have it in complete privacy. Ruth agreed, but she wished tomorrow afternoon didn't feel so far away.

When it was time for bed, Ruth felt firmly settled with a decision she'd been considering for weeks now. It had never felt completely right before now, but a great deal had changed today, and now it felt as right to her as it had to marry Thomas.

According to their usual routine, Thomas took clean clothes with him to the bathing room so he could get cleaned up and change. Even though he slept in his clothes, he'd insisted that he felt better wearing clean ones to bed—not to mention that doing so would help keep the bed linens cleaner. While he was in the other room, Ruth would always change and was generally brushing through her hair or braiding it when he came back into the room. She would then take her turn in the bathing room and generally returned to find him sitting in bed with a book, or already settled on the pillow as if he were ready to go to sleep.

Ruth entered the room to find him in bed looking up at the ceiling, with one arm behind his head and the other over his chest. It was a typical pose, and she'd come to find it endearing. Was he wondering how to tell his parents about the foolhardy, impulsive manner in which he'd gotten married? Was he worrying about how they would respond? Even though she believed it was a likely guess, she didn't want to talk about that right now. Instead, she just stood at the edge of the bed, waiting for him to notice that she was doing so.

When Thomas turned to look at her, she wasn't disappointed by the pleasant surprise in his expression. "What is this?" he asked, first looking at her hair. She generally brushed it through and braided it again for bed to avoid having it get tangled while she slept. But tonight she had left it hanging around her shoulders, if only so he would notice that tonight was different. She then saw his eyes take in the nightgown she wore, which was very different from the excessively prudish and very worn gown she'd always slept in.

To answer his question matter-of-factly, she said, "When we were getting new clothes made for me, the seamstress suggested some nightgowns appropriate for a newly married woman. I nearly protested getting any such thing, but I feared that doing so might appear suspicious. So when the clothing was delivered, I just . . . put them away . . . believing that eventually . . . when the time was right . . . we would finally have . . . our wedding night."

"Ruth," he said and slid out of the covers to sit on the edge of the bed, holding his hand out toward her. She took his hand but remained standing, looking down at him. "We were able to say some wonderful things to each other today, and I'm happier than I can tell you that we've come so far, but . . . I don't want you to think that means everything else should change immediately as a result. There are some things you've never shared with me, and I hope that one day you will, but I know I would be a fool to presume that after . . . whatever happened . . . you would—"

"You told me that whenever I was ready, Thomas. And I am. So, unless there is some reason that *you* would prefer to wait, or—"

Thomas silenced her with a kiss, kneeling on the bed so that he could reach her lips with his while she remained standing. "I love you, Ruth," he said. "And you love me." He kissed her again. "We are husband and wife." And again. "That's all we need to make this right."

Ruth reached tentatively beneath his shirt and allowed her fingers to find the scar he'd once shown her. She looked into his eyes while she touched it with reverence, searching for words to tell him that to her it represented how close he'd come to never being a part of her life at all.

"You touch it as if you could heal it . . . and every other wound of my life." He kissed her yet again. "Maybe you can."

"I touch it in gratitude for knowing that I almost lost you; before I ever knew you, I almost lost you. And I will never forget how very blessed I am."

"Nor I," Thomas said and put his hand over hers, and kissed her again.

* * *

In the glow of a low-burning lamp, Thomas settled his head more fully into the pillow and just watched his wife. He easily concluded that he'd never seen anything so beautiful, and he felt blessed just to think of being the man privileged to have such a view every night and morning for the rest of his life.

Noting the distant look in her eyes as she gazed toward the ceiling, he lightly pressed the back of his hand to her face and asked, "Where are your thoughts, my love?"

Ruth turned her head on the pillow to look at him and touched his face in return. "Everything is so perfect right now," she said. "I fear if I admit to my thoughts, I will mar this moment."

"My darling," he said, "if something is troubling you, I don't want you to be troubled alone. Everything will be more perfect when we have no secrets from each other."

He saw some kind of challenge in her eyes. "If I tell you my secrets, will you tell me yours?"

Thomas was surprised—though he knew he shouldn't have been—at how quickly the one thing came to mind that he didn't want to tell her. They had talked of many things, almost *everything*, but he'd kept this memory to himself, not wanting to even allow it past his lips. But he trusted her, and he found some added measure of confidence in the idea of facing his parents with knowing that he and Ruth had no secrets between them.

"Yes," he said. "As long as we can then put them away and never speak of them again. I will hold your secrets." He kissed her, then resumed his comfortable position. "And I will let you hold mine."

"I can agree to that," she said and looked at the ceiling again. She took a deep breath and put his hand over her belly, although when she was lying on her back as she was now it wasn't so easy to notice. "I'm pregnant," she said as if he didn't know. "And it's not your baby."

"After all we have now shared," he said vehemently, "it is more my baby than anyone else's."

"Your attitude means more to me than I can say," she murmured. "But . . . we both know the reality." Thomas kept quiet as he realized she was trying to tell him something she felt the need to say, and he needed to allow her the time to do so.

Thomas listened with growing compassion as she finally did what he'd been wanting her to do for weeks now. But he hadn't wanted to ask. He had hoped that when she felt ready she would tell him, and now she was; she was telling him the story of how she'd ended up pregnant and alone. At first it sounded wildly romantic. They'd both been employed at the same manor house and had frequently crossed paths. He'd said all the right things and had been very convincing, although she confessed more than once to feeling uncomfortable over certain things, of ignoring instincts that had told her he wasn't a good man.

"I thought he loved me," she admitted, and tears leaked from the corners of her eyes, running into the hair at her temples. "And I believed that I loved him. I know now that what I felt was nothing but a girlish attraction; infatuation. And I think now that he knew it. I think he was skilled at manipulating a woman's feelings with his smooth words." She chuckled humorlessly, and more tears fell. "Or perhaps that's simply what I tell myself to excuse my own naiveté and foolishness."

"Innocence is a virtue, Ruth. Of course we gain wisdom through experience. But he willfully deceived you and took advantage of your inexperience. I see no cause for you to continue punishing yourself."

"Perhaps," she said with a little sob and still more tears that Thomas wiped away with the edge of the sheet. "I might not have known of love, but I was taught right from wrong, and I knew it was wrong to share a bed with him before we were wed. I believe God will forgive my sin; Jesus taught such forgiveness in the Bible. But I wonder if my mother ever will."

Thomas watched as she got that faraway look in her eyes again, and he listened as she spoke the details of the experience they had grown comfortable enough with each other to share. As the story of her experience progressed, Thomas began to feel a tightening in his chest and a sickness in his gut. He waited for her to finish while he silently assessed everything he now knew, not wanting to say anything that would hurt or offend her. When he knew what he had to say, he sat up and turned to look down at her, leaning on his hand.

"Ruth," he said, "since the day we met you have been talking to me of the sin you committed and blaming yourself for making an enormous mistake. I have believed your biggest mistake was trusting this fool and believing that he loved you. But . . . Ruth . . . what you have just told me is . . ." He struggled to find the words. They had grown comfortable speaking of intimate things, but this was still very difficult to say. "Ruth, what you're telling me is . . . well, it sounds evident to me that you made no choice at all. You didn't want to do it," he stated, now knowing it was a fact. "You asked him repeatedly to stop and he refused. He hurt you."

Thomas saw something akin to terror rise in her eyes, as if she had just faced a horrifying beast from her worst nightmares. As if his words had pierced open a memory she had locked tightly away, she gasped to try to catch her breath, and the wretched sob that rushed out of her turned to a deep groan when she pressed her own hand over her mouth as if to keep it from escaping and waking the entire household.

Thomas's heart pounded, his throat went dry, and tears stung his eyes. He didn't know what to say but knew she was beyond hearing any words of compassion he might utter. For now, all he could do was hold her close and allow her to feel the pain that had just been unleashed. She held to him with a fierceness that implied he could save her from a fire-breathing dragon threatening to devour her from the inside out. She wept and moaned and was unable to speak for more than an hour. Or was it two? Thomas's mind raced in circles around what he'd just learned. He loved Ruth more and loved the baby no less. They were both innocent victims of a man who was nothing less than the worst kind of villain and blackguard. He felt a seething hatred for this man. Prior to now, he had strongly disliked him, but with the truth coming forth, it was difficult to not feel an anger he feared could drive him to commit a criminal act should he ever come face-to-face with the man.

Forcing his mind away from this unproductive anger and hatred, Thomas focused instead on his wife. As her weeping finally began to subside, he held her close and repeatedly brushed his lips through her hair and over her face, whispering quiet reassurances that he was glad to know the truth, he loved her so much, he would always be there for her, it was all in the past.

At last she became completely still, and he did the same, wondering if she was asleep. But out of the silence she said in a voice husky from weeping, "Thomas, there is something else you must know. I knew that I needed to tell you, but it's such a strange subject to bring up, and . . . I've not known what to say exactly."

"Just say it," he said, leaning up on his elbow to look down at her. Even with her eyes red and swollen from the anguish she'd just endured, she looked absolutely beautiful in the glow of lamplight illuminating her face.

Ruth pressed a hand to his face and whispered, as if it were a great secret, "He looks like you, Thomas; so much like you that it's eerie."

Thomas put the pieces together in his mind. "The night we met— when you saw my face, you were frightened. You said I looked like someone you knew. We never talked about it again. But you're telling me . . . it's him? The man who did this to you . . . looks like *me*?"

Ruth nodded. "You've told me you have no brothers or cousins, so I can't make sense of it. But he looks *exactly* like you."

"Exactly?" Thomas couldn't comprehend such a thing, but it was evident from Ruth's tone and expression that she couldn't either. "Not similar?" he clarified. "Exactly?"

"At first I truly wondered if you were him, playing some kind of cruel trick on me. But it didn't take long for me to be able to see the difference."

"How?" he asked. "If we look exactly the same, how could you tell the difference?"

"Your goodness, my love. It not only shines in your eyes, but it fills your countenance. I know now that I would never have any difficulty telling the two of you apart. If there was *any* question on that count—which there is not—he has a large mole, right here." She touched Thomas's left forearm which had no mark at all.

Somewhat snidely, Thomas said, "Perhaps if I had some kind of hideous scar it would be easier for you to know the difference." He plopped his head back onto the pillow, disconcerted at the very idea that some man out there could look so very much like him.

"You already do," she said and touched the scar on his upper chest.

"So I do," he said, feeling a little better for some reason, even before she continued.

"Thomas." She leaned over his chest and looked at him closely, their noses almost touching. "When you asked me to marry you, I can't begin to tell you how overcome I was by the irony—that the man who had hurt me and the man who had offered his life to rescue me could appear at a glance to be the same man. The night before, you spoke of fate and destiny and the hand of God in our lives. I had to believe this was no coincidence. I am more convinced every day that God brought us together. I pray to God every day that I never see *him* again, but every day I see the goodness and love in you and I feel happy, and safe. I wanted you to know all of that, but . . . it was difficult to know how to tell you that . . . if this baby looks like its father, it will look like you."

Her words sucked the breath from his lungs, and he had to gasp to retrieve it. He felt as if destiny were swirling around them, catching them up in some kind of strange storm while protecting them within its peaceful center. In an instant, while his loathing for this man who had hurt Ruth didn't lessen, he was overcome by a strange gratitude over the physical resemblance that could never be rationalized away as coincidence. To know the baby would likely share something of his physical features was comforting to him, even if he knew it would never carry his bloodline. He *felt* like the baby's father, and he never wanted anyone to ever question whether or not that was the case. This would aid their cause and make it easier to forget that another man had ever existed in Ruth's life.

Many minutes of silence passed while Thomas just held Ruth close to him, grateful to be able to do so. Even though he felt overcome with many emotions in regard to all she'd just told him, he felt relief in knowing that she was no longer holding anything back from him. He was startled to hear her say, "Now, it's your turn, husband. I've poured out my heart and soul to you, and you promised to tell me what it is that haunts you. You told me there was something that haunted you worse than nearly dying on the battlefield. I've wondered what that could be, and perhaps my imagination is worse than the truth." She touched his face and pressed her fingers into his hair. "Please tell me."

Thomas knew he had to make good on his promise. A part of him *wanted* to tell her; he wanted to not carry this burden alone, and perhaps it would feel like less of a burden if he were able to share it. He began by voicing his biggest concern. "I think that men are hesitant to talk of what they experience in war because they don't want to taint the minds of their loved ones with images that are difficult. I feel that way. I saw a great deal that I will not ever speak of for that very reason, but I understand the need we have to share. And so I will summarize it this way."

Thomas looked at the ceiling, finding it easier to say such things when he wasn't looking at Ruth. "Men speak of going to war with all its duty and honor as if it's a great privilege and opportunity. But the reality reduces some of the best of men to the very worst of themselves. I was horrified by the depravity of it; the way that men could just . . . maim and kill each other for the sake of a cause that few—if any—of the soldiers on the battlefield actually understood. I saw such horrible things with the dead and the dying; I never imagined the human body could be decimated so utterly. I often thought it was those who died quickly—or died at all—who were the lucky ones. Those who survived often had such horrible wounds and loss of limbs that they would never be the same. But there were also those whose wounds were not visible. Some men's minds were simply not strong enough to see such atrocities and recover. It felt criminal to me that a man might be raised—whether a gentleman, or a farmer, or shopkeeper—to be docile and kind, and then be given minimal training, thrown into a uniform, and expected to be a warrior. And after it's over, these same men are expected to return to their lives as if nothing had ever happened or changed. I personally came home feeling overwhelmed by this appalling injustice and inhumanity. I felt angry that a few powerful men could cause so much misery for so many men who have no power at all."

Thomas turned to look at Ruth, who had tears glistening in her eyes. He touched her face. "You helped heal that in me," he said. "I felt so purposeless, so useless. It was as if I desperately needed even some tiny way to help restore some good in the world to help balance out all of the ugliness I had seen. You were an answer to my prayers, my dear, in ways I could never put into words."

"And you to mine," she said and kissed him. She looked deeply into his eyes and declared with confidence, "There's something else; something you've not told me yet. It's more personal."

Thomas looked abruptly back to the ceiling, both comforted and unnerved by how well she could read him. He had to think a few minutes about how to tell her the memory that disturbed him more than any other. His temptation to avoid it or pretend it wasn't there was counteracted by their agreement to be free of secrets and to share one another's burdens. Still, details were not necessary, and he sought for a way to summarize and have it done.

"War is inexplicably horrible," he began, "but there is still a way to reason it out. Battles are fought because of tyranny, political disagreements; the list goes on and on, but it *is* war and people end up on one side or the other, depending on their loyalties." He looked at Ruth and said it aloud for the first time ever. "But the thing that disturbs me most happened between men who were on the same side—at least as far as the war was concerned."

"All English, you mean," she said, and he nodded.

"There was a young man who is one of those who *never* should have been expected to be a soldier. What I found disgusting and repulsive was the way that men who wore the same uniform bullied and tormented him because he was . . . different. The reasons for his differences don't matter, Ruth. It's the same thing we see all the time in the way the upper classes look down on those who serve them . . . or those who are poor. It's the issue at the heart of religious differences that divide nations. It's the injustice of men putting themselves above other men simply because they are *different*."

Thomas felt the anger starting to surface, but he'd expected it, and in truth he knew he couldn't effectively speak of this *without* feeling angry. Trying to get quickly to the point, he said, "More than once I stepped in to break up some ridiculous fighting where this young man was unfairly outnumbered and was just plain being treated badly. More than once I spoke to our commanding officer, who dismissed the issue as if a soldier—any soldier—ought to be able to hold his own among his comrades. *Comrades?* I could hardly believe he'd used the word! It seemed to me that this man agreed with the bullies and would have liked to persecute the victim himself."

"What is the name of this poor, dear man?" Ruth asked.

Thomas closed his eyes and almost winced at saying it aloud, but speaking the name seemed to honor the young man somehow. "Oscar. His name was Oscar."

"Was?"

Thomas took a deep breath. "He took his own life." Ruth gasped, and he hurried to finish what needed to be said. "And it was me who found him dead."

"Oh, my darling," she said and touched his face.

Thomas squeezed his eyes closed tightly and felt tears leak from their corners. He felt Ruth wipe at them, and she kissed his cheek, but he couldn't look at her until he'd finished saying all he needed to say. "I blamed myself, Ruth. I kept thinking there was something I could have done—*should* have done—to help this poor young man. Of course, I knew there was nothing to be accomplished from regret, and I've sincerely tried to make peace with the matter. I spoke to the chaplain about my feelings more than once while I was recovering from my wound. I wrote a letter to Oscar's parents, which the chaplain promised to see delivered. I simply offered my condolences and told them I had admired their son's unique qualities and that in my eyes he was a hero and a casualty of war. I *did* feel a little better after I had done that, but when I returned to Brownlie Manor, that young man's face haunted me; his *death* haunted me. I felt a restlessness in me . . . as if I needed to do something worthwhile in this world, something right, make some positive gesture toward humanity in order to redeem myself. I became obsessed with the feeling. And then . . . in an instant . . . the feeling went away . . . and I found peace."

Thomas opened his eyes and looked at his beautiful wife, her hair hanging around her shoulders, her face glowing in the lamplight.

"I don't understand," she said.

"My prayers were answered when I was led to a woman who needed my help, and the moment I made the decision to give my life to her, I was overcome with peace." He saw her eyes widen and fill with moisture, but he pressed on. "I can't explain it; I don't know what one thing has to do with the other—or even if it does. I only know that I had been praying for peace and desperately feeling the need to do something good. And I knew that marrying you was the right thing to do. For the first time since Oscar's death, I felt purpose and meaning in my life. I felt hope. I look back now and wonder if a spark of love ignited that very first time we met. Perhaps it did. Still . . . I don't know how to say this and have it make sense, but . . . I thought you were beautiful; I believed we could make a good marriage. But the spark of love I felt at that time was not attraction; it was not romantic love. It was not the kind of love that should drive a man to marry. I felt intrigued by you and drawn to you. But what I felt most, Ruth, that I find so hard to understand—let alone explain—is some kind of godly love. It was as if I felt God's love for you, and for this child, and I was being shown that you'd been led to *me* because this was right for both of us. I felt so in awe as I looked at you and realized you were likely thinking that my marrying you was some kind of sacrifice to save you, and all I could feel was that *you* were saving *me*." Thomas shook his head. "Does that sound crazy?"

"No, my love," she said and kissed him. "I can understand why you have trouble putting such feelings into words, but no words are necessary. I know because I felt it too. I feel it still. I just . . . never dreamed that we would grow to love each other so . . . completely . . . and in so short a time."

"Nor did I," he said with the rise of more tears. "I feel so greatly blessed."

"You cannot possibly feel any more blessed than I," she said and kissed him again.

Thomas rolled her back onto the bed and watched as her hair splayed over the pillows. "There," he said. "Now I have no more secrets; there is nothing in my heart that I have not told you."

"And I can say the same," she said.

"Then all will be well," he declared and gave her a long, savoring kiss. "I promise you, my darling," he said as he pressed his hand over where the baby grew, "that all will be well—for all of us."

"I believe you," she said, tears glimmering in her eyes.

* * *

Ruth tried not to blush when she and Thomas arrived in the dining room just as breakfast was nearly over. Yvette was absent, but everyone else was there. While everyone said good morning all around, Thomas helped Ruth with her chair, then sat down himself, winking at her while no one was looking.

"It's always nice to sleep in once in a while," Quin said, mostly focused on a newspaper he was reading.

"That's rich coming from you," Thomas said lightly to his father. "I don't recall that you've ever slept in a day in your life."

"I do enjoy the morning," he admitted and turned the page of the paper. "Whereas your mother does very much like to sleep in."

"How *is* Mother?" Thomas asked.

"Tired but otherwise fine, I believe," Quin said. "I checked on her before breakfast. She had another of those dreams."

Ruth wanted to ask what he meant exactly, since everyone else seemed to know. She was glad when Thomas said to her, "She occasionally has strange nightmares that can upset her and make it difficult to sleep. It's always the same dream, but she doesn't like to talk about it, so . . . we don't."

Ruth nodded, wanting to ask about the content of the dream, but by the way Thomas had put it, the content of Yvette's dreams was her own secret, and it was up to her whether or not she ever chose to tell Ruth. Recalling that later today she and Thomas would be telling his parents that they'd been lied to, she wondered if Quin or Yvette would ever want anything to do with her again.

Bertie had breakfast all cleaned up before Ruth and Thomas were finished eating. Since Bertie was obviously busy getting ready to go into town after lunch, Ruth volunteered to check on Yvette and see if she needed anything. Bertie gave Ruth a few simple instructions regarding Yvette's preferences, and Ruth knocked lightly at the door before she opened it, not wanting to wake Yvette on the chance she was still sleeping.

"Come in," she heard Yvette call, and Ruth entered, carrying a tray with tea and scones and butter and jam.

"Oh, it's you, dear," Yvette said, seeming pleased, although Ruth couldn't help noticing that she looked dramatically different than she had yesterday. It wasn't just the fact that she was wearing a nightgown and sitting in bed with her hair down. She looked visibly tired, with dark circles around her eyes and a slightly sallow look to her face. Thomas said she had always been like this, and there was nothing medically serious going on. But Ruth felt concerned.

"Bertie is busy with other things, so I offered."

"It's a lovely surprise to see you," Yvette said, adjusting the pillows behind her so that she could sit up more comfortably in bed.

Ruth set the tray on Yvette's lap and asked, "Is there anything else I can get for you?"

"Not at all," Yvette said and patted the edge of the bed, inviting Ruth to sit down, so she did. "I don't want you to have to wait on me, my dear."

"You mustn't think of it like that," Ruth said, knowing this woman was well aware that she'd had prior experience serving such ladies as Yvette Fitzbatten. "As family we simply help one another when there is a need. Your husband thought you would prefer having your breakfast here, and so I've brought a little something for you. That's all."

Yvette smiled as if she liked that explanation. "You're a dear girl," she said to Ruth, who poured Yvette a cup of tea while Yvette buttered a scone. "And Thomas seems very happy. I know that men often come home from war very much changed, and I've worried that even if he *did* survive, he *would* be changed. But he seems well."

"It was difficult for him," Ruth said, knowing that Thomas would be all right with her speaking of it in generalities. "He has admitted to being haunted by much of what he saw, but he has come a long way toward healing. And yes, I believe he's doing very well."

"I'm certain that has a great deal to do with you," Yvette said and took a bite of her scone. "His eyes light up when he looks at you, my dear. For years I watched women try to get his attention, but not one ever caught his eye. But you . . . you're different."

"He is very good to me," Ruth admitted.

"And you to him, it seems."

"I try," Ruth said, "although it doesn't take much effort. It's easy to be kind to a man who is so kind."

"And that would well describe how it is with his father," Yvette said and sipped her tea. "That makes the two of us very blessed, indeed."

"Indeed," Ruth said, hoping Yvette would still feel the same later today.

They chatted until Yvette had finished her simple breakfast and announced that she was feeling a little better and would get dressed and come downstairs before lunch.

"I'll bring you some fresh water," Ruth said. "And I'm glad to help you with your hair or—"

"Now, there's no need for you to be doing that kind of thing," Yvette insisted.

"Bertie is busy with the baby," Ruth said, "and I already explained this. We're family and I'm glad to help. I know for a fact that many of the dresses a lady is expected to wear cannot be fastened without help, and it's the same with putting your hair right. I'm *glad* to help."

Yvette smiled, seeming both pleased and relieved. She'd likely already thought of exactly what Ruth had just pointed out but didn't want to be a bother, what with Bertie having part of the day off to go into town with her husband. Ruth was glad to be able to assist her mother-in-law, and she enjoyed the simple conversation they shared while Ruth helped her into a blue-striped day dress and then helped style her hair, putting into place the little lace bonnet that went well with the style Yvette liked best for herself.

"You are competent as well as kind," Yvette said, examining her reflection in the mirror. "I've always thought I should be a little more self-reliant, but it is true that many dresses are made in a way that requires help. I often coerce Quin into doing such tasks." She laughed softly. "I've told him he'd make a fine lady's maid."

"It's surely the duty of every good husband," Ruth said in the same lighthearted manner, "to competently see to at least a *few* duties of a lady's maid."

"Indeed," Yvette said.

The two ladies went downstairs together, where they found lunch being served. Since the men were all helping transport food and dishes from the kitchen to the dining table while Bertie was feeding the baby, Yvette whispered to Ruth, "And it doesn't hurt if a man knows how to find his way around the kitchen, either."

"Indeed," Ruth said, just as Yvette had said it a minute earlier.

The women both giggled and Quin said, "What are the two of you conspiring about?"

"Nothing," Yvette said, and Ruth noticed how Quin's eyes were drawn immediately to his wife and he approached her with a quick kiss and a smile.

"How are you feeling, my dear?"

"Better, thank you," Yvette said.

Ruth was so entranced by the tender exchange between two people who had been married so long that she was surprised to find Thomas standing directly in front of her. "And how are *you*, my dear?" he asked. A sparkle in his eyes reminded her of all they had shared as husband and wife, and she hoped she wasn't blushing. When he smiled almost slyly she felt certain that she was.

"I'm very well," she said. "Your mother and I have been having a lovely chat."

"She's a dear girl, Thomas," Yvette said. "If I believed in arranged marriages, I would have picked her out for you myself."

Thomas chuckled. "I'm glad we have your approval, Mother," he said, but Ruth shot him a brief glance of concern, hoping the truth wouldn't change Yvette's feelings—or Quin's.

After lunch was over and cleaned up, Barclay and his little family were on their way into the village. The wagon had barely passed by the cottage before Thomas said to his parents, "We have something we need to speak with the both of you about. I wonder if we could sit and talk."

"Why, of course," Quin said, and the men both guided their wives into the parlor. The two couples sat facing each other on opposite sofas, and Ruth suddenly felt so nervous she almost wanted to back down on her conviction about his parents knowing the truth. But it only took a second's thought to know they *had* to be told. She drew on the reasoning she'd presented to Thomas initially. This just had to be done, and the consequences would have to be faced. She thought Thomas looked remarkably calm, and she decided that either he hid his nerves better than she did, or he knew his parents well enough that he didn't fear their reaction the way she did. Of course, even if they were upset, they would never stop giving Thomas the love and acceptance they'd always given him. Since Ruth had only met them yesterday, she couldn't be certain the same applied to her. At the moment, the only good thought she could hold on to was the fact that very soon the truth would be out and she wouldn't have to wonder any longer about what their reaction might be.

Chapter Nine

RETURN TO BROWNLIE MANOR

RUTH TOOK HOLD OF THOMAS'S hand, grateful for the way he squeezed it reassuringly, which helped disguise the fact that it was trembling. She knew it was up to him to set all of this straight, and she wished they had discussed how exactly he intended to go about it. While she was wondering, Thomas simply said, "Some of what we told you yesterday . . . about how we met . . . and got married . . . wasn't true."

Ruth saw Yvette's eyes widen, and Quin's eyebrow went up. But neither of them spoke. Thomas went on. "Afterward Ruth and I talked about it, and . . . we both agree that even though we have valid reasons for allowing people to believe that things are not exactly as they appear, the two of you are family, and we need to be completely honest with you. We know we can trust you, and I apologize on behalf of both of us for trying to deceive you at all. We should have been honest right up front. I want you to know that I haven't lied to you since I was seven, and I never will again. You must believe me when I tell you that my reasons for doing so yesterday were based in the best of intentions on behalf of my wife."

No one moved or made a sound. Ruth felt her own trembling increase from the inside out. She recalled the way her father's gruff temper had been his most typical response to any difficulty—large or small. And she recalled her mother's demeaning fury that had come in response to Ruth's admission to being pregnant. The very idea of facing such a response from Thomas's parents almost made her nauseous. At least she had Thomas at her side, and she knew that *his* feelings for her wouldn't change. But she didn't want to be a stumbling block between him and his parents.

Quin finally let out a loud sigh, exchanged a long glance with his wife, and crossed his arms over his broad chest. "Well . . ." he drawled, "I think I can speak for your mother and myself when I say how relieved we are to hear you admit it."

"What?" Thomas blurted.

Quin went on. "We knew you were lying, son." He chuckled as if he found the situation humorous. "You were never very good at it." He looked at Yvette and said, "I'd wager he's not much better at it now than when he was seven."

"Perhaps a tad more convincing," Yvette said before they both looked again at Thomas.

"You knew?" Thomas asked and got no response since the question had obviously already been answered. "Why didn't you say something?"

"We were hoping you'd come clean," Quin said. He leaned forward a little, looking directly at Thomas. In a voice that was more severe, he added, "Son, we don't know yet what your motive was in lying to us; I assume you're going to tell us. But we hope you know you *can* trust us."

"I do know that," Thomas said. "I lost sight of it, but I *do* know it. And I apologize. I hope you can forgive me and—"

"Thomas, dear," Yvette said. "Our only concern was in wondering why you didn't feel you could trust us enough to tell us the truth. Of course it's forgiven."

Ruth heard Thomas take in a deep breath and let it out slowly. She sensed his relief but couldn't quite share it just yet; they hadn't been told the truth. And that was the part that frightened her most.

"Thank you," Thomas said and tightened his hold on Ruth's hand while he put his other arm around her. "I want you to know that it was my good wife who set me straight. She knows how close we are and felt certain we could not and *should* not try to pretend anything less than the truth with you. Of course she was right."

"Good for you, my dear," Quin said to Ruth. She nodded but couldn't speak. Quin turned to Thomas and added, "You should know that you are not required to tell us the truth, or your reasons for feeling the need to allow people to believe that things are different than they appear. Tell us it's a private matter and we will leave it at that, and you know we will always be here for you—for both of you."

Thomas looked at Ruth as if to silently ask her what might be best. She knew in her heart that she needed Quin and Yvette to know everything. She didn't want to spend her life trying to skirt around the issue or trying to remember what they knew and what they didn't. If they felt any disdain toward her regarding the situation, she needed to know. She also knew it was up to her to tell them this part. Drawing a deep breath of courage, she faced Thomas's parents and said, "I was already pregnant when Thomas and I were married. The baby is not his."

Quin's brow furrowed, but Ruth couldn't discern the reason. Yvette gasped and put a hand over her heart. This was the moment of reckoning. They now knew that their son was pretending to have fathered a child that had no Fitzbatten blood, and the implications could be enormous in such a family.

"Oh, my!" Yvette said and frantically fanned her hands in front of her face as if she might swoon. Ruth held her breath, already hearing the rest of the conversation in her head. Their concerns about the family bloodline and many other matters were certainly valid, but Ruth had no idea what could ever be done about it.

"Oh, my!" Yvette said again, and Ruth felt her gathering the words while Quin just watched his wife, seemingly concerned only for her well-being at the moment. Although Ruth could well imagine that once Yvette calmed down, Quin could be very upset over the news Ruth had just divulged—news that had put his wife into such a state.

Ruth watched as huge tears welled up in Yvette's eyes. She looked directly at Ruth, who steeled herself for the inevitable onslaught of concerns and problems that could result from this situation. Yvette became so overcome with emotion that she could barely squeak out the words, "Oh, my dear, did someone . . . hurt you?"

Ruth took a sharp breath, feeling some degree of the grief that had assaulted her just last night when she'd finally admitted the whole truth to Thomas. She wondered how this moment might be if she'd not already told him. While Ruth was trying to compose her own response to Yvette's question, she looked at the faces of her mother and father-in-law and found not even the tiniest bit of the anger and disdain she had been imagining she should expect. She saw nothing but perfect compassion and acceptance. She was so stunned and taken aback that she couldn't speak. Even attempting to offer a nod in response to the question brought up all of the pain she'd been trying to suppress and ignore, even weeks before she'd met Thomas. She felt inexplicably relieved when Thomas tightened his arm around her, urging her face toward the perfect hiding place against the high collar of his shirt, as if he sensed her rising emotion and her reasons for being unable to speak.

"Yes," she heard him say in response to his mother's question. And to her added relief, he kept talking, which not only offered his parents the explanation they needed, but his voice helped disguise her attempts to keep her weeping silent.

Ruth listened as Thomas explained how Dawson had come to him for help in regard to his niece and what his initial intentions had been in providing the funds to see her through the pregnancy so that the baby could be adopted and she could have a fresh start. She then listened with growing amazement as he told his parents that after he'd met Ruth, something had sparked to life inside of him, and he had known beyond any doubt that marrying her was the right thing to do. He told them with conviction of how quickly he'd grown to love and admire her more every day, and that he'd never been happier. He declared firmly his intention to raise this child as his own and for no one to ever know otherwise.

Ruth was surprised to feel Yvette's hand on her arm and turned to see that she was now sitting on the opposite side of Ruth from Thomas. Ruth felt surprisingly unembarrassed by the evidence on her own face of how hard she had been crying. Yvette too had tears on her face as she opened her arms with a silent and gentle invitation. Ruth hesitated only a moment and began to cry all over again as Yvette gave her the acceptance and compassion Ruth had so desperately needed from her own mother.

"Everything will be all right, my dear," she heard Yvette whisper, and she felt the woman's dainty hand smoothing her hair over and over with gentle affection.

Ruth regained her composure enough to say, "I know it will . . . only because I have been blessed to be loved and accepted by such a good man." She eased back a little so she could look at Yvette, and Thomas handed Ruth his handkerchief as if he'd been waiting for the right moment. "When I think of the many women who have faced my plight, I wonder why I—of all of them—would be so blessed."

"God has clearly guided you and Thomas together," Yvette said. "Who are we to question His ways?"

Ruth nodded and sniffled and fought not to break into yet another outburst of tears. "And I never dared hope to receive such kindness and acceptance from you. How can you not be concerned about the bloodline of the family going forward?" She glanced at Quin and back to Yvette. "If this child is a boy, will he not inherit all that—"

"Now, let me tell you something, my dear," Quin said and came to his feet. Ruth was taken offguard by the way he stood in front of Thomas and motioned for him to move. "Let me sit down, son. There's something I need to say to your wife."

Thomas stood up and Quin sat in his place. Ruth turned toward her father-in-law, more than a little unnerved. She exchanged a quick glance with Thomas, who apparently intended to remain on his feet and looked decidedly nervous.

"Ruth, my dear," Quin said, and she turned her attention fully to him as he took her hand into his. "It's readily evident that you and Thomas love each other very much. Yvette and I agreed that we could see it from the very first minute we met you."

Ruth stole another quick glance toward Thomas and saw her own astonishment in his expression. Given that they'd not actually confessed their feelings of love to each other until after his parents had arrived, she wondered how this might have gone if they'd *not* confessed them—or even fully acknowledged them.

Ruth turned quickly back to look at Quin, since he obviously had more he wanted to say. "We talked about it last night, and we both agreed that whatever it was the two of you were trying to keep from us, you couldn't hide the fact of your love—and that's the most important thing. If the two of you love each other as you do, and your commitment is strong and true, then anything else can be worked out. We taught our son the importance of trust and respect in a marriage, and it's evident the two of you share that as well. I think I can speak for my wife when I say that we're glad you've told us the truth. We don't want you to feel alone in any of this, and we certainly don't want either of you to ever feel like you need to hide anything from us. If there is a problem to be solved, we will solve it together. We are family."

Ruth felt overcome by what he was saying, but she wanted to repeat her point that the child she was carrying had no Fitzbatten blood, which made the word *family* feel somewhat precarious. But Quin was quick to say, "Now, let's talk about this baby, my dear, because there's something I want both you and Thomas to understand without question."

Quin looked up at Thomas and said almost facetiously, "Sit down, son. You're making me nervous."

"Sorry," Thomas said and took a chair, looking as baffled as Ruth felt over what his father intended to say.

Ruth looked again at Quin, who said, "When Thomas was born—and he may have told you this—there were complications, and we knew then that he would be our only child. After all these years it's still a sensitive topic for us. We would have liked to have a large family, but it was not to be. At one time we considered adopting children, and in the end the answers to our prayers seemed to be that such an option was not right for us. Thomas was always a good boy and brought us a great deal of joy and pride. But I want to tell you something that Yvette and I both decided very firmly many years ago when we were talking through all of these things, and speculating over what might be—or what might have been. What if the only child we'd given birth to had been a girl? What if something happened to Thomas and our only living children were ones we adopted? There is an endless list of possibilities. We decided then that it didn't matter. We believe that somehow God guides children to be born and raised where they need to be. Even those who only suffer in this world—for all that we would like to be able to change it—we believe they will surely be among the most blessed in heaven.

We could talk of such beliefs for hours and we likely will, eventually. For right now, the only thing you need to know—the only thing that matters—is that if Thomas has chosen to be this child's father, then we are certainly this child's grandparents, and it *will* be a Fitzbatten!"

Ruth's view of Quin became blurry through a rise of new tears. She heard a loud sniffle and turned just as her own tears fell and her vision cleared enough for her to see Thomas with tears shimmering in his eyes.

"There now," Quin said and wrapped Ruth in a fatherly embrace. "Everything else will take care of itself."

Ruth laughed more than cried as she returned his embrace. After a long moment of silence while everyone seemed to be taking in Quin's firm conclusion, Thomas said, "Well, I'm glad *that's* settled!"

Quin laughed as if he felt nothing but joy and handed Ruth *his* handkerchief, since the one Thomas had given her was clearly very wet. "Yes, it *is* settled," Quin said to his son. "And no one beyond us will ever know anything different than what you told the household before you left."

"Dawson knows the truth, of course," Thomas said.

"There's no need to worry about that," Yvette said. "You couldn't squeeze gossip out of that man any more than you could squeeze honey from a stone."

"So true." Quin laughed again.

"Is there anyone else who knows?" Yvette asked Thomas.

"Only Ruth's mother," he told her.

"She won't have told a soul," Ruth said. "She was far too ashamed to want *anyone* to know. She sent me to my uncle for help, and he went to visit her to tell her that Thomas and I were married."

"Then everything is taken care of," Quin declared. "And if anyone bothers to notice the child doesn't resemble a one of us, we'll just give credit of its resemblance to an ancestor a few generations back; those things do happen."

"Actually," Thomas drawled, and she saw him catch her eye as if to ask her approval in sharing this one last piece of information. She nodded discreetly, and he said, "Ruth tells me that the father bears a striking resemblance to me."

"Truly?" Yvette said. "What an odd coincidence."

"Not coincidence, surely," Quin said. "Not in God's eyes, at least."

"I'm sure you're right," Yvette said. She then added with all the delight of a prospective grandmother, "Oh, we're going to have a baby in the house again! I can't think of anything more wonderful!"

"Indeed," Quin said and laughed with equal pleasure. Ruth met Thomas's eyes and saw perfect contentment there, mingled with the glow of his love for her. She truly couldn't imagine how she could be so thoroughly blessed.

* * *

That afternoon while Quin and Yvette intended to lounge in the garden and enjoy the fair weather, Thomas saddled his horse and helped Ruth mount behind him before he galloped across the countryside, immersed in the contentment of childhood memories. He loved the way Ruth kept her arms around his chest and held to him while he felt the side of her face against his back. Having her with him this way—in this place—perfectly combined the past with the hope of a bright future, and in the present all he could feel was peace and a blissful contentment he'd never known. He had hoped for it and believed that by simply observing the example of his parents he would find a love as true and strong as theirs. But he knew now that fate didn't always deal so kind a hand. And yet, in his case, happiness had practically leapt in front of him, and all he'd had to do was choose to collide with it.

Thomas rode to the sea at Ruth's request, where she removed her shoes and stockings and tucked her skirt and petticoats up beneath her bodice somehow to shorten them and keep them from getting wet while she walked in the waves and laughed like a child. He removed his boots and stockings and joined her, walking hand in hand along the shoreline, looking out over the endless horizon of sky and water while they talked of all that had changed between them just since yesterday and the joy they both felt, not only in the love they had come to share but in his parents' kindness and acceptance.

He made it clear—because he felt she needed to know—that he would have stood by her no matter what his parents might have said or done. But they were both grateful to have the support of Quin and Yvette, knowing it would make everything easier.

Only the growling of their stomachs urged them to leave the sea and head for home. Thankfully, Ruth had gotten past feeling quite so nauseous these days; nevertheless, she'd brought some scones with her, which she ate as they headed for home. Still, he teased her about her appetite, and they both knew that a couple of scones wouldn't stave off her hunger for long.

When she was finished eating, Ruth asked, "Now that we've said all that needs to be said—between us and with your parents as well—I have to ask if you would prefer a son or a daughter."

"I would prefer many of both," he said with a laugh.

"I will have to take on that task one at a time," she said, hugging him more tightly. "But, with this baby . . . do you—"

"It doesn't matter, Ruth. I agree with what my father said. And I believe that as long as a child is born legitimately within this marriage, it will have every right and privilege it should be afforded. I want this child to be healthy and strong, and I want you to be the same." He laughed and put one hand over hers where it held to his chest, while he kept the reins firmly in his other hand. "Boy or girl, I shall spoil this child terribly and we will find joy from being its parents each and every day."

Ruth laughed with him. "I love you, Thomas Fitzbatten."

"And I love you, my darling," he said, and the setting sun accompanied them home.

* * *

When Quin and Yvette indicated they would like to stay at the cottage for a month or so, Thomas and Ruth decided they would return to Brownlie Manor with them when the time came. Until then, they all enjoyed the simplicity of life at the cottage, with occasional jaunts into the village or to the sea. They picnicked and worked in the garden, intermittently assisting Barclay and Bertie with the cooking and chores and continuing to work on some repairs and mending that needed to be done. Yvette assigned herself the task of mending some draperies that needed a little help here and there, but she liked them and saw no reason to have them replaced. She often required extra rest, but Ruth gravitated to Yvette's room on those days, and the two women could talk endlessly while they worked at sewing projects, some of which included items for the forthcoming baby. And Ruth was pleased with the way Thomas occasionally held little Warren and seemed less and less nervous about doing so.

Barclay and Bertie decided they would have the christening of little Warren before the family returned to the manor so they could join in the celebration. It was tradition in the area that following the actual christening at the church, practically everyone in the village would gather to celebrate Warren's new life, all bringing food to share, and there would often be music and dancing late into the evening, which required the building of a large bonfire.

During the christening, Thomas held Ruth's hand and thought about what it might be like when their child was born. A part of him wanted to remain at the cottage and share the birth and christening with the people surrounding them now, people he'd come to know better and Ruth had come to know during their recent stay, which included church attendance and shopping excursions in the village. They were good people, for the most part, and he felt confident that Ruth and the baby would be well cared for. But the babies in his family had been born at Brownlie Manor for generations, and there were many people there who would surround them with great support and acceptance. It was just different. He missed the manor and looked forward to returning, and he loved the cottage and dreaded having to leave. But they would return and bring their children here regularly. He wanted regular visits to the cottage to be a part of his children's lives, just as it had been for him. And Ruth agreed. They had talked about it and a thousand other things during long walks, picnics, and late-night conversations with their heads sharing the same pillow. As Ruth came to share Thomas's vision for the future, his notion of what exactly mattered to him in that future became more clear. And Ruth had become such an integral part of everything he anticipated for the future that he could barely remember—and could hardly bear trying to—what his life had been like without her. He thanked God every day for the seemingly miraculous way she had been brought into his life, needing his help at the very moment he'd needed to be needed. He couldn't think about what this man who looked like him had done to Ruth without feeling upset on her behalf, but with time he found it incredibly easy to forgive this man. If not for him, he might never have found her. And if he had, he wondered if he would have had the good sense to see what a truly remarkable woman she was.

Thomas lingered in the church after the christening until almost everyone else had left. He just kept looking up at the stained glass and offering his silent oblation of gratitude for all his blessings.

The remainder of the day was filled with laughter and enjoyment. When Thomas wasn't at Ruth's side, he could never go very many minutes without looking for her. He loved the way she had come to know most of the local women by name and how she mingled among them with a gracefulness and refinement that belied the serving class in which she had been raised while still fitting in among them perfectly. She was kind and good to everyone equally, which was one of the things he loved most about her. And when he would see her turn to look for him and catch his eye, her smile almost made him giddy. By the way she often unconsciously put a hand over her heart, or on top of the growing mound where the baby grew, he believed she felt it too.

As darkness fell and the bonfire roared, the musicians gained momentum in their tunes, and people began to dance. Ruth prodded Thomas into dancing with her, and he thought how much he preferred a gathering such as this over some stodgy social in a stuffy ballroom where people were looking down their noses at each other and whispering, and the dancing was all so formal and perfectly proper. Here he could feel the music, and the dancing of the flames almost become a part of his spirit. Here he could watch Ruth spontaneously laugh and twirl, keeping her hand in his, as if the dance itself were some kind of ancient ritual that publicly declared their love and devotion for each other, with the sky above them, and the earth beneath, and the heat of the fire nearby. Oh, how he loved her!

* * *

It was difficult to say good-bye to the cottage—and to Barclay and Bertie and little Warren. Thomas caught Ruth crying more than once as they packed up their things and prepared to say their good-byes. But he caught his mother shedding some tears, as well. These good people who cared for the cottage were like family, and the time they'd spent here had been as pleasant as it was eventful. Thomas was not the same man who had brought his new bride here many weeks ago, nor was Ruth the same woman. And his parents seemed happier than he'd seen them in many years. Ruth had brightened their lives, and the prospect of a new baby in the family was a favorite topic of conversation. They all seemed to have completely forgotten that there was anything negative whatsoever about the origins of this child.

The carriage ride to the manor took most of one day, allowing for some stops to stretch and eat and freshen up. Barclay had sent a messenger two days prior to let the staff know they would be returning, and Thomas began to think more about how much he'd missed his home as the view out the carriage window became more familiar. He'd been here so short a time after returning from the war before leaving again, and he couldn't help feeling that it was good to be coming back.

Ruth didn't appear to be sharing his sentiment, however. It became increasingly evident that she was more than a little nervous. He was about to mention it when Yvette said to Ruth, "Are you all right, my dear?"

"It's just . . . strange," Ruth said. "I'm not sure I know how to be."

"Be yourself," Quin said. "That's all you need to know."

"But . . ." Ruth looked at Thomas, biting her lip. "I don't want to put myself above the servants when it's not so long since I worked among them; I mean . . . not in this house, but . . ."

"It's all right," Thomas said, glad to see that she had no qualms about being completely honest with her feelings—even to his parents.

"You're not putting yourself above them. We *are* the family who owns the manor and the estate and we employ the staff. But we've never seen that as putting ourselves above them."

"I know," Ruth said. "You've told me how you are about all that, and I admire it. I just don't . . ."

"What?" he pressed.

"I'm not sure," she admitted.

"Listen to me, my darling." He turned more toward her on the carriage seat. "If you need something, just ask. Be kind and generous as you always are, as you were with Bertie and Barclay at the cottage. And that's all. If you want to put on your oldest dress and work in the garden, so be it. If you want to go help in the kitchen or the laundry, feel free. But you don't *have* to do *anything*. Within a day or two you'll be completely comfortable—if not by the end of the day. You'll see." He added lightly, "And if Dawson gives you any trouble, Father will give him a good talking to."

Thomas had meant it to be humorous, but Ruth made a sound as if the idea caused her some kind of physical pain. "How can I have my uncle working for me? He oversees the serving of meals and everything in the household that's—"

"Ruth," Thomas said, "your uncle cares very much for you and he's happy for you. I don't think any of us—least of all him—are worried about you putting on airs or placing yourself above him. Besides—" Thomas tried again to lighten the mood—"he's the reason we met. I recognized you when I saw you in Portsmouth because you'd once been to the manor to visit him."

Ruth sighed, and he realized his attempts to calm her nerves were likely only making them worse. Yvette reached across the carriage and put a hand over Ruth's. "If you're concerned, just stay with one of us all of the time until you get a feel for how things are done. Don't forget that I was once in your place, coming home to the manor for the first time as the bride of the Fitzbattens' only son. If I survived it, you certainly can. You're much stronger than I ever was."

"And your mother-in-law was a beast," Quin said with a laugh.

"Oh, certainly not a beast!" Yvette said to her husband. "Your mother was . . ."

"Formidable," Quin said.

"She was . . . opinionated," Yvette said with a kind tone.

"And not afraid to say so," Quin said.

"And we all loved her anyway," Yvette declared.

"Yes, we did," Thomas said.

"Oh, you've told me about your grandparents," Ruth said to her husband. "Of course you all lived in the same home."

"We did," Thomas said.

"Amazing that with a house so big you can't get away from your in-laws," Quin said lightly.

"I'm not worried a bit about that," Ruth said, smiling at him. "In fact, I should very much miss you if I didn't see you each and every day."

"The feeling is mutual, my dear," Quin said with a wink. Yvette nodded and smiled in agreement.

Ruth felt her stomach quiver when Brownlie Manor came into view through the carriage window. In the distance it was breathtaking. She'd certainly seen it before, but never like this, and never with any possibility of an idea that it would become her home in the truest sense. She wondered for a moment how she might be feeling if her marriage to Thomas was not coming along as favorably as it was. If they had formed some kind of agreement of mutual respect without feeling any real affection for each other, she would have been grateful for all he'd given her but certainly not happy or at all comfortable about her place in the family. As it was, she felt some anxiousness, but she knew that Thomas would always be by her side—both literally and figuratively.

Some of the servants came outside by way of a formal greeting when the carriage halted near the main door. But the moment Thomas stepped out and helped her do the same, she already felt the difference from other homes where she had worked. The greetings between the staff and the family were certainly respectful of their separate positions, but the mood was far more relaxed, and Ruth already felt a little more at ease. Thomas introduced her to the most prominent members of the staff who had come out to meet them, but their names went out of her head almost as soon as she heard them.

She just greeted them with polite hellos and resisted the urge to hug her uncle, knowing it wouldn't be proper at the moment.

On their way into the house, Ruth whispered to Thomas, "Does the staff know . . . that my uncle is—"

"I believe so," he said. "If not they'll know soon enough."

"Isn't that strange?" she asked. "For your wife and the butler to be related?"

"Positively scandalous," he said with a chuckle, as if nothing could make him more proud or delighted than to stir up community gossip in such a way. "Perhaps with such scandal at our house, we'll be able to live in peace and avoid the social attention of all the pretentious snobs who would be the very ones to find something wrong with my choice of a wife." He kissed her hand as they walked. "I say she's perfect, and to the devil with them."

"Sometimes I wonder if you married a servant girl just to spite people like that."

"No." He chuckled. "You know why I married you. Spiting them is just an added bonus."

Ruth attempted to keep a sense of direction as she walked with Thomas to his rooms—which would now be theirs. She felt confident that with time she could find her way without getting lost, but she made him promise to not allow her to go anywhere in the house without him until she could get her bearings. He swore that he would see her well taken care of.

Ruth was pleasantly surprised at how much she immediately liked the bedroom and adjacent sitting room she would share with Thomas. She'd expected his accommodations to be beautiful—as everything in the house was—but she'd not anticipated how taken she was with the decor, which she declared was the color of roses complemented by the glow of the sun on a bright day. The draperies and carpets and bedcovers of deep red and gold gave the room a regal effect, and she told Thomas as she turned to look around herself, "I feel like a queen."

"As you should," he said and motioned her toward the largest of the room's windows. "I'm rather fond of the view."

Ruth stood next to Thomas at the window and gasped to see an endless stretch of manicured shrubberies and blossoming plants and bushes, with artistically laid out pathways winding among them. "Oh, it's lovely!" she said. "We must go walking there."

"And so we shall," he said and kissed her. "Welcome home, my darling."

"It's very beautiful," she said.

"But you miss the cottage," he stated intuitively.

"I'm certain—as you have pointed out more than once—that I will grow to love it here, as well. Wherever you are shall be my home."

"You know this has always been my home," he said with a sudden seriousness.

"Of course."

"It feels strange now to realize that without you . . . I don't know if it would ever feel like home again."

Perhaps attempting to lighten his mood, Ruth said, "But I've only been here a matter of minutes, Thomas."

"And you belong with me," he said, wrapping her in his arms, almost as if he feared he might lose her otherwise.

"Is something wrong?" she asked, returning his embrace.

"No, of course not," he insisted but held to her tightly. "I'm just so glad to have you here with me." He took hold of her shoulders and looked at her. "Perhaps I've fully realized now how very lonely I was during those days I spent here before we were married. I don't ever want to feel that way again."

Ruth touched his face and kissed him, promising they would never be apart. He smiled and kissed her again, but she could still see a sadness in his eyes that puzzled her.

Hoping to distract him—and also to do something she felt needed to be done right away—she asked, "Do you think it would be possible for us to speak privately with my uncle before supper?"

"I don't see why not," he said.

After they had both freshened up, Thomas took Ruth's hand and led her in a different direction from the way they'd come to his room. She counted herself lost within a minute, but eventually they ended up in a hallway near the kitchen, from which pleasant aromas drifted. Ruth could hear the noise and bustle of supper being prepared. Thomas stopped at a door that was left partially opened and knocked on it.

Ruth heard her uncle call, "Come in," and Thomas pushed open the door. Ruth noted that this was the room from which the entire household was likely managed. Her uncle sat at a table with a ledger book open in front of him. He looked up, clearly expecting a member of the staff, but coming abruptly to his feet when he saw them.

"Sir," he said, "and . . ." He hesitated, clearly not knowing what to call Ruth.

"Ruthie is what I believe you've always called me," she said and moved around the table to hug him tightly. As he returned the hug, she added, "I wanted a proper greeting without everyone looking on."

"How delightful," he said and hugged her again while he said lightly to Thomas, "She appears to be doing well, sir. I trust she's minding her manners."

"She's the epitome of a model wife," Thomas said, winking at Ruth.

"When a woman is treated like a queen," she said, "it's not hard to behave like one."

"I could introduce you to at least a dozen women in the county who would disprove that theory," Thomas said. "Unless you define behaving like a queen as arrogant and snobbish. And your uncle could attest to that."

"I could indeed."

The three of them sat to talk for a while with the door closed. Ruth was glad to hear that at the time of her uncle's visit, her mother and brothers had been doing well. Her mother had been glad to hear of Ruth's marriage and was determined to keep her ill-timed pregnancy a secret to the grave. When Ruth asked if her mother was still upset about the matter, her uncle diplomatically told her that it would likely never sit well with her.

"In other words," Ruth said, "she'll never forgive me."

Ruth appreciated the way her uncle took her hand. "I never saw eye to eye with my brother, Ruthie—nor with his wife. Let us simply be glad for how well things have worked out, and perhaps also be glad that you live a fair distance from her." He smiled as if he could erase all of Ruth's sadness by doing so. "In my opinion, child, you are the best of everything that ever came out of the family, and I'm glad to have you here."

Ruth nodded in response, so grateful for his kind words that she couldn't speak without her voice breaking. She was glad to have Thomas change the subject.

"And how has the staff responded to my marrying your niece . . . as far as you can tell?"

"Everyone who matters to me seems pleased and happy. If anyone *isn't* happy about it, I doubt that you or I care."

"How right you are, my good man," Thomas said.

Ruth laughed softly, glad to be free of her previous moment of sorrow in regard to her mother. "I swear the both of you take pleasure in going against convention just to spite others."

Thomas laughed as well and said to her uncle, "I told her I never do anything just to spite others, but sometimes it's an added bonus."

The men laughed heartily, and Ruth appreciated the camaraderie they shared as much as she appreciated how comfortable the situation felt. Even if a little awkward formality was required between her and her uncle at times, she could manage as long as their relationship could be this way privately. There was undoubtedly a strangeness to the situation, but she tended to agree with the men—as long as everyone who mattered to her was pleased and happy about it, she had no reason to care much what anyone else thought. Even if a tiny part of her hoped that her mother might one day forgive her, something bigger and deeper down inside her knew that she likely never would. But with Thomas in her life, even that would be all right.

Chapter Ten

THE RIGHT THING

WITHIN A WEEK OR SO, Ruth found herself able to keep time with
the rhythm of Brownlie Manor. Since everyone in the family got out
of bed and began their day at different times, the servants brought
breakfast to each of their rooms upon hearing the bell rope pulled.
Ruth was completely familiar with such an efficient system and
understood how the staff would know from which room the bell was
coming. But she was used to being at the other end of this process,
waiting for the signal to do an assigned task. She tried not to feel
guilty for being waited on and simply expressed appreciation each
time someone did something to assist her in any way. She could recall
very few times she'd been verbally thanked for her service in the past,
but she quickly noticed that with the Fitzbattens it was more unusual
for one of them *not* to express gratitude toward the staff for their
efforts. She wondered if she ever could have lived her life in a house
in which it wasn't that way—which was more typical.

Ruth enjoyed sharing breakfast with Thomas in their sitting
room, and sometimes she would go back to bed—being especially
tired due to her pregnancy—and he would leave to do whatever it
was that he did. He told her that he sometimes rode about the estate
with his father, either for pleasure or to oversee estate matters in one
way or another. And he and his father apparently worked closely
together in overseeing the books and financial matters of the estate.
They took the welfare of their land and the people who depended
upon it to make a living very seriously. They trusted the overseer, who

always kept matters in hand, but when Thomas or his father were at home, it was expected that they would be actively involved. Ruth was glad to leave him to his business while she rested, or read, or visited with Yvette, who often remained close to her bed until afternoon. Occasionally she shared lunch with the family, but more often than not she was asleep at the time they were eating and would have her lunch alone at her convenience.

Lunch was generally a casual meal served in a lovely little dining room that was fondly called the breakfast room, which Ruth found slightly comical since it was where they ate lunch. But the room had large windows, and on sunny days it was filled with light. Ruth enjoyed the relaxed atmosphere of lunch, and she enjoyed hearing Thomas and his father talk about the estate. They shared local gossip as easily as any group of women might. Once in a while her uncle joined them for lunch, and she appreciated feeling that a member of *her* family was welcome to share a meal with them now and then.

Dinner was a more formal event, and they often changed clothes for the evening meal. At first Ruth found the tradition a little silly, but after a few days she came to appreciate this time of day when everything else felt at a distance, and—as Thomas and his parents had all pointed out—the bounty of life could be fully appreciated. Ruth was able to appreciate it more, given how her new family talked openly of how they could never find joy in the finer things of life if they didn't know that every person who lived and worked on their estate was being treated fairly and having his or her needs well met. Ruth thought of the people she'd known in her life who indulged in ridiculous extravagance while others nearby were going hungry. She'd come to accept that it was a way of life, that people simply had to make do with their lot in life. But living here at Brownlie Manor, she'd come to realize that those who had been blessed with an abundance of worldly wealth could choose to help those in need, and she felt a secret pride to be part of a family who made that choice. Although Thomas had made it clear that he didn't want anyone to know, she had become aware of many quiet and often secretive ways he found to assist people in need. The Fitzbattens made donations to reputable charitable organizations by sending money through their solicitor, but they also did things that were closer to home. It was her knowledge of such things that made it possible to sit at a fine meal with her husband and his parents every evening and be able to relax and enjoy herself.

Ruth thought often of the life she'd become accustomed to at the cottage, and she wondered how Barclay and Bertie and little Warren were doing. She missed them but attempted to remedy that by writing a lengthy letter and having it posted. After getting a letter from Bertie in response, she wrote again, enjoying the prospect of maintaining a relationship with these new friends, even from a distance. This too added to her belief that she could be happy and content at Brownlie Manor.

Having worked in similarly enormous houses before, Ruth was able to quickly assess and memorize the particular configuration of her new home, and only once when she was on her own did she lose her way for a moment and have to turn back to get to a different hallway in order to find her intended destination.

Ruth quickly connected names to the faces of the members of the staff she interacted with, and she was glad to feel comfortable among them for the most part. She quickly put Thomas's suggestions to the test, and one day she set to work in the garden, partly as a way to occupy her time and feel productive, and partly just to see what might happen. The gardeners—Fletcher and Ernie—greeted her kindly and asked if they could be of any assistance to her, but they didn't protest over her efforts to help, and she enjoyed some conversation with the men as well as some lovely time to herself while she worked alone for a long while at pulling up tiny weeds from around some blooming rose bushes. The weeds never grew too big in such a well-maintained garden.

Ruth continued to go to the gardens to work whenever it suited her, and she also showed up in the kitchen or the laundry and insisted on helping. She even went to the stables now and then to help tend to the animals.

She enjoyed getting to know Chip and Herman, who were the men most commonly working in the stables, and she also got to know Gib, who drove the carriages and cared for them. She'd met him before, and, besides her uncle, he was the only one who knew her secret. But he was kind and genuinely seemed to like her, and she knew that if Thomas trusted him, she could too.

Ruth got to know Mrs. Darby quite well; she was the head cook, full of life and energy and a constant flow of stories. Candy was her assistant. They were both competent and efficient, and they both loved to talk. Ruth enjoyed doing simple tasks to help them and mostly just listened to their chatter.

Ruth also became rather well acquainted with most of the maids and butlers, and it wasn't uncommon for her to share a minute or two of conversation with any member of the staff as they crossed paths for any given reason. She became especially friendly with two maids—Selma and Liddy. Both were near her own age and were kind young women who were thrilled to be working with someone who knew and understood their lives well.

On a rainy morning that was especially chilly for summer, Liddy brought breakfast for Ruth and Thomas to their sitting room, and Ruth initiated some light conversation with the girl before she left. When Ruth was alone with Thomas and they'd begun eating, she was surprised to hear him say, "You're getting quite a reputation, wife."

"For what?" she asked and set down her teacup a little too loudly.

"No need to get snippy with me," Thomas said.

"Sorry." Ruth took another sip of tea, trying to wait patiently for him to go on.

"It's just that I hear everyone seems to like you very much, and it's the general opinion of the household that they're glad you're here."

Ruth relaxed a little. "I'm glad to hear it. I'm also glad that it's all right with you that I work with the servants when it suits me. If I had a husband who expected me to sit in parlors all day and look pretty while doing useless needlework, I think I'd go mad."

"And what if I did?" he asked.

"What?"

"Expect you to live like some kind of ornament, doing useless tasks."

"I already told you—I'd go mad."

"But you wouldn't *really* go mad," Thomas said, seeming intent on getting a serious answer. "You're stronger than that. What would you do if your husband forbade you to interact with the servants the way you do and got angry with you if you did so?" Ruth couldn't answer, and Thomas added, "It *could* have been that way. You knew absolutely nothing about me when you agreed to marry me."

"I knew you were kind," she said, "and that you have a reputation for treating your servants fairly."

Thomas shrugged. "But I was on my best behavior, and rumors can be misleading."

"Do you think I *wasn't* on my best behavior?" she asked, hearing that snippy tone in her own voice again. "What if I'd turned out to be a sore disappointment of a wife? What if—for all our good intentions—we felt entirely awkward with each other and had to accept that our marriage would be one of duty and sacrifice?"

"What if it had?" he echoed.

"What *if* it had?" she echoed back, hearing something in her voice that she knew was out of place for the conversation.

"You don't have to snap at me, wife," he said. "I was simply wondering."

Ruth stood and moved to the window. *"Why* are you wondering?" she asked, her back turned to him. "Are you trying to tell me something?"

Ruth heard him move behind her and felt his hands on her shoulders. "I'm trying to tell you that I'm very happy it all worked out even better than I ever could have hoped. I suppose I just can't help wondering . . . why that is . . . when it seems more likely—given the way we came together—that it could have been otherwise. I'm trying to tell you I'm grateful, Ruth. I just hope you feel content here."

"I *do* feel content here," she said, putting a hand over his on her shoulder while she continued to watch the rain fall. "Even though . . ." She hesitated and wondered why.

"Even though what?" he asked and turned her to face him.

"I suppose I just . . . feel more like one of them . . . like I belong in the stables or the kitchen. Sometimes I find myself thinking that if I don't get my work done and do it well, I'll be out of a job, and I have to remind myself of the way things really are." She looked up at her husband. "Sometimes it feels like a dream, Thomas. And I think I'm afraid that dreams end when we wake up and real life is there to greet us."

"This *is* your real life, Ruth," he said.

"I know." She looked down. "But much of the time it doesn't *feel* real, and sometimes that makes me afraid it won't last. I can't say there's any reason why I have such a fear; it's just what I feel."

"Fear is not known for being rational," he said. "But surely with time you will become more accustomed to your new life, and it will feel more real. And perhaps in the same right, I will come to accept that you really are here with me . . . and that having you in my life is not a dream."

Ruth looked up at him, her heart quickening. "Are you saying you feel the same?"

"Feelings can be difficult to compare, but I often wonder why I would be so blessed."

"Oh, it is I who am blessed," she murmured and was glad for the way he kissed her.

"Is that real enough for you?" he asked and kissed her again. "If you think you're dreaming," he muttered with a chuckle, "I could just keep . . ." He kissed her again and again.

Ruth touched his face and pushed her hands into his hair while he continued to kiss her, proving to her that the life she lived with him was indeed real. As long as he kissed her like this every day, surely she would eventually come to stop fearing that it was too good to last.

* * *

After breakfast Thomas met his father downstairs and they went out to the stables together and mounted their waiting horses to share a leisurely ride about the estate. They had debated whether or not to go out as planned, given the rain, but it lightened to a drizzle, and they set out, joking about how a decent Englishman couldn't be intimidated by a little rain. They chatted between stops they made whenever they saw someone out working. While making kind inquiries among the tenant farmers about their families and their circumstances, Thomas and Quin helped round up a small herd of sheep that had gotten past a broken fence, and they helped pull some weeds in the vegetable garden of a kindly widow whose deceased husband had been a friend to Quin for many years. When the rain worsened, they took cover in the barn of a pig farmer, and when the farmer picked up a pitchfork to pitch hay while they conversed, Thomas picked up another and helped him. Since there were only two pitchforks, Quin jokingly ordered them about and told them how they might be more efficient in their work, which made them all laugh.

After a number of stops—including lunch with one of the farmers and his family—Thomas and Quin rode toward home at a slow pace, sometimes talking and at other times just enjoying the silence as a light drizzle came and went.

"Ruth seems to be settling in well," Quin said, and Thomas's mind went back to his conversation with his wife earlier that morning.

"Yes, I believe she is, although I believe it will take time for her to feel completely at home. As comfortable as she is with us—and Mother—she admits to feeling like she's more at home among the servants."

"Nothing wrong with that," Quin said. "If she never stops feeling that way, so be it. There's nothing like having too much money to distort a man's view of what's truly important in life. Your sweet Ruth may be the very thing that helps you never forget."

Thomas liked the way that idea settled in, and he looked forward to repeating Quin's words to Ruth. "I do believe you're right, Father."

"She's the best thing that ever happened to you," Quin said. "You should never forget *that* either."

"You're right about that, as well."

Quin laughed in his jolly way. "To have a fine son who admits that his father is right now and then is about the best a man like me could wish for at my age."

Thomas chuckled, and they rode on in comfortable silence. Thomas's mind wandered to the things Ruth had said earlier. For entirely different reasons, he had to admit—at least to himself—that he too sometimes wondered if it was all too good to be true. He'd been so happy with his everyday life—now that Ruth was at the center of it. But he felt a nagging fear that it wouldn't last. What was it inside himself that tempted him to believe a man wasn't entitled to be this blessed and have it last? His greatest fear was presently focused on the fact that Ruth was daily getting closer to giving birth. There were a few months yet to go, but they would pass quickly, and her time would inevitably come. He looked forward to having the baby arrive, and he loved imagining life with a child at the center of everything. Thomas knew that some women did very well at giving birth, while others suffered complications and difficulties—and there was no way to know into which category Ruth fell until she actually went through it. He'd heard many gruesome tales about what women went through to give birth, and he knew it would be naive of him to ignore the fact that a certain percentage of women died in childbirth, and many others of childbed fever in the days afterward—a mysterious ailment that frightened him so horribly that he felt like a child afraid of the dark if he dared to even think about it.

"What is pulling your thoughts so far away?" Quin asked, bringing him back to the fact that he was not alone.

Since he'd never made a habit of hiding his feelings from his parents, he easily admitted, "I suppose I just have moments of worrying . . . about when the baby comes. I couldn't bear having anything happen to Ruth."

"We will make certain she has the very best of care, and we will pray that everything will be all right. Beyond that, such things must be left in God's hands."

"Yes, of course, but . . ."

"But it's impossible not to feel concerned. I know."

Thomas sensed that his father had stopped himself from saying more, and he could easily guess that Quin's mind had gone to how difficult it had been for Yvette to give birth to Thomas. He'd heard the story of his own birth many times, and there was no need to have it repeated. But Thomas knew that Quin had feared he would lose Yvette, and that her fragile state had begun with Thomas's birth. Perhaps it was knowing this story that contributed to Thomas's anxiousness. He thought of how he could bear having Ruth become fragile, as long as she lived to share a good, long life with him. He thought of how he could bear the possibility of Ruth never being able to have more children—just as it had been with his mother. He only wanted her to come through it alive and well.

Thomas was grateful when his father started a conversation that drew his thoughts far from his worries, and he felt certain that had been Quin's intention. They returned to the manor to find Ruth and Yvette sharing tea in his mother's favorite parlor. Their chatter and laughter filled the room, and Thomas thought of what Ruth had said earlier about a man wanting his wife to sit in a parlor and look pretty. He knew in that moment that he didn't *only* want that of her, but it was still nice to have such moments now and then. Because she certainly added beauty to the room.

* * *

Every week Ruth wrote a lengthy letter to Bertie, and she wrote a shorter one to her mother. Every week she got a letter back from Bertie. But summer turned to autumn without her ever receiving so much as a single written word from her mother. She worried about the welfare of her mother and brothers and she wrote many times that even a brief note regarding that would be appreciated. Still, she received nothing. Her uncle informed her that he'd finally gotten a brief response to a letter he'd sent some weeks earlier to his sister-in-law, wherein she had stated that everything was fine, but little else. Ruth thanked him for letting her know and ended the conversation. She knew he felt badly that her mother would write to him and not her, but she didn't want to add any emphasis to that fact, especially when she feared that she might break down and cry.

Later, when she was alone, Ruth *did* cry. She'd never felt terribly close to her mother, which made her wonder why the woman's anger and lack of forgiveness—implied by her ongoing silence—would even bother Ruth at all. But it did, even though she figured there was absolutely nothing to be done about it.

The following morning, Ruth was surprised to hear Thomas say at breakfast, "I've been thinking about this situation with your mother, and there's something I would like to propose."

"Yes?" she asked expectantly, unable to imagine what he could possibly be thinking.

"The idea occurred to me early on in our marriage, if you must know, but it didn't feel right to do anything about it then. Perhaps it seemed better to give the matter some time. But now I can't seem to stop thinking about it, as if it's nagging at me, and I feel that I just need to do the right thing."

"Yes?" Ruth said again in a higher pitch, wondering what on earth he meant by *the right thing*.

"And since we likely have only a few weeks of autumn left before it might start to turn cold, and the fact that your time with the baby will be getting closer once winter sets in and you'll be more uncomfortable and—"

"What on earth has all of this got to do with my mother?" she asked, unable to remain patient another second.

"Because it's so much more difficult to travel in the winter," he said, as if it should be obvious. When she only stared at him, he added, "I think it's time I met your family, Ruth. And since your mother isn't answering your letters, I believe we have good cause to just . . . go and see for ourselves that all is well."

"You can't be serious!" she said, unable to imagine why on earth he would want to travel two days by carriage to meet the difficult woman she had told him about.

"I'm *quite* serious," he insisted, "I can assure you."

"Why?"

"Because it's the right thing to do, Ruth," he said, putting his hand over hers on the table. "However difficult she might be, or however fragile your relationship with her, she is my mother-in-law, and I should meet her and assure her that you're being well cared for. Whether that is of any consequence to her or not, I must do the right thing."

Ruth took in a deep breath and let it out slowly. "It's just like you to get all honorable and such. I shouldn't be surprised."

"Perhaps I shouldn't have been so slow about it."

"Or perhaps—in spite of all your best intentions—we should decide against it. I appreciate your efforts, Thomas; I really do. But I'm not so sure it's a good idea." She looked down. "And in all honesty, I'm not so sure I *want* you to see where and what I come from."

"Do you sincerely believe," he said, sounding almost angry, "that I would think or feel any differently about you based on *that*?"

"No, I don't!" she countered in the same tone. "But that doesn't mean I want to take you there."

"Fair enough. But I still think it would be the right thing, and I think we should just . . . do it . . . before the baby comes. I would like to meet your brothers, as well. You must remember that I'm an only child. I confess I'm somewhat fascinated with the idea that you have so many brothers. You've never told me anything negative about any of them; in fact, you've hardly told me anything about them at all. I should like to meet them."

"Fine," she said and brushed the front of her dress abruptly, as if that might conclude the conversation. "We'll go. But don't be expecting anything good to come of it."

"Are you telling *me* that . . . or yourself?"

Ruth felt surprised by the question but couldn't deny the truth in it. "Maybe both," she admitted and tried to focus on her breakfast.

* * *

The journey to Ruth's childhood home went relatively well. The weather was fair, and the inn they stayed in to break their journey was very nice. But Ruth couldn't deny that the traveling was more uncomfortable given the increasing aches and pains of pregnancy, and she dreaded facing her mother more and more as the miles passed. She could only think of their last exchange—which had been nothing less than traumatic for Ruth. The fact that her mother hadn't responded to her letters only added a sting to those memories. She talked through her every thought and feeling with Thomas—more than once—and he simply assured her that even if her mother kicked them out and the visit lasted only a few minutes, they would at least know they had tried. Then they could let the matter rest more peacefully. She wanted to believe that was true, but she would be glad to have it over.

They arrived late afternoon in the town less than a mile from Ruth's home. It felt strange to be coming back here in her new circumstances of being married to a man like Thomas, and she couldn't help contrasting it with the hundreds of times she'd come into this town throughout her life. Thomas got them a room at the inn, where they were able to freshen up and rest for a short while before embarking on the brief drive to their ultimate destination.

In Ruth's nervousness she said to Thomas, "The house is much smaller than the cottage."

"So you've told me."

"I dare say it could be smaller than our bedroom."

"You've told me that as well," Thomas said. "You talk as if I've never stepped inside such a house. Your implication makes me sound like a snob. My father and I had lunch in a very small house with a farmer and his wife not four days ago."

"I didn't mean it like that," she said. "You're not a snob. Well," she chuckled, "you are rather snobbish toward rich people who *are* snobs."

"Am I?" he asked, sounding genuinely surprised. She only stared at him until he added, "I suppose I am."

"And proud of it, apparently," Ruth said, glad for a distraction from her growing nervousness.

When the carriage came to a halt she had difficulty taking a deep breath. But she did her best and said, "Let's get this over with."

Thomas chuckled and stepped out of the carriage before he offered his hand to help her. By the time Ruth had both feet on the ground, the door of the house had opened and her mother was standing in its frame, wiping her hands on an apron.

"Promise you'll protect me," Ruth said softly.

"I promise," Thomas said and offered his arm.

They walked the short footpath to the door while Ruth could see in her mother's countenance more curiosity than anger. It occurred to her that perhaps the reason for her mother's anger was the very fact that she *hadn't* come to visit with her new husband. Thomas was nothing if not insightful. With any luck he would be right and she *wouldn't* regret this.

"Hello, Mother," Ruth said when they were close enough to be heard.

"This is certainly a surprise," Keely Dawson said in a toneless voice. Her eyes moved quickly up and down and back forth, surveying both Ruth and Thomas as if to make a quick assessment.

"We thought it was time we came to visit," Ruth stated when her mother said nothing more. "And it's likely high time you met my husband."

"It likely is," Keely said.

Knowing it was up to her to make the introduction, she hurried to say, "Mother, this is my husband, Thomas Fitzbatten. Thomas, my mother, Keely Dawson."

"A pleasure, Mrs. Dawson." Thomas took one step forward and held out a hand. Keely looked at it as if she wasn't quite certain what to do, but she finally lifted her hand, which he took and kissed quickly before letting it go and stepping back to stand at Ruth's side. "I apologize that our visit has been delayed so many months, and I take full responsibility. I've very much wished to meet you, and we thought it would be wise to make the journey while the weather is still fair. And we wanted to make certain that all is well with you and your sons."

"Everything is fine," Keely said, and Ruth could imagine her mother ending the entire conversation with that. In her mind she could see her mother thanking them for the visit and closing the door. But Keely added—without any indication of enthusiasm, "Come in, if you like. I wasn't expecting company so the house looks the same as it always does."

"Thank you," Thomas said.

Ruth added, "You always keep things tidy, Mother. There's no need to be concerned." She didn't add that she'd told Thomas she didn't want to send word of their coming in advance for fear it would guarantee her mother not being at home. Or perhaps she would just hide and *pretend* not to be at home.

"Make yourselves comfortable," Keely said as she closed the door. "I'll put the kettle on."

"There's no need to go to any trouble," Ruth said.

"I'll put the kettle on," Keely repeated.

While the kettle was heating, and then while sharing tea, the three of them exchanged a minimal amount of mildly awkward conversation. The only meaningful thing Keely said was to Thomas. "My brother-in-law tells me you're a fine man and my Ruth couldn't ask for a better husband. I'm glad to know that."

Ruth saw Thomas barely nod in receipt of the compliment. He replied by saying, "Your brother-in-law is one of the finest men I know."

"He *is* a good man," Keely said.

She asked Ruth a few questions about how she was doing, although she seemed to want to ignore the pregnancy. Ruth asked the same questions of her mother and also asked about her brothers, and she was assured they were all fine.

The awkwardness lessened as Ruth's brothers who still lived at home came in after a day's work. They were excited to see Ruth and to meet her husband, and the mood improved dramatically.

According to a plan they had discussed in advance, Thomas announced that they needed to be going before any preparations for supper began. Ruth knew her mother would feel very uncomfortable with guests for supper when she'd had no opportunity for preparation, and she also knew that whatever her mother would have intended to cook, there likely wouldn't be enough for two extra people.

Ruth's brothers all hugged her tightly, and they shared zealous handshakes with Thomas. Ruth didn't know if it was her brothers' actions that might have inspired her mother, but she was surprised to get a hug from Keely as well. Holding on as long as she could manage, Ruth said quietly, "It's so good to see you, Mother."

"And you," Keely said. "I'm glad to know you're doing fine."

The door was open, and Ruth was about to step out when she realized that Thomas had pulled an envelope out of the inner pocket of his coat. With her brothers' attention elsewhere, Thomas said quietly to Keely, "I want you to have this . . . to make certain you are comfortable and have everything you need. And if you have any intention of trying to call it charity, or of declaring your pride in caring for your family, let me stop you by declaring *my* pride in caring for *my* family. It's the right thing to do."

Ruth held her breath, waiting for her mother to still find something unkind to say in response to his offering. But she said nothing at all. Still, there was something in her expression that betrayed a glimpse of gratitude, and perhaps relief. Thomas set the envelope on the table within Keely's reach and said, "It was so good to finally meet you."

"And you," Keely said. "Travel safely."

"Thank you," Thomas said and stepped out the door behind Ruth.

As they walked away, Keely once again stood in the doorway. Ruth was surprised to hear her call, "You'll let me know when the baby comes?"

Ruth stopped and turned, "Yes, of course."

Keely nodded and waved, and a moment later Ruth was sitting next to Thomas in the carriage and it was rolling away. Once out of her mother's view, Ruth couldn't restrain her tears. But Thomas seemed to have expected it and put his arm around her.

"Thank you," she said. "I *am* glad we came; so very glad."

"As am I," he said and kissed the top of her head.

She looked up at him. "Why didn't you tell me you were going to give her money?"

"Because you would have tried to talk me out of it," he said, and she knew he was probably right. "But your mother shouldn't have to scrimp to get by at her age, and don't tell me it isn't my responsibility, because it is. If I worked in a mine or a shop, I would send her any portion of my wages we could afford."

"My uncle was right about you," she said, settling her head on his shoulder. "You're a fine man and I couldn't ask for a better husband."

Thomas made a scoffing noise that indicated his discomfort at being talked about so favorably. Then he chuckled and kissed the top of her head again.

"I think I should be angry with your uncle for not bringing you to work in my household years ago. I would have fallen in love with you and stunned the entire county by marrying one of the household maids."

"I'll let you and my uncle argue about that when we get back, but please do it when I'm occupied elsewhere."

"I'll give it some thought," he said and chuckled again.

* * *

The following day being Sunday, Thomas and Ruth attended church and then called on each of her brothers who were married and still lived in the area. These visits were much more relaxed, and Ruth enjoyed being with her family.

Less than a week after returning home from their journey, Ruth received a letter from her mother. It was brief and by no means sentimental, but in it she thanked them for their visit and for the *kindness* Thomas had offered. By the way it was worded, Ruth knew she was referring to the money, and it made her wonder what circumstances she might not be aware of. When she showed Thomas the letter, she thanked him again for his insights and generosity, and she couldn't deny that she felt more at peace over the situation with her mother and was glad to not have it nagging at her any longer.

Chapter Eleven

LURED AWAY

As AUTUMN WAS SUDDENLY SWALLOWED by a harsh winter storm, Ruth felt the security of Brownlie Manor envelop her more fully. The warmth and coziness of its parlors and sitting rooms, and the comfort of its beds and sofas became all the more evident with the harsh winter winds howling outside, and with Ruth's pregnancy making her more and more uncomfortable.

Occasionally Ruth tried to imagine herself in a cold and condemning home for unwed mothers where babies were discreetly taken away and given to wealthy people who couldn't have children of their own. The very thought of how her life might have been if Thomas hadn't married her could bring on tears immediately. But even being in such a terrible place with the prospect of giving up her baby would have been far better than the alternative—and that would have been her fate had Thomas not been willing to intervene.

Unable to bear the thought of any other possibility than what had become reality, Ruth focused on all that was good in her life and found herself longing to get this baby out of her and have the experience of childbirth behind her. The local doctor—a man well-known and trusted by the family—came to check on her more frequently as her time drew closer. He always assured her that everything was in tip-top order and he believed she would do marvelously. Still, Ruth knew it would be difficult at best and she wanted it to be over. She also knew that Thomas and his parents were all more nervous about it than any of them were willing to let on. They skirted around the actual topics of labor and childbirth, and their conversations tended to focus more on how lovely it would be when they had a baby in the house.

During a stretch of fair weather when the skies were brilliant blue but the air was biting cold, Ruth felt like her belly was growing more round and tight every day. She'd given up even trying to go down the stairs and had all of her meals brought upstairs to their rooms. Thomas always ate with her, and a few times his parents did, as well. Between them and a few of the servant girls she'd gotten to know fairly well, Ruth rarely lacked company. But she longed for fresh air—even if it was cold.

As another harsh storm set in, Ruth's labor began. While the pains became more intense and frequent, she could see through the windows that the snow was not necessarily coming down in large quantities, but it was being blown around by a fierce and angry wind that seemed to be in harmony with the pain she was experiencing.

As daylight turned to darkness, she couldn't see anything out of the windows at all. The pain worsened severely, and she began to believe it would never end. When it was finally over and the baby was placed in her arms, she silently thanked God for the way His divine hand had made it possible for her to keep her child and see it raised in a proper home with a good family. Never had she felt happier than in that moment.

* * *

For Thomas, only certain experiences related to his years at war compared to what he felt during the hours of Ruth's labor. His father insisted they wait together in a parlor far away from the bedroom where Yvette would stay with Ruth. Thomas was glad to know his mother was with her, just as he was glad for the comfortable friendship Ruth had formed with Selma and Liddy, who had been asked ahead of time to be present to assist the doctor with whatever he needed. Knowing she was in capable hands and surrounded by women who cared for her eased Thomas's anxiety somewhat, but he wanted to be there himself. He wanted to hold her hand and suffer with her, in spite of having been told many times that it was far better for him to keep his distance.

Thomas could hardly sit still—or even sit at all—as the hours dragged on while the wind outside grew more ferocious. He knew his father was nervous as well, but Quin put on a good show of remaining calm. Thomas knew his father was likely exercising great self-control in order to keep Thomas from turning into a raving lunatic.

When a maid finally came into the room, her weary eyes betrayed her utter exhaustion. If the *maid* looked like that, he wondered what condition Ruth might be in. For a moment he imagined he could hear this young woman saying that something was wrong, that something had happened to Ruth or the baby—or both. His heart pounded, and he almost felt light-headed.

Thomas was about to shout at the maid to tell him whatever she'd come to say when she uttered with a quivering voice, "It's over, sir, and mother and baby are fine. The doctor says you can go and see them now."

"Oh!" Thomas muttered. "Oh!" He impulsively hugged the maid, lifting her off her feet for a moment before she scurried away. He hugged his father, who was laughing and wiping at his eyes.

"Go along, boy," Quin said. "I'll come up in a while."

Thomas took the stairs three at a time and ran the long hallways, slowing down only a few steps from the bedroom door, where he took a long moment to catch his breath and utter thanks to God that it was over and everything was fine. He knocked at the door before turning the knob, even though it was his own room.

"Come in, come in," he heard the doctor say as Thomas peered around the door to see Ruth propped up against pillows, illuminated by the glow of lamps on both sides of the bed. She had a pale, sunken look about her that reminded him of battle-weary soldiers he'd seen in hospital beds. He was so focused on her face that the movement and noise coming from the bundle in her arms nearly startled him. He stepped slowly toward the bed, and Ruth looked up at him when his presence caught her attention. Her countenance brightened, which didn't disguise her exhaustion, but the light in her eyes completely erased any similarity to his reminders of war. What she had just experienced had not damaged her spirit or broken her; it was quite the opposite. She was different, but in every possible good way. He could never find words to describe such a change, but he could see it; he could feel it.

Ruth reached a hand toward him, and he sat carefully on the edge of the bed as he took it and kissed her brow. "Oh, my darling," he said and looked into her eyes. "You're all right?"

"I am very sore and tired," she muttered in a weary voice, "but yes, I am more than all right." Her eyes moved toward the baby cradled in her other arm, and his eyes followed and widened as he saw the impossibly tiny hand reach up out of the blanket. "It's a girl," Ruth said, and Thomas let out a little laugh on the wave of a sharp breath.

"A girl," he repeated and leaned over to try to get a better look at her.

"Sit beside me," Ruth said, and he did so carefully, putting his arm around her so they could both clearly see the baby.

Thomas tentatively touched the baby's dark hair and laughed again to see her scrunched up face. "We have a daughter," he murmured and pressed a kiss into Ruth's mussed hair.

"Yes," she said and held more tightly to him with her free hand. "We have a daughter."

When Thomas realized Ruth was crying, he had difficulty holding back his own tears. He held his wife close while they wept together with relief and joy, and the ironies and miracles surrounded the three of them in a warm blanket of comfort.

* * *

Ruth came awake with her head heavy from whatever it was the doctor had given her to help ease the pain that had been making it difficult to sleep. Her first real awareness was the evidence she felt in her body that she'd given birth, but her mind went immediately to her beautiful little girl, and the pain seemed irrelevant. She'd made it through and she would recover. She was surrounded by every possible comfort and all kinds of assistance at her beck and call. And most importantly, she was encircled in love. She found it difficult to believe that she'd once felt certain this child would only bring heartache and grief into the world, but now she had to wonder if there had ever been anyone happier about the arrival of a baby than Thomas and his parents. The baby was barely a day old and she'd already been doted upon and admired with great fervency.

Ruth wondered where her baby was now and felt an aching to hold her. She didn't know how long she'd slept, but she knew it had been late in the evening when the doctor had given her a spoonful of some foul-tasting liquid, and now—even with her eyes still closed—she could tell it was daylight. She forced her heavy eyelids open with some effort and saw no one. She turned her head on the pillow to survey the room, wondering if she was alone—although she recalled both Thomas and Yvette promising that someone would stay nearby in case she needed anything.

Ruth squinted against the light when her eyes came to focus on the largest window in the room, through which she could see snow falling in light, gentle flakes with an absence of any wind to disturb their descent. And framed perfectly in the center of the window—like a living and breathing work of art—stood Thomas, turned mostly toward the window as if he might be looking out at the snow. But his eyes were fully focused on the infant in his arms. Her baby girl was wrapped in a delicately crocheted white shawl that hung down from where it was enfolded around the baby.

Ruth's heart quickened with unspeakable joy to see the adoration and delighted intrigue sparkling in Thomas's eyes, and she loved the way he gently swayed back and forth as if he'd already become an expert at holding and soothing an infant. While she watched, he began whispering something to the baby, but Ruth couldn't hear what he was saying. She smiled to conclude that it must be important by the way his expression changed from intense to animated—along with a little chuckle—and then to complete adoration.

When he'd apparently said all he meant to, Ruth couldn't keep from intruding any longer. "It would seem," she said, and he looked toward her, "that I must now share your affections with another woman."

"It would seem," he said, moving closer, "that my heart has grown more than large enough to hold all the love I have for *all* of the women in my life."

Thomas put one knee on the bed and placed the baby in Ruth's arms, as if he knew without asking that she would be wanting to hold her. "Oh," Ruth said with a little laugh, "I was thinking that she couldn't possibly be as beautiful as I'd remembered, but I do believe she's even more beautiful today than yesterday."

"I do believe she is," Thomas said, sitting on the edge of the bed. "Mother says that babies change every day when they are so young, which makes me want to look at her all the time so that I don't miss anything. It's too bad we have to sleep."

Ruth agreed with a nod while she touched her daughter's hands and face and hair, reassured that everything was as perfect as she remembered.

"How are you feeling?" Thomas asked and kissed her brow.

"Like I had a baby," Ruth said lightly, "but I'm certain it's nothing time won't heal."

Ruth sighed and pressed her lips to the baby's little face, inhaling the sweet fragrance of a newborn, wanting to remember these moments forever. "I can't think at all of what to name her. I hope you have something in mind, because I have thought and thought and can't come up with a single name that feels right."

"Nor can I, to be truthful," Thomas said. "I've just been calling her my joy—for she certainly is."

Ruth looked up at Thomas, feeling suddenly enlightened. "Then perhaps that's what she should be."

"What?" he asked, not grasping what she meant.

"Our Joy," Ruth said. "Perhaps her name *should* be Joy."

Thomas smiled. "I think you might be right." He looked at the baby and asked as if she might answer, "Is your name Joy, my little darling? Is that all right with you?"

The baby stretched in her sleep, making a funny face and a comical sound that was somewhere between cooing and grunting. Her parents both laughed and Thomas declared, "I do believe it's settled, then." He turned to look at Ruth's face and added, "You make a beautiful mother."

"I look a terrible sight," she said, lightly scoffing.

"No," he said severely, touching her chin with his finger, "you look all courage and strength and maternal beauty. And I will never forget what you went through to bring this beautiful child into our family."

Ruth couldn't help but be overcome with tears as her mind passed through the reality of the present to how it could have been. She knew at some point that she had to stop comparing, and she had to stop looking back and only look forward. But in that moment she just had to say, "If I'd had to let her go to someone else, I do believe she would have given them a great deal of joy. I'm so glad that we get to keep all of the joy to ourselves."

"I'm glad of it too," he whispered and kissed her. The baby made another of those noises and he added, "So very glad of it."

* * *

Thomas rarely left Ruth's side unless she was sleeping, and he felt equally hesitant to be very far away from Joy. His parents were pleased with the choice for her name, and they doted on the baby with all the love they seemed to have been saving up from not being able to have more children themselves.

Ruth's healing was slow but steady. The doctor checked in regularly to assure them that everything was fine; she just needed time. And the passing of weeks proved him right. Gradually Ruth regained her strength and color, and the soreness she felt began to improve.

Joy quickly lost the distinctive appearance of a newborn and began to fill out with adorably chubby cheeks and legs and little wrinkles in her fat wrists that Thomas loved to kiss. She was frequently prone to silly facial expressions and making funny noises, and when she slept she often had dreams that would make her smile as if she were remembering heaven with fondness.

Winter continued to be harsh, but Ruth and Yvette remained inside with every possible comfort, watching over Joy continually. The men went out as necessary to see to business as usual in estate matters. But Quin teased Thomas about how fatherhood had taken control of him; he had picked up on how anxious Thomas always was to return home as quickly as possible, as if being away from

Joy for the better part of a day might do him in. Thomas reminded himself often how blessed he was to not have to be away from his wife and daughter nearly as much as most men would need to be in order to go out and provide for their families. He especially felt a new compassion for men who had to leave home and go to war or to sea and leave their families for long stretches of time. He knew it wasn't in him to do so; he felt as if it would kill him.

Christmas came and went, and everyone agreed it was the best Christmas Brownlie Manor had ever seen. Not wanting to take Joy out in the cold, they made the decision to have her christened when spring came, and they would have a celebration like the one they'd participated in while they were staying at the cottage when little Warren had been christened. They would invite every person who lived on the estate and worked in the house, and every person in the village whom they had any association with at all. Thomas and his parents agreed that having a child born at Brownlie Manor was surely the greatest cause for celebration that had occurred in years, perhaps decades, and they would make the most of it.

Ruth wrote a long letter to her mother about Joy's arrival, including many details of the event and saying that she wished they didn't live so far away so that Ruth's mother and brothers could see the baby. She invited them to come and stay at any time, insisting they were always welcome, and promised that she and Thomas would bring Joy to meet them in the summer either way.

Ruth invited her family to the christening, making it clear there was more than enough room for everyone to stay at the manor and that Thomas's parents would very much love to meet them. Ruth was disappointed but not surprised when Keely wrote back to politely decline the offer, saying it would be impossible to leave their home unattended for so long, but that she appreciated the invitation. She expressed happiness and congratulations that all had gone well with the birth and that the baby was doing so well. Ruth hoped that might be her way of saying she was coming to accept the situation and that eventually she might forget about the unsavory facets of the past.

Ruth's hopes were heightened by the beautiful crocheted baby shawl Keely had made and sent along with her letter. Yvette admired the quality of the piece and declared there was surely love in every stitch. Ruth wrapped little Joy in it and felt certain it was true. And perhaps with that love also came healing and forgiveness. Ruth wrote her mother a long letter in return, thanking her for the beautiful gift and sharing some details of her new life. This began a more regular exchange of letters between Ruth and her mother, and with each one, Ruth felt the healing between them deepen.

When spring finally came and the christening took place, Thomas felt his contentment settling in more deeply. His parents were doing well; in fact, his mother was doing better than she had in years. Joy was healthy and growing and eagerly offering smiles and laughter to anyone who would give her attention. Ruth was fully recovered from giving birth, and, perhaps even more gratifying to Thomas, he could see tangible evidence that she had recovered from the difficulties that had taken place in her life before he'd met her. She'd said nothing for months about any of that, as if she never even gave it a thought. It was becoming easier every day to truly believe and feel that Joy was *his* daughter, that she always had been, and she always would be.

The christening celebration proved to be everything they had hoped it would be, and all of the planning was carried through to perfection. Thomas felt deeply happy to see the farmers and tradesmen and household servants—and their families—all eating and laughing together while the children all ran and played with each other, healthy and strong. He imagined Joy and her younger siblings one day participating in such festivities, which only deepened his contentment.

When it got late and the bonfire was lit, Thomas danced with his wife while Joy was passed around and cared for by many different people who knew and loved her. There was only a brief moment when Thomas had to suppress the thought that this was all too good to last. He ordered any such ideas out of his head, along with any sorrow he might feel to think of the many people in the world who were not nearly as blessed as those who were celebrating together this warm spring night. He knew he couldn't alter the plight of human suffering, but he could do his part to keep his own little corner of the world as safe and prosperous as humanly possible. He was doing that and he felt happy. And when Ruth looked into his eyes and told him how very much she loved him, he had to believe that he would be blessed enough for all of this goodness to last a lifetime.

* * *

A little more than a week after the christening, Thomas was surprised to receive a letter from his dear friend, Theodore Grayson. Teddy had been at Thomas's side throughout his entire time while serving in the military, and he had saved Thomas's life on the battlefield. The last time Thomas had seen Teddy had been in the hospital in which Thomas had been recovering from his near-fatal wound, and Teddy had been headed home. Teddy had promised to someday visit Brownlie Manor, but as of yet he hadn't been able to accept Thomas's open invitation to do so. They had exchanged some letters, and Teddy knew that Thomas was now married and a father, but in this newest letter Teddy made no mention of that. The missive was brief and seemed hurriedly written, with an apology for asking such an enormous favor of Thomas, but stating that he was in need of some help that could only be discussed face-to-face. He reminded Thomas—as if it were some kind of joke to lighten the urgent tone of the letter—that Thomas had told Teddy more than once that he owed Teddy for having saved his life and that one day he would repay the debt. In his mind Thomas could hear Teddy's voice as he lightly made reference to that promise, but there was a seriousness of tone in the way he added that he had hoped to never have to call in that favor; however, circumstances had made it necessary to ask for his aid if it were at all possible.

Thomas showed the letter to Ruth, and she read it through more than once while Thomas hurried to pack a few things, feeling the need to leave at once and meet Teddy in London as quickly as possible at the inn where Teddy had said he would be staying until he heard from Thomas.

Ruth sounded panicked as she said, "I understand why you need to go; he saved your life, and he's a dear friend. But . . . I feel afraid. Something feels . . . wrong."

"Something *is* wrong, obviously," Thomas said.

"That's not what I mean."

"What *do* you mean?"

"I . . . can't explain it," she said. "It just feels . . . wrong; I feel frightened to have you go."

Thomas stopped his rushing about to sit next to his wife and take her hand. "I'm certain it's nothing dangerous, or he would have indicated that. He's a good man, not the kind to get mixed up in anything unseemly. Perhaps he's in need of money, or maybe it's a health matter. It could be a member of his family who needs help. It's impossible to know without talking to him; that's why I must go as he's requested."

"Of course," Ruth said, but she didn't seem convinced.

Thomas kissed her and said, "I'll likely be gone less than a week. I'll write if there's some reason that makes it necessary to stay longer than that, but I can't imagine that will happen." He wrapped her tightly in his arms. "It will be difficult to be away from you for so long."

"Yes, it will," she insisted, holding to him as if she might never be able to again.

"And what will I do without seeing Joy every day?" he asked and realized he couldn't think about this too hard or he *wouldn't* go. "Tell her not to change too much before her papa comes home."

"I'll do my best," Ruth said. Thomas kissed her again and resumed his packing. He only took minimal items and a change of clothing that could fit into saddlebags. He wanted to be able to travel as lightly and quickly as possible.

Thomas said his good-byes to his family members quickly, not allowing himself time to think about being away from any of them. As he rode away from Brownlie Manor, he looked back over his shoulder several times, until he was too far away to see it anymore. He prayed that it wouldn't be too many days before he returned again to his beloved home and family and that all would be well with them in his absence. And he prayed that all would be well with Teddy.

* * *

Ruth watched from an upstairs window as Thomas rode away. As soon as he'd gone out to the stables, she had purposely come to find this window at the end of a hallway, which she knew afforded the best view of the road. She watched until he was completely out of sight, then she went to her room and curled up on the bed and cried, glad that Joy was taking a sound nap. She wasn't at all surprised by how thoroughly dependent she had become on her husband, but having him leave made her dependency feel almost frightening.

Ruth was glad to be alone long enough to have a good cry, but she was also glad when Yvette came to her room, having guessed that Ruth would be upset over Thomas leaving. At first she just wrapped Ruth in the arms of her motherly love and let her cry, and then she insisted that they find something to do to distract themselves. It wasn't as if Thomas didn't spend hours away from the house every day anyway.

Ruth was grateful for Yvette's company and distraction, and Quin too was kind and compassionate about Thomas's absence. But supper felt all wrong with Thomas gone, and when bedtime came and Ruth found herself trying to sleep without her husband next to her, she felt utterly dismayed. She read until she could hardly hold her head up, and then she was finally able to sleep. With the coming of morning she mentally tallied that she had one night down, and if she planned on him being gone for a week, she only had six to go.

Nine mornings later, Ruth was in a near-constant state of panic. Quin and Yvette had remained calm when Thomas hadn't come home after a week, but within another day Ruth had noticed signs of Yvette being anxious over his absence but trying to hide it. And now Quin was pacing instead of eating his breakfast, muttering about the possibilities of what could have kept Thomas from returning by now—or at least sending some kind of message to let them know what he was doing. Quin seemed angry with his son for not being more considerate in letting the family know, but Ruth could easily see through the anger and knew he was worried. She was worried too; they were all worried. Her mind went wild with all of the possibilities regarding what kind of trouble Teddy might have gotten himself into and she worried that Thomas could very well be caught up in the same trouble—or worse. The very idea of him never coming back made her physically ill. All she could manage to do was take care of her daughter and barely force herself to eat enough to ease her hunger. If not for knowing that she had a baby to nurse who depended upon her, she doubted she would have been able to eat at all. It had been little more than a year since she'd met Thomas Fitzbatten, and now she doubted that it was possible to ever live without him.

* * *

Thomas felt disturbingly concerned about Teddy when he arrived at the inn to which he'd been beckoned and found that not only was Teddy not there, but according to the innkeeper and all of his employees, no one fitting Teddy's description had been there for as far back as anyone could remember. Since Teddy had very distinctive pale blond hair and a scar to the side of his nose that was impossible to ignore, there was no mistaking him for anyone else. He had *not* been at the location to which Thomas had been summoned, and he certainly wasn't there now.

Thomas got a room at the inn, deciding to stay a night—maybe two—to see if Teddy showed up. On a hunch, he sent a high-speed messenger to Teddy's family home in Yorkshire and decided to remain at the inn until he got a response.

That night there was a fire at the inn that started in the room next door to Thomas's. Thankfully Thomas had been awake and had smelled the smoke and was able to help put the fire out and get everyone outside to safety. No one was hurt, and the damage was only to the one room, which meant the inn would stay in business, for which the innkeeper was very grateful.

During his second day there, efforts to repair the fire damage were already underway, Thomas went to some local pubs that he thought Teddy would likely visit if he were staying in this part of London. He spoke with several people, but no one had seen anyone fitting Teddy's description. Thomas found it odd when he considered the likelihood that if Teddy had been in this part of the city for even a short period of time, he would have surely gone to one of the pubs at least once or twice. He knew this because he knew Teddy. But he found it even more odd that when he was crossing a busy street—after having looked both ways—he was nearly run down by a carriage and four that was going far too fast for such a street. If not for being very alert and acting quickly, Thomas could have been seriously injured. While a kind man was helping him get up off the street where he'd thrown himself in order to avoid the collision, the sheer lack of coincidences came together in Thomas's mind. He didn't know what was going on, but he suddenly felt disposed to looking over his shoulder as he walked back to the inn, wondering if the trouble Teddy had written to him about had latched itself onto him, and it was far more serious—and dangerous—than he'd ever imagined.

Thomas could hardly sleep that night while he tried in vain to put the puzzle pieces together in his mind. What was he doing here? Why were all these things happening? And where was Teddy? His mind vacillated between being convinced this was all just strange coincidence and then being absolutely certain someone was out to get him—quite literally. He wondered whether he should have chosen to stay somewhere else. He was glad when daylight arrived so he could at least see what was going on around him, but he felt eerily alert—to the point of being frightened—while he ate breakfast in the dining room of the inn, wishing the messenger would return and give him some information that might help him know what to do.

Thomas hid away in his room for the remainder of the morning, often peeking carefully between the closed curtains to the street below, as if he might see something that could help him assess whether or not he was actually in danger. He was eating lunch in the dining room when the messenger arrived to inform him he'd spoken with Teddy Grayson's father, who had reported that Teddy had been gone from home for a few months—supposedly in France staying with an aunt and uncle there.

Thomas gave the messenger some extra money for his efforts and settled his bill with the innkeeper once he'd firmly decided he really had no idea what to do, but it didn't feel right to stay at *this* inn for another night. He couldn't imagine what Teddy might be up to while his family believed he was in France. He stewed over it for hours before it occurred to him that perhaps Teddy *was* in France and this had absolutely nothing to do with him. But who would have possibly lured him away from his home with a letter that had been very convincingly written in what had appeared to be Teddy's hand, and with enough knowledge of their relationship to know that Thomas would rush to the aid of his friend? And to what purpose? He had never once in his life been involved in anything unseemly. He'd never even been drunk enough to not remember anything that had happened. Not once!

That night Thomas stayed in a different inn located in a completely different part of the city. And again he had trouble sleeping while he pondered and stewed and tried to discern whether his instincts were alerting him to danger or just playing games with his imagination. He decided distinctly on the former when he realized that someone was coming into his room—and he or she had opened the door with a key. His heart pounded while he thanked God for the fact that he *was* awake and at the same time pleaded for protection in order to make it home safely. He felt suddenly worried over what might be happening at Brownlie Manor. Had he been lured away for reasons that had something to do with his family? His position? His wealth? Then a heart-stopping question burst into his mind, making it difficult to concentrate on how he was going to handle the possibility of someone being in the room who might be there to harm him. He *did* have a secret. A very big secret. He was pretending to be the father of someone else's child. Could this possibly have anything to do with that? Was there any way the man who had hurt Ruth could be behind such a ruse?

Thomas abruptly left off wondering about such things when his eyes adjusted to the shadows and he saw that the dark figure in the room was pointing a pistol toward the bed. Thomas rolled abruptly in the other direction and onto the floor at the very second the shot rang out. If he'd been asleep, he would have been dead. Someone was *actually* trying to kill him! For a second that seemed like minutes, Thomas wondered if his attacker—realizing he had failed—might come at him again. Did he have another weapon of some kind? But

Thomas heard footsteps hurrying out of the room, and half a minute later—while Thomas was still frozen with disbelief on the floor—the innkeeper rushed into the room, carrying a lamp that illuminated the area enough for Thomas to be assured that no one else was there.

"What happened?" the innkeeper asked, astonished.

Thomas tried to explain, all the while wishing he were wearing his boots so that he could at least make some attempt to chase down the would-be murderer. But he was surely long gone by now. There were nooks and crannies aplenty in the alleys and alcoves of the city. The assailant would surely never be found—which made the innkeeper's insistence on talking with the police feel completely irrelevant to Thomas. His sole desire was to leave this very minute and get home to make certain everything was all right. The moment he was able to get away, he retrieved his horse from the livery where he'd left it, even though he had to wake up three people in order to do so. He started riding toward Brownlie Manor as quickly as he could possibly manage, wishing with all his soul it wasn't so many hours away. While he rode, his mind replayed over and over what had just happened, as if to convince himself it really *had* happened. He couldn't believe it!

Thomas's fear magnified a hundredfold when he realized someone was following close behind him, and since it was still dark and he'd long ago left the city, he couldn't see through the inky blackness enough to have any idea if it was the danger he feared it might be. He could only hear hoofbeats pounding in steady time with those of his own horse—and growing closer. A shot rang out, and he actually heard the bullet whistle past his ear, a sound he recalled all too well from being on the battlefield. Instinctively he veered off the road and into the trees, figuring he was far better off there than out in the open. Another shot crackled the air, and Thomas felt the sting of a bullet just as he half fell and half dove from his horse onto the ground. Then everything went black.

Chapter Twelve

THE IMPOSTER

RUTH WAS AWAKENED FROM A nap by Selma, whose words shocked Ruth out of her sleepiness like a splash of cold water.

"He's home; your husband is home."

"Oh, my!" Ruth sat up and slipped her feet into her shoes. "He's all right?"

"I saw him with my own eyes," Selma said. "I believe he's in his office. He's been here a good hour or more, but you was sleeping so good and I didn't want to wake you."

"Why did he not wake me himself?" Ruth asked without expecting Selma to have an answer. It just didn't seem like Thomas to not came straight to find her after being gone for ten days.

"I'll watch out for the little one when she wakes up," Selma said.

"Thank you," Ruth called back on her way out of the bedroom door. She ran the length of the halls and down the stairs, imagining—as she had since he left—the moment of being in his arms again. She opened the office door without knocking, surprised to see Thomas going through a drawer in his desk in which she knew his most important papers were kept. The key to unlock the drawer, which was normally tucked beneath some things in a different drawer, was on the desk, which was unusually disheveled, as if he'd been searching frantically for something. In the one or two seconds she had to take in his frenzied manner and the appearance of the room, she concluded that something was terribly wrong. This, added to the fact that he'd not come to find her right away—and that he'd been gone far longer than he'd said he would be, without sending any word—all came together to make her feel a mild panic that was lessened only by the very fact that he was here and alive and well.

"Thomas!" she said, and he looked up. Immediately her panic deepened into a heart-pounding fear and a stark dread in the pit of her stomach. He looked different; something in his eyes was all wrong. As soon as she thought it, his eyes widened with shock, as if he had been completely surprised to see her there.

"Ruth?" he said, and her heart pounded faster. His voice was wrong; his attitude, his bearing. Something was wrong. It was subtle, difficult to define, but it was wrong. She noticed that his clothes were new; they were different. Why would he have purchased entirely new clothing when he usually preferred wearing what was old and comfortable?

"Who were you expecting?" she asked while the handful of seconds since she'd opened the door felt like as many minutes. "I'm your wife," she said as if she needed to convince him. Through the span of another second or two, one part of her mind asked *why* she would instinctively feel the need to convince him. Why? Because his expression told her he didn't know.

Heaven be merciful, she thought and gripped the open door tightly with one hand, as if doing so might keep her upright. Her mind frantically considered the possibilities, with *madness* standing out high on the list. She'd gone mad. She was hallucinating. She was mixing old memories and fears with new ones.

"Of course," he said with a little laugh that sounded more like Thomas. "Forgive me, my dear. I needed to make certain some things were in order, and . . . I got distracted. How are you, sweetheart?"

Sweetheart? Never once had Thomas called her *sweetheart!* But Lucius had! No, it wasn't possible! It couldn't really, truly be possible! Ruth added up all of the evidence, combined with her instincts. What clinched it for her was the way he just stood there. *How are you?* he'd asked. Thomas would have dropped everything and leapt over the furniture if necessary to take her in his arms. No, Thomas would have run upstairs before he'd done anything else and wakened her with a kiss. This wasn't Thomas! It wasn't Thomas and she knew it! But she felt a sense of danger, and instinctively knew she needed to tread carefully.

Ruth felt the need to test him, and at the same time she knew that whatever his reasons for this charade, he must never suspect the most important truth. She doubted he would know the age of a baby without being told, and she didn't want him to add up months and even suspect that he had anything to do with her baby's existence. Since he seemed surprised to see her there, he likely hadn't even known there was a baby. While there were a thousand unanswered questions—the most prominent being *why* he was here instead of Thomas, and *where* was Thomas—in that moment she felt a deep maternal need to protect her child.

"The baby finally smiled while you were gone," she said, knowing Joy had been smiling a great deal for months—and Thomas would have contradicted such a comment.

"That's wonderful, sweetheart," said this man who was here in this house, pretending to be her husband.

Ruth closed the door behind her, knowing as she did so how foolish it was to put herself alone in a room with such a man. "*What* are you doing here?" she demanded.

Lucius looked exaggeratedly innocent, and Ruth impulsively needed absolute proof. She crossed the room and unbuttoned his shirt, even though doing so made her cringe slightly.

"Oh, sweetheart," he said in a seductive tone Thomas never would have used. She pushed his shirt and waistcoat aside and gasped. No scar!

Ruth took a step back and raised her hands as if they'd betrayed her by getting anywhere near him. Her shock was so deep that her mind seemed to demand further proof. Without even thinking, she grabbed his left arm and tore at the cuff, making the button pop off.

"What are you doing?" he snarled, trying to pull his arm away.

"You *know* what I'm doing," she said, recalling well the distinctive mole that Lucius had on his left forearm. But now, in its place, was a hideous burn scar.

"I had a nasty dispute with a fire poker," he said, jerking his arm from her grasp.

"Thomas only left here ten days ago," she snarled and took several steps back. "No burn that severe would heal that quickly.

And apparently you didn't know about the scar on his chest, and you didn't know about *me* being here."

"So, what *are* you doing here?" he asked, almost snarling in a way that made it evident he'd given up his attempts at pretense any longer. "I'm thinking you must have either been terribly in love with me, or at the very least found me extremely attractive. You went out and married a man who looks just like me?"

To hear him talk now made her realize he'd been *trying* to talk like Thomas, but his natural intonations sounded nothing the same. But where would he have learned how Thomas talked? Where he lived? Where his private papers were kept? That a man who looked so much the same even *existed*? And how could it possibly be only some bizarre coincidence that—of all people—*she* would be the one standing here facing Lucius now, fully aware that two men looked so very much like each other? Two things seemed starkly obvious. The first being that Lucius had obviously figured out the possible advantages of his identical resemblance to Thomas, and he was here with the intent of creating mischief of some great proportion. And secondly, Ruth was here—in this house, with this family, fully aware of this man's true identity. She'd like to think that God had placed her in this position to help protect the family of which she'd become a part. And if that was the case, she needed to exert her greatest courage and do everything in her power to protect those she loved.

Forcing back the hurricane of torment she felt brewing inside her at the implications of what this might mean in regard to Thomas, Ruth focused on the moment and stated firmly, "Whatever you are trying to get away with here, I will not let you do it."

"*You*," Lucius snarled, stepping abruptly toward her, "will do or say *nothing* to even imply the truth about who I really am, or I assure you that you will regret it."

Ruth stepped back, clenching her skirt with fists that were attempting to hold all of the fear rushing into her. She was almost believing she could still stand up to him until he added, "If you so much as breathe a hint to *anyone* about this, who knows what might happen to that precious baby of yours?"

"You wouldn't!" she hissed.

"Oh," he lifted a brow, and his eyes betrayed an evil in him that she had once come to know well, "you of all people should know that I *would*! I have worked long and hard to be here now, and I will not leave without what rightfully belongs to me, and *you* are not going to stand in my way. The equation is simple, sweetheart: you stay silent and everyone in this place will stay safe. The choice is entirely up to you."

"You are a heartless fiend!" she declared, trying to keep her voice down while she felt like screaming. He had her and he knew it. She would never do anything to risk the safety of her baby or anyone else here. He might not have known she would be here, but he'd quickly figured out that the most powerful threat to hold against a mother was the well-being of her child.

"I may well be." He chuckled with self-sa'tisfaction. "But given my good fortune of looking like Thomas Fitzbatten, I am now a *very wealthy* heartless fiend."

Ruth found it more difficult to maintain any facade of courage and strength as the horror of the situation began to break past the barriers of shock that had been holding it back. She heard her own breathing become audible as she demanded, "Where is Thomas? What's happened to him?"

"Well," Lucius said as if talking about the weather, "if this is going to work, there couldn't very well be *two* of us, now could there?"

Ruth stumbled backward and fell awkwardly into a chair, gasping for breath. "What have you done to him?" she asked breathlessly.

"I, personally, have done nothing to your precious Thomas. I left that up to one of his old army friends who puts a much higher priority on the profits of bribery than friendship."

"Teddy would never—"

"No, I'm certain you're right. Teddy would never do anything to harm Thomas, but thankfully Teddy is enjoying a very lengthy holiday in France, which created the perfect opportunity to let Thomas believe that Teddy needed his help."

"How in the world . . ." Ruth couldn't finish the question due to the fact that she was barely managing to breathe. While her mind was frantically trying to accept the possibility that Thomas might actually be dead, she realized that Lucius was now bragging about this horrible scheme of his. She fought to keep her emotions subdued and to listen, feeling the need to get as much information as she could. He certainly held power over her in his threat against the safety of her child and others she cared about, but she could never let this go on indefinitely, and she needed all the knowledge she could possibly acquire in order to have any hope of eventually finding a way to wield some power over *him*.

"Imagine my surprise," Lucius said whimsically as he leaned against the desk and folded his arms over his chest, "when one day in London a man stopped me on the street and called me Thomas, and he was astonished to realize that I was *not* Thomas, and I didn't know who he was talking about. I asked him some questions and bought him a drink, and I soon realized he was someone who knew a great deal about this Thomas—having served in the army with him for quite some time—and between us we had a potentially profitable endeavor that was too good to pass up. There was a great deal of work to be done and many questions to be answered, but between us we eventually figured out the details and discovered things I would bet not a single person in this house could even guess." He laughed maniacally as if he reveled in the power of knowing a secret no one else knew, and Ruth felt terrified of what that secret might be.

"I wondered if I could actually get away with it . . . if I could be convincing enough to make these people believe I'm Thomas." He chuckled. "Well, I've done *that*. Even his parents believe I'm their precious son."

"You didn't convince *me*!" Ruth snarled.

"I didn't *know* about you," he said as if that fact made him angry. "But I know better than to think *you* would stand in my way, especially when you have so much to lose."

"I cannot believe that even *you* would do something as atrocious as this!"

"You'd best believe it, sweetheart, because it's happening, and you have great incentive to keep my secrets."

"I cannot even begin to imagine how you . . . did this."

"Well," Lucius went on, unable to resist his natural tendency to brag about his accomplishments, "my new friend had in his possession more than one letter from Teddy Grayson; it was easy enough to find someone who could forge the handwriting for a price. And now, while I pretend to be Thomas Fitzbatten, I will make certain I walk away from here with the fortune I deserve. But don't you worry, sweetheart, I won't be here long. Once I've got what I've come for, I will mysteriously leave and you can go on with your luxurious new life—although the Fitzbattens might have to cut back a bit given the dramatic decrease that's about to take place in their bank accounts and such." He laughed again, while Ruth was so stunned by the horror of it all that she couldn't even make a sound. "But I'm certain you'll still have enough to live better here as a widow than you would have lived anywhere else, and—"

Ruth acted on a sudden surge of grief and terror and anger that pumped energy and strength through her veins, making it possible for her to hurry out of the room and up the stairs, desperately needing to be completely alone before the numbness and shock fully wore off and her true feelings took over. She could feel the threat of something akin to a volcanic emotional eruption as she ran up the stairs, down one hall, around a corner, and down another. She went into what she knew was a long-unused guest room and closed the door, knowing no one would be in this section of the house, no one would hear her, no one would find her. She pressed her back to the door, and the eruption began with sharp gasps of breath and a tangible pain smoldering in the center of her chest. She pressed both hands over the pain and dropped to her knees, unable to remain standing another second.

Ruth heaved with helpless sobbing over the probable death of her husband while at the same time her mind frantically bounced around from one horrible realization to another. She couldn't show any evidence of her grief to anyone. She couldn't breathe a word of suspicion or imply even a hint that anything was wrong. The life of her child depended on it. Her absolute belief that Quin and Yvette should be warned about what was taking place battled with her belief that they would not be capable of pretending this intruder was their son. And if Lucius was not convinced she'd kept his secret, she could never underestimate the lengths he might go to in order to succeed in this sick and loathsome game he was playing.

Ruth prayed fervently while she attempted to expel enough weeping to lessen the pressure in her head and chest. She struggled to regain a measure of composure and forced herself to breathe normally and attempt to appear calm and in control. She reminded herself with renewed horror that she had to pretend she was happy to have her husband back. If she behaved differently, the household would become suspicious.

Steeling herself to play this role perfectly for the sake of those she loved, Ruth returned to her own room, sneaking in quietly in order to have a few minutes to smooth her hair and use some face powder to try to conceal the fact that she'd been crying. She found Selma in the nursery with the baby, thanked her for her help, and sent her away to see to other things. Ruth just wanted to be alone with Joy and hold her close and try to believe that Thomas couldn't really be dead. It seemed impossible, felt impossible. But surely that was just her own disbelief trying to convince her. Wanting something to be true wouldn't necessarily make it that way, and eventually she was going to have to accept that fact. Right now she just had to think about how she was going to get through the rest of the day without creating any suspicion.

That evening at supper, Ruth was astonished to see Lucius behaving very much like Thomas—at least in his general attitude and mannerisms. His parents and the servants didn't seem to even notice that something wasn't right, but then not one of them would have even conceived of the possibility of another man looking and behaving so much like the Thomas they all knew and loved. Surely the idea wouldn't even occur to them, and therefore if anything felt off, they would likely disregard it.

The man pretending to be Ruth's husband smiled at her across the table and told her how lovely she looked. He talked about how good it was to be home and told an elaborate story about the reasons for Teddy summoning him and how he'd been able to help solve the problem, even though it had taken longer than expected. Ruth felt dazed and barely able to remain upright while she couldn't stop wondering what had happened to Thomas. If her husband was truly dead, she couldn't imagine how she would ever survive. She was worried about Quin and Yvette, and everyone on the estate who depended on them. She was worried about Joy. And the whole thing just made her sick to her stomach and a little light-headed.

Unable to bear it any longer, Ruth finally stood and said, "I'm not feeling very well. I think I'll just go up to bed."

"You have been awfully quiet," Quin said.

"Is there anything we can do?" Yvette asked.

"No, thank you. I'm certain I'll be fine. I probably just need some rest."

Ruth moved toward the door, longing to get out of the room and be alone. But Lucius stood and said, "I'll walk up with you, my dear."

Ruth wanted to scream at him; she wanted to scream at Thomas's parents and tell them this man was an evil imposter. But she forced a smile and said, "Oh, that's not necessary. You can—"

"Oh, I insist," Lucius said and put a hand on her back to guide her out of the room.

When they were a safe distance up the hall, she whispered, "Get your hand off of me immediately." He did so, which helped her feel a little less powerless. A new and horrible thought occurred to her, and she added in the same sharp whisper, "You will *not* be sleeping in the same room with me. Pick a guest room and mind your manners if you want me to keep your secret. We'll just tell the servants I'm not sleeping well and it was disturbing *your* sleep."

"Fine," he said, almost as if he would do anything she asked. "Although I confess I am going upstairs with you because I have no idea how to find *my things*, and perhaps you can direct me to a proper guest room. Remember all of the incentive you have to help me make certain everything goes smoothly."

"Extortion? Threats? Blackmail? Oh yes. Great incentive."

"I'm only here to get what should have been mine," he said, which wasn't the first time he'd made such a reference. She wanted to ask what he meant, but her anxious desire to be away from him stifled any such conversation.

Her most pressing question seemed more important. As they started up the stairs, she asked, "What have you done to Thomas? You can't really be so heartless as to kill a man in order to take his place."

"*I* would never do such a thing," he said, which gave her a moment of hope, until he added, "But your beloved's so-called friend who helped make all of this possible assured me he would make certain the real Thomas didn't show up and foil my plan. Exactly how he meant to go about that I can't say."

"You're a fiend," Ruth snarled.

"It's not the first time you've called me that," he said, as if he found the total sum of his cruelty amusing.

"And it won't be the last," she said, grateful that no more conversation took place except for her giving him a few simple instructions on how to summon the servants and what they would expect from him. She guided him to a guest room that would be the most logical for Thomas to occupy if there was any reason for them to spend the night in separate rooms, and even though it made her sick, she took some of Thomas's clothes to him, her only motivation being to avoid any attention that might make Lucius feel the need to carry out any of his threats.

Ruth went to the nursery and took over the care of her baby, and once she and Joy were alone, she wept and held her daughter close, wondering what might become of them now.

* * *

For the next few days, Ruth claimed to not be feeling well and remained in her rooms, where she had contact only with Selma and Liddy, who brought her meals and helped just a little with the baby. She believed she would be better able to carry off the charade if she just remained at a distance from Lucius. The whole thing had her so upset she doubted her own ability to maintain her composure and dignity; therefore, it felt safer for everyone if she just pretended to be ill. Doing so also helped justify her puffy, red eyes that were a result of the seemingly endless tears she cried over the loss of her husband. With every passing hour it became more and more difficult to convince herself that he was coming back.

Yvette came to check on her more than once, and Ruth assured her it was nothing serious but she did feel the need to rest. Given

Yvette's long history of frequently feeling under the weather, she didn't ask for any other explanation. During their conversations, Ruth learned—much to her horror—that Quin and the man Yvette assumed was Thomas were working together to make some changes in the financial management of the estate. Apparently she believed her son had returned—from his time spent with Teddy—full of ideas to make the estate run more efficiently, and Quin—of course—was completely trusting of all that his supposed son was doing, even if he didn't fully understand it. It took all of Ruth's willpower to not tell Yvette the truth, but she knew that eventually Thomas's parents *would* know, and the very thought only made Ruth feel horribly ill.

During one of Yvette's visits, she talked to Ruth about having strange dreams again and rambled for quite some time about how upsetting they could be. And for the first time ever, Yvette told Ruth the content of her recurring nightmare. Long after Yvette had left, Ruth stewed over the entire situation, unable to push away an idea that was as preposterous as it was perfectly logical. She just didn't know what to do about it. For now, she could only muster enough strength to pray and to grieve and to care for her baby.

Ruth eventually realized the only possible hope for ever freeing herself—and her family—from Lucius's evil grasp was for her to obtain as much information as possible. Lucius had easily taken to bragging about his exploits to her in the little time they had talked privately. As much as she loathed the idea of even being in the same room with him, she mustered her courage and strength, determined to be the very best actress possible.

While Yvette was plagued with a recurring nightmare, only Ruth was aware that they were all living in the midst of a very real threat that was so thoroughly haunting and ironic that she doubted any of them would ever recover.

* * *

Thomas could barely recall the reasons why he would be waking up in the woods, in the dark, with his head pounding and plagued with dizziness. His thigh was throbbing, and he reached down to find it sticky with blood, but in the dark he had no idea what that actually meant. He lay there drifting in and out of consciousness until the sky began to lighten. He considered it a miracle that whoever had shot him hadn't come searching for him to make certain the job was finished.

When he was finally able to sit up, he assumed he must have hit his head—very hard—when the bullet that hit him knocked him from his horse. The wound—for all that it hurt—wasn't very deep, and it had stopped bleeding. It appeared that the bullet had only grazed him, which would hopefully make it possible for him to find his way out of here and stay alive. But he had to assume that whoever had been tracking him—and had tried unsuccessfully multiple times to do him in—would be searching this area of the woods, leaving nothing to chance. His assailant surely wouldn't assume Thomas was dead without finding proof of a body.

Praying and trying to think clearly, Thomas removed his cravat and tied it tightly around the wounded leg, mostly to absorb any blood should it start bleeding again. He instinctively moved deeper into the woods, going carefully and quietly, praying with every tentative, limping step, constantly looking in every direction and listening keenly.

Thomas lost track of how long he had wandered in the trees with no sense of direction, with nothing to eat, while growing increasingly weak. When he came upon an obscure little dwelling, he thanked God for what seemed a miracle and prayed that whoever lived there would be inclined to help him rather than turn him away. It occurred to him that his unknown enemy might have found this place first, but he felt desperate, knowing he had no choice but to take the risk.

Thomas knocked at the door, and it was answered by a scraggly looking man near his father's age. Thomas was trying without much success to explain his plight when he lost consciousness. He woke up on a makeshift bed to find a woman—probably this man's wife—offering him some broth.

Thomas felt weak and little hazy while he gratefully accepted the food and listened to this man and his wife arguing as if he weren't there. Through the course of a couple of days, Thomas learned that this man was a gamekeeper on a large estate, and while he considered himself too much of a Christian to turn away someone in need, he wasn't necessarily happy about Thomas being here. However, since Thomas had money to offer them in exchange for food and a place to sleep for a few nights while he got his strength back, the gamekeeper became a little less surly. The gamekeeper's wife was more compassionate, but she offered her kindness to Thomas very quietly, as if she feared that any evidence of it would displease her husband. Thomas found this man's view of being a Christian rather ironic, but he focused his attention on his gratitude for their help. Without it he likely would have starved to death while wandering aimlessly, hopelessly lost in the woods.

Thomas's anxiousness to get home and make certain all was well compelled him to leave, even though he still felt weak. Yet he also felt rather terrified of trying to make his journey, knowing there was someone out there who wanted him dead. While he couldn't begin to comprehend his assailant's motives, he had absolutely no doubt of his vicious intent.

Despite the time spent in the gamekeeper's little home, Thomas never once heard the man's name spoken—or that of his wife. The churlish man simply called her *woman*, and she in return hardly spoke to her husband at all. The gamekeeper grumbled continually, and his wife just listened, as if that was the best way to keep the peace. The man said a great deal *about* Thomas, as if he weren't there, but actually said very little *to* him.

Only when Thomas was getting ready to leave—supplied with some bread and dried fruit by the gamekeeper's caring wife—did the gamekeeper reluctantly mention, "I assume the horse that wandered here the day before you arrived might be yours. You might as well take him."

"Thank you," Thomas said to both the man and his wife, "for everything."

The man grunted while his wife nodded and smiled, as if she might miss his company. Free now of pain, dizziness, and hunger, Thomas was able to follow the gamekeeper's directions and find his way out of the woods and onto a road he recognized. But he knew he needed to stay away from any main roads where he might be seen. With the necessity of traveling so discreetly, Thomas was forced to travel more slowly, managing to acquire food in villages along the way while staying mostly in the woods. He preferred the cover of wooded areas and cursed the openness of long stretches of moors and meadows that offered him nowhere to hide. He felt on edge every waking moment and slept very little, usually on the ground next to stone fences or large trees.

When Thomas finally found himself on Fitzbatten land, he felt far more than simple gratitude; he felt as if the Red Sea had parted on his behalf. He was home! Now he could find his way with no difficulty whatsoever, although his instincts told him he might be in danger here more than anywhere else. If someone *was* trying to kill him and his previous efforts had failed, then his home would be the logical place where his assailant might likely lay in wait for his return.

Thomas waited in a wooded area until it was past two in the morning, knowing it was the most likely time for every person in the household to be asleep. He made his way to a little-used door and knew exactly how to get in and where to find a lamp. He crept quietly with the lamp in his hand, its wick only high enough to barely illuminate his way. He still couldn't fathom that he had to sneak into his own home by cover of darkness because his life was in danger for reasons he couldn't begin to imagine. Not understanding what was happening or why, he feared for the safety of his family as well and refused to take any unnecessary risks.

Thomas wondered in that moment if his family might have reason to believe he was dead. He had lost track of how long he'd been gone, and he had no idea what news might have reached their ears. He had many unanswered questions, and many reasons to feel afraid. But right now he only needed to see Ruth, to be with her, to hold her, to let her know he was safe and alive and well. As he crept up the back stairs—taking each hallway corner with extreme caution—he prayed she would not be terrified by his unexpected appearance in the middle of the night.

Thomas breathed in relief when he arrived undetected at the door of the room where he knew Ruth would be sleeping. He crept into the room and closed the door behind him, hardly making a sound. He waited and listened, relieved even more to hear her gentle, even breathing. He stepped slowly and carefully toward the bed and held the lamp higher, turning up the wick to cast more light upon her beautiful face. She looked like an angel, sleeping with her hair strewn over the pillow.

Fearing she might have good cause to scream when she saw him, he set the lamp on the bedside table and knelt carefully beside the bed. He couldn't recall the last time he'd thought about the fact that the man who had once been so cruel to her had looked so much like him. But he thought of it in that moment, fearing she might wake up and see him and be reminded of horrible events from her past. Telling himself he just had to do it, he gently put a hand over her mouth to prevent her from making any sound, at the same time whispering, "Ruth. Ruth, wake up. It's me, Thomas."

Her eyes flew open in terror, and she responded exactly as he'd feared, trying to push him away while his hand muffled her attempts to scream.

"Ruth, it's me. Don't be afraid. I'm here. I'm all right." She stopped fighting but still looked terrified, and he wondered why. "I'm going to move my hand. I just didn't want you to make a sound that might wake anyone else." She nodded, and he moved his hand. "You thought I was dead?" he asked, attempting to understand why she still looked so afraid.

While he was expecting her to say something and wanting to just hold her in his arms, she leapt from the bed and in one stealthy movement grabbed the fire poker with one hand and the letter opener from the desk with the other. With her weapons poised, she looked at him as if he were the devil himself.

"Ruth?" he said. "It's me. It's Thomas. Forgive me for frightening you. I don't know what you've been told, but . . . I'm here. It's me. It's really me." He took a step toward her, but she raised the fire poker to a more threatening position. He stopped and held up his hands. "I would never hurt you, my darling. What's happened to make you think I would hurt you?"

Ruth looked at what appeared to be her husband standing there in the lamplight and wondered if she was truly going mad. Now that she was fully awake, she had to ask herself if this was Lucius once again, trying cruelly to push her to the edge of insanity, or if she was looking at some ghostly apparition. Then it occurred to her with a rush of wind coming into her lungs that there was another possibility. She recounted all the words he'd said while she'd been too dazed with sleep and too panicked to fully hear them. And she allowed herself to rationally assess his appearance. Lucius was crafty and impeccably deceitful, but he could not have made his hair grow a couple of inches since she had seen him at supper, and his freshly shaven face couldn't have produced days' worth of growth in that same amount of time.

Suddenly weak with relief, Ruth teetered slightly and allowed the fire poker to fall to the floor while she absently set the letter opener back on the desk at her side. "Thomas," she breathed.

"It's me, darling. I swear to you that it's me. I'm not dead. I'm here."

Ruth tentatively stepped toward him while he kept his arms out to his sides in a gesture of surrender. In the lamplight she searched for the love and goodness she had always been able to see in his countenance, qualities that had never been present with Lucius. She gasped when it became readily evident, but standing close enough to touch him, she still had to look up into his eyes for a long moment in order to be certain. "Thomas," she said again, her heart pounding as she comprehended the miracle. He was alive! He was here! She touched his face to be assured that he truly hadn't shaved for days. She touched his hair and his face again while he just watched her and waited, as if he would give her all the time she needed to be certain it was him.

Still unable to fully perceive this as truth, she frantically unfastened the top three buttons of his shirt and pushed it aside, gasping again to see the scar. She knew its every detail by heart. She touched it and laughed while tears stung her eyes. Still needing to be completely certain, she firmly took hold of his left hand and pushed up the cuff that was already unbuttoned. His forearm looked as it always had. No scar. She laughed again as her relief deepened, and with complete certainty that he was indeed her Thomas, she threw herself into his arms, relishing the feel of his tight embrace.

"Oh, Ruth," he murmured near her ear. "My precious Ruth. I feared I would never see you again."

"Oh, I feared it too," she said and took his face into her hands, weeping with joy and relief. He kissed her and that too assured her it was Thomas. As much as she loathed the fact that she had once been kissed by Lucius, she distinctly knew Thomas's kiss. He kissed her again and again, and she had to keep telling herself she wasn't dreaming.

Chapter Thirteen

THE OTHER MOTHER

THOMAS LUXURIATED IN THE RELIEF of having Ruth in his arms, and he became thoroughly caught up in kissing her the way he'd dreamt of doing all the time he'd been away. Then, like a stone being thrown into a still pond, his silent recounting of her reaction to seeing him and her frantic search for evidence that it *was* him assaulted him with ripples of concern and a growing fear. He pulled back and took her by the shoulders.

"Ruth," he said sternly, "why did you doubt that it was me? Why did you need to see the scar? And my arm? Why would you need to see my arm?"

He saw her eyes fill with terror at the same moment he felt her slump within his grasp like a rag doll. He picked her up and carried her to the bed, where he sat beside her. He touched her face to make her look at him and he insisted, "You must tell me. What's happened?"

"He's here, Thomas," she said, her voice quivering.

"What?" he demanded. "Who?"

"Lucius. He's here." She clung to him and wept, her whole body trembling. "He's here, Thomas . . . pretending to be you." Thomas could hardly breathe while he clung to her and listened to what could only be a nightmare unfolding. "By some horrible coincidence he discovered his resemblance to you . . . and he knew about your friendship with Teddy. The letter you received was fabricated . . . forged. You'd already been gone too long and I was so afraid, and then . . . he came. I knew within a minute that it wasn't you, but . . . he threatened me to stay quiet, and—"

"Has he hurt you?" Thomas demanded, looking into her eyes to be certain she told him the truth.

"No," she said firmly. "Not in the way I know you're thinking. He's not laid a hand on me. But he's made it very clear that if I say anything to anyone he will do harm to your parents, or . . ." she sobbed, "the baby."

"Heaven help us," Thomas muttered. "So you must have believed I was dead."

"I wondered. He implied that you were."

"Well, it certainly explains what's been happening to *me.*"

"What *has* been happening to you?" she asked sharply.

"Someone has been trying to kill me," he said, and Ruth put a hand over her mouth. "Even as I say it I can't believe it. I quickly realized something was wrong in regard to the situation with Teddy. He wasn't there; no one had seen him. He's supposedly in France. But things kept happening that put me in danger, and . . . I'll tell you the details another time. I can only say it's truly a miracle I made it here alive. Once I realized that someone wanted me dead, I knew that getting home would not be easy. That's why I came in the middle of the night. I feared something might be amiss here, but I never would have dreamed . . ." He touched her face and hair. "And all this time you thought me dead." Given what he now knew, a brand-new thought occurred to him. "But my parents—"

"Everyone else believes you're alive and well and happily making changes in the management of the estate—especially with the finances."

"No!" Thomas gasped, and he felt light-headed as the scheme all came together clearly in his head. "No, it can't be!"

"I've been so afraid, Thomas. I've wondered if this nightmare would ever end."

"I don't understand how this could happen, Ruth. You told me that he and I look very much the same, but how can my own parents not know the difference? How can all of the servants, most of whom have known me my whole life, *not* know the difference?"

"Thomas," she said and took his hand as if she were about to deliver bad news. He couldn't imagine what might be any worse than what he'd already been told. "I think I know at least part of the reason for that, but I certainly do not have all of the answers, and I can't begin to understand how it might have happened."

"What? What are you talking about?"

"Lucius told me he is here because he rightfully deserves to be."

Thomas scoffed. "Why would he ever believe *that*?"

"And he told me he was adopted, and the father who raised him treated him very poorly, which might perhaps explain why he's such a cruel man."

"Wait, Ruth. What are you trying to say?"

"Thomas," she whimpered, and fresh tears slid down her cheeks, "I think he might be your twin brother."

For a long moment Thomas was too stunned to move or even breathe, then he sprang from the bed and pushed his hands brutally through his hair. "No!" he muttered with clenched fists. "No, Ruth. No! It can't be possible! My parents would have no reason to do something like that. They always wished they could have had more children. There was plenty of money and plenty of help. They *never* would have given away a child. Never!"

"I know that, Thomas," Ruth said with compassion. "I do. And I know this is difficult for you to hear and a great deal for you to take in. I felt the same shock when I first realized the possibility, and I've had time to think it through . . . to consider . . . the facts."

"Facts?" he countered. "You're speculating."

"Thomas." Ruth stood and took hold of his upper arms. "I know this is upsetting; the entire situation is upsetting. But we must get to the truth. We must if we ever hope to put all of this right. Even if the truth might be difficult to hear . . . or understand."

She led him back to the bed and urged him to sit beside her. His shock had subsided enough for him to be able to hear what she had to say, but he could feel a deep turmoil and confusion roiling inside him, just beneath the surface.

"These are the things I absolutely know to be true, Thomas. He looks *exactly* like you. *Exactly*. He's been very cautious around everyone else, but when we've been alone, he's talked freely. It seems he believes I will heed his threat to remain silent and he has no fear of my knowing exactly what he is up to. Apparently he crossed paths with someone who knew you well in the military. This man mistook him for you and started up a conversation about the uncanny resemblance. And apparently this man—whoever he is—was easily convinced to join forces with Lucius in this scheme for him to replace you and therefore take control of all your wealth. This man—I don't know his name—knew a great deal about you; your preferences and personality. He even coached Lucius on your mannerisms and such."

"Unbelievable," Thomas muttered breathlessly, his heart sinking further into turmoil while his mind grew more confused with information that was beyond his ability to grasp.

"Because this man knew your friend Teddy as well, he knew that a letter requesting help on Teddy's behalf was the perfect way to get you away from the estate so they could make the switch."

"And while Lucius is here pretending to be me, one of my so-called friends from days gone by has betrayed me in the worst possible way. For all we know it was he who has been tracking me, trying to do away with me."

"It's possible," Ruth said.

"Or there could be more than just the two men in on it," Thomas speculated.

"Perhaps, but I've gotten the impression that . . . it's just the two of them. He said something about secrets being better kept when shared between two comrades."

"Or when the lives of loved ones are threatened," he said, looking at his wife, wondering what she'd done to deserve being caught up in the middle of this horror.

She looked away and said, "There's something else, Thomas. I understand why you believe that it's impossible for you to have a twin. I know your parents well enough to believe exactly the same. But Thomas"—she looked at him again and tightened her hold on his hand—"what if they never knew?"

"How could that even be possible?" he demanded, barely able to breathe at the very idea.

The tears he saw in Ruth's eyes frightened him, and he steeled himself to hear what else she might say. "After he came back . . .

and he'd said what he did about . . . believing it was his *right* to take over the estate, I spent every waking moment trying to figure out how that could be possible. I couldn't start asking questions or do or say anything even slightly suspicious. He watches me like a vulture when we're in the same room, and he seems to remember everything everybody says. I didn't want to put anyone in danger, so I kept my thoughts to myself, but . . . one morning your mother and I were talking privately, and . . . she told me she'd had that dream again. I have known about her recurring nightmare, but this was the first time she told me *what* she dreams about."

Thomas knew exactly what she meant and suddenly found it difficult to breathe. He wondered why this—more than anything else—would threaten to suffocate him. Perhaps it was this combined with everything else he'd just been told. He put both hands over his chest and lowered his head, gasping for breath. He felt Ruth's hands on his shoulders; he heard her asking if he was all right. But he could only focus on getting three words out of his mouth; three words his mother had used as a title to her recurring dream. It had always seemed strange to all of them, and his father had credited the dream to Yvette's deep desire to have more children when it was medically impossible after Thomas's birth had been so difficult. But now something eerie and unnatural was oozing from Thomas's memories of hearing his mother recount the dream, and the title she'd given it. He finally managed to draw enough breath to mutter, "The missing child."

He looked up at Ruth but kept his hands tightly pressed over his chest. "But . . . how . . ."

"I don't know, exactly, but . . . your mother telling me about the dream seemed an answer to my prayers, even though I couldn't begin to comprehend what it might mean. The next time we were completely alone, I steered the conversation gracefully toward her experience of giving birth to you. She talked about her pregnancy and childbirth the way I've heard many women do. Some of it was amazing; some of it painful. But I just let her reminisce . . . and I listened . . . and I said nothing to even hint at my suspicions; I asked no questions to initiate her response one way or the other."

Thomas felt a growing horror as what he'd believed only minutes ago to be a complete impossibility was starting to feel possible, even if he couldn't put all of the pieces together. But already he saw a certainty on Ruth's face, and he didn't even know what she was going to tell him of his mother's innocent confessions.

"Thomas," Ruth went on, "she spoke of how huge she felt during her pregnancy, of comparing the size of her belly to other women, and she knew it would be a very large baby. But after you were born she commented on how you were smaller than most babies. Both scenarios are the case with twins. Bertie told me as much with all her rambling about her midwife training. And I know what you must be thinking because I thought the same thing: How could a woman give birth to two babies and not know? Your mother says she can hardly remember anything after you were born until sometime the next day. She said she was given something for the pain the moment it was over. And of course your father would not have been in the room."

"You're implying, then," Thomas said, surprised at the calm in his own voice, "that the doctor . . . and . . . or someone else assisting with the birth . . . took one of the babies away . . . without anyone else knowing."

Thomas felt so heavy with shock he could barely see his wife as she said, "Yes, that's what I believe. Of course I have no proof, but . . . it seems . . . the most logical explanation. If Lucius knows he was adopted, and someone believed him to be you . . . he figured it out."

"How can we know for certain?" Thomas asked, still unconvinced, still not wanting to change what he'd believed to be true his entire life.

"I don't know. Your mother told me that both the doctor and the maid who had assisted him are deceased. Perhaps the secret died with them."

"Or perhaps not," Thomas said, his mind drawn abruptly to the other side of this situation—however improbable it seemed. "What of the parents who adopted Lucius? Would they not have any idea where he'd come from?"

"Perhaps," Ruth said. "But since you are here . . . Lucius cannot lay claim to anything that is yours; the truth can be told."

"And how do you think that truth will affect my parents? To be told—to be *shown*—that one of their sons was stolen from them? If it *is* true, I need to *know* it's true. If it *is* true, Ruth, he is my *brother*. And he is the father of your child."

"*Our* child," she corrected scoldingly. "Whatever the truth might be, it does not change what you promised me long before she was born. *You* are her father."

"Does Lucius know?" Thomas asked, perhaps fearing that as much as anything else.

"No!" Ruth said vehemently. "Back when we were together, he was entirely certain that pregnancy could not occur from only one encounter; in fact, he scoffed at my fears, which made me all the more surprised to discover I *was* pregnant. I can assure you I have been a very good actress in regard to protecting our daughter. But then . . . he doesn't actually know the date of her birth, although I doubt he kept track of how long it's been since . . ."

He knew what she meant and he was glad she didn't say it. Going back to the point he'd been making, he said again, "If it's true, I need to know. I need to understand what happened and why. And under the circumstances I can't very well ask my parents, although if what you say is true—and it surely must be—neither of them know."

"Then how will you find out?" she asked as if she feared letting him out of her sight.

"From the people who raised him," he said. "I don't suppose you would know where or how to find them?" She looked as if she didn't want to tell him, and he added, "I have to know, Ruth."

"His father is dead, but . . . back when I believed he was in love with me . . . he spoke of his mother."

"Then I must talk to her," Thomas insisted. "But before I leave I will tell you everything you need to know to ensure that what's rightfully ours remains ours. There are things no one except my father and I could ever know, and Lucius could never question Father about it without giving himself away. I will leave you with all of the leverage and protection you need, my darling, and I will return as soon as I can find this woman and speak with her. If you tell me where to find her, it will surely save a great deal of time."

"But there's someone out there trying to kill you," Ruth protested.

"And I am a trained soldier. Now that I know what's going on, I can take with me what I need to remain more easily hidden and protect myself. I'll be fine. You must trust me."

Ruth sighed and closed her eyes. "I know exactly where you can find her."

"Then I must go," he said, "before anyone sees me." She looked panicked, and he took her face into his hands. "But not yet," he said and kissed her with such consuming fervor that all of the drama surrounding them temporarily faded away.

Ruth looked into his eyes with a desire that mirrored his own. Oh, how he'd missed her! And how grateful he was to have come home to her in spite of all the forces conspiring against them!

"No, you mustn't leave yet," she said and initiated another all-consuming kiss.

* * *

Before Thomas left, Ruth attended to the wound on his thigh, which was already healing. Miraculously, it was not very serious. While she did so he told her more of what had happened, and she couldn't ignore the long list of miracles that had brought him home to her.

Thomas cleaned up a little and put on fresh clothes, burning those he'd come home in, which he figured was the best way to not leave any clues the maids might find to indicate that someone other than the man they believed to be Thomas had been here.

Ruth felt terrified to let him go and told him so more than once, but he promised her he would be very careful, and she felt appeased by the evidence of all he had survived thus far. Surely God would not have kept him alive just to have something awful happen now. But she couldn't disagree with his reasoning in needing to understand all that had happened and put things right.

Before he left, Thomas stood over Joy's crib and watched her sleeping. He pressed a gentle hand over her wispy hair and whispered how very much he'd missed her. He held Ruth tightly for a long moment before he kissed her and told her how he loved her. And then he was gone.

Ruth attempted to get some sleep but found it impossible. She still felt afraid and uncertain, but knowing that Thomas was alive and well had given her new strength and great hope that all of this would soon be over. He had also left her armed with information that would preserve the estate and easily prove to his parents that Lucius was not who they believed him to be. She preferred, however, that Thomas would return quickly and be the one to put everything right. For now, she only had to pretend for a little while longer.

* * *

Thomas was grateful for his experience and training in the military that had aided him in being able to get home safely, and that now helped him as he went in search of the woman who had raised his supposed twin brother. Now that he was properly armed and had all he needed in his saddlebags, he felt more confident in being able to travel discreetly and with haste.

While he rode, Thomas mentally rehearsed all that had happened and everything Ruth had told him. He still felt very much in shock and completely horrified to think of this man living in his house and fooling even his own parents about his identity. The thought made him sick. On the other hand, learning of the possibility that he might have a brother was so overwhelming that it made his head hurt.

After less than a day's travel—stopping in a wooded area to get some rest—Thomas slowed his horse as the little house that was his destination came into view. He approached with trepidation as a new thought occurred to him. If Lucius was indeed his twin brother, then it was only a tiny twist of fate that had left him to be raised with an abundance of love and wealth. What he was seeing before him could have been his own life. The woman he was seeking out might have become the only mother he would have ever known.

As he rode closer, it became regretfully evident that the house was in sorry shape. He could see a haphazardly patched roof, peeling paint, and a broken window with boards nailed across the opening. The entire structure was overgrown with weeds, with no flower or pleasing piece of foliage in sight. He wondered if the woman still lived here. What if she had died since Ruth had known of her whereabouts? Or what if she'd left? Would he ever find her? The thought frightened him. He didn't know how to face his parents without having some answers to give them. He had prayed nearly every moment of his journey here to know how to put all of this right. He had much yet to figure out, but first and foremost he needed answers, and there was no one but the woman who had raised Lucius who might have them.

Thomas dismounted and tied his horse's reins to a low-hanging branch. He looked around and knocked at the door three times without getting a response. He walked around the house, already feeling his disappointment settling in. But as he turned the corner he saw a woman some distance away, bent over and pulling weeds in what appeared to be a small vegetable garden. His heart quickened and he walked closer, calling "Hello" as he approached.

The woman turned, startled. He doubted she received many visitors out here. He then had several questions answered within the breadth of a second. "Lucius!" she gasped, and her eyes widened with unmistakable fear. Was the woman afraid of her own son?

"No," he said and made no attempt to move closer, recalling how Ruth had reacted when she had believed he was Lucius. "I'm not Lucius."

The woman stepped closer, and Thomas couldn't help but notice the deep lines in her face and the life-worn look of her eyes. Her clothing was meager. Her gray hair was thin and haphazardly tied back from her face with a ribbon.

Thomas knew he should say something else; he should explain himself. But he was mesmerized with imagining how his life might have been. She startled him from his thoughts when she said, "I've wondered if this day would come."

Thomas considered what that meant, not as surprised as he thought he would be. He found it remarkable how much he had adjusted to the idea so quickly. "Then you knew," he said, "that he had a brother . . . a twin."

"Yes, I knew," she said, then added with kindness, "but it's evident that you didn't."

"No, I didn't . . . until yesterday."

"You look a little pale, young man," she said and put a gentle hand on his arm. "Why don't we go inside and have a cup of tea?"

"That's very kind, thank you," he said, not only wanting to sit down and get out of the sun but also, more importantly, wanting to glean everything from this woman that he possibly could.

Inside, the house was dark and dingy and in as poor a condition as the outside. And yet it looked surprisingly clean, and he noticed a great many books. She asked him to sit down next to the table in the tiny kitchen. He did so, then noticed she was having trouble lighting the stove to heat the water in the kettle.

"Here, let me," he said, coming to her side. He lit the stove and blew out the match, then found her staring at him. He didn't even know her name, and she could have been his mother.

"It's easy to see you're not him," she said.

"How is that? I've never met him personally, but I'm told we are identical."

"There's a kindness in your way that he never had; well, not since he was a boy. I daresay his father beat it out of him."

Thomas winced inwardly, marveling at the fate that had left him to be raised by a kind and good man, while his brother had apparently endured unspeakable cruelty. It didn't make him feel any less loathing for the criminal and heinous acts Lucius had committed; however, he certainly felt compassion while contemplating his brother's unfortunate upbringing. Perhaps he could begin to understand why a man might grow up to be so cruel and selfish.

With the water in the kettle heating, the woman sat down, and Thomas sat across from her. Not knowing what to say, he was glad when she just started talking. "I don't know how you found me, but I assume you came looking for answers, and I'm certain you have the right to know—although I'm not sure I know much. I can tell you that I gave everything I had to love that child. When I took him on as my own, I loved him with all the love a mother has to give. I tried. I know in my heart I tried. But I'd married a man who had hidden his true nature from me until he had me wed and bound to spend my life seeing to his needs. He insisted we needed a son, that he couldn't do his work without a son at his side, that the family name had to be carried on. And after a couple of years it became evident I couldn't give him a child. He told me he knew of a way for us to get a child but wouldn't tell me how. I felt afraid of what he might do, knowing his lack of integrity. Months went by and I tried not to think about it. Then one night, with no warning, he went out to the pub—or so he told me—and didn't come home until very late. And he had a baby with him. It was so newly born that it hadn't even been bathed." She shook her head and closed her eyes. "I was worried about whose child it was . . . who he belonged to. My husband informed me that the baby was a twin and the parents didn't know they'd had more than one son because the mother had not been doing well during the delivery. He said the money we had put away couldn't have bought us anything finer. He bragged of how our son had aristocratic blood and would grow up fine because of that, as if nothing else might have an influence on him for good or ill. But I'm absolutely certain he didn't know where Lucius had come from; not the identity of the family, or where they lived. We never would have known how to find you, which I always thought was best, knowing my husband's lack of scruples. I can only imagine what kind of scheming he might have gotten up to if he *had* known."

The woman sighed heavily, and her eyes had a distant look. "And Lucius became very much like him." She let out a smaller sigh that betrayed deep sadness. "I often wondered why my husband had been so keen on wanting a son, when it turned out the only kind of father he knew how to be was a cruel one. But that's the way of things, I suppose. If a man wants a son in order to carry on his legacy or some such thing, my husband certainly accomplished that. Lucius turned out to be so much like his father, if not worse. I do believe it's gone on for generations in that family. And I learned long ago there was no way to find any sense in my husband's way of thinking."

The water in the kettle started to boil, and she stood to gather the makings for tea. Thomas had been told that Lucius's father was dead, but he still asked, "Your husband has died?"

"Yes, praise heaven. All of his drinking took him to an early grave. It's the best thing that ever happened to me."

She sat back down and poured tea into mismatched cups. "My name is Abigail, in case you're wondering. We skipped past a proper introduction. I prefer to avoid the surname. It never brought me any good."

"I'm Thomas," he said and cradled the warm teacup in his hands.

Abigail sighed and continued her story without any prompting. "I think it was about the time Lucius became taller than me that I finally resigned myself to accept that no amount of love from me would ever undo the damage his father had done. I just did my cooking and housekeeping and kept out of their way as much as I could, glad when Lucius left to join the navy, and even more glad when my husband passed."

"Do you ever see Lucius?" Thomas asked.

"He's been home a handful of times since he became a man; not one visit has had any pleasantry, and I was always glad to see him leave." She shook her head. "It's a terrible way for a mother to feel, but that's the truth of it." Abigail looked up at Thomas. "And I suspect he must be causing some kind of trouble for you now. I can't think of any other reason you'd come looking for *me.*"

Thomas took a sip of tea and cleared his throat. "He is currently living in my home and pretending to be me, and since he has apparently—by some sick twist of fate—become friends with someone I knew well during my military days, he has learned enough about me to pull it off. He has everyone fooled except my wife, who is terrified of the danger he might pose to my family."

Abigail looked stunned, and again she shook her head. "I thought I'd heard it all. But it sounds like something he would do." She reached across the table and put her aging hand over his. Her touch warmed him, and he took hold of her fingers. Noting how old she looked, Thomas wondered if she was truly much older than his own mother, or if the difficulty of her life had aged her. Perhaps both.

By the way she gazed at him, he felt certain she was sharing his thoughts. But she said, "I'm so sorry for what he's put you and your family through. If there is anything I can do to help make it right . . ."

Thomas was more grateful for her offer and her kindness than he could say. At the moment he was more preoccupied with a different thought. "You could have been *my* mother. And I wonder how *I* might have turned out if I'd been raised by a father so heartless and cruel."

Abigail leaned as far over the table as she could manage and still remain seated. "There is something you *must* know, my boy. And I know it to be true because my husband grumbled about it many a time, as if we'd been cheated out of something, even though—as far as I knew—he had no way of knowing where Lucius had come from. I could never understand such thinking. Never." She shook her head.

"What must I know?" he asked.

"You were born first. By all religious traditions and the law, the birthright of your family is yours. I was told the doctor made certain of that."

Thomas had not even wondered about such a thing, but now that he knew, he felt deeply comforted. It made a difference that he believed would fully sink in, given more time. But it also brought up another point. "So, the doctor was responsible. It was he who stole a child from my parents and sold it."

Abigail sighed. "That's how I understand it. I'm not even sure how my husband knew him, but he did. And he was told that only one other person knew the truth, and she'd been sorely threatened into secrecy."

It was now Thomas who sighed. "As I understand it, the doctor and the maid who assisted him are both now deceased."

"Then God will see justice met," Abigail said and took a sip of her tea.

"And what of justice here in this world? There are no words to describe the hatred I feel for a man who I now realize is my brother. What he has done . . . what he is doing . . . is unconscionable. Yet who am I to judge how he must feel . . . knowing that he was stolen and sold to be raised with such cruelty in spite of all the love you tried to give him?"

"No amount of pain makes it right for a person to pass pain on to others."

"I agree wholeheartedly. What he is doing is criminal, but my parents do not even know of his existence. I can prove my own identity easily enough. There are things I know that Lucius could never know, things that would immediately prove to my parents who I am. But . . . the complications; the . . . impact."

"If I may offer an opinion . . . In spite of how difficult it might be to learn the truth, in the end I believe truth brings peace. If I were in your mother's place, I would want to know. Perhaps a part of her already knows something's not right."

The missing child he thought. "Perhaps."

Abigail insisted he stay for lunch, and Thomas insisted that he help her prepare it. By the time they'd eaten and cleaned up their meal, he felt instinctively at peace over saying, "Abigail, come home with me."

She looked only a little surprised. "If you need me to help prove the truth of the situation, I'm happy to do all I can, but I—"

"I *do* need your help," he said, "but I'm not asking you to come with me for that reason alone. I'm asking you to come and live in our home." She put a hand over her heart and was apparently unable to speak. "What do you have here? Who? Do you have friends nearby? People who help care for you? Who would miss you? If that's the case, just say so. I can help make certain your needs are met even if you choose to stay. But if you *don't* want to stay . . . come with me."

Abigail moved unsteadily to a chair and sat down. Thomas scooted a chair beside her and put an arm around her shoulders. "Talk to me, Abigail. Talk to me as if I'm your son." She looked up at him in puzzled wonder. "Can I not in some small way be a son to you and help care for you? Please . . . tell me the truth about your situation here."

Tears rose in her eyes before she looked down. "There is no one, nothing. My husband never allowed me to have friends . . . or go to church. I feel as if I'm just . . . biding my time until I leave this world. But," she looked up at him, "how can I be a burden to *you*? How can you . . ."

"You would be no burden, I can assure you."

"But . . . you hardly know me. How can you know I'm not going to be difficult and cause you trouble?"

"How do you know I'm as kind as you seem to believe? How is it you have trusted me enough to invite me into your home and tell me your darkest secrets?"

Her expression told him she had perceived his point, but he added for good measure, "Sometimes I believe God brings people together—even in the strangest ways—so they can enrich each other's lives. But we have to be careful not to let such opportunities slip away." He took her hand and kissed it. "My dear Abigail, come home with me. We will try our best to make things right with my brother, and after that you may work in the garden if you choose, or you may help in the kitchen if it suits you. I will give you your very own sitting room, and you may sit there all day with your feet up and read. We have so many books in our library that no one could read through them in a lifetime." He saw her eyes light up, and he added with a touch of humor, "Or you may live out your days making a nuisance of yourself, and we will all politely ignore you and make sure you have plenty to eat, a comfortable room, and a warm bed in which to sleep." He paused to give her a moment to take in his offer but added earnestly, "Come home with me. Don't let me spend my life thinking of you here alone and wondering if you are all right."

"If you're certain," she said, and the light in her eyes sparkled with the moisture of tears.

"Absolutely. If some time passes and you change your mind, we can make other arrangements; but it's my wish to see that you're cared for."

"You surely got the best of whatever Lucius got the worst of."

"And do you think our personalities have not been impacted by our upbringing?" he asked, surprised by how the words almost choked him. He knew there was grief bubbling inside of him, but he called forward all of his discipline to keep it in check for now.

Thomas left Abigail with the promise that he would return in the morning about nine o'clock with a carriage and they would take whatever belongings she wanted to bring along. He asked if he should acquire some trunks, but she said there was nothing she wanted to take that wouldn't fit in the bag she already had. "I've read all the books I own more than once, and there's little else of value."

Thomas traveled away from Abigail's home vigilantly, all his senses on high alert. He went to the closest village, where he got a room at an inn, using a false name. That night, alone in his room,

Thomas wanted to cry like a child. But tears wouldn't come. He only felt heavy with a numb shock that wouldn't allow all his mind had learned to get anywhere near his ability to feel. He managed to get some sleep, deeply comforted by the thought of being able to help Abigail. Her life had been filled with pain and disappointment; she deserved something better. He hoped she could be happy at Brownlie Manor. He wondered how Ruth and the baby were doing but didn't feel excessively worried about anything happening to them. He knew Lucius's goal was to maintain his charade, and Ruth was giving him no reason to believe she wouldn't protect his secret. But Thomas felt deeply worried about his parents. He wondered if they had any suspicions at all that the man living in their home and eating at their table was not the son they had raised. If they did, he hoped they would keep quiet about it. Either way, upon his return they were in for an enormous shock, and he feared what it might do to them—especially to his mother.

The following morning Thomas made a conscious decision *not* to shave. If Lucius was shaving every day—as Ruth had told him he was—then having the beginnings of a beard on his face would be an easy way to distinguish them from each other at a glance. The very thought of that necessity knotted his stomach.

While eating breakfast, Thomas again recounted his worries for his loved ones before considering again the danger *he* might be in. He'd been extremely careful, but it occurred to him that this mysterious friend of Lucius's would know very well where Abigail lived. He felt a sudden urgency to get to her and rescue her right away, but he also felt the need to take some extra precautions.

It wasn't yet eight-thirty when the hired carriage came to a halt in front of Abigail's home and Thomas got out. He looked around, heeding his instincts, and went cautiously to the door. The loaded pistol he carried tucked into the back of his breeches beneath his coat was somewhat of a comfort. He prayed he would never have to use it.

Thomas knocked at the door and immediately called, "Abigail. It's me, Thomas. I'm a bit early, but—"

"Come in," he heard her call, and he opened the door and stepped inside. He saw her standing across the room with her back to him, and the hair at the back of his neck prickled. Before he could think how to ask if she was all right, she turned and shouted, "Run, Thomas! Run!"

Thomas heard a pistol cock behind him and wondered if it was too late to run. "I wouldn't do that if I were you," he heard a man say in a voice that was indeed familiar. *Albert Baldwin.* Thomas quickly recounted memories of all the time they'd spent together defending each other's lives regularly and sharing what he'd believed was sincere friendship. But Baldwin had not only sold him out to Lucius, he had been trying to kill him—or so it seemed.

Thomas met Abigail's eyes and tried to silently assure her that everything would be all right. But she was staring wide-eyed and terrified at the man holding the gun. Thomas attempted to turn and face Baldwin, perhaps needing to see for himself that a man he'd once trusted with his life was indeed holding him at gunpoint. Or perhaps he hoped that if he could look him in the eye, he could convince him to stop this madness.

But Baldwin threatened hotly, "Don't move! Don't turn around!"

"I'm not moving," Thomas said, keeping his hands high and clearly visible while trying to figure out how he might reach for the gun hidden beneath his coat without getting himself shot. "But let Abigail go. This has nothing to do with her."

"No one is going anywhere," Baldwin said. "Funny thing how I came here because her *son* asked me to take care of some business on his behalf, and I arrived yesterday to see a horse outside and wondered who might have come to pay her a visit. Imagine my astonishment—and my good fortune—to realize it was *you*. I have no idea how you walked out of those woods alive, because I saw you fall off the horse after I shot you, and I saw you dead on the ground."

Thomas lifted his face slightly toward heaven and silently thanked God that Albert Baldwin didn't know how to tell the difference between an unconscious man and a dead one. Thomas's horrible bump on the head had apparently been a life-saving miracle.

"Obviously, I should have been more thorough," Baldwin said. "Lucky for me, fate seems to be on my side." He chuckled maliciously. "And I can make certain the job gets done this time."

Knowing what he knew that Baldwin *didn't* know, Thomas took advantage of the opportunity to get information he could have gotten from no one else. "So that was the plan, Baldwin? Betray an old friend because you stumbled upon a seemingly impossible secret? Kill me for the sake of profit?"

"Sorry, mate," Baldwin said as if he'd just beat him at a hand of poker. "It was just too big of a temptation to pass up. But enough chatting. I must finish my business and be on my way."

Thomas heard Baldwin move, if only from the rustle of his clothing. He saw Abigail's expression become more terrified, and he knew that Baldwin was about to shoot him.

"Abigail, get down!" Thomas shouted at the same moment he dropped to the floor, reaching for his pistol. In the same second he heard a gunshot and wondered desperately if his preparations had worked in their favor—or against them. He heard Abigail cry out, followed by footsteps approaching him. He rolled abruptly onto his back, pointing the gun upward, only to groan with relief to see one of the police officers who had come with him in the carriage.

"Oh, praise heaven!" Thomas said as the officer held out a hand to help Thomas to his feet. It was then he saw the man on the floor who had clearly been shot by the other officer, who was standing near the door.

"He was about to shoot you in the back," the police officer informed Thomas.

Abigail ran to Thomas as if they'd known each other a lifetime. "Oh, you're all right," she muttered through a surge of tears. "I feared he would kill you."

"I'm fine," he assured her before he looked at her face. "But you're not!"

"Oh, I've had worse," she insisted, touching the nasty bruise on her cheek.

"Did he do this to you?" Thomas asked, and she nodded.

Thomas turned as one of the officers asked him, "Do you know this man, Mr. Fitzbatten?"

The face of the man was heavily bearded, and the clothes and hair were scruffy, but Thomas unmistakably knew him. It was indeed

Albert Baldwin. They had been part of the same regiment; they'd fought together, often side by side, for well over a year. And now this man had betrayed him in ways Thomas couldn't even think about right now or he would surely lose any hope of composure. This so-called friend had been trying to kill him for weeks now, all the while conspiring with Lucius to do away with him and take all that was his. And now he had been intending to shoot Thomas in the back, using Abigail as bait—and hurting her in the process. Suddenly, Thomas felt so sick he had to rush outside and into the trees, where he lost his breakfast and heaved for several minutes after his stomach was empty. He followed the sound of running water and knelt beside a small stream, splashing water onto his face and rinsing out his mouth. He then bowed his head in prayer and thanked God for what he could see now was clear guidance that had led him to convince two police officers to accompany him. The local police were well aware of the reputation of Abigail's son, but it had taken some time to convince them that he was *not* Lucius and that his intent was to help Abigail. They had finally given in to the logic that no man wanting to do someone harm would come to the police for help. And now the men who had come with him, waiting discreetly in the carriage until Thomas had entered the house, had saved his life, and perhaps Abigail's, as well.

Having expressed his gratitude to God, Thomas hastened to return to the house to be certain of Abigail's well-being. This had obviously been a traumatic morning for her. He walked through the open door of the house to find one officer examining Baldwin's body, as if searching for evidence, and the other officer seated with Abigail, asking her questions and jotting down notes. Thomas listened as she explained how she had stepped outside earlier that morning to get some water from a pump near her back door when a man had come from behind the house and struck her in the face, knocking her briefly unconscious. She had awakened inside her home with her hands tied; and Baldwin had threatened her with dire consequences if she failed to behave normally when Mr. Fitzbatten arrived. Thomas was wondering how Baldwin had known he would be returning; however, he didn't have long to wonder when Abigail explained that she'd been told that Thomas had been discreetly followed. The perpetrator had known that Thomas had hired a carriage and would be coming back here this morning. Obviously Thomas hadn't been nearly as careful as he had thought.

"It is astonishing beyond belief," Thomas said, alerting Abigail and the officer to his presence.

"It is indeed, sir," the officer said. "Downright disturbing the things some people will do."

Thomas didn't envy the occupation of upholding the law. Serving as a soldier had exposed him to enough depravity to last three lifetimes. He couldn't imagine being exposed to crime and its victims on a regular basis.

When the police told Abigail that she was free to go, the officers agreed that one of them would ride back into town in the carriage with Thomas and Abigail to acquire assistance, while the other remained with the body. Later, another officer would return to retrieve his partner as well as Baldwin's body.

Thomas helped Abigail gather her things, which had been mostly packed the previous evening. Now that a man had been shot there after assaulting her, she was even more anxious and relieved to vacate her rotting and dilapidated home.

Before taking her things out to the carriage, Thomas paused to put his hand over Abigail's and ask, "Are you certain you're all right? I'm sure your head must be hurting, and you must have had quite a scare. I don't want you to—"

"I'm fine, Thomas," she said while contradictory tears brimmed in her eyes. "But I am very glad to be leaving this place."

"Then let's hurry along," he said, suddenly anxious to get home and be certain his family was safe and well. Now that he'd gotten everything he'd come for—and more—he was anxious and ready to put all of this behind him.

Chapter Fourteen

MIRROR IMAGE

THOMAS WAS GLAD TO BE able to leave the ugly scene at Abigail's home behind and to be assured by the driver of the hired coach that he could have them at Brownlie Manor by evening if they rested briefly at one of his usual stops to change horses. Since Thomas preferred arriving after dark to heighten the likelihood of remaining safely undetected, the timing was perfect. There were a couple of places he needed to stop first once he got closer to home, knowing he needed a plan in place and some assistance from the law. Having police officers accompany him this morning had proved to be an invaluable decision. He felt the same precaution was in order as he returned home to confront the man he now knew was his brother. And if everything went well, he could get there while the family was at dinner. That was the one time of day when Thomas knew where almost everyone in the household was likely to be.

During the journey, he was able to put his plan more fully into place in his mind, but when thinking about it too long only began to make him agitated, he was glad for Abigail's company and the opportunity to get to know her better. And he felt more and more at peace over his decision to bring her home with him. In a house the size of Brownlie Manor—with so much abundance to go around— he felt certain it was only right and proper to see her cared for. In a strange and deeply ironic way, she was like a part of the family. And he would rest easier knowing she would be able to live what was left of her life without fear or depravation. She had already known far too much of that.

When the carriage finally arrived at the manor—along with its extra passengers—Thomas had the driver take it around to a rear entrance where wagons came to deliver food and supplies that were taken into the cellars and pantries near the kitchen. Thomas went carefully and quietly to the door and opened it just a little, listening enough to hear the distant bustle of activity in the kitchen. He peered inside and saw no one, so he hurriedly motioned those who were with him to come inside and go down a side hall in the direction he was pointing. He guided everyone into a pantry that had been built to help manage enormous amounts of food used for very large social gatherings—and since gatherings of such magnitude rarely happened at Brownlie Manor, he knew no one would come into this room on an average evening. With most of his little crew safely tucked away there with all they needed, Thomas went with one of the accompanying police officers around a corner, where he peered carefully into a partially opened door to see exactly what he'd hoped for. Dawson was seated at his desk—alone. It was typical of him to be here while the family had supper so he could be easily found if a problem arose. But he would have his own supper later in the kitchen with the majority of the servants.

Thomas slipped into the room with the officer and closed the door before Dawson even looked up, understandably astonished. Before Dawson could speak, Thomas hurried to say what he'd prepared and memorized, knowing he had to convince Dawson very quickly of the situation in order to get his cooperation.

"Don't speak," Thomas said as Dawson came to his feet, his expression showing a confusion that bordered on fear. "Just listen for one minute. I know this is very strange, because I'm guessing that a clean-shaven version of me is sitting in the dining room right now. It's a very long story, Dawson, and I don't have time to give you all the details right now. But you must trust me. That man is not the Thomas you have seen grow up here in the manor. He is my twin brother, who was deceitfully taken away the night of our birth without our mother's knowledge."

Dawson gasped, and his eyes widened, but he remained quiet, willing to listen as Thomas had asked.

"My . . . brother . . . discovered the truth, and this has all been a scheme to have me killed and to take over the wealth of the estate. It is truly a miracle that I am alive and here now, Dawson, and I need your help to put things right. Given the fact that you now know there is a man who looks exactly like me, I need you to absolutely know that the man you're talking to now is the Thomas you've always known. Ask me anything. Anything."

Dawson took a long look at the police officer standing at Thomas's shoulder, as if to accept the implication of Thomas feeling the need to take such a precaution. He was thoughtful a long moment before he said to Thomas, "The name of your first horse."

"Buck," Thomas answered.

"The reason you needed a doctor when you were eleven."

"I tripped while running in my father's study and got a nasty gash on the top of my head that needed stitching."

"The serious illness you contracted as a child that nearly killed you."

Thomas felt confused but stated the truth. "That never happened."

Dawson drew a deep breath. "It *is* you," he said. "And I must say I'm deeply relieved because I've been wondering what on earth was wrong with you; you haven't seemed at all like yourself."

"I guess he *wasn't* himself," the officer said with a little chuckle, but neither Thomas nor Dawson responded with any humor.

"This is Officer Norton," Thomas said, ignoring the officer's comment. "There are two other officers down the hall in the unused pantry—along with a woman I've brought with me; I will tell you all about her reasons for being here later. Is the family still at dinner?"

"Yes." Dawson glanced at the clock on the wall. He kept the timing of such things very accurately. "I estimate they'll be going to the parlor for coffee in ten or fifteen minutes."

"Perfect!" Thomas said. So far so good. "Right now we are going to the hallway outside of the dining room, and you are going to ask my father if he could come out; tell him you have a small matter that's come up with one of the tenant farmers, and you simply need some instructions on how to deal with it. You are going to be completely normal and calm, as if nothing is out of the ordinary, and you are not even going to glance in the direction of the man pretending to be me. Can you do that?"

"I certainly can!" Dawson declared as if he were ready to go into battle to defend all that mattered to him.

"Of course you can," Thomas said. "That's why I knew I could come to you; I knew you were the right person to help me. Now, after I've finished talking with my father—and we can all hope the shock doesn't undo him—I want you to come back to the pantry and get the people I've left there and take them to a hallway near the parlor without anyone seeing you. After my father knows the truth and goes back into the dining room, he's going to suggest everyone go to the parlor for coffee, and that's where I will make my appearance. If you listen at the door, you will know when it's right to let them come in. Officer Norton will stay with me. Does all of that make sense, Dawson? Do you know what to do?"

"Yes, sir. I know what to do." His eyes narrowed and he asked, "Does Ruth know?"

Thomas said what seemed obvious, which was something that would only further prove that he was the real Thomas. "That's the first time I've heard you not call her Ruthie." Dawson nodded and showed a hint of a smile, as if he'd been testing him. "Yes, she knows," said Thomas. "We spoke a couple of nights ago. She's known since he arrived that it wasn't me, but he's threatened her into keeping quiet. Let's hope and pray we can all get through what needs to be done without anyone getting hurt."

"Yes indeed, sir," Dawson said and opened the door to peer out into the hall and make certain it was empty. Again, Thomas could hear a great deal of noise coming from the kitchen, but the servants would use an adjacent hallway to take things back and forth to the dining room.

The three men moved stealthily toward their destination, which was a door that led to the dining room from a hallway the servants wouldn't use. They discussed in greater detail the plan and exactly what Dawson needed to do and say. Thomas's heart was pounding as they came to the door. Dawson paused, met Thomas's eyes firmly, and took a deep breath before he opened the door and went in.

Thomas could hear Dawson say, "Begging your pardon. I do apologize for interrupting, but there is a small problem with one of the tenant farmers, and I wonder if I might speak with Lord Arrington for just a moment on how he would like me to handle the situation."

"Of course, of course," Thomas heard his father say.

Thomas eased back and into an adjacent hallway that was only dimly lit. Officer Norton shadowed his every move and hovered close to him, as they'd previously agreed. His job was simply to keep Thomas—and everyone around him—safe. The other officers would be nearby before Thomas made any declarations. He was so nervous at the prospect of actually confronting his brother face-to-face that he couldn't even think about it. For now, he needed to deal with telling his father something too horrible for any parent to comprehend. And then he had to dread the fact that his mother would soon have to know the truth as well.

After hearing the dining-room door close, Thomas hovered in the shadowy hallway where he could see Dawson and his father speaking. He had to remind himself to keep breathing as Dawson said gravely, "My lord, there is something terribly amiss that I must prepare you to hear, which has nothing to do with a tenant farmer. I ask that you prepare yourself for a shock, and perhaps it would be best if you sit down." He motioned toward a nearby chair.

"I daresay you're actually frightening me, Dawson," Quin said, and Thomas knew his father was not a man easily frightened.

Quin sat in a chair not far from where Thomas and Norton were remaining in the shadows. In order to keep watch, just as Thomas had asked him to do, Dawson remained standing where the two hallways intersected. Thomas stepped out of the shadows, which startled Quin, but his eyes widened and his mouth dropped open before he could speak. He made no effort to stand, as if he were momentarily incapable of doing so.

"Hello, Father," Thomas said, knowing he needed to speak quickly. "There is a great deal I need to tell you without much time to say it. I ask you to remain composed and hear me out. I know you're wondering how it's possible that you just left the dining room where

I am apparently sitting, and yet here I stand, looking very different. I have discovered a horrible truth, which is at this very moment putting us all in danger. The man in the other room is not the son you raised, Father, but he *is* your son. He is my twin brother." Quin gasped and put a hand over his chest, but Thomas didn't give him time to speak. "He was stolen by the doctor the night of our birth, and raised by a good and loving mother, but also a cruel and harsh father. That man is dead, and the woman is here with me now."

Thomas saw a vague glimmer of moisture in his father's eyes as it was apparently sinking in that he had *two* sons and that one of them had been maliciously taken away. But Thomas knew they couldn't stop to feel all of that now.

"Father," he said, sitting in the chair beside Quin and placing a hand on his arm, "remember how you taught me there are times when a man has to remain calm and in perfect control when faced with difficult circumstances, and at a later time the necessary emotions can be felt. This is one of those times. I need you to remain perfectly composed in spite of what you are learning, because we have a very minimal amount of time to solve this problem." He motioned toward Norton. "I have brought the police with me; there are two other officers who will come to the parlor shortly. Before we go any further, I want you to be absolutely certain that *I* am the son you raised. I'm the one who knows your father told you that the secret of a long life is to have a good heart, but you don't speak of it often because you want to regard it as a secret. I'm the one you took hunting when I was thirteen, and I almost shot my own foot while bumbling with the rifle, and I had a nasty fall. And you told me it was all right for a man to cry when he was afraid or sad, as long as he maintained his dignity. I'm the son who knows how you almost cut off your finger chopping wood when you were a child, and I'm the one who knows that when you made the decision to marry Mother, you were so afraid she'd turn down your proposal that it took you nearly a month to work up the courage to ask for her hand."

Thomas saw the moisture in his father's eyes increase—if only a little. Quin nodded and said, "Only my Thomas would know such things." He gasped as if struggling to breathe. "But that means . . . the

man who has been here . . . for how long? Pretending to be you? He's
. . . He's . . . what, Thomas? Who? I don't understand."

"There will be time to let it all settle in and to talk through all
of the facts I've learned. Right now you only need to know that he
discovered my existence when someone I served with in the army—
and whom I considered to be a friend—thought that Lucius was me.
The two of them concocted this scheme. They lured me away with
a forged letter, and my so-called friend has been trying to kill me.
Lucius—my brother—is pretending to be me in order to take control
of the estate with all its wealth. Have you not noticed his newfound
interest in our accounts and financial matters?"

"Good heavens!" Quin muttered breathlessly.

"The important thing right now is to make the distinction
between the two of us clear and get him out of here—for all our
sakes. I need you to go back in there and behave as if everything is
completely normal. He will be watching very closely for any hint of
something feeling even the tiniest bit abnormal. Do you understand?"

"Does Ruth know?"

"She does," Thomas said. "She's known all along, but he
threatened her to keep quiet."

"Threatened her with what?" Quin sounded incensed. But
Thomas far preferred that his father feel anger right now as opposed
to all the other things he would inevitably feel when all of this fully
settled in.

"The baby's safety . . . and yours and mother's."

Quin shot to his feet and Thomas did the same. "Tell me what
to do." He glanced at Norton, then Dawson, as if he found some
comfort in their presence. He looked squarely at Thomas. "Tell me
what to do, son, and I'll do it."

"Go back in there and behave as you normally would. After
you've all gone to the parlor for coffee, as you always do, I will come
there with the officers and Lucius's . . . mother . . . to confront him.
See if you can discreetly speak to Ruth on your way to the parlor. Tell
her to stay close to Mother, and you should do the same. I've thought
this through carefully, and I believe it's important that you both
see the evidence with your own eyes—even as difficult as it might

be." Thomas had yet to do the same, and the very thought left him terrified, but he tried not to think about that. "I fear what this will do to Mother, as fragile as she is." He paused in his determination to see all of this through, and as he met his father's eyes, he could see they mirrored all the sadness and horror he felt over the situation. He said more softly, "Perhaps this explains the reasons for and the meaning of her recurring dreams."

"Good heavens!" Quin said again. They shared a silent moment of reckoning before Quin squared his shoulders and cleared his throat. "Very well. We shall come to terms with all of that later. Right now we must get this blackguard out of our home."

"Father"—Thomas put a hand on his arm again—"he is a blackguard and a villain in ways that I cannot even tell you, and he must face the consequences of his crimes. But he is still your son and my brother; I fear this will not be easy for any of us."

Quin nodded firmly. "Then we'd do well to get it over with before I have time to think about it too much."

Quin quickly embraced his son with a brief desperation that confirmed his gratitude in knowing that Thomas was safe and well— even if he'd only just discovered that he might not have been.

Quin hurried back into the dining room, and Thomas heard him bellow in his typical lighthearted way, "Sorry about the intrusion. Nothing to worry about."

Thomas and Norton went stealthily to the parlor while Dawson went back to the pantry to retrieve those who were waiting there. Thomas uttered one more silent prayer that this would all go well and they would all remain safe. He also prayed once more that his parents would not be undone by the truth—or the drama surrounding it.

* * *

Ruth felt a little nervous when Dawson came into the dining room to ask to speak with Quin; but she'd been on edge ever since Lucius had shown up here, and she'd come a long way in being able to appear perfectly calm even while her insides fumed and roiled with fear. Since Thomas had returned, she'd felt less fearful in some respects and more fearful in others. She'd started expecting him to appear at any unexpected moment. And even though it was what she wanted more than anything, she felt constantly prepared to be startled while knowing she needed to appear to everyone else as if nothing in the world was wrong and she had nothing more important to think about than the quality of the dessert they were eating. She was glad to know that Joy was safely in the nursery and being cared for there. In fact, Lucius had hardly even gotten a glance at Joy, since Ruth rarely chose to be anywhere near him unless the baby was being watched over elsewhere.

When everyone was finished eating and they were all moving together toward the parlor for coffee as they usually did, Ruth considered pleading that she didn't feel well so she could go upstairs. She had no desire to sit in the same room with Lucius any more than was absolutely necessary, and she figured she'd served her time sufficiently for one day. She was about to deliver her excuse for not joining them, when her father-in-law appeared beside her and put an arm around her shoulders while they walked. Lucius and Yvette were walking a short distance ahead, chatting about something that Ruth couldn't hear.

Ruth tried not to gasp when she heard Quin whisper, "I just spoke to Thomas . . . in the hall; he's here."

"You know!" she whispered back, at the same time glancing at Lucius to be assured he hadn't overheard. Thankfully he wasn't paying any attention to anything except whatever he was telling Yvette.

"I do now," Quin said softly, sounding angry. "I can't think too much about that at the moment," he added. "Just know that it's all about to end. Thomas will be making his appearance while we are in the parlor, and he's brought some police officers with him. He asked me to tell you to stay close to Yvette, and I will as well. This is going to be very difficult—however it turns out."

"Indeed," Ruth said, her heart thudding while her skin felt cold and clammy and hot all at the same time.

"Now, let's just appear normal," Quin added with a convincing wink and a smile, which helped Ruth feel more calm.

According to Quin's instructions, Ruth attempted to sit on a sofa next to Yvette, but Lucius took her hand as if she really were his wife and urged her to sit next to him on a different sofa. She knew there had to be some minimal attempt to behave as if they were married when others were around, but she cringed every time he touched her. Quin caught her eye discreetly as if he understood, and he sat close to Yvette, putting his arm up on the back of the sofa behind her.

Ruth expected to have to wait for something to happen, certain that every ticking second of the clock would make it more and more difficult to remain calm. But they were barely seated when the door opened. And while they expected to see a maid enter with a tray, they instead saw Thomas walk into the room with two police officers flanking him and a third nearby, just behind him. Ruth's relief was so deep she could hardly breathe. Thomas met her eyes for a fleeting moment as if to silently reassure her that everything would be all right, then he turned his full attention to Lucius, and the silence in the room became palpable.

Thomas entered the room, already certain that everything he'd been told about his twin brother was true, but when he saw the man with his own eyes, he found it difficult to draw breath into his lungs. There was a strange eeriness in seeing him sitting there next to Ruth. It almost felt as if Thomas were standing outside of himself, looking at his own life through different eyes. A mirror could not have borne a more solid resemblance. He assumed that when a person grew up with a twin at his side all the time, such a phenomenon would be accepted from the beginning. But in this situation, Thomas had to consciously jolt himself into remembering what he was here to do and simply do it. Just as he'd told his father, he needed to remain calm now and face the emotional impact of the situation at a more appropriate time.

Ruth noticed Thomas first and gasped. Lucius looked up, and Thomas looked into his brother's eyes for the first time. For a brief second Thomas could see this man's pretense to be someone he was not, and he comprehended the scope of his abilities to lie and manipulate. But his facade vanished instantaneously when he saw Thomas standing there, and Thomas knew now exactly what Ruth had meant when she'd said there was something in his eyes that made it easy to tell them apart. For a long moment while he was completely taken off guard, the evil and malevolence in Lucius's eyes was boldly evident.

Lucius shot to his feet and put his facade back in place, pretending to be Thomas as he demanded, "What on earth is this? Who is this . . . imposter?"

Thomas was glad to see Ruth take advantage of the distraction to move to the other sofa, next to his parents. She was out of Lucius's reach there, and he felt certain they could all benefit by remaining close together.

"There's no point in pretending any further, Lucius," Thomas said as if they already knew each other well. In a strange way they did. Lucius had studied Thomas's life enough to be able to live it, and Thomas had been learning a great deal about Lucius. "I can prove very quickly that I am Thomas and you are not, and that you have been here pretending to be me for selfish and wicked purposes."

While Lucius looked alarmed and apparently at a loss for words, Thomas heard his father whispering to his mother in some attempt to explain. He heard his mother start to cry, which was certainly no surprise. But right now Thomas had to focus on his brother. He didn't dare even glance away, not trusting him to any degree and not having any idea how he would respond to all of this. He surely had to feel cornered, facing the realization that his plan to kill the man he was impersonating had failed. He was also facing three police officers who were each holding pistols at their sides. The officers had warned Thomas that when criminals were cornered they often behaved rashly and without reason—which most often meant dangerously.

Thomas hurried to say what needed to be said, reminding himself that he'd given this plan a great deal of thought and he'd tried very hard to err on the side of compassion. He didn't want any reason for himself—or his parents—to regret how this was dealt with. "I know everything, and I can't blame you for being angry over what should have been. It's upsetting for all of us. We can't change the past, but . . ." Thomas reached inside his jacket and pulled a paper from the pocket. He held it toward Lucius.

"What's that?" Lucius snapped. "A warrant for my arrest?"

"You've certainly broken many laws," Thomas said, "but since no permanent damage has actually been done, I'm willing to let all of that go, on one condition. Take this and leave. Leave and don't ever come back."

"What is it?" Lucius snarled with skepticism.

"It's a legal document. I met with my solicitor and with the banker on my way back here. Given my longtime relationship with them, they were kind enough to accommodate my after-hours visit and prepare the necessary documents. This gives you half of everything that's mine. Everything."

Thomas heard Ruth and his father gasp. Yvette was still crying. Thomas ignored them and kept talking.

"Through no fault of anyone here, you were cheated out of a great deal that could have made your life better. Take this. I give it to you with all the sincerity of my heart. In spite of what you've done and how angry it makes me feel, I cannot deny that you deserve this. Take it. These officers will keep you in their custody until morning, when they will escort you to the bank and you will be given more money than you could ever imagine. I realize, as I'm certain you do, that it's only a twist of fate that made our lives what they are. So I consider it only right that you have half of what is mine. You can live lavishly for the rest of your life and leave wealth behind for your posterity. I only ask that you go somewhere far from here and never come back. We may be brothers, but . . ." at the mention of the word, Thomas heard his mother whimper more loudly, and he had to force his mind to block out what this was doing to her. "But," he went on, "too much trust has been broken for us to ever have contact with each other peacefully. So take it and go."

"It's a trick," Lucius said. "It has to be."

"It's not a trick," Thomas said. "I assure you I am an honest man and I'm trying to give you a way out. I could legally have you arrested for a great many reasons, but I'm not pressing charges. This is the best chance you'll ever get for a good life. Take it."

Lucius stepped forward to take the paper without taking his eyes off of Thomas. He stepped back, snapped the folded document open, and took quick glances at it while keeping a close eye on the men facing him.

"It all looks very convincing," Lucius said snidely, "but forgive me if I don't trust you. I think I *will* go now, but I won't be going with any police escort." He reached abruptly inside his jacket, toward his back, and pulled out a pistol, which he promptly pointed at Thomas. While Thomas put up his hands, he considered the possibility that Lucius had been carrying a loaded weapon with him every minute he'd been in this house. The thought added one more reason to feel sick about this entire travesty.

All three officers pointed their weapons at Lucius, and Thomas wondered what Lucius had believed would happen. He supposed this was the part where the criminal was cornered and behaved rashly and without reason. But with a gun pointed at him, Thomas had to try to calm his pounding heart and the knots in his stomach while he prayed he would come out of this in one piece.

"I offer you half of everything and you respond like *this*? Do you think shooting me will help your cause?" Thomas asked, sounding far calmer than he felt. "If you commit murder in front of all these people, what will that get you?"

Lucius waved the document triumphantly. "I can run very far and fast, can I not?"

"The money is yours," Thomas said, "but the bank will only give it to you if you pick it up accompanied by police officers who will escort you out of the country. Even if that weren't the case, do you think the police wouldn't be there waiting for you if you were wanted for murder? You can either take the money peacefully or not take it at all."

"You!" Lucius said through clenched teeth, taking a step closer and pointing the pistol more fiercely at Thomas. "You had *everything*! I had *nothing*!"

"Do you blame me for that?" Thomas asked, but Lucius just looked angrier. When he said nothing more but didn't lower his weapon, Thomas added, "You were raised by a mother who loved you very much."

"What does *that* mean," Lucius began, "when a man has to—"

"Lucius," Abigail said, stepping through the open doorway from where she had been listening in the hall. Lucius looked taken off guard but kept the gun perfectly pointed toward the center of Thomas's chest. The officers standing by with their weapons drawn gave Thomas *some* comfort, but there was no guarantee that Lucius couldn't pull the trigger before one of them did. And that was *certainly* not how Thomas wanted this to end. The very possibility made him want to rush the women out of the room, but he couldn't move, and he was afraid to speak now that Abigail had made her appearance. He prayed she could have a soothing effect on Lucius so this could be over.

"What are you doing here?" Lucius demanded of her in a tone Thomas couldn't even comprehend using with his mother. It was no wonder she feared him.

"Thomas found me," she said in a gentle voice, showing great calmness and courage. Thomas suspected she'd had numerous opportunities to develop such characteristics while living with a violent husband and a son who had followed in his adoptive father's footsteps. "And so did your friend . . . the one who helped you do all of this. He tried to kill Thomas . . . right there in the house . . . but the police were there, and they killed *him*."

Lucius looked surprised, alarmed even. But he said nothing, and his hold on the pistol didn't waver.

"Your plan failed, Lucius," Abigail said. "But Thomas is being more than fair. He is offering you a way out . . . a way to live your life in a way most men could only dream of. Take his offer, Lucius. Don't let your pride and anger deny you this opportunity."

Lucius looked long and hard at Abigail before his eyes scanned every person in the room, as if he were silently assessing the situation. His gaze came back to rest firmly on Thomas, and they stared at each other through a long, grueling minute—man to man, brother to brother—while both of their lives teetered precariously at the edge of a cliff of uncertainty. And the outcome would all be determined by—as Abigail had put it—Lucius's pride and anger, or the lack of it.

Thomas sucked in his breath when Lucius corrected his aim and something deeply evil and determined filled his eyes. "I could never live in peace knowing that *you* were raised with all of *this*." He waved around the hand holding the document. *"Never!"*

Lucius cocked the pistol and Thomas squeezed his eyes closed, knowing that his family was seated behind him, which meant that if he dropped down to avoid getting hit, one of them would likely get shot instead.

"Lucius, no!" Abigail screamed, and a shot cracked the air.

Thomas opened his eyes when he realized he was still standing. Lucius was on the floor, blood oozing into the fabric of the waistcoat covering his chest. His eyes were open and glazed. Thomas knew from his experience on the battlefield that Lucius had likely been shot right through the heart; he was already dead.

Everything around Thomas felt hazy and distant as he looked at the body and saw himself. Knowing how close he'd come to getting shot, the comparison made it difficult for him to breathe. He was vaguely aware of his father hurrying the women out of the room and Norton saying, "He gave me no choice, sir. I've been doing this long enough to know when a man's intent on pulling the trigger."

Thomas forced breath out of his lungs but had trouble drawing more air in. He could only stare at Lucius's dead body on the floor while one of the officers checked his neck for a pulse, then shook his head to indicate that he couldn't find one.

The officer said to Thomas, "Sometimes they do it because they'd rather die than face up to the consequences of being caught. And they know a copper'll shoot 'em." The man shook his head. "Not an easy part of the job for us; that's for sure."

Thomas started to feel lightheaded and became aware of Norton's hand on his arm, guiding him to a chair. "Are you all right, sir?"

"I . . . will be," Thomas said. "Thank you . . . for everything."

"I'm glad to see you alive and well," Norton said. "And I'm glad you came to us instead of trying to handle it on your own." He glanced at the body. "But no criminal I know of was ever given such a grand chance to get away free and clear. It's a shame he was too proud to just go."

"Yes," Thomas said, feeling disconnected from himself, "it's a shame."

Thomas was immeasurably grateful to find Dawson standing beside him, asking if there was anything he could do. This good man remained his calm and collected self, hovering near Thomas while the police finished their business and asked a few remaining questions.

When Thomas was no longer needed, he left the matter in Dawson's capable hands, knowing he would make certain that the officers had all they needed until everything was taken care of and the body was removed from the home. Thomas's last thought before he left the scene of the drama was to tell Dawson to let the police know that he would see to a proper burial.

As soon as Thomas left the parlor where the shooting had taken place, he was surprised to find Abigail pacing in the hallway, all alone.

He quickly said, "Surely there is a place you could find to sit and rest so that you—"

"Oh, I can't sit down," she insisted and stopped walking. "Not right now." He was surprised by the way she faced him directly and took both his hands into hers. "I'm so very grateful that you're all right."

"I am grateful for that too," he said, "but I'm very sorry for your loss, Abigail, and so, so sorry you had to see that."

Tears rose in her eyes as she admitted, "If I'd not seen him die, I'm not sure I ever would have believed it." She sighed and bit her trembling lip. "If I think of the child he once was and the hopes I had for him, I could feel great sorrow. But when I think of what he'd become . . . and what he was capable of . . . I can only feel relief. Is that a terrible thing for a mother to admit, Thomas?" She whimpered softly, and tears fell down her face. "That I'm relieved to know my son is dead?"

"If it is," he said gently, "then you and I shall be terrible together. I think I should feel some kind of sorrow or regret to know my brother is dead—even if I did only recently discover that I had a brother—but I feel nothing except relief. My only sorrow for myself is in wishing that he and I could have been like brothers, but it never would have been that way."

"No," Abigail said, "it never would."

Feeling her teeter slightly, Thomas insisted, "You must rest. Come and sit down with the family and—"

"Oh no," she insisted. "Not now; not tonight. They are in a great deal of shock. I would prefer to wait to meet them until that has settled somewhat. You can let me know the best time. For now, I just need a place to—"

"Wait right here," Thomas said and guided her to a chair before he quickly found a maid, who assured him she would see that Abigail was taken to a comfortable room for the night and given everything she needed.

Thomas kissed Abigail's brow and promised her they would talk in the morning. She thanked him and left with the maid. Thomas stood alone in the hall, attempting to gather his complex thoughts and calm his churning emotions. In truth, he *did* feel sorrow. He would have far preferred to think of his brother somewhere out in the world living a life of luxury—even as amoral as Lucius seemed to be. Thomas had hoped there was some spark of something redeemable in him, that if he'd felt compensated somehow for all he'd suffered he might have changed his ways. He had never imagined it ending like this. But recalling the harsh evil in his brother's eyes just before he'd died, Thomas knew there could have been no other outcome. Therefore his relief was real and likely his most prominent emotion—relief that Lucius no longer had to be contended with or feared, and relief that Thomas was alive and safe, along with everyone else in the household.

Thomas recalled that Ruth and his parents were in a nearby drawing room, where they'd been told to wait until he finished up matters with the police. As his mind went to them, his sorrow deepened. He had greatly feared how this would impact his parents. Now they knew the truth, and had just—in a matter of minutes— learned of the existence of another son and then seen him shot and killed. It was too horrible to comprehend. He knew they needed him, but he had no idea what to say or do that would help. It occurred to him there was *nothing* to be said or done that would help. They would all have to grieve, in their own way, over what had taken place—and it would take time. All he could do was be there for them and do his best to fill in the details of the story they didn't yet know. He hoped that when the time was right, Abigail and his mother could help each other find some peace and solace, but that remained to be seen.

Chapter Fifteen
TRUTH

THOMAS TOOK A DEEP BREATH and went to find his family. The moment he came through the door, Ruth rose from where she'd been sitting on the floor near his mother's side and rushed into his arms, holding him tightly. He returned her embrace with all the fervor and desperation he felt in having just faced the possibility of death.

"Oh, my darling," she said, holding his face in her hands. "You're all right. You're really all right."

"I really am," he said. Realizing how strange and traumatic this all must have been for her, he asked, "Do you want to see my scar?"

She touched his chest where she knew it was, but she offered a faint smile and looked into his eyes. "I don't need to see it."

Thomas kissed her quickly before turning his attention to his parents, and Ruth slipped her hand into his. Quin was slumped into the corner of an overstuffed sofa, making no attempt to hide the fact that he'd been crying—and quite a lot. Given that Quincy Fitzbatten was a man known for maintaining his dignity and composure, Thomas knew at a glance how deeply this was affecting him. Yet, for all that Quin looked undone, Yvette was far worse off. She was lying on the sofa with her head in Quin's lap, a handkerchief pressed over her mouth that did nothing to hold back the steady sobbing she couldn't control.

Ruth slipped away from Thomas and returned to where she'd been sitting on the floor beside Yvette. Ruth gently stroked her mother-in-law's hair and shoulder and whispered soothing words. Thomas picked up a chair and moved it directly in front of his parents, right next to where Ruth was sitting on the floor. He sat down and leaned his forearms on his thighs, making firm eye contact with his father, who nodded but couldn't speak.

Thomas turned his attention to his mother and realized that with her eyes squeezed shut and the intensity of her sobs, she might not even know he was there.

"Mother," he said, taking hold of her hand.

Yvette's eyes flew open, and she gripped his hand tightly. "Thomas!" she exclaimed and sat up. "Is it you?" She touched his face and looked into his eyes. "Is it really you?"

"It really is, Mother. You can ask me anything."

"There's no need," she said, sitting up and moving to the edge of her seat, throwing her arms around him. "After what I just saw in there, I have no doubt that it's you. I just can't believe that . . ." She tightened her embrace and whimpered. "There's so much I can't believe, but . . ." She drew back and looked at him gravely. "I wondered if something wasn't right after you—or the man I thought was you—came back. There were moments that . . . you just . . . didn't seem . . . yourself."

"Well, that's certainly true!" Quin snarled.

"I just passed it off, thinking you were dealing with a great deal of stress, or . . . well . . . I confess I didn't think too deeply about it, figuring it would work itself out. Now I see that . . ." She sobbed again. "I should have questioned it. I should have—"

"No, Mother," Thomas said, placing his hands on her shoulders. "Questioning it would have only put you in danger. And how could you have ever comprehended the possibility of such a thing? That someone could look enough like me to take my place? You mustn't blame yourself for this; not for any of it!"

"Ruth and your father have been filling in the details of what happened," she went on to say. "And I can't believe it . . . I can't believe that . . . all these years . . ."

"You had *two* sons?" Thomas guessed what she seemed hesitant to say.

Yvette tightened her gaze on him. "That I wasn't crazy!" she said and surprised him. "Don't you see?" his mother cried. "I've been dreaming about him since the two of you were born, and . . ." She became too emotional to speak and looked to Quin as if to silently ask him to explain what she couldn't.

"Soon after you were born, her nightmares started," Quin said to Thomas, and Thomas felt Ruth take his hand. "She told me then that she had the strangest feeling there had been two babies and that one was missing. I went so far as to question the doctor and the maid who had assisted him. Of course they both boldly denied knowing of any such thing and said that surely it was a strange side effect from the medicine your mother had been given to help ease the pain. The doctor told us that the medicine could sometimes cause hallucinations. But neither the feelings nor the dreams have ever ceased. We never told anyone else; your mother feared people would think her mind to be unstable or some such nonsense."

"And *now*," Yvette said, "to realize that it was true. All along it was true! And my *other* son has been living here in the house during these past several days . . . a part of our lives . . . and we had no idea. And now he's—" She pressed her handkerchief over her mouth and wept, but she moved it and took a harsh breath in order to say, "But how can he have become such a man? So cruel and deceptive!" She gasped as if a thought had just occurred to her, and she turned to Thomas. "That woman . . . who was here . . . that's his mother? The woman who raised him?"

"Yes, her name is Abigail. She's a good woman, and she's lived a hard life. She had nothing and I felt it was right I bring her home with me. I hope that's all right."

"Of course it's all right," Quin said. "If you felt it was right, then it had to be done. We certainly have plenty of room."

"I should talk to her," Yvette said, but she was only barely managing to speak at all due to her ongoing grief. "That poor, dear woman. I should—"

"I've made certain that Liddy will take care of her tonight, Mother," Thomas said. "There will be plenty of time for all that."

"Oh!" Yvette put a hand over her heart. "It's all so . . . I . . . I . . . don't even know what to think."

"Perhaps," Quin said to her, giving her shoulders a squeeze, "we should go up to bed and we can talk . . . and give all of this some time to settle in."

"I'm sure you're right," Yvette said and dabbed at her eyes as more tears flowed out. Thomas couldn't even imagine the raucous mixture of emotions she must be experiencing. While he felt utterly overwhelmed and confused with a cacophony of thoughts, he had no idea how all of this must appear through his parents' eyes—especially his mother's.

Quin and Yvette each embraced both Thomas and Ruth, expressing their gratitude that they were all safe and well, and they promised to talk in the morning.

When the door had closed and Thomas was finally all alone with Ruth, he took her in his arms and held her fiercely, feeling all over again the fear of dying that had consumed him when Lucius had been pointing a pistol at him.

"Oh, my darling," he muttered and pressed a kiss into her hair while she held to him in desperation and cried against his chest. "It's over now. It's all over now."

"Never leave me again," she insisted and held to him even more tightly. "Promise me you will never leave me again."

"I promise," he said and took her face into his hands, examining her tear-filled eyes and the perfect love that shone in them. "I love you, Ruth. I love you now more than ever. And our little Joy. Oh, how I love her! I've missed the both of you so much! Everything I've ever wanted or hoped for is right here with you."

Thomas kissed her the way he'd wanted to ever since he'd entered the room earlier to see her sitting next to his brother—a man now dead. Suddenly exhausted and perhaps a little weak from the tidal waves of emotion and fear that had been crashing around them, Thomas took Ruth's hand, saying, "Perhaps we too should go upstairs. I know we have much to talk about, but first I need to see our daughter."

Ruth laughed softly and put her arm around his waist as they headed out of the room and toward the stairs.

"What?" he asked, questioning her laughter.

"Not once did Lucius ever want to see the baby, nor did he show the slightest interest in anything to do with her. For that reason alone, I would have known he wasn't you."

Thomas decided to ask something he knew that he should. "So . . . he didn't suspect . . . that she . . ."

"Not in the slightest," Ruth assured him. "I don't think it even crossed his mind. She's *our* daughter, Thomas."

"Indeed, she is," he said with all the conviction he felt on that count.

Ruth felt as if her head would burst with the tears she desperately wanted to cry. She held tightly to her husband as they walked together, taking into herself every tiny piece of evidence that it was indeed Thomas, and that he was here, and alive, and real. It was a miracle!

They entered the nursery to find Selma sitting on the floor, playing with little Joy, who had a number of toys scattered around her. Thomas laughed and hurried to pick up the baby, playing a little game he'd come up with weeks ago in which he would pretend to drop her just a little even while he held her completely safe and secure. The dropping motion made Joy giggle, which made Thomas laugh. Ruth watched and couldn't hold back her tears. The nightmare was over, and as horrible as the events of this evening had been, she felt no guilt in acknowledging her relief that Lucius was dead. She never had to fear him again, never had to wonder if he would find another way to hurt them with his malicious schemes.

Ruth laughed away her tears while observing Thomas's silliness with little Joy. When he'd finished the typical allotted time for their dropping game, he just held her and talked to her as if she were his equal. She tentatively reached out a chubby hand to touch the hair on his face as if she didn't know what to make of it.

Thomas said to her what seemed obvious. "You're not very fond of the beard, are you, little lady? I'll shave it off in the morning and your real papa will be back again."

As if he realized what he'd said as soon as he said it, Thomas turned to look at Ruth, and she saw her own relief and gratitude mirrored in his eyes. The real Thomas was truly back again.

* * *

Ruth lay close beside her husband in the darkness, so grateful to not be alone in the huge bed, and even more so to know that Lucius was not in the house, posing an insidious threat to her and those she loved most. They talked far into the night in spite of their exhaustion. He told her all that had happened since he'd last spoken with her, and she filled in many details for him of what it had been like to have Lucius in the house. More than once they wept together over the drama and irony they'd experienced. The situation had brought a great deal of sorrow and betrayal to the surface, and they both felt certain it would not be easy for any of them to recover. They were both largely concerned for Thomas's parents—especially Yvette. But exhaustion finally forced them to agree that they could do nothing about that until tomorrow and that they both needed to get some rest.

Ruth awoke to daylight and found Thomas leaning his head on his hand while he watched her. She smiled to see him and thanked God for the miracles that had kept him alive and brought him home to her. He leaned over to kiss her at the same moment that she realized that Joy was lying between them, exploring the texture of a little cloth doll with her mouth—and getting the doll very soggy in the process.

"Good morning, my little queen," Ruth said to her daughter.

"You are the queen," Thomas said, touching Ruth's face as if to make certain she was real. Ruth knew exactly how he felt and touched his face in return. "Our daughter is the princess."

Ruth kissed her daughter's head but couldn't stop staring at Thomas. In the tranquility of this moment she didn't want to bring up everything that had been so difficult, but she knew it had to be discussed, just as she knew he had to be thinking about it every bit as much as she was.

"I can't believe it, Thomas—any of it. Now that it's over, it all feels like a bad dream, but I know it was real, and I never could have imagined that anything so . . . bizarre . . . and so . . . awful . . . could have happened to us . . . to our family."

"How well you express my own thoughts," he said and kissed her brow. He rolled onto his back and looked at the ceiling, letting out a burdened sigh. "A thought occurred to me this morning when I got Joy out of her crib and . . . I don't know why I didn't think of it before. I suppose it's all been so overwhelming that . . . it just didn't occur to me; perhaps it's occurred to you, but . . . I find it both disturbing and yet . . . comforting, somehow."

"What, Thomas?" she urged gently.

Thomas turned his head on the pillow to look at her. "Joy *does* have Fitzbatten blood in her veins." Ruth gasped and realized that the thought hadn't occurred to her either, but now that he'd said it, the irony took her breath away. "She may not *literally* be my daughter, but she is as much a granddaughter to my parents as she would have been if I *were* her father."

"I can't believe it!" Ruth said, leaning up on her elbow. "How can such a thing possibly be a coincidence?"

"You don't believe in coincidence any more than I do," he said with vehemence and sat up as if what he had to say couldn't be said lying down. She sat to face him, and he took both her hands into his. "Ruth, my love," he said, "now that this is all over . . . now that I'm starting to be able to think more clearly . . . and put all of the pieces together . . . I firmly believe this was meant to be, more than any of us can comprehend. I am deeply convinced more than ever that God's hand brought us together."

"What do you mean?" she asked, furrowing her brow.

"Ruth," he said as he leaned a little closer, "set aside for a moment the fact that you and I have grown to love each other so dearly and that we share the best marriage either of us could have ever hoped for. Set that aside and consider the probability of a woman being in your position, related to someone who would come to *me* for help, and that you knew when you met me that another man existed who looked exactly like me. What if *any* other woman had been here in this house as my wife when Lucius showed up pretending to be me? *You* knew immediately it wasn't me; you knew *exactly* who it was. And you knew Lucius well enough that you were able to put the pieces together and help me find the woman who raised him."

Thomas tightened his hold on her hands, and she saw a sparkle of tears in his eyes. "Ruth, my darling, I believe you not only saved us all from the possible destruction that Lucius could have wreaked upon this family . . . this estate . . . but you also made it possible for us to discover the truth, to unearth long-buried secrets that were causing pain for my parents—and for Abigail. Secrets we had no idea existed. Now there will be no more secrets, and I pray this will—in time— bring healing to those who have been impacted the most."

Ruth didn't realize she was crying until Thomas pulled her into his arms and held her tightly while Joy continued to play with her little doll and make happy gurgling noises from where she lay close beside them.

"Eventually the secrets would have come out, Ruth," Thomas said while he continued to hold her tightly. "I fear they would have caused pain and destruction in one way or another. But it's over, and because *you* were here, I believe it all turned out very differently than it might have. Oh, Ruth!" He took her face into his hands and looked gravely into her eyes. "I thank God for the day He brought you into my life; into *our* lives. You have saved us all."

Ruth shook her head. "No, my darling. It is I who was saved."

"Think what you want," he said with a smile and kissed her.

Ruth put her head on his shoulder, thinking about everything he'd just said, feeling even more overwhelmed by all that had happened. A thought occurred to her, and she looked up at him. "You said there would be no more secrets. Does that mean you want people to know that Joy is—"

"She is *my* daughter!" he said as if he would defend the idea to the death. "There is no reason for *anyone* to ever know otherwise. Besides my parents, only your mother and Dawson know the truth, and I want it to stay that way forever."

Ruth sighed. "I'm glad, but . . . I have to ask . . . *should* your parents know . . . and Abigail . . . that Lucius is the one who fathered Joy?"

"Do you think it would give any of them any comfort to know one more horrible fact about how completely heinous Lucius could be? It's possible my parents could figure it out, given that Joy may look a great deal like me as she grows. But we will deal with that if and when it comes up. Otherwise, that situation is as we have agreed, and it's laid to rest."

Ruth nodded and drew in a long breath of relief.

"As for the other . . . the fact that Lucius is my brother . . . and all things related to that—including what's been happening these past weeks—all this will be made known so there is no cause for speculation. There is no one left alive who can be hurt by this. The truth must be known. I will discuss it with my father, but I think he will agree." He drew her head to his chest and pressed a hand over her hair. "But there is no need for you to worry over such things, my dear. We are together and all is well; everything else will take care of itself with time."

"I love you, Thomas," she said, holding to him tightly.

"And I love you, my dear Ruth." He kissed the top of her head. "More than ever."

* * *

When Selma brought breakfast to their room, she informed them that she had also taken breakfast to Abigail, who'd assured Selma that she was doing well and had everything she needed.

"I'm glad to hear it," Thomas said to Selma. "Would you mind very much letting her know that I will come to her sitting room to talk with her just as soon as I've finished eating?"

"Glad to, sir," Selma said and left them to eat their meal.

Thomas thoroughly enjoyed his breakfast, even though he wasn't thinking at all about the food. He was rather preoccupied with a deep gratitude for being here—back in his own life—sitting across the small table from his wife while she nursed the baby and ate her own breakfast at the same time. He marveled at how adept she'd become at doing such things. She'd taken to motherhood so gracefully, and he loved the way she insisted on keeping the baby in her own care the majority of the time, even though there were plenty of reliable people on hand who would gladly help her. Thomas was so glad to simply be here with both of them.

"May I come with you?" Ruth asked, breaking a long silence.

"Where?" he asked, confused.

"To speak with Abigail."

"I was hoping you would, actually." He went on to tell her about the strong feelings he felt toward Abigail. He'd realized the moment he saw her that she could have very well been the mother who had raised *him*. He felt an obligation toward her that he couldn't define, as much as he felt a deep respect and kinship with her. And he was glad to be able to share his feelings with Ruth. He'd previously told her all that had happened in finding Abigail and the drama that had taken place in her home, but he'd not yet shared the full depth of his feelings or his reasons for bringing her home with him.

Once they were all done eating, Ruth changed the baby's diaper and dressed her in something soft and pale yellow, which Thomas declared made her look like sunshine. They went together to the door of Abigail's sitting room, and Thomas knocked lightly before they heard her call for them to come in.

"Oh!" Abigail said, sounding mildly alarmed to see that he wasn't alone.

Thomas closed the door behind him and tried to calm her nerves. "I thought you should officially meet my wife and daughter. This is Ruth, and as you can see she is lovely."

"She is indeed!" Abigail said and nodded.

Before Thomas could officially finish the introductions, Ruth handed the baby to Thomas and stepped toward Abigail, taking hold of her hands. "My dear Abigail," she said, "welcome to our home. I do hope you will find as much happiness here as I have."

"You are so kind," Abigail said, her voice cracking. "Everyone has been so kind," she said more to Thomas.

"I should hope," Thomas said. In order to divert any awkwardness, he hurried to add, "And this is our daughter, Joy."

"Oh, she's beautiful!" Abigail said, and Thomas saw in her eyes what he'd come to see from his mother and most of the maids who encountered the baby. They all wanted to hold her. He didn't know if *all* babies had that effect on women, but Joy certainly did. He handed Joy over to Abigail, who looked surprised but delighted, and they all sat down.

Thomas held Ruth's hand while they observed Abigail and Joy taking each other in while Abigail talked to her in a silly voice and smiled warmly as if she'd not seen her son shot to death by a police officer the previous evening.

"Oh, she *is* a precious little one!" Abigail declared. "So friendly with strangers, too."

"She seems to like anyone who will give her attention," Ruth affirmed. "It seems everyone in the household has grown to love her."

"I can see why," Abigail said while Joy became fascinated with the shiny buttons on Abigail's dress. "And she certainly looks like her father."

Thomas was glad that Abigail's focus was completely on the baby when he unconsciously put a hand over his mouth to hold back a sudden onslaught of emotion he feared might come out of his mouth as a very unmasculine whimper. He didn't at all begrudge the fact that he was not actually Joy's father. What he felt was more like a warm rush of destiny. Abigail would likely never know that the son she'd raised was the father of this baby, but she would be a part of Joy's life. And perhaps without Abigail even realizing it, Joy might make up in some way for all of the sorrow that Lucius had brought into her difficult existence.

Thomas felt Ruth squeeze his hand tightly and turned to see that she'd noticed his reaction. But she didn't look concerned; her eyes told him she knew exactly what he was thinking and feeling. She gave him a serene smile that told him she understood. He was able to swallow his emotion, and they both turned their attention back to the sweet observation of Abigail getting to know her granddaughter.

"How are you this morning?" Thomas asked Abigail when the silence began to feel a bit strained.

"I am feeling a great mixture of emotions," she said, continuing to hold Joy, "as I'm sure we all are. I'm worried about your poor mother, Thomas. And I confess that in spite of how glad I am to be here, I fear your parents might not be comfortable with my presence in the home. I want you to know if that's the case, I will completely understand and I will go elsewhere."

"If I had believed my parents would not want you here, I wouldn't have asked you to stay," Thomas said. "But I promise you we will make sure. I want you to feel comfortable here. If it turns out that you don't, then I'll make arrangements for you to live elsewhere. Either way, I will make certain your needs are met. I don't want you to ever worry about that."

"Your kindness warms me, Thomas," Abigail said and held little Joy closer, as if doing so was somehow healing for her. "As horrible as what happened last night may be, seeing the way you have handled all of this—and your kindness to me—has restored my faith that there is goodness in the world. I will forever be grateful for that."

They talked a while longer, and they each shed a few tears as the rawness of their emotions occasionally bubbled to the surface. Thomas was glad that Abigail felt comfortable enough to share her feelings so openly, and he was proud of Ruth—though not surprised—by how compassionately and warmly she behaved toward Abigail.

When Thomas felt a need to check on his parents and see how they were coping with all of this, he asked Abigail if she would like to walk in the gardens or see the library. She insisted that she preferred to remain in the comfort of what she called her luxurious rooms until the household was fully aware of all that had happened. And she wanted to have a conversation with his parents, although she told him if they didn't want to see her she would understand. Thomas assured her they would surely want to talk to her and that all would be well. She didn't seem to believe him, but, then, she didn't know them the way he did, and life had given her many disappointments and much disillusionment. He told her that a maid would check in with her and bring some lunch and make certain she had all she needed, and he would be back this afternoon.

Thomas went with Ruth back to their room, where she changed the baby's diaper—and her clothes—since the diaper had leaked, which it usually did. While she was doing so, Ruth said to him, "I really like Abigail. I hope she'll stay. It feels like she should be here."

"I agree," he said, "and I'm very glad you feel the same way."

"Do you think your parents will feel differently?"

"I think my parents are severely traumatized right now, and we need to take all of this one step at a time. But I truly believe they will want Abigail to stay. Right now, let's just go see how they're doing."

As they walked together down long hallways to get to a different wing of the house, Ruth said, "I can't imagine how your parents must be feeling—to suddenly realize, after all these years, that they had another son, and then to see him die."

"I keep wondering the same," Thomas admitted. "But I think it's equally disturbing to consider how they must feel about realizing what Lucius has been doing. His evil motives must surely be heartbreaking to a parent. Abigail has known of his dubious character for years and has come to terms with it. For my parents, that must be difficult to accept. They saw the way he behaved last night, but it must be difficult to comprehend."

Ruth sighed. "I wonder how Adam and Eve must have felt when they realized Cain had killed Abel."

Thomas stopped walking as the comparison chilled him. This story he'd known from his youth suddenly felt very real and personal. As usual, Ruth seemed to understand without him needing to explain. She added with tenderness, "At least your parents didn't have to deal with *that*. At least you're here and alive."

"Yes." Thomas started walking again, and she joined him. "We have been given many miracles."

Thomas knocked at his parents' bedroom door, knowing it was typical for his mother to remain in bed long past this time of day, and he doubted his father would be anywhere but with her under the circumstances. When there was no response after he'd knocked again, Thomas carefully peeked inside, only to find no one was there and the bed had been made. They checked the sitting room and found no one there, either.

"That's strange," Thomas said to Ruth and held her hand while he carried the baby in his other arm as they went down the stairs. They came across one of the servants, who told them that Thomas's parents were in the breakfast room, having tea.

Thomas stepped into the room and felt a little unsteady. He leaned a shoulder against the doorjamb and tightened his hold on Ruth's hand. This was not at all what he'd expected to see; in fact, he'd never seen his mother quite like this in his entire life.

"Good morning, my dears," Yvette said, glancing toward them as she set down her teacup. Quin glanced over the top of his newspaper and nodded a typical greeting. "I've been wondering when you'd show yourselves," Yvette continued. "It was a dreadful business last night, and I'm sure we need to talk about it, but I've been worried about you."

"I've been worried about *you*," Thomas said.

"We both have," Ruth added.

"I can't say I'm not rattled by the whole thing," Yvette said, "and I'm certain it will take time to adjust, but . . ." Joy distracted her by making a noise that seemed to be a declaration that all attention should be averted to her. "Oh, look at Grandmama's little angel today!" Yvette said and rose from her chair, whisking across the room to take the baby from Thomas. She began speaking to Joy in a silly voice; Joy had a way of making *everyone* talk in silly voices. Thomas exchanged an astonished glance with Ruth, glad to see by her expression that he wasn't the only one disarmed by Yvette's behavior.

Thomas guided Ruth to a chair, and they sat next to each other. They both watched for a minute or two while Yvette fussed over the baby and Quin kept reading the paper.

Thomas finally had to say something. "Mother," he began with trepidation, wondering if she'd had some kind of final breakdown that had completely wiped away the horror from her mind, "forgive me, but . . . this is not what we expected from you. I don't want to sound insensitive, however . . ."

"You're wondering," Yvette said, "how the fragile woman you've known all your life could actually be doing so well after what happened last night."

"That would sum up my question, yes."

Yvette told Quin to put his newspaper away and handed him the baby, which made Quin smile as *he* started talking to her in a silly voice. Yvette moved a chair and sat on it so she was directly facing Thomas and Ruth, and she took each of them by the hand. But it was Thomas she looked at as she spoke. "My dear boy," she said, "I don't want you to mistake my present mood for any kind of flippancy over the gravity of what's taken place. I cried half the night, and I'm certain I will yet cry many tears. I also prayed and prayed, and your father prayed and cried with me. This strange thing that has happened to us is completely unimaginable, and there is so much to grieve over; but in spite of what we have lost, much has been gained, and we have been very blessed."

Yvette leaned a little closer and tightened her hold on their hands. "The thing that you must both know . . . is that I woke up this morning feeling a peace inside of me that I've not felt since my baby was stolen from me and a hole was left in my heart that I could never understand or make sense of. The past cannot be changed—as horrible as some aspects of it are—and I'm certain it will take time for all of us to come to terms with what's happened. But I have realized that what it says in the Bible is true."

When she didn't enlarge on what she had just said, Thomas ventured a query. "I'm certain that most if not all of what is said in the Bible is true, Mother. Could you perhaps be a little more specific and enlighten us?"

Thomas felt the warmth of witnessing a miracle as he watched his mother close her eyes and lift her face heavenward. With a serene smile, she said with quiet conviction, "'And ye shall know the truth, and the truth shall make you free.'" She sighed and opened her eyes. "Don't you see? I've been burdened with this terrible secret . . . this lie . . . all these years. And now I know the truth. We are all together and we are safe, and the rest will sort itself out with time."

Thomas exchanged another astonished glance with Ruth before he turned to just watch his parents both coddling the baby and laughing at her funny little expressions. All of his fears and worries and the personal trauma he'd felt over recent discoveries now fell into perspective as he witnessed his mother's wisdom—and her happiness. He felt certain she was right, that there would yet be grief to face and overcome and it would take time. But for the moment he could only sit with Ruth's hand in his and take in the miracle of this moment. It all could have turned out so differently, so horribly. But it hadn't.

A few minutes later Quin informed them that he had spoken to the household staff when they'd been gathered for breakfast. He'd explained everything and answered their questions. Thomas wasn't surprised to hear that many of them had been rather upset; comments of astonishment had been made about having had a man in the house who had not actually been Thomas, and the story of one of the Fitzbatten twins having been stolen and sold had everyone reeling. Many had also expressed their gratitude that Thomas was safe and at home again, and the evidence of how much these people were like family settled freshly into Thomas.

Quin went on to tell Thomas that he'd sent for the undertaker, who had already come and gone, and arrangements were being made for a service to be held in two days' time. The mood became more somber with talk of the fact that there had been a death in the family—even if none of them had realized Lucius was family until very recently. Quin got a little choked up, and Yvette shed a few stray tears, but they both commented that as horrible as his death was, they feared that given what they knew of his character, any life he would have lived would have likely been filled with unhappiness and perhaps even more disaster. Knowing he was at rest gave them a sense of peace Thomas doubted they would have felt if Lucius had simply left and they'd had to live wondering where he might be and what he might be doing—and whether he might return to cause even more grief.

When Quin and Yvette had informed Thomas and Ruth of all they needed to be told, Yvette asked about Abigail, wanting to know more about her and expressing concern for how all of this was affecting her. Thomas couldn't hold back a smile when Yvette said, "Oh, I do hope she won't be put off by us and want to leave. I haven't actually met her, but I do so feel that she should be here with us. It just seems right."

"It does indeed," Quin said, then changed his tone of voice to talk to Joy, who smiled at him, making him laugh in his jolly way.

When a maid came into the room, Thomas asked if she would go and get Abigail and bring her here. He could well imagine Abigail's nervousness and wondered if he should have gone to get her himself. Not many minutes later she entered the room but hovered tentatively in the doorway, saying nothing. He wasn't at all surprised—although he knew Abigail was—with the way Yvette sprang out of her chair and rushed across the room to put her arms around this woman, with an embrace that implied they were lifelong friends.

"Oh, my dear Abigail," Yvette said. "We are so very sorry for all you have been through."

Thomas noticed how Abigail hesitated only a moment before she eagerly returned Yvette's embrace, and then neither woman seemed inclined to let go.

"As I am for yours," Abigail said, and he could tell she was crying.

Yvette finally let go and took hold of Abigail's shoulders in order to look her in the eye. "We do hope you'll want to stay here with us. It's such a ridiculously large house with so much wasted space. Please tell me you'll stay. We have so much in common, my dear; so much catching up to do. We'd have such fun! Tell me you'll stay."

"If you're certain," Abigail said quietly, and Yvette hugged her again and laughed.

Yvette escorted Abigail to the table, where they all adjusted their chairs so that they were seated around it in order to easily see each other's faces as they talked openly about the events of the previous evening. Lunch was served there, and long after they'd eaten they all kept talking. Joy was discreetly nursed beneath a small blanket when she got hungry, and once she'd fallen asleep, Selma took her upstairs to her bed. The adults continued to converse and marvel over the strange events that had brought them all to this day. Thomas squeezed Ruth's hand beneath the table, glad for the secret he shared with her that he considered to be one of the most important pieces of the puzzle, the element that had saved them all in the end. She smiled at him, and he knew she shared his thoughts. It was one of a million things he loved about her. And he would love her for as long as he drew breath, and far beyond that.

Epilogue

THOMAS SAT COMFORTABLY ON THE blanket he'd spread out in the meadow and leaned back on his hands, turning his face toward the sun. The designated picnic spot was only a short distance from the cottage, and the familiar, vague smell of the sea was in the air. Thomas closed his eyes and listened to the mixture of sounds that represented what he considered perfect evidence of the goodness of his life. Ruth and Bertie were talking about how to make the best shepherd's pie. Barclay was tickling Thomas's young daughter and making her giggle. Quin was chasing little Warren around in the tall grass, growling like a wild animal, which was far more silly than frightening. Warren was thoroughly enjoying this game with Quin, who was much like a grandfather to him. Joy was in the midst of their little game and letting out high-pitched shrieks of laughter the way only a little girl could. Yvette and Abigail were chattering in a way that had become typical between them. They had become the best friend to each other that neither of them had ever had, and they were practically inseparable. They burst into a bout of girlish giggling that made Thomas smile even though he kept his eyes closed and allowed the sun to continue warming his face.

His reverie was interrupted by the nearby sound of some kind of havoc taking place, and he opened his eyes and looked down to see Thomas Quincy Fitzbatten III gleefully emptying the picnic hamper and tossing its contents haphazardly. Thomas laughed and hurried to save their lunch from his son before he picked him up. He lifted him skyward and turned in a circle in the meadow, making the baby giggle, which made Thomas laugh.

In the midst of their little game, Thomas caught his breath to see a little blue butterfly flitting around them, as if it wanted to participate in the laughter. The brilliant color of its wings reflected the sunlight. Its beauty was remarkable, and its apparent significance in his life made his heart beat a little more quickly. The tiny creature disappeared as quickly as it had shown itself, seemingly flying away into thin air with the speed of its flight. But it left a deep impression on Thomas as he held his son close to him and briefly pondered the other times he'd seen a blue butterfly and the good fortune and blessings that had followed its appearance. Given the reality of the present moment, he couldn't think of a single thing he could want for, and he thought it was more accurate that he simply needed to stop and take notice of all that was good in his life and never take it for granted.

Thomas turned and caught Ruth's eye. She smiled at him with an adoration in her gaze that had only deepened since the day she'd admitted to her love for him. He could only stare back at her for a long moment, overcome with disbelief that such a woman could love him so deeply, so truly. He felt the essence of happiness all around him in that moment, but she was at the center of it. And she always would be.

About the Author

ANITA STANSFIELD HAS MORE THAN fifty published books and is the recipient of many awards, including two lifetime achievement awards. Her books go far beyond being enjoyable, memorable stories. Anita resonates particularly well with a broad range of devoted readers because of her sensitive and insightful examination of contemporary issues that are faced by many of those readers, even when her venue is a historical romance; readers come away from her compelling stories equipped with new ideas about how to enrich their own lives, regardless of their circumstances.

Anita was born and raised in Provo, Utah. She is the mother of five and has a growing number of grandchildren. She also writes for the general trade market under the name Elizabeth D. Michaels.

For more information and a complete list of her publications, go to anitastansfield.blogspot.com or anitastansfield.com, where you can sign up to receive email updates. You can also follow her on Facebook and Twitter.